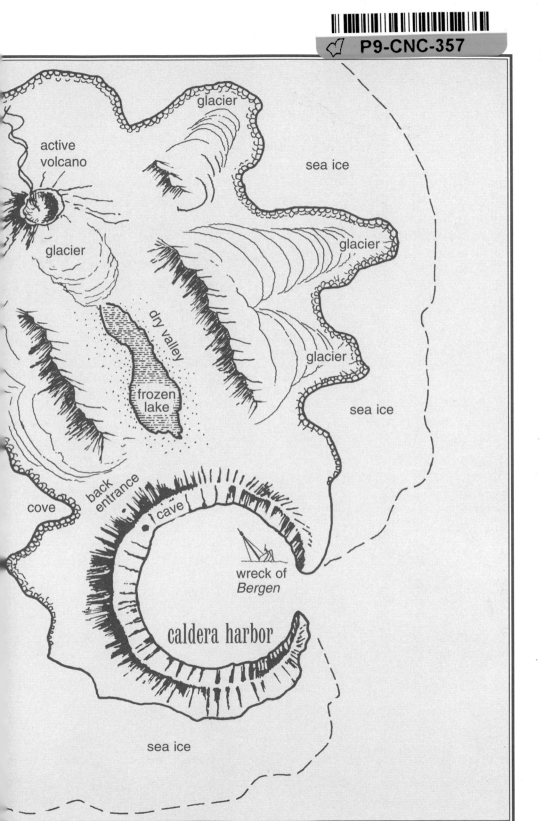

ICE
REICH

Also by William Dietrich

The Final Forest
Northwest Passage

ICE
REICH

WILLIAM
DIETRICH

WARNER BOOKS

A Time Warner Company

Copyright © 1998 by William Dietrich
All rights reserved.
Warner Books, Inc., 1271 Avenue of the Americas,
New York, NY 10020
Visit our Web site at http://warnerbooks.com
W A Time Warner Company
Printed in the United States of America
First Printing: October 1998
10 9 8 7 6 5 4 3 2 1
Library of Congress Cataloging-in-Publication Data

Dietrich, William.
    Ice reich / William Dietrich.
      p. cm.
    ISBN 0-446-52339-9
    1. Deutsche Antarktische Expedition (1938–1939)—Fiction.
    2. Antarctica—Discovery and exploration—German—Fiction.
    3. Göring, Herman, 1893–1946—Fiction.   I. Title.
PS3554.I367I28   1998
813' .54—dc21   97-39152
                                        CIP

To my mother
and, always,
for Holly

He who may have failed back there has his chance to make good here . . .
Admiral Richard Byrd

Great God! This is an awful place . . .
Robert Falcon Scott

PART ONE

1938–39

CHAPTER ONE

The flying was bad. The corpse made it worse.

The whore named Ramona was wrapped in a red Hudson's Bay Company blanket and slung beneath Owen Hart's bush plane like one of those newfangled aerial torpedoes. Hart could hear her down there as the plane bucked in the rough air, the frayed ends of the hemp rope that snugged her in place beating an incessant tattoo against the bottom of his cabin door. He'd reluctantly agreed to transport the macabre cargo, but when it had become apparent at Fairbanks Field that the body wouldn't fit inside the already-stuffed cargo area, her cousin Elmer had persuaded him to tie Ramona to the undercarriage struts. "That way you won't have to smell her," the Eskimo pointed out.

Hart understood what the old man was trying to do in sending Ramona back to her birthplace at Anaktuvuk Pass, but all in all it seemed a bad business. In the pilot's experience women were generally bad luck, and he assumed dead women were doubly so.

It wasn't just the extra drag that made things difficult, but the weight. The single-engine Stinson was so badly overloaded he'd had to delay takeoff until late afternoon for the August air to cool sufficiently to give him the necessary lift. It was an old bush trick, waiting for thicker air. But now the light was slowly fading, Barrow had radioed of deteriorating weather in the north, and the plane rattled tiredly as its propeller clutched at the broad Alaskan sky.

He flew over an earth seemingly untouched by human hand or imagination. The boreal forest of pine and birch and boggy muskeg rolled north from Fairbanks for two hundred miles before ending at a tall wall of mountains. The trees stopped and beyond the Brooks Range was the vast Arctic plain, the North Slope, its tundra a great shaggy carpet already turning orange and scarlet at summer's end. And beyond *that* was the frozen Northern Ocean, the ice at this time of year holding offshore and the waves lapping lonely beaches of gray sand. There wasn't a damn thing in that awful emptiness that any man could really want—except perhaps freedom, or the room to hide from past disappointments.

Disappointments. He figured the woman strapped beneath his fuselage had had a few.

Weary, used-up Ramona—the whores were called "slot machines" in the bush—had worked the miners, trappers, and fishermen in Nome and Fairbanks and Ketchikan and Juneau. Old Elmer had said her spirit could be free of bad memories if she could come home. That seemed reason enough for Hart, who had no home.

"Christ, she was ugly," he'd said to Elmer as the Eskimo heaved her up against the bottom of the fuselage while Hart tied his slipknots. "How in hell did she ever make a living?"

"You shouldn't speak so of the dead," grunted Elmer, who only did this kind of lifting in moose season. "You should have seen her smile in the old days, before her husband took her to the camps and died drunk at cards."

"Hard to imagine her young," Hart said flatly. He pulled on the rope. "There, she's tight."

"You're a good man, Owen, for taking her."

"Well, she's got about as much money as any other passenger

I've met in this godforsaken icebox. At least I'll have company while I fly myself broke."

Elmer misunderstood. "Yes, you'll have Ivan." That was the name of his half-blind, half-crippled, ear-chewed husky. The dog was as pug-ugly as Ramona and smelled about as bad, yet Hart was taking the mutt to Anaktuvuk anyway: probably to die as well. The animal was no good on a team anymore.

"Shortwave says the weather's getting bad up north," Hart noted.

"You'll have an angel on your shoulder," the Eskimo assured. Hart knew that Elmer believed in angels as solemnly as he did the return of the salmon or the cycle of winter.

Now, in mid-flight, Hart found himself wanting to believe in Elmer's angel as the Stinson began to buck and the weather worsened. He was usually a safe flier, which meant a cautious one, and of course that was what cost him his shot at the big time in 1934 and sent him like a whipped dog to the North.

"I didn't hire you, Owen, to advise me what I shouldn't do, I hired you to find a way I *could*," the millionaire Elliott Farnsworth had told him as Hart had slewed their plane around to race away from the storms of Antarctica. In retreating, the pilot had ruined the explorer's first great chance to fly across the southern continent. Farnsworth had lived to come back three years later and try it again, finally making what should have been a fourteen-hour crossing in twenty-two days after putting down for periodic storms. And Hart had been dismissed long before that as the pilot without grit, the man who hesitated, the exacting, overcautious cold-weather flier whose heart had chilled at the critical moment. Farnsworth, having spent so much, had not hesitated to complain bitterly in the press.

Now here was bad weather again, clouds rolling down the barren slopes of the Brooks Range like a mirror reflection of surf hissing up a steep beach, and once again Hart had a woman to think about. "Hang on, lady," he whispered to Ramona. The Stinson hit a pocket and bounced and there was a bark and a yelp at the back,

"Shut up, Ivan!" he called. "You're the only damn thing in God's Creation uglier than that whore!"

The earlier woman had been named Audrey. He'd found her in California when preparing with Farnsworth. Actually, she'd found *him:* approaching him on a Long Beach float, both the tethered seaplane and her halo of hair afire from a golden dusk. She was a kind of woman he'd never known, exhibiting the poise that comes with effortless beauty and drawn to the dock not so much by the money as by the sense of limitless adventure that millionaires like Farnsworth exuded. She glowed from the electric atmosphere of pre-expedition camaraderie and fed on its energy, funny and fascinated.

And in the ensuing weeks he'd lost his heart and maybe something else. Because when the critical moment came at the bottom of the world, he'd finally been afraid. Not at the risk of losing himself so much as of losing her, of never coming back to all she represented: the perfume of her, the soft caress of her hair, her implicit promise that life was not just grim struggle but sweetness as well. And in *not* risking he'd lost her ever more completely, of course, lost her in a rush of shame and hurt pride and devastating regret. Since then, he'd come to regard all women with a tight wariness.

The Alaskan light was wan, the sun down somewhere behind the mountains, and only lingering chinks of silver glimmered through. Unconsciously adopting a half grin—his trademark reaction to worry—Hart leaned forward and calculated his chances. He had the lean build of the rangy Montanan he was, not so much muscled as wiry—a cowboy body, she'd called it. He was handsome in a rugged way, dark hair falling toward smoke-gray eyes and a nose bent just slightly from being cracked on the cockpit rim of a flipped over barnstormer. His cheekbones and chin were as hard as the country he was flying through, but his grin conveyed reassurance. If he wished it a woman would return his look, before glancing uncertainly away.

He didn't want to turn back, not with a corpse on board that needed to freeze into the permafrost. If he found the mouth of the

pass in time he might be able to fly under the weather to
Ramona's home. He'd hit the range a bit east of the opening and
now skirted the foothills to search, storm clouds stacking above
him like dark towers. The plane lurched in the rising wind and
Elmer's husky let out a low howl.

It had been this way in 1934 when Farnsworth tried to become
the first man to fly 3,400 miles across Antarctica. The expedition
was dogged by ill fortune. First the Northrop monoplane *Polar
Star* had wrecked its undercarriage when the ice shelf being used
as a makeshift runway prematurely broke up: only the wings,
caught by ice floes as the aircraft dropped toward the water, prevented the plane from disappearing into the sea completely. The
millionaire steamed back to the United States to make repairs—
Hart seeing Audrey again, sinking helplessly into the pool of her
green eyes—and then returned dangerously late in the season, toward the end of the Antarctic summer.

This time weather was the enemy, week after week of storm
and overcast. The millionaire's mood turned as foul as the climate
and he finally ordered his men to pack for home. Of course it was
then that a bowl of blue sky opened up like the doorway to
heaven. "We're going!" Farnsworth roared excitedly. The crew
heaved supplies on board the plane as Hart and his employer
crouched over the maps a final time. In little more than an hour
they'd lifted off, sprinting south. Then, three hours into the
flight, a wall of cloud loomed over the polar plateau and Hart
swung away.

"Dammit, man, what are you doing?" Farnsworth cried, looking up from his chart.

"That's suicide weather, Elliott." The featureless white of the
Antarctic plateau had dissolved into the rushing fog of an ap-
proaching storm. "You didn't pay me to let you go down in that.
We're going back."

Farnsworth protested that the front looked weak. Or that they
might fly through it, or over it, or around it. That they were turning their back on history. He'd sputtered and raged and finally
just seethed on the long painful retreat home, as the weather first

chased them and then hung back over the white horizon, a taunting ghost. Back on Snow Hill Island the financier muttered "damned yellow" within hearing of the crew. Owen had stalked away in his own bottled anger, neither man really knowing if a path could have been found or if a break in the clouds would have proved a sucker hole leading them to whiteout and death. And in making his call Hart *had* committed a kind of suicide, giving up a sliver of Lindbergh-like fame for doubt, for whispers, for airfield second-guessing. No one would talk about it directly, of course. Especially not the woman. Audrey was incapable of knowing what to say because Hart didn't know himself. And ultimately, as if each was marooned on a fissuring shelf of ice, they drifted apart.

So Hart finally came to Alaska where he didn't have to face anyone not talking about it. Where the country was as fierce and empty as his heart. Where the almosts and what-ifs and do-overs wouldn't haunt him quite as badly. Maybe. Where he could wonder all by himself if the arrogant millionaire was secretly right— that he'd looked out over a frozen wasteland and allowed it to swallow his senses, squeeze his heart. And then turned away.

"Snow." He grimaced, watching the flakes whip past his windshield. Alaska was wrapped in gauze, the view losing definition, and Hart knew his chance of finding Anaktuvuk Pass was blurring with it. Still, as he drifted down closer to the forest, the wilderness offered a shred of familiarity: the dark black-green of the trees, the dull pewter of taiga lakes, a familiar scale of height and distance. In Antarctica, by contrast, there had been a glorious clarity of atmosphere that destroyed depth perception: a seemingly airless infinity above sterile whiteness without a hint of life. The continent, bigger than the United States, boasted an emptiness as intimidating as a cell, its clouds boiling down from the high polar plateau. Alien, primeval, Creation before the fire.

As the Stinson skipped from pocket to pocket of air, wings flapping as they picked up a rime of ice, the engine roared and then groaned. Only the toes of the Brooks Range were visible now and they'd turned white. He skittered west, looking for the

John River, which rose near Anaktuvuk, and hoping he wouldn't overshoot and pick up the Alana, a river that dead-ended in the mountains. He cursed himself for being so anxious to lift away from Fairbanks and cursed Elmer for saddling him with a decomposing corpse. The cockpit windows were frosting, so he cursed the Stinson's balky heater as well. It was hard to believe the warmth of Fairbanks had given way to this, but that was Alaska. Where was Elmer's angel?

Ramona, you're a hard-luck case even when you're dead.

There! A ribbon colored white and lead-gray, leading into a knot of storm. Hart banked and began following the river. It led to a gap in the foothills and he pressed on, five hundred feet above the John. The water was unfrozen and low at this time of year. Its exposed bars had turned white with snow flurries.

The air had stabilized since he'd crossed the edge of the storm but light and visibility continued to fade, leaving him in a box of cotton. He dipped lower toward the broad gravel channel, snaking the plane and sensing more than seeing the squeeze of enclosing hills. Still no Anaktuvuk. Ivan was whimpering, his toenails skittering as he scraped for purchase in the bucking plane. "Dog," said Hart, "I think we'd better put down."

He'd been foolish not to do so earlier, he realized. The fog of snow had cost him the ability to judge exactly how close he was to the ground, increasing the possibility he'd slam into it when he tried to land. He needed a dark log to serve as reference point but had left all trees behind. He was in a developing whiteout, the same effective blindness he'd feared in Antarctica. "A sane man would have fled to Brazil," he chided himself, not for the first time.

If he could drop a reference marker from the plane he could judge his approach to the ground. Something big, something colorful, something . . . red.

Ramona's blanket was red.

He debated it for only a moment. Crashing would do her no better good—she'd be chewed up if the undercarriage broke and the plane skidded down on top of her—and the snow might cushion her fall. She was beyond caring, wasn't she? The only danger seemed to be the possibility of angry relatives if she was busted up too much. Right now they seemed less threatening than the unyielding flank of a mountain.

Banking as steeply as he could, he turned downriver, anxiously watching a snow slope solidify off his wing tip. Then he continued turning until he was pointing north again, satisfied he could maintain that orbit. There was a gravel bar below, far superior to boggy tundra for a landing. He unlatched the plane door and pushed it open against a shriek of wind and cold, holding it with his leg. Leaning out, one hand on the stick as he circled, he began tugging at the slipknots that held Ramona in place. Ivan kept up a low, rumbling moan.

Hart clung to a fistful of blanket. At the point where the John's channels joined, he let go. Ramona slumped, the wind caught her, and she was gone.

The Stinson bounced upward and circled. There! The red blanket was bright as a cherry against the snow, closer than he'd imagined: nervously, he pulled up a few feet. Then he aimed for her cigar-shaped form, wanting his undercarriage to touch just past her. Flaps down, power reduced, he glided down, fighting small gusts. The heavily laden plane was sluggish. He aimed as if to ram her and then hopped over Ramona at the last minute, striking the bar beyond. The plane bounced once, twice, set down, stumbled over a rock, began to slow. He'd made it!

Then it all went wrong. The right wheel banged into a snow-hidden hole and shattered, a wing tip caught, and the plane jerked sideways, pivoting out of control. The propeller chewed into gravel and disintegrated, one piece cracking the windshield. The engine screamed, coughed, died. And then it should have been quiet except that Ivan was barking excitedly. Hart blinked. He'd been thrown onto the control panel. Cargo had lurched forward to occupy the space where his head had been and he reached up to shove it back.

The plane was awkwardly tilted. He popped open the door on the elevated side, pushed clear, and dropped to the wet, snow-dusted ground, sweating. He sat a minute on the hard gravel and then stood unsteadily and backed off to survey the damage. His propeller had become two wooden stumps. One wing was crumpled. The wheels and struts were gone and if Ramona had still been strapped on she'd have been crushed. His plane was finished, and so was he. He had no money to repair the damage, and, after this, precious little reputation to get a loan.

"Damn, damn, damn." The world was a white blur of gusting snow. He assumed he was near Anaktuvuk but had no idea how far. There was no real danger, he thought: the storm would soon blow over this time of year. He'd just have to wait.

He dug out his parka and some jerky, throwing a bit to the dog. Then he sat in the cockpit. *Jesus!* Well, he could still probably find a flying job in the Lower 48, running a mail route and going crazy from boredom. Or he could chuck the whole business and stay up here and fish. To hell with it. To hell with everything.

CHAPTER TWO

A low growl from Ivan prodded Hart from sleep. The dog had its nose up: it sensed something, or maybe smelled it. The light was dim and the pilot peered into the thinning snow, trying to spot what the husky was so uneasy about. Then the curtain of flakes shifted and a huge shape ambled along the edge of the bar. Grizzly!

The bear's cinnamon coat was flecked with snow, the muscles of its neck and back rippling along its hump. Hart groped behind his seat for his sheathed Winchester .30-.30 and levered a shell into the rifle's chamber. The bear took no notice of the click. Then Ivan began barking excitedly and the grizzly's muzzle came up, not so much fearful as puzzled. Slowly it put its nose down and began ambling casually downriver, as if to retreat without admitting it. Hart glanced around the cockpit. The airplane's metal skin suddenly seemed not only cold, but thin. He was relieved the bear had moved on.

Then he remembered Ramona. Of all the luck! It would be less than easy to explain to the village of Anaktuvuk Pass that not only had he used one of its natives as an aerial bomb, he'd allowed her to be devoured by a wild animal as well. Death had not robbed her claim for final decency. He'd have to go get her.

He climbed out of the plane with the Winchester at the ready and began walking back toward Ramona's body, his skin prickling with unease. The grizzly's tracks were huge, like dinner plates with claws. Soon the Stinson was invisible in the fog behind him and he began to turn around periodically, looking for stalking bear. The rush of the river hid all other noise and he couldn't smell or see a thing. Perhaps his own scent would scare the animal off, letting him retrieve the body in peace. "Bear!" he shouted, to encourage the animal to continue on its way. The noise seemed inconsequential.

He saw the grizzly before he saw Ramona. It was a twitching boulder at the limit of his vision, bent over the red blanket and working at the body with a massive paw. He waited to see if the animal might lose interest but the grizzly showed no sign of doing so. Slowly he raised the rifle up, its stock cold against his cheek, and fired deliberately a few feet to the right of the bear's muzzle, watching splinters of gravel fly. Its head jerked up in surprise, grunting.

"Go away, bear!" Hart shouted, without much hope.

He fired again past the animal's head, the bullet kicking up a splash in the river. Rather than flee, the grizzly snarled and reared up on its hind legs, trying to make out this intruder with its dim eyesight. The pilot waited to see if the animal would charge or run, meanwhile sliding replacement shells into the chamber.

Then the bear attacked.

Hart was nearly certain he saw a ripple in the grizzly's shoulder where the first shot struck home, but the animal didn't slow at all. Roaring, it devoured the intervening space between them in a few heartbeats, the beast a wall of furred fury that swelled to consume all of the pilot's vision. He levered and fired, levered and fired, levered and fired, nightmarishly without seeming effect, praying that the bucking Winchester wouldn't jam. There was a click, a signal the last shell was gone, the bear was close enough to smell . . . and then it abruptly collapsed as if someone had jerked a string and its bones had melted to hot wax. The grizzly crashed and slid, groaning, its angry muzzle exhaling one last cloud of steaming air. Then it was still.

Hart went to Ramona. It was difficult to tell which damage had been done by the fall and which by the bear. The blanket was filthy and half unwrapped, a dangling arm scuffed or bitten. Kneeling, he folded the arm back inside and re-covered the body, retying the ropes holding the shroud in place. Then, hoisting the deadweight over his shoulder, he staggered slowly back to the plane.

The husky was scratching to get out. Hart let him, to stand guard, and then pushed Ramona into the cockpit and clambered in beside her. He'd refused to do this in Fairbanks but now the body didn't bother him. *Still comforting lonely men.* Cradling the rifle in his arms and carefully leaning against the opposite door of the plane, he dozed. This time he didn't dream.

He woke to a brilliant morning. The overcast was breaking up and the sun blazed with enough heat to make the snow sweat. He climbed out stiffly, drank from the river, and chewed on a piece of jerky. No bears were to be seen, or anything else for that matter. The treeless whiteness of the scene made him think of the moon and he tried to guess how far it was to Anaktuvuk. The natives knew he was due the day before and radios would be crackling back and forth.

Prudence suggested waiting so long as snowmelt didn't push up the John River. He watched the old dog trot down the sandbar, sniff at the bear, and then come quickly back to settle down under the broken wing of the plane. In clearing weather Hart felt even stupider for having crashed his Stinson. He should have turned back to Fairbanks or Bettles, Ramona or no.

He joined the dog and dozed again, then woke shortly after noon to the sound of an engine. A plane! It came up valley out of the south, the glint of metal growing. Karl Popper's orange and silver bush plane, by the look of it. It roared low over the sandbar and circled once, a passenger peering out the side window, and then went on toward Anaktuvuk.

Popper would put down at the village and walk in with the Eskimos to fetch Hart and the cargo. The pilot waited. Clouds drifted in again, first white and then gray. The sun was shut away, the air cooled and rain began to spatter down. Uneasily, he noticed that the river had come up almost a foot with the warming weather. The bar had shrunk and the willows on the far shores were starting to be tugged by the rising current. If he waited too long it would be too high to ford. He wished the Eskimos would show up.

It started raining harder, washing away the thin snow. Hart crouched under the wing, considering. Finally he decided to cross over and start walking up the valley. He was getting awfully hungry anyway.

The rifle went over his shoulder again and the remaining jerky in a pocket. Then he picked up Ramona. The feeling of unwanted responsibility was beginning to be replaced by the companionship of shared experience. She was now too stiff to drape over his other shoulder and so he had to carry her rigid form in his arms, like a log. "You're gaining weight," he said with a grunt.

After crossing the river, he'd gone only a few hundred yards when Ivan let out a low growl. Another grizzly? Hart set Ramona down carefully and unshouldered his rifle. The brush ahead of him moved. He levered a fresh shell into the chamber and aimed.

"Are you already so hungry that I look like food to you?" a voice called out. Shrouded in furs, a figure emerged from the brush and slogged toward him. Two others followed farther behind.

Hart lowered his rifle. "I thought you might be a bear."

"Ah, a white man," the Eskimo said. "When they come to hunt, nothing is safe. I hide in Anaktuvuk." He put his arms up over his face in mock fear.

"I'm hauling cargo, not hunting," Hart said sheepishly. He told the Eskimo his name.

"Isaac Alatak," the Eskimo replied. "And I'm told by Mr.

Popper you've stopped hauling and started hunting, judging by what he saw from his airplane. Is not one bear enough for you?"

Hart accepted the inevitable ribbing. "More than enough."

The second man caught up to them. "I've heard of dedicated sportsmen, but cracking your plane up to get at a grizzly is a bit much, Hart." It was Popper. "I think you need another hobby."

"Or another career. Thanks for coming to fetch me, Karl."

"Well, I was paid. For a change." He jerked his head toward the third figure.

That other man hung back a few steps and said nothing, preferring to observe the soaked pilot.

"I'm bringing a body to Anaktuvuk," Hart said. "Ramona Umiat. She died of TB." He pointed to the form lying in the mud at his feet. Startled, he saw part of the blanket had unwrapped again and her arm had once more come free. "She's had a rough time, I'm afraid."

The Eskimo squatted down and touched the still form. Then he crossed himself. "What have you done with my sister, white man?"

Hart winced at the relationship. "I'm sorry. I got caught in the storm. Couldn't make the village."

The Eskimo looked mournfully at the battered body. "Foolish day to fly in, white man. Foolish time for such a sacred responsibility. You need to learn caution. Always the white man is in such a hurry."

Hart opened his mouth, then said nothing.

"I don't think Mr. Hart crashed on purpose," the third man said. Hart was surprised. From the tone of his voice it was obvious he was not Eskimo, or American either. He had a German accent. "Perhaps he was prudent enough not to fly your sister into a mountainside. *Sprechen sie Deutsch,* Hart?"

"Some, from my youth," the pilot replied in German. "I grew up in a German settlement in Montana."

"Yes, I've checked your ancestry," the stranger said, continuing in German.

The reply gave Hart pause. "And you are . . . German? You

come here to climb?" Sometimes krauts came to Alaska for the mountains. They were nuts for mountains.

"An opportunity," the stranger replied. "I'd planned to contact you in Fairbanks but you'd just left. Despite the weather. A decision that seems counter to your reputation."

"Reputation?"

"Antarctica."

There was silence a moment. "The weather was fine when I left," Hart said. "When you fly you have to make decisions."

"I respect that," the stranger said.

Alatak produced a small hatchet and began slashing at the willows. "I'll make a sling for my sister while you practice your German." Popper bent to help but Hart, mystified by the stranger, made no move. He was too numb.

When it became apparent he wasn't going to speak, the German did—this time in English. "My name is Otto Kohl. I'm a German-American trade representative. I've come halfway around the world to speak with you. When Anaktuvuk radioed that your plane was missing I feared I'd wasted my time on a dead man. Mr. Popper, though, convinced me to hire his plane and have a look for you. Lucky for you that I did."

"I would've been all right."

"Perhaps." Kohl looked away down valley. "Could you show me your plane? I'd like to make a complete report."

Hart was taken aback. "A *report?* You from the government?"

"Not exactly. Is your plane near here?"

Hart looked at Alatak. "Go on," the Eskimo grumbled, knowing it wasn't far. "We'll finish here."

Wordlessly, Hart led the way back through the brush to the bank. The river was rising swiftly and the bar was almost gone. A channel had opened under the fuselage and the crippled Stinson was rocking in the flow. As they watched, it slid a few feet downstream. "I'm going to lose my whole damn cargo."

"Yes," Kohl observed. "Fortune is curious, isn't it?"

The pilot turned to study his companion more closely. He looked near fifty, with a trim mustache, pale, soft skin, and an irritating self-assurance for such wild surroundings. Well, it wasn't *his* plane that had been lost.

They stood there a moment in silence, rain drumming on their heads.

"Who the hell *are* you?"

Kohl smiled. "I'm based in Washington but represent the German government." He pointed to the plane, beginning to tilt. "I could report to the Reich that you incautiously flew into bad weather and landed poorly, exhibiting neither courage nor wisdom." He waited for Hart to react, but the pilot said nothing. "Or I could report you have a knack for survival in polar weather conditions, even saving a passenger from a grizzly bear, albeit a dead passenger."

"Why should I care what you report?"

"Let me be blunt," the German replied. "Your misfortune may prove to be our opportunity because it may predispose you to accept what I'm about to offer. You're well aware that my government is controversial. You may be aware it has limited experience in Antarctic exploration: Germany has yet to make any lengthy presence there, unlike the British or Norwegians or you Americans with Admiral Byrd. You're certainly aware that under National Socialism, my country is moving quickly to claim her rightful place as an equal in the rank of nations. You, on the other hand, are in financial difficulty, I suspect. You've just lost your primary possession. You lost some of your reputation as a flier in 1934 and this incident will hardly restore it. Yet I'm here to offer you another chance. To be part of history."

Hart stood watching his plane. As if drawn by a giant unseen hand, it sank toward the center of the channel.

"Why me?"

"Simple. You're an expert at Antarctic flying. You're what we need."

"I was fired in the Antarctic. My boss said I chickened."

"And did you?"

There was a silence.

"I've done some checking," said Kohl. "You were fired for *cau-*

tion. We Germans can be determined, even headstrong, but we know prudence is a virtue as well. In any event you know about Antarctic oils, fuels, clothing, and navigation."

"Wait a minute," Hart said, still absorbing what the German was saying. "I fly my plane into the ground and you *still* want to hire me?"

Kohl shrugged. "You strike me as a man who accepts the options he has and chooses well. And, frankly, for us your situation is ideal. We want to make clear to the world that our mission is one of peaceful exploration. As an American, a foreigner, your presence will reinforce that." The German eyed him intently. "In your present situation, may I assume politics are a nonissue?"

"I don't follow politics." Hart tried to think. He hadn't made up his mind about the Nazis. Hitler was a dictator, certainly, but he'd put Germany to work. Lindbergh had visited and come away impressed. But Hart knew why Kohl had come all the way to Alaska. Not everyone wanted to work for the Reich. Not everyone had forgotten the Great War. "I'll think about it."

"Certainly. Think all you want, as we hike back to Anaktuvuk. Think tonight as you eat, and then sleep. Think, and ask me any question you care to. And then you must decide because Mr. Popper and I are returning to Fairbanks in the morning. We have room for an employee."

Kohl smiled, but there was little warmth in it.

They went back to where the Eskimo had slung Ramona between willow branches. The German and Hart took one end, Popper and the Eskimo the other. The dog led off. As always the tundra was miserable walking, spongy and ankle-twisting, but the trudge was warming.

"This expedition, will it be reported?" Hart asked Kohl in German.

"Reported?"

"In the newspapers. If it succeeds, will the world know about it?"

"The men who make it will be as famous as they wish," the German replied. "As successful as they dare."

They reached Anaktuvuk after midnight, the tethered huskies of the village barking excitedly at Ivan's approach. Despite the late hour half the village came out to meet them, taking Ramona's battered body away for cleaning and wrapping and final rest. Her condition caused some looks at the pilot but no one spoke. Word of the bear had spread.

Hart took Popper aside. "This guy is offering me a job in Germany," he said. "What do you think of him?"

Popper shrugged and spat. "He paid me in cash."

Later, at the mission house, the two bush pilots ate some soup and bread and warmed themselves in front of the stove. Hart thought about what Kohl had said. The German's arrival seemed so well timed. He wondered if Elmer's angel was real after all.

"Sorry about your plane, Hart," Popper said.

"It's simpler in Antarctica," Hart said drowsily. He was trying to resummon that world.

"What do you mean?"

"No one lives there. No one stays there. It has no memory."

"No memory? Bah! Every place has history."

"No," Hart said. "Here there's history, because people are here to remember, but not there. It has no past. Only a great, yawning now."

"Sounds *too* simple to me."

Owen smiled. "Maybe you're right." He sighed. "But when everything is now, you can always start over."

CHAPTER THREE

Berlin was a brown city set ablaze with the red of Nazi banners, their fabric caressing hard stone. To Hart, arriving in the fall of 1938, it seemed a richly conservative metropolis crackling with the excitement of the dangerously new, a resurgently smug place with a sense of watchful unease. A place on stage, a grand opera that was dramatically unfolding. Boots and high heels, black uniforms and silver furs.

"Welcome to the future," Otto Kohl greeted him.

The two had parted company at Fairbanks. Kohl had gone ahead to Washington and Germany while Hart remained in Alaska to check out of his rooming house, store his meager belongings, and wrap up his simple affairs. Being single and bankrupt gave life a certain simplicity, he reflected. And now he felt infused with new purpose. *Antarctica.* He'd thought he would never go near the place again. Yet suddenly it promised both adventure and redemption. And with a bunch of krauts, no less!

He'd felt a curious German mix of arrogance and apprehension even on arrival in Hamburg. There'd been a sense of entering something captive being hurtled toward a great unknown. The energy of Germany was palpable. There was the drumbeat of reawakening industry, made visible by the shroud of steam and greasy smoke above the port city's factories. There was the officious, pompous bustle of uniformed bureaucrats, stamping this, peering at that, smelling of sausage and beer. There was the shriek of ferry and steamer whistles, the clang of trolleys and the excitement of crowds admiring an example of the beetle-shaped "people's car" that Hitler had invented. Yet the Germans were quieter than he'd imagined: not diffident, even a bit boastful about their astonishing transformation since the Nazis came to power, but cautiously restrained all the same. As if there was an unspoken lid on laughter and enthusiasms. There simply were a lot of uniforms.

Adding to the surreal quality were the many Berlin shop fronts still boarded up from the anti-Jewish terror of Crystal Night less than two weeks before. Hart had heard reports that some Jews were fleeing the country and rumors that others were simply disappearing into a vast new Nazi prison system. The pilot knew no Jews—at least he didn't *know* of knowing any—but the stories were unsettling. As hopeless as his situation had seemed in Alaska, he couldn't help wondering if accepting employment from these people was wise. He decided that he admired their resurgence but questioned their judgment. His task was to separate the application of polar expertise from politics, to remain focused on exploration and science.

The Germans lived up to their reputation for efficiency. Kohl was brisk at the Berlin train station: snapping orders to a porter to collect the pilot's bag, leading him at a near-trot to the taxi stand, issuing crisp instructions about the hotel, and giving him a clip of new Reichsmarks for meals and expenses. A courier would arrive at the hotel the next morning at nine o'clock with suitable clothes, Kohl explained. Hart would then be free until four when the German would pick him up to meet Reich Minister Hermann Göring. They would journey to Göring's estate of Karinhall at the outskirts of Berlin and dine that evening with the officers of the Antarctic expedition, preparatory to sail-

ing late in the year for the southern continent. The expedition
was timed to take advantage of Antarctica's brief "summer" of
good weather, the opposite of seasons in the Northern
Hemisphere. It was very much Göring's expedition, Kohl explained, and the powerful minister was giving it his personal attention. He had a curiosity about the world.

Hart was welcome to tour Berlin but was not to take notes or
pictures, speak to anyone more than necessary, or discuss the expedition. "Circumspection is a key to our success," Kohl had said,
pushing Hart into a taxi. The pilot found himself at the swank
Adlon Hotel on Unter den Linden, not far from the Foreign and
Propaganda ministries.

An Interior Ministry courier arrived promptly the next morning as promised, greeting Hart at his hotel room door with a stiff-
armed salute and a "Heil Hitler!"

Hart looked at him with bemusement. "For God's sake, put
your arm down." The messenger looked miffed, as if a compliment had been batted away, unacknowledged. He delivered a
written invitation to the Reich Minister's Karinhall and a box
with a suit, shirt, and tie. A handwritten note from Kohl told
Hart to be wearing them at four.

To kill time the pilot wandered outside. The traffic and bustle
of a huge city intimidated him so he crossed to the Tiergarten
Park, barren and empty in November. He walked briskly, enjoying the empty cold. Then he returned to his room, gave himself
a full hour to struggle into the new suit, descended to the lobby
fifteen minutes early, and waited uncomfortably. He felt the
concierge sneaking glances at him.

As if driven by a clock, a black Mercedes limousine arrived
outside the hotel doors promptly at four and the chauffeur opened
the rear door with a click of booted heels. The rearmost seat was
filled but the facing one was empty, so Hart climbed in to find
himself sitting backward, knee to knee with Kohl and a beautiful young blonde in an evening dress and fur wrap. The door
clicked shut and the car purred forward.

"This is Leni Stauffenberg, the film actress," said Kohl, who looked as assured in his business suit as Hart felt uncomfortable.

The woman flashed a stunning but distant smile, sufficient to serve notice that there was an insurmountable wall between them. She had no interest in mere pilots.

"The Reich Minister enjoys the company of lovely women from the film industry," Kohl explained. "After being widowed he married the actress Emmy Sonnemann, you may know. It was the most stunning ceremony of the new regime."

"I preferred the '36 Opera Ball," Leni said. "I was told he spent a million marks on that one."

"Miss Stauffenberg later caught his eye in perhaps her finest work, *Conquest of the Crest.* Remarkable climbing picture. Have you heard of it?"

"We don't get German movies in Alaska."

"Of course." Kohl smiled thinly.

"I almost froze making that picture," Leni said. "That bastard Reinhardt insisted on shooting everything outdoors. I got caught in an avalanche! I nearly died!"

Hart studied her. He couldn't imagine this woman on a mountain, let alone in an avalanche. He wondered what her intention was in attending this dinner. She gave no sign of being attached to Kohl, and Göring, while famous, was not only married, he was fat. Maybe the Reich Minister had something to do with the German movie business.

Noting his curious scrutiny of the actress, Kohl felt compelled to issue a caution. "I should mention, it's best not to be too inquisitive about the Reich Minister's social life when we're at Karinhall. The presence of his female guests is decorative, you understand. Suppose nothing else."

Leni poked her companion. "I'm not a *decoration*," the actress objected. "Hermann is simply a wonderful man," she said smugly to Hart. "Funny, enthusiastic. A child, really. You must let him show you his trains."

The pilot looked quizzical at this.

"Model railroad," Kohl said. "The biggest I've ever seen. But he's no child. He was an ace in the Great War."

"Well, Hermann makes me laugh."

"Leni, he shot down more than twenty men."

She laughed herself. "As I said, boyish charm. Have you looked at the pictures at Karinhall? He was really quite handsome back then. Still is, in a way."

"Well, the Reich Minister is a great man," Kohl grumped, somehow annoyed by this lighthearted affection he clearly deemed inappropriate. "Second only to Hitler. He runs not only the Luftwaffe but the Prussian Interior Ministry, the Forestry Commission, and the Hunt. He's President of the Reichstag and founded the Gestapo. A truly superhuman energy."

"They say he draws six salaries." Leni winked.

Kohl chose to ignore this gossip. "It's too bad about the wound he suffered at the Munich Putsch. The reliance on pain relievers. Hart, don't let the burdens that the Reich Minister shoulders deflect your honor to him. Your presence on this voyage as a foreigner is important to its image but sensitive. I've been working hard to assure the authorities you'll not be a problem. Göring is key. You must be certain to satisfy him. Keep your curiosity within limits. Be ready to do as instructed. Restrain your American . . . casualness."

"Oh, Otto," Leni scolded with a grin. "I think Mr. Hart will muster the proper respect."

Hart had only seen Göring in newsreels and thought the man looked clownish, but he kept that opinion to himself. "I'll do my best," he told Kohl, determined to be polite but not a toady. He was irritated that the German was treating him like a rube in front of the woman. "He'll have to take me as I am."

Leni nodded. "Good for you! That's the kind of attitude Hermann enjoys!"

The car raced through the suburbs, the trim German homes getting larger and farther apart as they journeyed into the forest surrounding the city. It seemed to Hart that all of Germany was like a model railroad: too tidy to be a place people really lived in.

Litter was absent, cars were washed, and the forest itself seemed groomed, its floor picked clean of branches and leaf litter. He had a sense of having entered onto a stage set, and the company of a movie star reinforced the notion. She drew Kohl into gossiping about Nazis whom Hart had never heard of. He half listened, watching the scenery.

It took nearly an hour to reach the gates of Göring's estate. An unmarked road departed from the main highway and the car turned down the oak-shaded lane. Then it slowed to weave around concrete pylons and approach a guard station. A white-painted pole blocked the road and gray-uniformed soldiers with strapped submachine guns dangling from their necks sauntered out as the limousine came to a halt. They barely glanced at the driver, clearly recognizing him, but they peered inside intently— first to Kohl, then Hart, and then with appreciation to Miss Stauffenberg. "Papers, please!" a handsome lieutenant barked, keeping his eyes on the actress. She ignored him.

The guards studied their passes as if this was the first time they'd seen writing. Then, with elaborate slowness, they handed them back. "American," the lieutenant remarked. The wings on his uniform showed him to be a member of the Luftwaffe, the German air arm that Göring had reportedly made into the most powerful in the world. "New York, perhaps?"

"Alaska," Hart replied.

"Ah, yes." Clearly the place didn't register. "Soon we'll have planes that reach New York. Perhaps I'll see it one day, from the air." His smile was cold.

"Mr. Hart is an employee of the German government!" Kohl snapped with unmistakable authority.

The lieutenant stiffened. "Of course. You are free to proceed! Heil Hitler!" He snapped his salute.

"Heil Hitler," Kohl grunted, dismissing the sentry. The pole was raised and the limousine jumped forward.

Göring's estate was a vast park of forest, lake, and meadow, the car following a winding drive to a final vast lawn. Its crown was Karinhall, a feudal half-timbered château modeled on a rural retreat of Göring's former in-laws in Sweden: an edifice of leaded glass and soaring towers and steep, slate-gray roofs. It reminded Hart of a gingerbread fantasy.

"Where's Hansel and Gretel?" he murmured, both impressed and uneasy at this proximity to power.

Kohl gave him a warning glance. Leni smiled slightly.

The light was quickly fading from the brief November day and the mansion's windows glowed a welcoming yellow. Two more guards, these in black uniforms, flanked a massive oaken door. A German shepherd stood alertly as the limo pulled up but did not growl or bark.

An orderly trotted officiously down the stone stairs to meet them, moving to Leni's door first. She took his arm, stood expertly in her heels in the pea gravel, and then ascended the steps as if floating, the silk of her dress lightly kissing stone. How does she do that? Hart wondered, following. The massive entryway seemed to open of its own accord and then they were in a large flagstone foyer hung with medieval tapestries. Two suits of black armor stood guard. There were no swastikas or Nazi regalia in sight.

"Welcome to Karinhall," the orderly said. "Mr. Kohl." He gave a nod of acknowledgment. "So good to have you with us again, Miss Stauffenberg." A smile this time. Then, more appraising: "And yes, Mr. Hart. The Reich Minister is of course especially fond of pilots. You're actually the *second* American pilot to visit. You know of Mr. Lindbergh?"

"I know of him," Hart replied dryly. Was there anyone in the flying profession who didn't?

"A great man," the orderly enthused. "A great man."

Servants materialized to take their coats and then they moved to the Great Hall, a soaring, timbered cathedral of a room. Its walls were studded with game heads, a fire roared in a vast fireplace, and a table as long as a bowling alley occupied its center. The feeling of a stage set was sustained, as if Karinhall was designed not just as a home but as a kind of artificial realm, trying to couple Germanic charm with overbearing power. For Hart the power was there but the charm was not.

"Clearly, Herr Göring's politics have paid off," he noted mildly, his head rotating back to eye the timbered ceiling.

"The Reich Minister stood by the Führer in the dark days after the Putsch," Kohl said. "He went broke trying to represent the party while Hitler was in prison. He's exhibited the economic vision to remake Germany. Vision enough to reach all the way to the bottom of the world."

"A great man," Hart said, trying to estimate the length of the table. Fifty feet? It was bizarre to find himself here after Anaktuvuk Pass.

Suddenly, unannounced, a figure strode through the doorway. Not just a man but a presence. Göring was big, for one thing, almost decadently fat, and his girth was clothed in a snow-white uniform with gold epaulets at the shoulders and buttons and braid accenting them below. The belt was black and its buckle silver, a Nazi eagle at rigid attention in gold relief. The clothes were ornate but to Hart he looked faintly ridiculous, like a New York doorman. It was certainly disconcerting that instead of jackboots the Reich Minister wore slippers lined with fur. His complexion was healthy but too pink at the cheeks, as if he used rouge, and the fat of his jowls softened the military bearing. Yet Göring's air of authority remained unmistakable. There was a sense of arrogant proprietorship. The habit of command.

"Gentlemen, Leni!" Göring reached out with fingers that were short and fat and studded with rings. Kohl shook and then Hart followed, surprised by a pumping grip both energetic and soft. There was a slight sense of decay in the touch and yet Göring's eyes were iron-hard, black and judging—quite disconcerting, really. The entire effect was strange, and despite his determination not to seem obsequious, Hart felt off balance.

"So this is our American expert on Antarctica. A fellow flier! I must tell you, Hart, the only pure place is in the air."

"Yes, Reich Minister," Hart managed. "I share your enthusiasm. The air, and perhaps Antarctica."

"Ah really?" Göring looked genuinely interested. "And what is so pure about the southern continent?"

"Well . . ." Hart thought for a moment. "The ice, of course, is as white as your uniform. No, not just white but . . . prismatic. The colors are unworldly. And the air is clearer there. You can see to infinity."

"Ah, infinity." Göring laughed appreciatively. "I think I saw that a few times from my biplane in the war, looking over my shoulder into the barrel of an enemy machine gun. I'm not sure I'd like to see so much infinity again." Hart found himself joining the others in complimentary laughter, a solar system in orbit around its fat white sun. "But then the kind of purity you talk of, Hart—the sublime cleanliness of a place never before trod by man—that, that must be remarkable."

"It can be inspiring or frightening," Hart said without thinking, instantly feeling he'd betrayed himself.

"So I understand." Suddenly Göring's softness seemed to stiffen and his eyes bored into the pilot's as if taking Hart's measure. Owen forced himself to stare calmly back. "My pilots, the men I recruit, are not easily frightened."

"No, they're not, Herr Göring." You Germans were dogged enough to search me out in Alaska and paid to bring me here, he thought. If you don't want me now, then to hell with you.

The German held his gaze for a moment more and then abruptly smiled. The appraisal was done. "Good! You know, Hart, that's the name of the stag, a name that originally comes from the German word for 'horn'—and so I approve of your ancestry as well! Just like Lindbergh! We Germans are all pioneers of the air. Now come, come, into my library. You must meet your fellow adventurers."

CHAPTER FOUR

The library was the size of a small hangar, its gold-lettered books ranked as neatly as soldiers. Most looked new and completely unread: this was a room to impress, not to work in. A fire burned here as well. Clustered around a side table were four men and a woman, sipping wine. Their evident leader—the captain, Hart guessed—wore his Prussian aura of command on weathered features, his steel-gray hair close-cropped and his goatee trimmed with precision. Next to him was a tall, blond, Nordic man of about Hart's age who looked like he'd stepped from a Nazi recruiting poster. And a shorter, more officious-looking fellow with a mustache and gold wire-rimmed glasses. The oldest, at least in appearance, was a balding, somewhat cadaverous male with thin lips, yellowed teeth, and long, tobacco-stained fingers. He was smoking a cigarette. The woman Hart studied for a moment longer. She was about Leni Stauffenberg's age but did not pretend to the actress's ostentatious beauty. Her dark red hair was cut just below her shoulders, flipped slightly inward in a simple style, and she wore a modestly cut print dress and low heels. She appeared to wear no makeup and seemed to have no need of it. Her skin was clear and her blue eyes bright and intelligent.

"Captain Heiden!" Göring greeted the Prussian. "Let me present to you one of our country's representatives in America, Otto Kohl, our American consultant Owen Hart, and of course our own beautiful Leni Stauffenberg—even more stunning," and here the Reich Minister grinned like a playboy, "in the flesh than on the screen. Who would have thought it possible?"

Heiden bowed with Prussian formality and took the actress's gloved hand, kissing it lightly. Then he turned and gave a shorter bow to Hart. "So good of you to agree to accompany us, Mr. Hart," he said. "I'm Konrad Heiden, captain of the *Schwabenland,* the seaplane tender that will take us to Antarctica. Your experience in polar flying should prove invaluable. Let me introduce our political liaison, Jürgen Drexler"—the handsome blond gave a nod—"our chief geographer, Alfred Feder"—here the shorter man bobbed his head a bit shyly—"ship's doctor Maximilian Schmidt"—the smoker smiled remotely behind a cloud of exhaled smoke—"and Greta Heinz, our polar biologist." The woman smiled and looked at Hart with interest, keeping one hand on the stem of her wineglass and the other at her wrist, as if the goblet needed special support. She glanced quickly at Leni and then away, shy of the movie star's polish, and seemed to avoid even incidental eye contact with Kohl. Almost imperceptibly Drexler sidled an inch closer, as if to suggest a relationship. She gave no sign she noticed. She was attractive, Hart decided: not so much glamorous as interesting.

"Glad to meet you," Hart said. "It should be an intriguing adventure."

"Captain Heiden has had experience in the Arctic but this will be Germany's first great thrust toward the South Pole," Göring said. "We've had explorers there before—Erich von Drygalski even rose in a balloon just after the turn of the century, becoming the first Antarctic aeronaut—but the effort wasn't sustained. This time we're being systematic about it: we're staking our claim and planning to do Antarctic research. The expedition will have geopolitical implications as well." Göring turned toward the others. "And Mr. Hart has been assuring me about the beauty of the place. How I wish I could accompany you, to escape the cares of my office!"

"But Hermann, Germany would miss you so much!" Leni exclaimed, as if she thought Göring was really going to slip away to sea. She leaned toward him and grasped his arm.

"And I would miss Germany!" the Reich Minister said, beaming. The others smiled at this banter.

"So, Hart, I assume you didn't fly in the war," Drexler said, clearly sizing him up. The German was slim, athletic, and even in repose seemed to have the grace of a cat.

"I don't look *that* old, I hope," Hart replied.

"Ah!" Göring cried. "The unintended insults of arrogant youth." The group laughed.

"I did some flying on the barnstormer circuit," Hart said, "then flew in competition and in the Rockies, learning cold weather skills. Hired on with Elliott Farnsworth. And was fired when I wouldn't fly him into bad weather."

"Sometimes heroism must be put in abeyance," Drexler observed.

Unsure of what to make of that remark, the pilot turned to the geographer. "Alfred, do you know exactly where on the continent we're going?"

"I do," the man said with a certain self-satisfaction. "And the rest of you shall know when we get there."

There was an awkward pause and then Göring laughed explosively, drawing the others in. "Ha!" he crowed. "The white part, Hart! You're going to the cold part!" He laughed some more, patting Feder on the back. "I do like a man who can keep a secret."

Hart smiled, mystified by any secrecy.

Schmidt spoke up. "The truth is, Owen, like all explorers we don't know *exactly* where we're going. We've selected an area of interest with an eye to competing national claims and are looking for a possible permanent site for research, but this is of course an investigation of a new world." He took a puff. "You and your fellow pilots will be our eyes, from the air."

Hart nodded. "Well, I've got good eyesight, Dr. . . . Schmidt," he remembered. "You've been to sea before?"

"No, I've volunteered for this opportunity because it will allow me to explore my medical interest: the body in environmental extremes."

"You mean cold?"

"Cold and simplicity. No group of people has ever really *inhabited* Antarctica, and few plants and animals exist there. What remains, I hope, is medical truth shorn of the complexities and prejudices of our warmer world. To understand polar perils is to take a step toward conquering them, yes?"

"Or avoiding them, as we prudent pilots might advise." The others laughed, and the pilot, encouraged by this good humor, turned to the woman. "And Greta, you're a biologist? Looking at polar bears perhaps?"

She looked amused. "If you've truly been to Antarctica you know as well as I do that there are no bears there. Penguins, of course. And seals. But I'm primarily interested in krill."

The pilot nodded politely. "Those little shrimp things? We saw clouds of them in the ocean back in '34."

"Whale food, Hart! Whale food!" Göring boomed. "The key to scientific management of Antarctic whaling. One of many keys to Germany's bright future."

"Then this mission may indeed have significance for our whaling industry, Reich Minister?" Kohl inquired, with the tone of one who already knew the answer.

"What whaling industry, Otto?" Göring growled. "The damned Norwegians have a near-monopoly down there. They've laid a territorial claim and tried to chase others out. Well, two can play that game. This expedition will lay its own claim and with it the justification for expansion of the German whaling effort. Whale fat and oils are vital to sustaining our expanding economy. And the greatest whales in the world are to be found in that region."

"So," Hart said, turning back to Greta. "You'll be taking a census of this whale food?" He was intrigued by her. He'd never heard of a woman going to Antarctica.

"That and more," she replied. "I'm interested in the relationship between the world of the great—the whale, for example—and the small. The latter is my field of expertise: plankton, protozoa, bacteria, viruses . . ."

"Germs," Hart said with a grin.

"Yes, germs. You might not think so, but they reside in Antarctica too. They're capable of adapting to every condition, including cold. It is this adaptability of life that interests me."

Drexler piped up. "Greta is a woman who can look in a microscope and see a universe. We're lucky to have her." Greta smiled to acknowledge the compliment.

A bit obvious, Hart thought. He wondered what their relationship was.

"Hermann," Leni said, "Mr. Hart expressed interest in your trains."

"Really?" Göring said, his mood clearly jovial. "Are you a railroad enthusiast as well as an aeronaut?"

"Uhm, well, I like trains." He glanced at Kohl, who nodded approvingly. Drexler looked at Hart with amusement.

"Ha! I tell my staff it's an organizational exercise," Göring said, smiling. "Designing the tracks, scheduling the trains: not so different from running a nation. But secretly, Hart, I'm convinced we men remain boys, relishing our toys. We leave it to women to be the grown-ups in the house while we play in the outside world. It's one of the reasons I'm so happy that I'm a man—if you can forgive that, Miss Heinz!" Again, the group joined in his laughter.

"And why I'm happy to be a woman."

Göring bowed.

Puffing a bit, the Reich Minister led his entourage up a winding balustrade toward the attic. As they began to ascend Hart found himself just behind and to the right of Greta. Still curious about her, he tried to think of something to say but Drexler smoothly moved in front of him and slipped beside her, forcing the pilot to pause a moment on the stairs to avoid a collision. The tips of the German's fingers brushed her elbow as if to guide her and he whispered a comment. She raised her wineglass to her lips as they climbed, moving her arm slightly out of reach, but she also granted him a look and smile. Hart fell back.

The party went through an arched wooden door and filed into a dim, cavernous room. When all were present Göring flicked on the lights. Under the eves sprawled an enormous track set with model trains lined up on sidings. The set was the biggest Hart had ever seen: scale-model miles of track and a score of locomotives. Curiously, scenery was absent as if irrelevant to Göring's vision; the layout did indeed resemble some kind of enormous organizational chart in its abstract complexity. Hart was struck by its sterility. There were no miniature people in it.

"Oh Hermann, let me operate one of the trains!" Leni begged. Göring chuckled at her interest.

"And Mr. Hart, you must direct another!" the Reich Minister said. He showed them the controls. With a few jerks as he adjusted the speed, Hart managed to begin moving his train out of its station. The actress succeeded too. The trains traveled around a vast oval, occasionally passing each other on different tracks. It took some concentration to hold their speed at curves and pause at crossings to avoid a possible collision. The others watched politely, chatting among themselves.

"Your skill as a pilot serves you well as an engineer," said a soft voice at Hart's elbow. He glanced sideways. It was Greta.

He nodded, smiling tightly. "I was warned I might be tested, but no one talked about model trains." He nodded toward the actress at the other end of the control box. "Herr Göring does have an enthusiasm for toys, it seems."

Greta shrugged. "She's just for show. Did you know that the Reich Minister took a bullet at the Putsch?"

"Causes him a great deal of pain, apparently."

"In many ways. It was in the groin. Direct your jokes and sympathies accordingly." She smiled mischievously.

Suddenly Göring's voice boomed. "Now, Hart, you must ob-serve airpower in action! Your direction is impressive but what if you're caught in an extremity? How does one keep the system functioning?" He paused dramatically, then pushed a button.

There was a rattle and something swooped down from the shadowy eves above. Hart thought for a moment it was a swallow. Then he saw it was a model of a German Stuka dive-bomber, gliding down across the train as it dangled from a sloping wire. Göring stabbed another button and a pellet fell from its belly, arcing in with expert aim to bounce off one of Hart's boxcars. "A direct hit!" Göring exclaimed. "In combat your train would be cut in two." He laughed. "The next war will be decided in the air."

There was another rattle and a second model airplane flew jerk-ily down and released again, this time striking Leni's train. "Oh *pooh,* Hermann!" she exclaimed. "You're such a bully!"

Göring's eyes were already on Hart's train again as it rounded a curve. A third airplane rode its wire down from the gloom, aimed for Hart's engine. The pilot considered a moment, then tightened his hold on the electric throttle. When the pellet fell, he slammed his train to a halt. The bomb bounced harmlessly across the track ahead.

"Flying by wire is too predictable," Hart said.

Göring smiled, but a bit less broadly. "Very true. A quick re-action, Mr. Hart. Unpredictability is the first lesson of war." He emphasized this last, as if he'd sought to make that point to the others. "But I would still have cut the track."

"No matter." The pilot threw his train into reverse. "As a man of prudence, I'd be backing out of that war zone as fast as possi-ble." The group laughed, Greta clapping her hands once in ap-plause.

"And yet there might be an even better strategy." It was Jürgen Drexler, catching the woman's eye. "If you would allow me to take a turn at the controls, Owen?"

"Certainly." The American surrendered the throttle and backed away. The trains began moving around the oval again.

Greta was watching the German with interest and Hart searched for something to continue their conversation. "I understand the Reich Minister is the most popular of Germany's leaders," he finally tried.

She kept her gaze on the railroad, speaking quietly so as not to be overheard. "He's a brave man, I think. But he's had much trauma in his life. Years of exile and poverty, a virtual political outlaw. The loss of his first wife. The wound. It explains perhaps the morphine, the weight, the clothes."

"He certainly likes to dress up."

Greta lowered her voice even further. "We Germans joke about it. The story goes that Göring's Forestry Ministry was going to harvest the Tiergarten to build him an adequate-sized wardrobe. But the chief forester had to report back that the trees were gone already, they'd all been sawed into his coat hangers! We don't laugh at him, we laugh with him, because we can identify with his appetites. Or at least we try not to judge."

"Yet he judges us." Hart saw Göring's hand stray toward the button that would release his model warplanes.

"We serve at his pleasure. It's different here in Germany, Owen. We're a society with a purpose, but to have such purpose you can't rely on the mob: it must be directed by a few great men."

"I don't think the American voter thinks of himself as a mob."

She shrugged. "Still, someone must be in charge."

Just then there was a familiar rattle and a Stuka swooped down, its rigid wheels like the talons of a raptor. Hearing the noise, Drexler calmly reached across the control panel and threw a switch. "I've watched you at the controls, Reich Minister," he explained. His train shunted onto a new line just as Göring released his bomb. The pellet landed squarely on the newly emptied track and Drexler's train rumbled calmly past the impact point.

"Ach! Touché, Jürgen!" Göring exclaimed. "I'm outwitted!" The political liaison's train accelerated. "And on you go to your destination!" He laughed.

With the Reich Minister's good humor the others laughed too. Drexler nodded in acknowledgment and stole a glance at Greta. She replied with an encouraging smile. Owen found himself irked by the demonstration.

"Do you consider yourself a man of strong opinions, Owen?" she whispered, still watching Drexler.

He looked at her curiously, wondering if he'd become a toy in some game he didn't understand. "I . . . am adaptable, I guess."

She nodded knowingly. "That's obvious."

"Meaning?"

"Meaning you're here. In Germany. With us."

"No," said Hart, shaking his head. "You don't understand. I'm not *with* you, not *against* you. I'm simply on my way to Antarctica. Where politics don't apply."

"Ah! Wait until you get on the *Schwabenland*. A confined society, a long voyage. Humans wear politics as tightly as their skin." She was teasing him.

"Is that why Jürgen is necessary?"

She shrugged, watching the blond German as he stole a glance at them again. "Jürgen reminds us why we're here. He sees things clearly."

Drexler brought his train into the station. "I was admittedly fortunate that your attack coincided with the availability of a siding," he told the Reich Minister. "But there is a lesson here, no? A lesson for us in Antarctica, perhaps. If one way doesn't serve, another may suffice."

"Indeed, your twist has demonstrated the endless complications of war," Göring agreed. "Which is why battle is not as simple as it appears in the history books. Well. My Luftwaffe is out of bombs. Perhaps we should adjourn for dinner?"

There was no disagreement.

Greta moved off to congratulate Drexler. Over her head, he nodded at Hart.

The group filed down the stairs to a baronial dining room with timbered ceiling and glittering candles, more suits of armor posted in the shadows like hovering waiters. Two more lovely women—one a model, another an aspiring starlet, Hart gathered—joined the group. Göring took his place at the head of the table with the two actresses at either side and the model at the foot, facing him. There otherwise didn't seem to be assigned seating. Greta moved toward a chair and Drexler quickly moved forward to touch the back of an adjacent one as if asserting the spoils of victory. But at the last moment she unbalanced things by slipping sideways around Feder—"Alfred, I'd like to map out a sampling calendar based on your expected arrival and departure dates," she murmured—and swiftly plopped down between the geographer and Hart, giving the American pilot a quick smile. Owen sensed someone else looking at him. It was Kohl across the table, frowning and giving a barely perceptible shake of his head.

"And Owen," Greta said, turning away from Feder. "I'd like to learn more from you about America!"

"Well," Hart said, surprised by her continuing attention, "America is a bit what I suspect *you* to be: energetic and adventuresome."

"Ah. And unsettled?"

"You're describing yourself?"

"Perhaps."

"Hmm. Well, the frontier has closed. But the nation is uncompleted. America is an experiment, still playing itself out."

"Then perhaps that *is* me," she said, smiling.

Course followed course, Göring commenting on the food like a gourmand as he explained its origins or spicing or preparation. Given his girth and enthusiasms, it seemed almost appropriate when he finally turned the conversation back to whales.

"The most astonishing creatures," the Reich Minister said. "I believe the Creator placed them here as much for the nourishment of the soul as for the nourishment of industry. Of course, it is the latter that preoccupies me at the moment. To a strong nation the whale is as important as steel."

"Important for what?" Hart dared, genuinely curious. While

he knew whaling continued in the world, he'd always thought it belonged more to a bygone era of sailing ships and *Moby-Dick.*

"Fat, of course," the Reich Minister said, winking and patting his own stomach in self-deprecation. The others laughed again. "For margarine. And oil. Not for lighting anymore, no, we're no longer harpooning to read by. For munitions, Hart. Whale fat is a valuable ingredient of glycerin. And sperm oil is preferred for precision machinery such as fighter plane engines. The whale is vital for waging modern war."

"So this expedition *isn't* just for scientific purposes?" Hart asked.

"Science and national destiny are inextricably linked in the modern world," answered Heiden, making a rare contribution to the conversation.

"Well said, Captain!" exclaimed Göring. "Knowledge is power!"

"Knowledge is also *progress,*" added Greta. "After all, what ultimately sets us apart from the whales is what we *know.*"

"But this *is* a peaceful expedition?" persisted Hart, despite a frown of disapproval from Kohl.

Göring grew serious. "Life is competition, Hart," he said. "I don't draw the distinction between peace and war that the naive do."

"I think Owen's real question is whether the *Schwabenland* is a warship," said Kohl, trying to steer the conversation to safer ground.

"No, of course not! Do you think we'd enlist an American in our navy? Your mere presence underlines Germany's peaceful intentions. No, no, no. We sail for knowledge, but knowledge with purpose: to explore Antarctica and to establish our rights."

"We stake our claim in peace," Heiden said.

"Exactly," the Reich Minister said. "And if the Norwegians get in our way, our spirits are prepared for war!"

CHAPTER FIVE

The *Schwabenland* looked like an unpacked steamer trunk, its holds popped open and Antarctic supplies strewn on the Hamburg docks. Crates, canvas bags, tanks, tubes, and coils of rope and wire were heaped as if in anticipation of Christmas. Wooden skis were bundled like firewood, tents came wrapped in their own ropes and pegs, and cargo sleds machined in Bavaria were precisely lined on the creosote dock timbers as if on military parade. Pallets of canned food shone dully under the gray German sky, freshly filled and without rust. There were ice axes, crampons, fur parkas, boots, nets, carboys, buoys, snow shovels, backpacks, camp stoves, a case of Scotch whiskey, and a box of Spanish oranges. *Be prepared,* Hart quoted to himself.

Perched on the vessel's stern were two twin-engined Dornier Wal seaplanes, mounted to catapults that stretched for one hundred and forty feet along its deck. "So these are the birds," the pilot whispered to himself. The flying boats were big: sixty feet long with a ninety-foot wingspan. Struts held the wing and engine housing above a narrow, boatlike fuselage that nested on enormous floats. On the tail was a swastika. The Wals looked a bit ungainly but Hart knew they were famous for dependability and endurance.

The *Schwabenland* itself was a seaplane tender of workmanlike appearance, the point of its bow descending vertically into the water and its rounded stern overhanging a huge rudder. Two cargo masts were busily employed swinging cargo aboard. There was a low bridge superstructure, a mid-deck with a single towering smokestack and lifeboats, and then a long stern deck dominated by the catapults. The ship looked twice the length of the tender Farnsworth had taken to the Antarctic. The Germans seemed to be sparing no expense.

Hart was met on the pier by a short and wiry master's mate, with curly hair and wry manner. "You the Yankee?" he asked, not waiting for an answer. "Yes, of course, I could see it a quarter mile away, the walk, the manner. Americans! God knows what possessed you to show up here."

"I was hired," Hart said.

"The universal excuse. Well, my name is Fritz. Eckermann's the surname, but it's just Fritz to you, right? Because you're going to be Owen to me, I'm afraid, no *Herr* this and *Herr* that. Ach, don't bother shaking hands with yours so full, you can kiss me later, here, I'll take that seabag . . . God in heaven, are you hoarding lead? No, I'm just kidding, I've got it, but Christ, you've packed enough for The Afterlife . . . Ah, it's books I suspect, you're a secret intellectual! Some are dirty, I hope? No? Well, it's a long voyage, pilot, you can borrow mine . . . This way! Will you look at this mess? Damnation, who ordered all this stuff? Not the people who have to put it away, you can bet on that! . . . Albert, move that massive ass of yours, we're coming aboard . . . !" And Hart was led up the gangway and through a hatchway to the initially bewildering warren of companion- and passageways typical of any ship.

The manifest assigned him a tiny stateroom to himself. "I'm impressed," said Fritz, giving an exaggerated groan as he dumped Hart's seabag on the floor. "Your own bunk and porthole. One more pooh-bah, right? Well, no bowing and scraping from Fritz

Eckermann, I'm afraid. When the revolution comes, we'll all be equal." He winked. "Come on then, you can sort your socks later. Captain Heiden wants to meet with you." He turned and led the way toward the bridge.

The expedition leader sat in a high leather swivel chair from which he could survey the city's harbor, meeting a steady stream of officers and sailors who had questions about the voyage. Heiden usually answered with a curt sentence or two but with Owen he took a bit longer.

"Welcome aboard the *Schwabenland,* Hart. Not quite as luxurious as Karinhall but I think you'll find her a good ship. A range of twenty-four thousand miles and a host of recent improvements. Fritz here will show you about but I must warn you: don't take his prattling too seriously."

Hart smiled. "It's bigger than I expected."

"It's no battleship but we've made some modifications. There's a meter-wide belt of reinforcing steel around the hull to fend off ice. The bronze prop has been replaced by a stronger steel one. We've added nine cabins—you have one of the new ones—and to make sure we don't suffer the fate of the *Titanic* we've added thousands of welded steel casks in the lowest hold for emergency flotation in case we're breached. We're trying to think of everything but I'm sure your experience will be most useful, so don't hesitate to suggest improvements. If there is a question or decision, I'm the ultimate authority. Understand?"

Hart nodded. "Then Jürgen's role is advisory?" he asked, taking the opportunity to satisfy his curiosity about the political liaison.

The captain frowned. "Drexler represents the Reich Minister," he said obliquely. "The state. He is in the *Allgemeine* division but this ship is mine. Now. You must meet our pilots; Fritz will introduce you. Please inspect the airplanes and equipment. And you'll dine in the officer's mess, as will the people you met at Karinhall. There will be a rotating watch once we're at sea. If there is a problem, see me. This is satisfactory, yes?"

And with that Fritz ushered him away. "This is satisfactory?"

the seaman mimicked as they descended from the bridge. "As if we have an alternative. You have no ticket back to America yet, yes? And no pay yet, am I right? That's what I thought. Ha! Welcome to Germany, Mr. Pilot, you may have signed on for more than you wished. Of course I never said that. Heil Hitler, blah blah blah."

"Where's your Germanic respect for authority, Fritz?" Hart asked.

"I lost it when I watched workingmen tremble before bosses who couldn't find the crack of their ass with both hands," he said. "Nazi big shots! I've seen more pompous fools and self-important blunderers the last few years than a toilet swabber in a Berlin ministry. Though to tell you the truth, pilot, this Heiden seems all right. Just don't *you* strike any airs with me."

In actuality, things *were* satisfactory. Hart found himself useful soon after his arrival in Hamburg. The voyage gave him purpose; he'd gone from self-imposed exile to foreign expert. He specified the airplane fuel-oil ratio Lufthansa was supplying for Antarctic cold and began prowling the cargo and comparing it to his experience on Snow Hill Island. He suggested substitution of wooden for metal runners on the sleds to make them less brittle, and seemingly primitive leather lashings in exchange for machined screws for the same purpose. Dehydration is a surprisingly severe problem in dry polar air and so he made sure there were sufficient canteens. He proposed canvas hoods that could be slung over the airplane engine casings until their oil pans could be warmed by portable kerosene heaters. And he inspected with misgiving the troublesome bubble sextants used to help estimate position in a high-latitude region where compasses became unreliable. "These will be hampered by the cold," he warned the German pilots, Reinhard Kauffman and Seigfried Lambert. "The bubbles will distort. You'll have to use them in conjunction with compass and dead reckoning, and above all keep an eye on the weather so you can use landmarks. It's easy to get lost down there."

The men nodded. Their initial wariness at meeting the American had given way to the international fraternity of fliers.

"Tell Heiden as well," Kauffman requested. "Your own caution will make him understand ours."

Quickly bonding into a team were Fritz, the irreverent German, and Hart, the amused outsider from America. The pilot was a safe and reliable audience for Fritz's observations on Germany and Fritz exhibited a wry candor the other Germans didn't share.

"Hitler is a want-to-be," the little sailor psychoanalyzed blandly while sucking on a cigarette under soggy Hamburg skies. "The little Austrian who wants to out-German Germany. He's seized on our worst traits, Owen. Everywhere there are rules now: do this, do that, papers please, stamp stamp stamp. His father was a customs official, you know, and now the whole nation is a fucking post office. Oh, Hitler is smart all right, he's a shrewd one, I grant him that. Look how far he's come! And he has the fault of all clever men: he believes his own speeches. Like our earnest Jürgen Drexler."

"Jürgen hasn't given any speeches to me."

"Give him time."

Hart smiled. "And do *you* understand his role aboard?"

"To out-Hitler Hitler, I suspect."

"The captain said he's in the *Allgemeine* division. What's that?"

"What all the Nazi pooh-bahs must belong to. The civilian branch of the SS, the Führer's elite. Drexler's a major. So be careful with him, Owen."

The political liaison never wore a uniform or referred to his rank. Yet when it came time to seek additional supplies his role became more obvious: his whisper of Göring's name sufficed. Hart judged him reflexively competitive, but also competent and seemingly straightforward. On the docks the young Nazi was all business, listening judiciously to the pilot's suggestions, asking intelligent questions, and acting quickly once a decision was made. He seemed a man of serious intent who assumed others shared that intent until they revealed otherwise. He also appeared to respect Hart's experience. Twice Drexler went out of his way to find the pilot and introduce him to visiting functionaries from

Berlin, including a reporter from Goebbels's Propaganda Ministry. "This is Owen Hart, our American consultant," he would say. "Mr. Hart is intimately involved in planning the success of our expedition."

Drexler's candor was limited, however. The pilot was puzzled that some of the crates were labeled only by number and stamped with a German eagle. His inquiries as to what they contained brought bored shrugs from the sailors. Cargo net after cargo net was slung into the hold.

"Fritz, what's all this gear?" Hart finally asked. "The *Schwabenland* is going to sink if we put much more aboard."

The mate considered a moment, then elaborately looked first one way, then another. "The German glance," he explained with a wink. His voice fell to a conspiratorial whisper. "Well, if you ask Heiden, he'll tell you it helps ballast the boat to keep the propeller below the ice. If you ask Drexler, he'll tell you it's peanuts for the elephant seals. But since you asked me . . . I've peeked at a bit of it and it seems to be field equipment, construction supplies, even guns. Yes, bang-bang, don't be surprised. I'm not sure all these things are going to come back off the ice. These Nazis don't like to be tourists, you know. They look for places to stay, room to grow. So it looks to me we've enough to start a research camp. Or a whaling station. Or a fucking Hamburg shopping arcade. But that's just me. I'm not a big shot. They tell me less than they do you."

Hart decided to pursue the question with Drexler. He found the blond German sitting alone one evening in a corner of the galley, looking weary but satisfied. Jürgen lifted his glass of cognac as the pilot came in.

"So, Hart," he greeted, "do you think we're ready for the southern continent?"

"As ready as anyone can be," the pilot said, taking a chair. "I can't fault your preparations. The rest is up to Antarctica."

"Well put. And do you feel at home with us?"

Hart considered. "I'm comfortable. It's a much larger ship than the one I was on before."

"It must be strange sailing on a foreign vessel. Do you get homesick?"

"No. My home is wherever I am. My parents were lost in the big Spanish flu epidemic of 1918. I have no other relatives, no house, no job, no plane. I'd have a hard time filling out an employment form, I'm afraid. It's a miracle you hired me."

The German laughed. *"Unattached* is one of the best credentials for an explorer."

"I suppose so."

"And no sweetheart back in America either?" The question was meant to be light, but it had a slight edge to it.

"No, not much luck in that department, I'm afraid. Or skill." He grinned ruefully. "But what about you? I sensed a relationship with Greta Heinz."

The German sipped his cognac. "Greta? She's a good friend. Maybe more someday, who knows? She's also a professional, like us. Tied up in her work. She's coming aboard because she's very, very good in her field."

"How did you meet?"

"Through her . . . well, Otto introduced us."

"Otto seems to introduce everyone."

Drexler laughed again.

"And what's your background, Jürgen?"

He grew serious. "I grew up in the German nightmare. You have no idea how disastrous for us the Weimar Republic was, how huge a failure democracy was. Money worth nothing, morality worth nothing, honor worth nothing. I was alone too, my father dead in the war, my mother . . . ill. In an institution. And then came the Party. My new family. My new father. My new hope! I know it looks strange to you outsiders, the torches, the marches, but the Führer has touched the very soul of the German people. The *soul."*

Hart nodded, considering. He searched for the right question. "Jürgen, I'm puzzled by so much cargo. Boxes and boxes of it. I don't know what it is, where it goes, the sailors keep mum."

"Well, we're going to a place far away, thousands of miles from resupply. It's better to be over- than underprepared. And if we find a site for a future base, we may cache supplies."

"So this is more than just an aerial survey?"

"In essence this is an *opportunity,* the dimensions of which none of us can guess as yet."

"I just feel I could be more help if I understood more."

Drexler took another sip. "I understand your American curiosity, Owen. But it's best not to ask too many questions. You'll be told everything you need to know to perform your job, and believe me, it will be easier not having to worry about what you *don't* need to know. I mean no disrespect by this. It's simply the way we Germans prefer to do things. I trust you understand."

Hart didn't but decided not to press the point. He had to live with these people for the next three months.

Later he asked Fritz to come to his cabin, presenting some bottled beers he'd liberated from the officer's mess. "For our philosophic musings," he explained.

Fritz pulled out some schnapps from his coat. "For our philharmonic bitching. You can tell me about Alaska and I'll tell you about this ship. Unfortunately for you, I have opinions on everyone and everything: loud and obnoxious ones if we toast enough times."

Owen summarized his conversation with Drexler, including the German's admonition.

"You should be flattered. If you were a German he'd simply tell you to shut up. They spoil you, Owen. Are you tired of it yet?"

Hart took a swig. "It's a cozy ship," he assessed. "And I like Germans. They're enthusiastic, energetic. Like Americans."

"Ha! As if that were a compliment!" Fritz tilted the schnapps bottle. "Well. Heiden is okay. He knows his seamanship, I'm told. Had some problems on an earlier voyage up to the Arctic— lost a ship—but the story is that it was ice and bad luck. We learn from our mistakes. Drexler I'm more suspicious of. Ambitious, the kind of ambition that gets other people hurt. The type of arrogant young prick they seem to stamp out of some Reich factory by the thousands these days. I tell you, Hart, the Party has put people to work—I grant them that—but they also attract the biggest collection of self-important pig-heads I've ever seen. And I never said that, by the way!" he shouted at a vent opening.

"Jürgen simply strikes me as serious. Committed."

"Or pretentious." Fritz stood stiffly, trying to comb his curly hair to one side with his fingers to approximate Drexler's straight blond cut. "We sail for the glory of Greater Germany! Crap. I sail for three months' good wages and to get out of this lunatic asylum, and you sail to erase your past. Drexler to curry favor, Heiden to make up for the ship he lost in the Arctic in 1912, this woman Heinz I bet to find a husband, or escape one. Ach, we all have one reason and pretend another, we lie so desperately we believe ourselves. We look for chance and call it purpose. What a lot of pompous asses all people are, Hart—*all* of us." He belched. "Probably me no better than him."

At lunch the next day Hart asked Drexler about his enthusiasm for a leader many Americans regarded with apprehension.

"Adolf Hitler has succeeded for one simple reason," the political liaison replied, pointing with his fork. "He's extraordinary. A man of vision who is above common appetites, but who recognizes those appetites in others. There is an oft-told story: Hitler goes to a small village inn and the mayor and notables assemble at a table with him. When the waiter comes, Hitler orders mineral water. All the others hastily do too, except one absentminded fellow at the end of the table who orders beer. The other men look aghast, but Hitler smiles. 'It seems you and I are the only two honest men in this village.' "

Feder barked a laugh.

"So why is the world so uneasy with him?" Hart asked.

"Because he represents change. Or, rather, correction. Hitler seeks only to correct the errors in the treachery at Versailles that followed the Great War. The Allied politicians, seeking their revenge, put Germans in France, Germans in Austria, Germans in Czechoslovakia—a bastard creation of a country that didn't even exist!—and Germans in Poland. Christ, Poland! Another geographic monstrosity! Another historical aberration! And that's supposed to solve something? Give Germany Germany. That's all Hitler is asking. Can't you agree?"

Hart was cautious. "European history is confusing to Americans, I'm afraid."

"Justice is not, I hope."

"And flags are irrelevant in an Antarctic storm."

The German smiled thinly. "Then why does every nation take them there?"

The docks were beginning to empty and the ship to settle lower in the water. Departure was drawing near. One night a gray military truck pulled onto the dock and a dozen muscular young men leaped off, shouldered seabags, and bounded up the gangplank to disappear without a word into the forecastle. They wouldn't appear on deck again until the ship had entered the North Sea, went the rumor around ship. Drexler was closeted with them.

"Naval marines, I'll bet," Fritz offered. "Or something worse."

Marines had never been discussed in conversations about the provisioning of the expedition, so Hart mentioned their sudden appearance to the political liaison. Drexler looked faintly disapproving.

"Those men are not your concern."

"But why marines in the Antarctic?"

"I didn't say they were marines."

"Then what are they?"

Drexler sighed. "Those men are simply security, Hart, specialists from the *Schutzstaffel,* the SS. Elite troops."

"Then they are *your* men?"

"They are my responsibility. But I'm a civilian in the SS, not a soldier. An advisor, not a general. They take guidance from me."

"Why soldiers in Antarctica?"

"They're mountaineers trained for extreme conditions, a precaution against rash action by Norwegian whalers or anyone else we might encounter. You know better than I how far we'll be

from civilization. It would be imprudent not to include such protection to ensure the safety of our mission."

"We won't encounter anyone. There's no one down there."

"That's not true. Half the world is ahead of us down there.
Really, Hart, this is exactly the kind of situation we discussed in
the galley. Our polar flight is your business. The makeup of our
complement is not." And with that he walked away.

Greta arrived a day later, only one day prior to sailing. Hart encountered her in a passageway, trailing another seaman who was
carrying a seabag to her cabin.

"Ah, so I see they let the other oddball on board," she said
brightly. "First an American horns in, now I arrive. What do you
think—is there room enough on this ship for a woman?"

"Oh, I'm sure you'll have no problem," said Hart. "They'll
soon be admiring your gumption."

"*Gumption?*" She was puzzled.

"*Guts.* Courage. It takes a lot of both to be going where you're
going."

"Oh, I have my chaperon. Jürgen is determined to look after
me." She laughed, but Hart wasn't sure she found that idea un-
appealing or ridiculous. "And a pilot guide from America!" she
added. "You won't let me get lost, will you?"

He smiled uncertainly. "You seem to know your way."

"Hardly!" She laughed again and was off down a passageway,
calling over her shoulder, "I can barely find my way around this
ship!"

Women are bad luck, he reminded himself as he stared after
her. Remembering her smile.

CHAPTER SIX

The *Schwabenland* left Hamburg at six in the morning on December 1, 1938, casting off in a chill drizzle. Europe was electric with tension as Czechoslovakia was absorbed into the Reich and civil war neared its climax in Spain, a war the fascists appeared destined to win. Hart was largely oblivious to such events, engrossed in the details of expedition preparation. With Teutonic efficiency, the aircraft mechanics had stocked two of everything. Hart suggested they get three. The pilots had requested two weeks' emergency rations on each plane; Hart had them double it to four. He also convinced Heiden to bring on board sixty parachutes attached to enough emergency food, water, and fuel to last a downed aircraft a month.

Soon they were plowing through snow squalls in the North Sea. Hart had a flier's stomach and little problem with the motion, but Feder and Greta were sick and stayed away from the officer's mess for the first few days. The seaplane tender soon turned down the Channel and passed other freighters, their running lights glowing in the gloom. None seemed to take special note of the German passing despite the Dornier seaplanes lashed to the catapults. Off Calais, however, a British destroyer emerged from a bank of fog and rounded on the *Schwabenland*'s flag, following for a few miles like a dog sniffing scent. Drexler ran out on the bridge wing and studied the warship through binoculars, as no doubt its officers were studying the German vessel. Then the British ship pulled away.

Hart liked the sea. It offered the same combination of freedom and simple emptiness as the air. And the ship was a cocoon, a refuge of warmth from the elements outside. The American's quarters were with the expedition leaders and pilots, high in the midcastle housing. Ordinary seamen were on decks below. The mysteriously ensconced SS mountaineers were housed in the uncomfortable forecastle, where the ship's motion and noise from pounding waves was at an extreme. True to prediction, the soldiers did emerge after the ship left Hamburg but they kept to themselves, clinging to the bow area of the *Schwabenland* as if an invisible leash kept them from roaming. Twice a day they assembled on the forward deck in shorts and T-shirts and did calisthenics. They looked like white, blond machines.

Hart prowled the vessel's passageways until he had a mental map of its layout, then scouted cozy places on deck shielded from wind. From there, catching the warmth of the occasional winter sun like a cat, he could watch the cresting swells for hours. Under dark skies the waves were like hills of obsidian, glassy but opaque. When the sun shone they turned molten emerald. The air outside was cold and refreshing, a contrast to the interior's smell of oil and cigarette smoke and overcooked German food.

Eventually Greta emerged on deck and remained there as long as possible, using the wind to blow away her nausea. At first she seemed to prefer to be alone with her thoughts. Sometimes Drexler would approach her, Hart would surreptitiously observe, and she would give a quiet shake of her head. But later she would chat with him for a bit and the other officers would occasionally join her too, sometimes making a joke to cover their awkwardness. Her gender made her exotic and her quiet beauty—it was more evident here at sea, away from the calculated flash of Göring's actresses—a magnet.

Without effort she became, along with Heiden as captain and Drexler as German philosopher, a focal point in the officer's mess. She would arrive for dinner dressed in practical working clothes—wool pants, boots, and a sweater, her red hair pulled back into a ponytail—and gamely enter the male conversation. Sometimes she smelled of perfume and sometimes of formaldehyde, but she had a light, gentle laugh that sounded in the dark and overheated mess like a bell in a cave. Her effect was amusing: the men would unconsciously straighten a bit, voices would quiet and soften, eyes would quickly dart her way and then turn to a studious examination of a salt shaker or coffee mug. She was aware of this and careful to let her own gaze flit from face to face, democratically pleasant. The woman was an antidote to coarseness, and Hart guessed most of the men in the officer's mess were secretly grateful for her presence. Yet he knew her position was not easy. She was trying to assert a place as an equal and yet adhere to the feminine reticence expected in 1938 Germany.

Her relationship with Jürgen Drexler seemed as "unsettled" as she'd described herself to be. Clearly she enjoyed his company: he was handsome, self-assured, and flattering in his attentions. The German was a man on the make, a comer who might go far in the new regime if this expedition was a success. An alliance with a bright, pathbreaking woman like Greta would likely make them a celebrity couple back home. And he was a dogged campaigner for her affection. Whenever possible, Hart noticed, Drexler would take the seat next to her in the mess. The others often left it empty as if waiting for his arrival. Yet the pilot wasn't sure what the woman made of this presumption. On a few occasions she made a point of sitting between two other men, reminding him of her move at Karinhall. The change, it seemed to Hart, gave her a bit of relief: Jürgen Drexler could be relentlessly persistent. Yet when Drexler talked late in the evening about their expedition— "to the crystal towers of Antarctica!"—he'd lose himself in romanticism and the biologist's eyes would take on a certain shine.

Still, Hart didn't see in Greta's manner an emotional commitment to the German. There was none of the easy partnership of a
romance or affair or betrothal. Her fingers were empty of rings
and she retained the cautious aloofness attractive women sometimes adopt as a necessary shield. Drexler was clearly seeking an
intimacy beyond simple friendship but she had a way of both admitting him and yet putting him off. All this was the subject of
idle gossip, of course—it was assumed the presence of both on
board was far from coincidental—yet no one claimed firm knowledge. The couple deflected curiosity.

Drexler's behavior persuaded Hart that he should keep a careful distance from Greta. If he was going to rehabilitate his reputation the last thing he needed was a rivalry with the expedition's
political liaison—or to get his mind wrapped around another
woman. Yet curiosity nagged at him.

One evening he took Drexler's intended seat next to hers in
order to see what would happen. She looked at him curiously, but
not without welcome. "Hello."

Hart smiled. "It looks like you've gotten your sea legs." He
nodded toward her full plate.

"And you appear to be finding your way as well." She studied
him.

His throat suddenly felt dry, but he managed: "Well, it isn't
that big a ship."

"Yes. And yet, I haven't seen that much of you."

"Everyone is busy and I'm trying not to interfere. You
seem . . . occupied."

She looked up at the dark circle of a porthole, the lift of her
chin showing the white curve of her neck. "Not all the time," she
said, trying to keep her tone light.

They let that hang for a moment.

"So, have you gotten things—the expedition, I mean—in
proper order?" she finally asked.

"Actually my contribution has been pretty minimal. I've done
my best, but the clichés about German thoroughness appear to be
true."

"Really?" She smiled at that. "How does it feel to be sur-rounded by meticulous Germans?"

"Depends on the German."

"Of course." She sipped some water, studying him over the rim of the glass. "Well, I suspect we benefit from the perspective of an outsider. There's talk about you on the ship, you know. Your past. Why you're here. I have my own theory."

"Which is?"

"I think you're a deliberate adventurer. Undaunted by the prospect of death but afraid of life. Fond of going to remote, lonely places." She waited for his reaction.

"Hmmm. That might describe anyone on this ship. Including you."

She laughed. "That's the problem with Professor Freud's psy-choanalysis. It's like a boomerang, coming back at the analyst."

"Yes, but still, it's fun to form conjectures. I must admit, I've been mostly stymied in your case."

She smiled. "How so?"

"Well—" Hart paused, afraid he was venturing onto unsafe ground. "Your presence on this ship is . . . puzzling. A lone woman among so many men, willing to risk everything for some scientific data. One wonders—"

"What?"

"I only meant that you're female. That's good, admirable, but I can't help wondering how you came to be here."

"I was invited, like you."

"I know that, yes, of course . . ."

"For my *expertise,* Owen. Like you." She sounded annoyed.

"I didn't mean . . ."

Drexler came in then, his cheeks flushed from some mission outside in the cold. He moved to the table where Greta was and then stopped, clearly a bit nonplussed at Hart's presence. Greta looked up at him with exasperation, as if he'd undercut her point by appearing. Then she studied her salad, poking it with her fork. "I am unclear what you *did* mean," she said quietly to Hart.

Quickly masking his own discomfort, Drexler moved to a

smaller table and took a seat next to Schmidt, pretending a hearty companionship. Greta glanced over at the blond German, who was studiously ignoring her.

Damn.

"You'd better eat that salad," Hart told her, his voice a bit rougher than he intended. "We'll be out of greens in another week."

"Yes, of course." She trimmed a small leaf with her knife and lifted it to her lips, slipping it in. Then she suddenly turned to him. "You must forgive me. I'm still finding my way aboard and am a bit awkward at it, I'm afraid." She abruptly stood up, gathering her dishes. "This motion destroys my appetite."

Hart started to stand too, anxious that he'd spoiled her supper, but as soon as he did so he knocked over his water glass, sending a small flood toward the pilot Kauffman. He lunged. "I'm sorry, Reinhard!" He groped for his napkin, glancing around in time to see Greta leave the galley. Drexler looked after her as she disappeared but didn't move.

Well, thought Hart. Next time I'll sit elsewhere.

After dinner Drexler paused at Hart's table. "No luck? Or no skill?"

Each of the expedition leaders was developing roles in the ship's new social order. Heiden was friendly but professionally distant: appropriately so, Hart judged. The success of the expedition was ultimately the captain's responsibility and so he was trying to cultivate an air of shared competence, not camaraderie. He had a Prussian briskness.

Drexler's manner was one of energetic dedication, an officious drive he probably thought reasonably masked his interest in Greta. Hart had heard little of this *Schutzstaffel,* or SS, but it clearly was an elite that drew deference from Germans. Jürgen enjoyed Göring's influence and Heiden's ear. Hart was impressed by his mind—Drexler seemed to retain any statistic about the Dorniers that was thrown at him—and his ability to put their voyage in grand historical context. "This is a first step toward making Germany a true global power!" he would exclaim with almost boyish enthusiasm. He conferred for long hours with Heiden, the two men bent over old Antarctic charts.

Alfred Feder, the geographer, was conversational, exhibiting a genuine curiosity about Antarctica. What had been the weather pattern? How cold in summer and winter? Which food, if any, could be hunted or fished for? What did the climate do to storage of supplies? Was fire a serious danger because of dry air? Yes, and of course the lack of unfrozen water! How did the British or Americans melt enough to sustain a base? Hart answered as straightforwardly as he could, not pretending knowledge when he didn't have it.

Schmidt, the ship's doctor, was more of a mystery. He had a sour closeness about him, seeming to tolerate people more than enjoy them. He smoked like a chimney and only dabbed at his food. His sallow skin reminded Hart of oiled paper. The physician held a clinic for the sailors two hours each day, receiving the usual litany of complaints ranging from seasickness to the inevitable venereal disease resulting from Hamburg shore leave. He quickly earned a reputation for being gruff and ungentle. "He's got the bedside manner of a veterinarian," the sailors reported.

Hart continued to run into Greta but she passed by with a distracted air, which satisfied him. In truth, he was a bit intimidated by her. Once he caught her looking at him, her expression opaque, and could think of nothing intelligent to say.

Then she approached again.

The pilot was sitting on a hatch cover, enjoying a watery sun in a hazy sky. To occupy himself he'd found some line and was splicing two rope ends together.

"You do that as if from long experience," came a female voice. He looked up, startled. She was carrying binoculars and a book about seabirds, the wind pressing one side of her coat against her figure and snapping the other end free like a flag. She pointed to his splices. "Were you a seaman as well as a pilot?"

She'd caught him by surprise, and he hesitated a moment before replying. "No, Fritz taught me." Her skin was rosy from the unaccustomed midwinter sun and wind, he noticed. "I'm a *land-lubber.*"

"A what?"

"It's an American word for someone who's never been to sea. I grew up in Montana, a mountain state. I'd never been on the ocean until my first trip south."

"I like the mountains too. Have you been to the Alps?"

"Afraid not. Not even in Leni's movies."

She smiled at the reference and, without asking, sat down, opening the book on her lap. The pages fluttered in the wind. Hart was a bit surprised at this overture; he thought he'd muddled things sufficiently at supper. Now here she was, pretending as if nothing had happened.

"Is it a good place, Montana?"

"A wonderful place to grow up for a boy. Riding, fishing, climbing, caving."

"Caving?"

"Spelunking. There were caverns not far from our place. Beautiful limestone ones. We were warned not to go in them but we'd sneak off anyway with candles and lanterns, crawling around and getting stuck. Lucky we didn't get lost. We'd come home pretending we'd gone someplace else but our mothers had to know. We stank of them."

"You had a lot of freedom then."

"They let us run wild. And you?"

She laughed. "Convent school. My father far away. Nuns. Sin. Guilt."

"My God."

"Oh, not so bad. But this is my chance to run to freedom."

"It's the only thing worth running to," he said.

For a moment she didn't say anything, then: "How did you become a pilot?"

"Took a dollar ride at a county fair and was hooked. I saved up during a summer of riding and roping and bought myself flying lessons. I became a barnstormer. A wild one, actually. At eighteen you think you're immortal. I had more guts than sense until I cracked up a couple times. Then I ran cargo, chartered, and did a lot of cold weather flying. I met Elliott Farnsworth at an air show, and the rest, as they say, is history."

"And no woman in this history?"

"That's a forward kind of inquiry."

"It's the only inquiry any woman cares to know. Surely you've learned that by now."

He grinned. "You're not very coy, are you?"

"I am when I want to be."

"Well. The girls *I* knew would tell you I've learned nothing about your gender. Yes, there were women—even *a* woman—but it didn't last. A pilot is about as stable as a hummingbird. And Antarctica is not a place conducive to romance."

She laughed at that, and Hart sensed she was laughing at herself. "Too bad!"

"Too cold. And if we're being so inquisitive, let me ask you about men in *your* history."

"Ah. Well. That's a complicated story." She looked across the waves. "I'm not married, if that's what you mean. I . . . I hope to do a lot of thinking down here."

"About Jürgen?"

She looked away. "No. About me."

Her tone made him cautious. "All right. Fair enough."

They were quiet for a bit. He sensed her approval at the quiet; it felt companionable to watch the swells hiss by. Finally she turned to him again. "Would you like to see my laboratory?"

It was on the main deck, just above the waterline. A single porthole offered natural illumination. A microscope was bolted to a wooden table, shelves held scientific books and journals in German, and cabinets stored beakers and tubes. Small translucent shrimplike creatures floated in jars of formaldehyde, all less than an inch long. "Krill," she explained, holding them to the light, regarding the specimens with a professionally flat rationality. "There are billions, trillions of them in the Southern Ocean. Combined, they outweigh any animal on earth: humans, elephants, whales. A hundred million tons, some have guessed. They're the key to the biological wealth of Antarctica."

"They look like ghosts," Hart said. "So pale."

"As clear as the cold waters. We have some nets aboard to try to produce an estimate of their abundance. That we scarcely recognized their importance until a few years ago is humbling, no? How little we still know of our own world."

"Yes." He took the jar and examined the creatures closely. They seemed gossamer in their translucence, naked somehow. "Yet we don't seem to be humbled. We're anxious enough to run the world anyway."

"You mean by whaling in Antarctica."

"By going there, by staying there, by establishing new orders. Look at Hitler. He wants to change everything."

"He's exciting," Greta said. "He started from nothing and now he's the most important man in the world. He has what most people lack: vision, and will."

"You sound like Drexler."

"Jürgen's not incorrect. He recognizes the path to the future, even if he can be a bit single-minded about it at times. It's exciting to feel a part of that. For an American, perhaps, it's different."

"Ah, you mean I'm not a patriot," Hart said wryly. "A hired gun."

"Just that you go for your own reasons. I, and Jürgen, and Captain Heiden, and everyone else aboard go for Germany. At least in part."

Hart thought back to Fritz's more cynical interpretation. "And I go for myself?"

"My guess is you're looking for yourself there."

"Oh. Freud again."

She shrugged guiltily, smiling.

"But there's more than that," he said. "I go for Antarctica."

"Yes." She put the jar back on the shelf. "And that's interesting. It must be quite a place, to draw you back."

CHAPTER SEVEN

The weather warmed as the tender sailed south. Mindful of the need to take advantage of the short Antarctic summer, Heiden bypassed the chance to get fresh produce in the Canaries—the Spanish oranges were already gone—and steamed on for the equator. Hart busied himself getting to know the two flying boats and their pilots, Kauffman and Lambert. The aviators seemed simple and straightforward men, in love with flying and excited at the prospect of being the first humans to see unexplored territory. In the calmer seas off Africa it was decided to give the airplanes a test flight and the *Schwabenland* turned to point the Heinkel K7 catapults directly into the hot breeze. The sea here was rolling but placid, like a cerulean desert.

"Would you like to go flying, Hart?" Kauffman asked him.

"Of course. I've never been on a catapult plane."

"Then you're in for a ride. We'll achieve a speed of one hundred and fifty kilometers per hour in a second and a half. Takes your breath away."

Kauffman took the pilot's seat, Hart the co-pilot's. In the compartment behind, Lambert served as navigator and Heinrich

Stern, the expedition's communications officer, was radioman. Sailors scrambled to ready the catapult and the Dornier engine roared to life, the plane trembling like an excited puppy. Kauffman checked the gauges, Hart following his gaze. All were familiar. Planes are planes, he thought. Then the German pilot brought the engine to full power and gave a thumbs-up. There was a bang and a hiss and the propeller craft hurled forward, shoving Hart back into his seat. As they left the catapult's end there was a brief, alarming drop toward the sea—a moment's hesitation as if the engine was gathering effort—and then they were away and soaring upward, banking to rotate over the ship. Hart whooped and Kauffman grinned. Toy figures on the deck below waved a cheer and the *Schwabenland* suddenly seemed very tiny in the immensity of the ocean.

The men took a bearing toward Africa and flew off in that direction, the blue bowl they navigated through featureless and hazy. Hart felt the sheer exhilaration of being in the air, cut free from the earth and sea.

"Do you want to fly her?" Kauffman inquired.

Hart nodded happily and took the controls. The seaplane was not nimble but steady, a high-powered workhorse that should perform well in the cold Antarctic air. He began flying in a broad loop back toward the ship. The vessel was lost for a while in the dazzle of the sun and then became visible again, drawing a dark line on a platter of silver. It looked so slow and stately from this height! Then, toward the horizon, there was a puff of mist. Kauffman pointed excitedly. "Whales!"

Hart brought the plane down to three hundred feet and roared over the leviathans, awed by the spectacle. The beasts were huge, barnacled and battered like jetty rocks. They broke the surface, exhaled with a powerful sigh, and then slid underwater to become racing blue shadows. When he flew over again at only fifty feet the whales sounded, tails flashing in the sunlight as they headed for the abyss. Hart realized he'd been holding his breath. "Magnificent!"

The German pilot held his thumb up in approval.

"I'm not sure I'm happy to be helping hunt them," the American added.

Kauffman shrugged. "God put them there for us."

"How can you be sure?"

"Because he gave us the skill to kill them. Harden yourself, Hart. Those are dumb animals. It's no different than a slaughter-house."

"It feels different, seeing them in the wild like that."

"Bah. They're beasts. Glorious creatures, but beasts nonethe-less."

"No, they're more than that. Greta Heinz should be here. She'd tell you."

Kauffman grinned. "Then let her. Have Heinrich radio the ship. We'll pick her up and chase them. By the time we turn the plane around they should be back to the surface. We can spot their blow for miles."

Hart surrendered control of the plane again to Kauffman for the landing. The German pilot betrayed no anxiety, only intense concentration. He let the pontoons clip the top of one swell, then another, and finally settled on the third like a great seabird. The plane sledded down its gentle slope and came to a halt in the wave hollow. Then they were bobbing on the ocean. The *Schwabenland* came up to create a lee pocket and the cargo crane rotated out. Kauffman scrambled out on top of the wing to catch the hook and attach it to the engine housing. The Dornier was lifted, twisting a bit like a dripping ornament, and then rose swiftly up, over, the crewmen grabbing the wet, slippery pon-toons . . . and they were back aboard.

Greta came running up as soon as they dropped from the plane's hatch. "Yes, the whales, I must see them!" She grabbed Kauffman's arm. "Reinhard, please take me up!"

Drexler had trailed her. "What's all the excitement about?" he asked warily. Kauffman was already issuing orders to the crew-men to ready the plane again.

"We spotted a pod of whales," Hart explained. "I thought Greta might like to see them. It's really an extraordinary sight."

"Jürgen, you must come too," she said. "To observe them from the air is an amazing opportunity."

The German looked doubtfully at the still-dripping aircraft. "I think I'll see them well enough from the ship."

"The *Schwabenland* will never catch them," Kauffman warned. "They're too far."

Drexler looked distinctly uncomfortable. "I think it would be too crowded . . ."

"We have room . . ."

"Please come, Jürgen. It will be so much fun." He smiled weakly at her pleading. "Come, this may be a once-in-a-lifetime chance."

Hart suddenly realized the man didn't relish being launched into the air. He was afraid of flying.

"Yes, come on up, Jürgen!" the American joined, unable to resist. "We could dive right on them and get a real close-up view."

Drexler's mouth set in a thin line. Hart's voice had decided him. "All right." Roughly grabbing a life jacket, he pushed past the American to jerk open the hatch.

"You can take Lambert's spot," Kauffman called after him. "The navigator's seat. Greta can be co-pilot next to me." Nodding wordlessly, Drexler crawled inside.

"I'll replace Heinrich on the radio," Hart said.

They followed Drexler, Greta peppering Kauffman with questions about the instruments as he buckled her in. Hart sat on the rear-facing radioman's seat opposite Jürgen. The German was staring straight backward, refusing to glance out the porthole at the sailors making final preparations. Then the engine coughed to life, spun, and roared. The plane rattled again, eager to go. Drexler's hands gripped the underside of his seat and Hart watched the knuckles whiten.

"Ready!" Kauffman's voice came over the earphones.

Another bang and with a lurch and a rush they were off. "It's so quick!" Greta exclaimed with delight. The plane banked, bouncing a bit in the warm air. Drexler shut his eyes.

Kauffman's voice crackled in Hart's ears over his headphones.

"I'll get a bit of altitude and start looking where we saw them before," he announced. Hart began peering out his own porthole, searching for telltale spouts.

It was Greta who first saw them again. "Look!"

"Amazing!" Kauffman exclaimed. "How far they've moved."

Hart unbuckled his seat belt and poked his head up into the cockpit. He could see dissipating mist ahead and a flash of foam as if the sea was breaking over rocks.

"Jürgen," Greta called. "You must come and see."

There was a long pause.

"Jürgen?"

Finally there was a click of an unfastened belt and Hart was roughly pushed to one side. The political liaison put his head between Greta and Kauffman and squinted at the ocean. He was pale, his skin glistening. "I see them," he managed. "And yes, they're impressive."

Kauffman passed over at three hundred feet again so as not to spook the animals. As the whales rose and fell, breathing rhythmically, their backs darkened and lightened with the depth of the water, making it look like they glowed with variable light.

"So beautiful," Greta enthused.

"Look at the slow, slow beat of their swim," Hart added. "It's like music, but to a different, longer, deeper time."

"I wonder how long they live?" Kauffman asked, swinging the plane around. The whales came in view again. "How long does it take to grow to such immense size? Nearly forever?"

They roared over again, the whale spouts shimmering with solar rainbows.

"Just remember that what we're seeing is Germany's next resource."

Greta looked at Drexler with exasperation. "Jürgen! Look!" Their peeling skin was like a worn hill, testimony to epic survival. "They're just oil to you?"

Drexler took a deep breath. "My personal reaction is irrelevant," he said, exhaling to battle his physical unease. "It's not that they're without beauty. It's that such beauty has no practical use."

"That's an awfully prosaic view of nature," Hart objected.

"It's a *realistic* view of nature." Drexler regained some self-assurance as he talked. It took his mind off where he was, suspended in air above the ocean. "You pilots never ask where the machine that carries you comes from. It comes ultimately from nature, from resources like those whales. To think otherwise is pleasurable but naive."

Hart frowned. He liked the man better when he was quiet from fright. Next would come a lecture on Nazi destiny. "Reinhard, let me fly again," Owen suggested. "I need the practice."

The German pilot hesitated. He'd been enjoying showing off for the woman but it would look piggish to refuse. "All right."

There was a laborious shifting of bodies, both pilots brushing against Greta as Drexler leaned back unhappily. Then Hart was at the controls. He banked again, steeper this time, and headed back toward the whales. "I think we should get closer," he said over his shoulder to Drexler. "If we can find some mark that identifies individuals—like the colors of ponies—maybe you'll think of them as more than bags of oil." He put the ponderous seaplane in a dive.

"Oh my!" Greta slapped out her hands to brace herself. The Dornier rapidly closed with the water until it looked as if the mammal spouts would spatter their canopy. She managed a laugh, anxious and delighted. Then Hart pulled up. "My stomach!" she exclaimed.

The seaplane zoomed upward as if climbing a hill, slowed, hesitated, and rolled to the left, banking steeply. Then it dove again. "Hart, stop it!" Kauffman snapped. "This isn't a barnstormer!"

"Of course." He pulled back and leveled, then banked a bit to peer down. The whales had sounded again. "Damn. They're gone."

Greta laid a hand on the muscles of his forearm. "You frightened me!"

"Just trying to get a good look." He glanced over his shoulder. Drexler was gone.

Kauffman ducked down to look back along the interior of the fuselage. Jürgen was on his knees, his head inside the plane's cramped lavatory. "Our political liaison is sick."

"How was your maiden Dornier voyage, Hart?" Heiden inquired over tea in the galley.

The captain was in a pleasant mood. It was the day after the whale sighting. The weather was still fine, progress good, and the airplanes appeared in excellent working order. They'd crossed the equator that morning and were entering the southern latitudes. There'd been a ceremony on board with Heiden as King Neptune, christening those who hadn't yet made the crossing. Drexler had recovered his equilibrium and was determined to take his dousing with good humor. He even seized the bucket to spray Greta, who laughed and hurled water back, Neptune backing off hurriedly. The seamen craned to look at the clothes plastered on her body before she ran below to change.

"I felt free as a bird," the American now replied. "I think you've got an agile airplane there. Reinhard let me put her through some paces."

"Yes, I heard your flying was quite . . . *exuberant.*"

"My stomach is still up there, I'm afraid," Drexler said, trying to make light of his experience. "Hart is quite the stunt pilot." He poured himself some tea. "In good weather."

No one missed the allusion.

"I've had a lot of experience," Hart said evenly. "In *all* kinds of weather."

"The Dornier's a good plane," Drexler went on mildly. "Range of a thousand kilometers, ceiling of four." He didn't forget what the pilots had told him. "It's part of Germany's leadership in the air." He took a sip of Earl Grey from England and looked at Greta. "I expect someday all of us will travel by air, everywhere. Aircraft will be as commonplace as the auto."

As if everyone would want one, Hart thought. Sick as a dog and now an aeronautical visionary. The man didn't back down an inch.

"Well," Feder put in, "it will be interesting to see how the planes perform in Antarctica."

"I suppose you'd stick to dogs, Alfred?"

"It worked for Amundsen," Feder replied, referring to the first man to reach the South Pole.

"Ach, the Norwegians again. A nation living in the past."

"I think you need to take the best of the past and the future," Hart said. "In Antarctica, wood sometimes works better than metal. Fur better than linen."

"And a gun better than an arrow," said Drexler. "That's why the airplane will let us explore more territory in a day than the Norwegians or British saw in a year."

"I don't disagree with that," said Hart. "I'm a flier. But airplanes have their limitations too. You can only see so much detail. Airplanes break down. Some days they aren't usable. I respect bad weather."

"Yes, a prudent flier," Drexler said. "So we've heard."

"A *live* flier," Hart countered.

"Jürgen, for goodness' sake," Greta said. "Owen is helping us and you pretend there is some contest of views."

"I'm just making a point. After he made his."

"He agrees with you and you insult him. You need to get to an iceberg to cool your head."

Drexler looked truculent at this scolding but said nothing.

CHAPTER EIGHT

The first icebergs were huge flat chunks from the ice shelf of the Weddell Sea, looking to Hart like mesas rising from a watery desert. They gleamed as if lit from within, shining with pearly translucence under a pale gray sky. In the emptiness of the Southern Ocean their exact size was impossible to gauge but as the *Schwabenland* steamed closer their immensity became apparent. The white cliffs of their sides were taller than a fortress wall and their bulk was enough to produce a harbor of calm water on their lee side. To windward, ocean swells ate caves into their bulk. The white was veined with blue like marble and just below the slate-gray water the bergs shelved into brilliant turquoise. Their top was snowy and unmarked: the perfect face of snowfalls stretching back ten thousand years.

The days were growing steadily longer as they steamed south. Hart spent the twilight after dinner watching the bergs slide by, wrapped in his flying jacket and wool hat.

"They look like cake, yes?"

Hart turned. It was cold at the railing and Greta was bundled in her Antarctic parka, the fur ruff of its hood framing her face.

Her eyes were the same blue as the fissures in the icebergs, but he didn't say that.

"You'll make me hungry," he joked lamely. He was pleased she'd joined him but he didn't say that, either. They seemed to have repaired the awkward dinner and he'd been secretly pleased at her defense of him at tea. Still, he was cautious.

"They're like wedding cakes," the biologist said. "Beautiful but sad. You know that something sublime is about to be consumed, or, in this case, melted. It heightens the beauty, I think— like leaves in autumn."

"Things are more beautiful when they're lost?"

"Yes, because the loss makes the feeling more intense. Sometimes life seems to me to be an endless slipping away."

"Well, things seem more beautiful when you can't have them," said Hart. "Sometimes life seems to me to be an endless anticipation of arrival. Like this voyage."

Greta smiled wistfully. "Ach, what a pair we are! Arriving, leaving, never in the moment! Perhaps we should take a lesson from the whales, who are *always* in the moment. It would be interesting to *be* them for a while, don't you think? To have every fiber of your being focused on the now, to drink in all the endless sensations, the colors, the feelings, the scents and tastes. It must be a comfort: not even realizing the inevitability of your own death."

"You seem less a biologist than a philosopher," Hart said, meaning to joke but feeling uncomfortable. He'd never met a woman who talked like this. He was intrigued by her mind but not quite sure how to respond.

"You seem less a pilot than an artist," she countered. "I catch you watching things but not in the way the other men do, as an obstacle or a prize. You have an eye for beauty."

"Yes, I do," Hart risked, looking at her. Tendrils of her red hair fluttered against her ruff in the breeze and her skin was pale and taut in the cold. She blushed, then looked up at him, her eyes searching his.

"Greta, I . . ."

Abruptly, she turned away and was gone.

*　　*　　*

The *Schwabenland* met its first Norwegian whaler the next day. It was a large pursuit vessel, part of a flotilla of harpoon ships that would kill and tow whales to a factory vessel or shore station somewhere beyond the horizon. Its harpoon was mounted like a cannon on its bow.

"I'd like to see the dart that's loaded into that thing," said the pilot Kauffman, watching with Hart from the wing of the bridge deck.

"I saw them hunt last time," the American said. "The harpoons are as long as a man and weigh as much as Fritz. The tip alone is as long as your forearm. They explode inside the whale with a charge of powder. It's spectacular and violent."

"I would have thought it overkill. But then we saw the size of those whales."

The foreign ship swung about from its routine prowl and steamed over. Heiden watched the whaler's approach through binoculars and then spoke to a mate. "Break out the flag," he said. The German ensign began fluttering from a mast.

The Norwegian skipper called by radio, speaking a heavily accented German. "This is Sigvald Jansen from the *Aurora Australis,*" he greeted. "We don't get many aircraft carriers at sixty degrees south! Are you lost, my friends?"

Drexler smiled thinly. "We should tell *him* to get lost. After we stake our claim he is going to find himself in Reich territory."

Heiden ignored this. "This is Captain Konrad Heiden of the German seaplane tender *Schwabenland,*" he radioed back. "We're on a scientific mission to explore the continent by air. Do you have any word on the extent of the pack ice?"

There was a moment's hesitation as the Norwegians digested this information. "No, we haven't gone that far south," Jansen's voice crackled. "Maybe that's where our whales are hiding! We've had poor hunting so far."

"Well, we're going to the ice so we'll keep an eye out for whales," Heiden radioed. "Of course if we see any, we'll think of them as *our* whales."

The Norwegian actually laughed at that. "Ha! I can tell I am speaking to Germans! We'll it's almost Christmas, my friends, and ocean and ice enough to share. I'd like to satisfy my curiosity about that ship of yours. I think I can find a holiday present if you'll allow us to row over."

Heiden looked questioningly at Drexler. The political liaison considered a moment, then nodded. "We may learn something."

The captain spoke into the radio. "Be our guest!"

They watched the Norwegians work efficiently to launch a boat and pull strongly across. Jansen proved a big, thickly muscled man with a blond beard and ice-gray eyes. He came stomping into the *Schwabenland*'s mess in an oilskin jacket and enormous black seaboots. "Ho, ho, ho!" he chortled, trying to imitate the Anglo-American version of Saint Nick. "Merry Christmas!"

Heiden shook the callused hand politely and began making introductions.

"He smells like a ripe whale," Feder whispered to Hart.

Drexler hung back, sizing the man up. Jansen noticed, and returned the scrutiny. "A political liaison?" the whaler repeated after Heiden's introduction. "Far from a ministry, aren't you?"

"Not far from political issues. As you know."

Jansen raised his eyebrows at that. "Really? I'd hoped we were." His bag, tied with red yarn, whomped down onto a table with a clink. "Merry Christmas." Bowing, Heiden unlaced it. Inside were several bottles of aquavit, a fiery Norwegian drink. "To keep you warm on your trip back!"

The German grinned. "And some Dutch courage to you, my friend," Heiden said, handing over a case of schnapps in return.

Jansen beamed. "I love religious holidays." He plopped into a chair and looked about curiously. "Nice ship. All this for science?"

"We're intending to explore new regions of the continent by air and establish formal claim," Drexler spoke up. "Our intention is to see more of Antarctica in a season than most explorers see in a lifetime. By airplane."

The Norwegian looked at the German with amusement. "Fair enough. But flying doesn't count, does it? I mean, you have to step ashore to lay claim. Politically speaking."

"We will," Drexler said. "Our Dorniers have skis, our launch has an engine, our rowboats oars. We intend to be everywhere, staking our claim."

Jansen laughed. "Yes, I can tell I am talking with Germans! Although the American there—Hart, is it? He has a bit of a different look—he sticks out like a crooked harpoon. Exactly who are you, young fellow?"

"I'm a pilot. I've flown in Antarctica before."

"Flown here before? And come back? With Nazis no less? Then you've got about as much sense as I do, locked in this stinking, miserable, butt-freezing, frustrating, bankrupt, glorious trade of whaling." He turned to Heiden. "It's not like the old days, you know. The whales are all gone. We've hunted them out."

"And yet you're still here," observed Drexler.

"As I've already told you, I've no more sense than the Yankee there."

"Of course," Drexler said dryly.

"Of course!" The Norwegian smiled broadly, scanning the room to see if anyone believed him. "It would be interesting to tour your ship. I've never seen a tender like this before."

"Unfortunately that's not possible," Heiden said. "Most of the ship is off limits because of the sensitivity of our scientific cargo. I'm sure you've seen her type before."

"Not down here."

"Yes. We Germans like to be first."

"Really? That's too bad, because we Norwegians have been here decades before you." Jansen's expression grew harder. "Be careful at the continent, my friends. It's cold down there. Lots of ice. We've learned to stay away from those latitudes." He looked grave.

"And why is that?" asked Heiden.

"A whaler ventured down that way last season. The *Bergen*. Wondered if the whales had been pushed that far south and radioed it had found a possible site for a rendering station. Then, poof! Was never heard from again."

"What happened?" the German captain asked.

"Who knows? Ice. Storm. I'm not about to go down there to find out! I'd advise you to exercise caution as well. But Germans! First in Austria, then Czechoslovakia, now Antarctica! Such ambition! I expect we'll meet again?"

"Only if you stay in these waters," Drexler said.

"Oh, we'll stay. These waters are home to us now." Jansen let his gaze flicker from German to German again, looking each of them squarely in the eye. "But then you already know that." He winked, stood, and clomped back to his waiting launch. "Merry Christmas!" he shouted again from the boat, waving as it rose and fell in the swells.

The German officers gathered on the bridge wing and watched the Norwegian whaler swing away.

"Like an animal peeing to mark his territory," Drexler assessed.

"He's probably saying the same thing about us," Feder remarked.

"God willing we'll be the first, not the last, of Third Reich explorers he meets down here," Heiden said. "He'll find more Germans than he likes and will have to adjust to it. Become an ally or an enemy."

"Better the former."

Heiden turned. The comment came from Fritz, pulling watch duty on the bridge.

"You speak from experience, Mr. Eckermann?"

"Yes, sir. Fished with them in '31. There's a bit of the Viking left. Best not to cross them, especially when it comes to boats and fish."

"And best for them not to cross us," Drexler said.

"Yes, the Norwegians are about to experience true competition," the captain agreed.

"And I wonder what happened to the *Bergen*?"

"I suspect Antarctica swallowed it."

*   *   *

The clouds darkened as they continued steaming south. The wind picked up. Snow began scudding across the deck and the temperature dropped, signaling their approach to the southern continent. The ship began to roll heavily and Hart stood lookout for icebergs, observing them pass like dark fortresses in the gloom. The weather continued foul for the brief night, the following day, and into a second night, while the ice grew steadily thicker. Christmas morning dawned with the ship pushing through thin pack ice, broken into floes the size of houses. It was loose enough that they could shoulder the ice aside, occasionally driving headlong into a floe and splintering it, cracks racing away from the bow of the ship. The ice rasped and banged against the hull. Drexler and Feder joined Hart on deck, watching the spectacle.

On some of the floes giant-sized seals snoozed, content on their mattress of snow. They obviously belonged here. "Crabeater seals, most of them," Greta told the men at the rail. "They get their name from eating krill."

"They look awkward."

"Not in the water," Greta said, smiling.

Drexler gathered some snow from the deck and threw a snowball at one. It raised its head and opened its mouth, giving a *grawkkk* as it yawned a sleepy protest. Then it wiggled forward into the water and slipped away like a dying note of music.

"*Jürgen,*" she scolded, "you shouldn't harass them."

"They're just seals, Greta. Slugs of the ice."

"Jump in the water and swim next to them and we'll see who looks like the slug," she jested. "They've adapted to this place in ways we can only envy."

Drexler harrumphed. "Yes, they can swim, but they simply *exist.* They are passive, meek, dim."

"You wouldn't say that if you encountered a leopard seal."

"Oh?"

"They're spotted, ten feet long, weigh as much as four men, and have huge jaws full of sharp teeth. They can move faster than any of us and snatch us in a minute. They prey on penguins and seals."

Drexler laughed. "Well, I'm not a penguin, and I'm not going to lose any sleep over a seal. I do admire the way you love these animals, Greta. But I'm more concerned about the future of *our* species."

She looked miffed. "Someday you'll meet a leopard seal, Jürgen, and then you'll see."

"Someday." He shrugged.

The ship broke into clear water again, dark and cold. Now the passing bergs were tall and sharp like small jagged mountains. They passed a cluster of penguins standing on one, some sliding comically down the ice like children on a slide.

Christmas dinner was festive, lit by the warm glow of candlelight. Heiden was in a good mood about their progress. Feder became first amusingly and then annoyingly drunk. Schmidt sat in a corner, chain-smoking his cigarettes and content to just watch the others. It appeared there were no presents but Hart passed out intricately knotted key or watch chains he'd tied from thick cord. Greta's was inked red and green. When he presented it her cheeks were flush from the libations and her eyes shining with the excitement of being in such an exotic spot for the holiday. She lit up as if he'd given her a necklace and, leaning forward, quickly pecked him on the cheek. "I'm embarrassed I have nothing for you!" she whispered in his ear. Then she slipped away.

Drexler watched, fingering his own key chain. "Very thoughtful, Hart. It's good you're finding time for clever crafts. I don't have anything for you either but I do"—and here he raised his voice—"have something as well for our female pioneer."

She turned, smiling in surprise.

"Alone of her gender but not alone in our hearts," said Drexler with a bow. "To Greta for her tolerance of this rude company"— they laughed—"I present this gift." He pulled a wrapped package from behind a chair and handed it to the biologist. She blushed.

"Jürgen, you know you shouldn't single me out this way." She carefully unfastened the bright wrapping and peeked when it was half off. "It's a book!" More paper came off. The Germans clustered around. "A book about whales!"

"Not poetry, perhaps, but better than the one about paramecia," Drexler joked.

"But from *you,* Jürgen?"

"He picked it out in Hamburg," Heiden said. "Too timid to buy a romance, so he headed for the biology section." The Germans laughed.

"I figured I couldn't go wrong, getting you something connected with your specialty," Jürgen said sheepishly. "When I saw the title, *Lords of the Ocean,* it seemed like the right choice."

Greta nodded, her eyes moist. "You devil. You are more intrigued by them than you dare admit!" She grasped the back of his neck and kissed him, quickly, on the lips. The assembly roared with appreciation. "Thank you." She looked at him shyly, grasping the book to her breast. Jürgen smiled.

Hart watched from the shadows.

The next morning there was a watery dawn of gray light. As the sun climbed higher the wind dropped and the overcast began to break. The *Schwabenland* was in a lead of cold black water between two masses of pack ice, picking its way slowly southward. More silver-colored seals lounged on the ice floes, indeed looking from a distance like giant slugs. Maybe Drexler had a point.

Then the clouds on the horizon slowly spun away to reveal a harder shape. A chain of white mountains rose from the sea, the snow on them so thick and immaculate it looked like a wall of sugar.

"Antarctica," Hart announced to the Germans.

CHAPTER NINE

Antarctica was like a dream that stung. Part of it seemed soft and hallucinatory: the gauzy shimmer of downy white peaks reflected in a cobalt sea, vast icebergs drifting out of a cold fog, the ethereal gloom of crevasses sunk like blue wounds into crumpled glaciers. Yet the continent was hard as well: the blaze of reflected light that dazzled the eyes, the bitter cold that seared the nose and throat, or the rime of ice on railings and deck. Nose hair froze, lips cracked, and even the blinked moisture of an eye could become sticky from the chill. During a gale the wind could become so bitter that it would seem to suck all oxygen away with it, yet on a still day the sunny radiance could leave one's body glowing while standing on a slab of ice. Most of all there was the clarity of the air. The ordinary slight humid haze of temperate lands was wholly absent and distant mountains stood revealed in incredible detail. Instead of sharpening perception this clarity seemed to confuse it. The mind lost its common reference points and the landscape seemed less real, not more. Antarctica was as vivid as fantasy, as substantial as reverie. Hart had fallen in love with it the first time. He found he still feared it as well.

"Where are we?" he asked Heiden. For all his recognition of the white wall of mountains that stretched as far as the eye could see in any direction, he could have been on the moon.

"New Schwabenland," the captain replied. "The newest part of greater Germany."

The immediate need was to go ashore, Drexler announced. The *Schwabenland* was the first vessel of the Third Reich to visit the southern continent, and a formal claim was paramount. They'd anchored in a bay bounded by two-hundred-foot-high glacial walls that the geographer, Feder, promptly named after their home port of Hamburg. Occasionally a chunk of ice would break away from the glacier face with a crack like a cannon shot, crashing into the dark clear water and bobbing away through the echoes of its own turbulence. A rocky point of land jutted from the southwest corner and it was there that they rowed in a lifeboat, the ever-silent mountaineers pulling at the oars. The boat crunched onto a beach of rocky cobbles and the passengers splashed through the shallows to mushy snow and granite outcrops. A gull-like skua flew overhead, shrieking a protest of prior occupation.

Feder had brought a movie camera, which he proceeded to erect on a tripod. Greta had her silver Leica. Drexler carried a small Nazi flag tied to a boat-hook pole. Since there was no breeze to flaunt the swastika, he had one of the soldiers hold the flag outward while Greta snapped a picture. Then he ushered Heiden in front of the movie camera, pulling down the captain's parka hood so that his steel-gray Prussian features were clearly visible.

"We claim this land for the German Reich in the name of Adolf Hitler," the captain proclaimed, his voice thin in the immense landscape. "May its challenge and resources inspire the German people for generations to come!"

Schmidt stumbled off to peer at small stains of lichen on the rocks. "Life at its most elemental," he muttered, scraping some off.

There was also a colony of Adélie penguins nearby, and a trio of avian ambassadors waddled across the snow to inspect these curious goings-on. "Look, they're already dressed for the New Year," Greta exclaimed in delight. Indeed, the penguins looked like a delegation in tuxedos.

"They're welcoming our protection and administration," Drexler said, winking. He strode toward the birds, which scuttled away warily. "Thank you for your hospitality, we bring you civilization in return," he said, bowing. Then he stood erect and gave a stiff-armed salute. "Heil Hitler!" Greta laughed and snapped his picture.

Hart sighed and walked over to inspect the penguin colony. There were hundreds of birds jockeying for nesting position on the bare dirt that had emerged from surrounding snow. The rookery smelled rank from bird excrement, which stained the area reddish brown. Periodically a group of the birds would walk or belly-slide to the water's edge, hesitate, and then follow a leader, their awkwardness instantly changing to grace as they glided away like sibilant torpedoes.

Greta came too, clicking away with the Leica. Hart felt slightly irritated with her for photographing the Nazi posturing and then reminded himself it was her country. She was oblivious to his mood, delighted at being ashore again. He slowed to wait for her to catch up.

"They look like little people," he said to her.

"This is their nesting time. No one knows yet where they go in winter, but in summer they swim to places like this to breed."

"It's funny to see them pause at the water's edge like we might, as if it was too cold."

"They're not pausing for the cold. They're checking for leopard seals. The leopards lurk just below the surface, looking upward for the silhouette of a penguin before they strike. Stay away from the edge yourself, if you venture onto the pack ice."

"Yes, ma'am," Hart said, mock saluting. "So why are the penguins clustered here?"

"They use pebbles to build their nests and return year after year to rookeries that have a supply of them. You can see them quarreling over the stones now."

Hart watched. Some penguins were simply searching the ground for rocks but others eyed the cache of their neighbors. Sometimes they'd stage a raid and snatch a pebble to much tumult and squawking. Often their own supply would be raided by still other penguins at the same time. It was a pointless competition that seemed, well, very human.

"They're not very bright," the pilot said.

"No, they're little more than hormone boxes, driven by instinct. Skuas and the gulls are the brighter birds. They'll work as a team at breeding time, one bird distracting a parent penguin from its egg while the other snatches it. But there are so many penguins that I guess enough survive."

"If only they'd cooperate with each other."

"Sometimes they do. See there? That penguin is giving his pebble to another. He's probably a male, demonstrating his attention to a female. Romantic, yes?"

Hart grinned. "The rocks we humans give are usually prettier. But yes, they seem to imitate us."

"That's why biology is so fascinating. I see us in them."

"Even krill?"

She laughed. "It's hard to love krill, which drift in the ocean like aimless clouds. But whales? We know so little about them, except their magnificence. Did you know some can dive more than an hour, more than two kilometers deep?"

Hart wondered whether she'd learned that from the book Jürgen had given her. With a slight air of irritation, he gestured toward the political liaison and his men, inspecting a nearby glacial fissure. "What do you think of them claiming the whales' home?"

She shrugged. "Such a claim lets people like me do science. And Jürgen says that if Germany doesn't act, some other nation will. In fact other nations have. The British, the Norwegians, you Americans, the Argentines, the Chileans . . . everyone planting flags."

Hart nodded reluctantly. "I suppose you're right. Still, Drexler seems so . . . arrogant about it all. Germany this, Germany that. So damned serious."

"He just made a joke with the penguins—he's not as severe as you think. And you're pretty intense yourself. No talk of home or family or sports. Do you know what I think? You two don't like each other because you're too much alike. Both loners, both rigid in your opinions, both interested in . . . well, very alike." She flushed a bit.

Hart was miffed by the comparison. "I just find him . . . *self-important.* Claim this icebox? For what? No one can really live here. The weather is fine today but wait for the first storm. The darkness of winter. It's insane."

"Then why are *you* here?"

"To explore. To fly. Not to give a Hitler salute to penguins."

"Maybe Jürgen can see humor where you can't," she retorted. "He's not so bad if you'd get to know him. And he befriended me. I had a . . . a mentor, a professor, who was killed in a car crash, and I had no support in my career as a woman, no means to establish myself at a university, and then I met Jürgen and suddenly I was offered this job in Antarctica . . . God, the opportunity! I could have kissed him! And he's sincere in his dreams. You never listen to him with an open mind."

"Did you?"

"Did I what?"

"Kiss him?"

"No. No! And what if I did! It's none of your business!"

"After that party you have to wonder what his motive is in having you aboard . . ."

"Good biology." Her voice was flat.

"I know you're a good biologist, but just see him for what he is."

"How dare you!" Her temper was rising. "Who did *you* kiss to get your berth on the *Schwabenland*? You haul this checkered past on board with you, and then act superior and condescending about a scientific mission—"

"A *political* mission."

"Both."

Hart sighed. She was angry and defensive and he knew he was making a mess of the situation: that he was alienating a woman who fascinated him, pursuing a woman who could only bring trouble.

"Look, I'm sorry. I . . . I just don't want to see you hurt."

"My friendships are none of your business!"

"Let's drop it."

"I couldn't care less what you think!"

He looked at her hopelessly. "Greta, please, I'm not criticizing you . . ."

But she was stalking away on the beach. He could see Jürgen waiting, a narrow look of curiosity on his face.

Hart thought Greta would cool down by the time they returned to the launch but she sat in the bow away from him, close to Drexler, leaning close to whisper to the German. Feder grinned at the pilot. Great, Owen thought: his ineptness would be the talk of the ship. He was told by the coxswain to take an oar because some of the German SS troops were staying on the beach to exercise their snow skills. He complied, pulling as hard as he could with his back to the German couple.

They began to fly. The initial reconnaissance was simple, the Dornier Wal the pilots had dubbed *Boreas* to the west, *Passat* to the east, each rocketing off the catapult to soar like giant petrels. Hart recognized none of the geography—they were in an unexplored area east of the Weddell Sea, below the Atlantic Ocean and Africa—but he found himself playing a useful role in his advice on icing, weather patterns, the dangerous downdrafts off the mountains, and the importance of careful navigation.

The immensity of Antarctica unexpectedly intimidated the German pilots. Within minutes of their launching the planes seemed swallowed in the wildest, most epic landscape they'd ever seen. Not only was there no town or road or light or landmark, there never had been. In all of human existence they were the first of their species to see this hostile shore.

The flights were mostly in clear, calm weather, not unusual during Antarctica's high summer of December and January. Hart and Feder would often have a chance to accompany them, the pilot working on his own launchings and landings. They began sketching out maps, Feder sometimes giving names that seemed sure to curry favor: the Hitler Range, Mount Göring, Goebbels Glacier, Bismarck Bay. The German pilots seemed particularly interested in anchorages and adjoining bits of snow-free land. Sometimes after they discovered one the *Schwabenland* worked around the coast to it, threading its way past towering bergs and through patchy pack ice. Hart realized they were looking for a harbor to return to. Drexler used a word he had apparently picked up from Hitler's speeches or writings: *Lebensraum,* living room.

Heiden's greatest fear was the unpredictable ice. Sometimes pack ice skidded before a breeze one way while the larger, deeper icebergs perversely went the opposite because their underwater bulk was being pushed by ocean currents. The *Schwabenland* was not a true icebreaker and could make progress only by searching out openings, or leads. The pilots scouted for them.

"Look for a rain squall," Hart told the aviators at one point.

"It's too cold to rain in Antarctica," Kauffman objected.

"It's the reflection of open water on an overcast sky. The ice shines light back up onto the clouds and makes them whiter than they are, but the dark open water throws a patch of shadow. It looks like an approaching storm, but go that way and you'll find a lead or polynya." Thereafter the Germans began making their way through the ice with more confidence.

The most bizarre part of each flight came when the airplanes reached the farthest point of their range. It was then that the mystery of at least some of the crates was solved. Each morning the sailors would load one into a Dornier. Inside were four-foot-long metal stakes with a small flattened oval and engraved swastika at one end. "This will substantiate our claim that we saw these lands before any other nation," Drexler solemnly told the pilots. "Drop them at the far limit of your penetration. They're designed to fall point down and stick into the ice."

Hart could barely restrain himself from laughing out loud at the conceit but he found that as aerial observer it was often his job to drop the damned things. The pilots would signal at the appropriate moment and he'd have to crank open a side hatch to a blast of shrieking air, watching through his goggles as the stakes tumbled until they were lost in ice glare. Afterward he could see no evidence of their existence; he suspected they'd simply been engulfed by the snow. But the pilots didn't care so long as the stakes were gone.

Meanwhile, Greta ignored Owen. Fine, he thought, I'm exhausted from the constant flying anyway. Let Drexler entertain her. Sometimes when returning to the ship in a Dornier he'd spot her in the launch, dragging a net or hauling up water. She'd come in late, wet and cold, and go wordlessly to her laboratory with her samples. She was quieter and more distracted at mealtimes, only summoning the energy to smile wanly at Drexler during his monologues about Greater Germany and a Thousand Year Reich. Fritz had been right: Hart was weary of the speeches. If Jürgen tried any harder, the pilot thought, he'll break a sweat.

CHAPTER TEN

A storm moved in. A pale sky taut as a balloon was invaded by a great scudding fleet of storm clouds and landmarks were devoured. The *Schwabenland* prudently dropped anchor and waited out the wind, midsummer snow giving a wintry cast to the decks. Ice rasped and clanked by as Heiden brooded on the bridge. The weather provided a welcome respite from flying and Hart seized the opportunity to nap. The hiatus also gave him time to think, however, and it bothered him that he thought so much about Greta.

He scarcely knew her. He wanted to avoid being distracted by her. Yet he couldn't get her out of his mind. He didn't understand it; she had none of the California glamour of Audrey. Half the time the woman simply upset him. Yet he missed her company, the ease of talking with her, the surprise of what she would say—and cursed himself for both missing it and being an ass every time he was around her.

Then New Year's came.

They stayed up late in the officer's mess, drinking toasts to

1939 by candlelight and playing scratchy records, some of them American, on the ship's sole phonograph.

"To *Amerika!*" a boozy Feder offered.

"To the crucible of history and our Führer!" an equally tipsy Drexler added.

"To peace on earth," Greta said. There was a grunted assent from the males.

"To Antarctica, the last untouched place," said Hart.

He surreptitiously studied Greta's face in the candlelight, trying to keep from making his fascination too obvious. Sometimes she'd glance at him and, seeing him watching her, look uncertainly away. Drexler noticed once and evenly stared at Hart a moment before turning back to fill her glass. The man hung on her like a cloak. And yet she didn't melt into him, Hart noticed, but he could tell the caution frustrated the political officer. She sipped champagne but lacked the gaiety she'd demonstrated at Christmas. She'd seemed subdued since their quarrel on the beach.

The champagne aboard had been cooled for the day in the galley refrigerator. When a bottle emptied Hart decided it was his turn to fetch another. He worked his way in the dark past the steel sideboard and hanging pots and opened the door, leaning into its pool of light to seize a bottle. As he swung around, closing the door with his elbow, the eclipsing illumination showed Greta frozen behind him. The door clicked shut.

"I guess we had the same idea," she whispered in the dark.

He hesitated a moment, gauging what to say. "Greta," he finally decided, "I'm just trying to be a friend."

He heard her sigh. "Owen . . . it's not you."

He waited, saying nothing.

"It's . . . just me, the expedition. Things are not going exactly as I expected. Jürgen and I are trying to . . . we knew each other before . . . it's complicated. I'm sorry."

"I'm sorry too."

She didn't move, a shadow in the dark. A tremulous breathing. What the hell, Hart thought.

He reached up, the tips of his fingers cold from grasping the champagne. He touched her hair, then let his fingers brush against her cheek. For a moment he thought he heard her heart and then realized it was his own. Still she didn't move.

Damn.

He reached around to cup the back of her neck and leaned forward, the scent of her filling his senses. He hunted for her lips and then he was kissing her, a bit awkwardly as she stiffened. Her own head tilted and she was hesitantly kissing him back, her arms still at her side. And then she jerked and took a step back.

"You shouldn't have done that." And with that she was gone.

He waited a minute, giving her some grace to collect herself and himself time to calm down. That was stupid, he told himself. You're no good at this.

"Where's the champagne?" a drunken Feder was calling.

Hart came slowly back into the mess, bearing the bottle and smiling wanly. Greta was gone. So was Drexler. The men were slumped, looking desultory. "The only woman and she left," Kauffman said, groaning. "All she does is remind you of what you're missing."

"Where's Jürgen?" Hart asked.

"Like a hound on a hunt, what do you think?" Feder laughed, gesturing at the door. "Or like a dog after an auto, wondering what to do when he catches it." He laughed again.

They had hangovers the next morning. The storm had passed, leaving a gray overcast. The ship slowly picked its way along the coast, aerial exploration suspended. Only a few even came to lunch. Hart looked out over the ice. Before Antarctica he'd never dreamed that water could freeze in so many different ways. There was a litany of navigator names for it: anchor ice, bare ice, brash ice, close ice, compacted ice, deformed ice, dried ice, fast ice, floe ice, frazil ice, grease ice, growler ice, hummocked ice, ice rind, multiyear ice, nilas ice, rafted ice, ridged ice, rotten ice, shuga ice, slush ice, strip ice, tongue ice . . . This was pancake ice, freshly frozen in platters several feet across that looked like giant pan-

cakes. The wind had jostled them together so that the edges over-
lapped like scalloped potatoes. Some pieces looked dirty and reddish on the bottom. The sailors speculated it was dust blown
from Africa, but Greta told them it was really algae that grew
there, something biologists had scarcely thought possible.

Hart sighed, listening to her. He assumed she was angry and
he supposed she had a right to be. He'd made a presumption
without clarifying her feelings. He felt like an oaf.

Still, he reminded himself, she'd hesitated before fleeing. He
missed her. The thought of being on board the rest of the voyage
and having her avoid him was intolerable. If she was committed
to Drexler, that was fine, he'd hardly expected anything else. He
enjoyed talking to her, however. Couldn't they at least do that?

He brooded about it all day, turning events over in his mind.
That evening he went to Greta's laboratory, intending to apologize for his forwardness. Taking a deep breath, he rapped on the
door.

There was a bang inside as something fell over and then a shuf-
fle of feet. "Just a minute!" she called, somewhat breathlessly.

Hart waited several seconds. When she pulled open the door
her sweater was rumpled and her hair awry. She looked startled to
see him. "Owen! What is it?"

She half stepped through the door to partly close it behind her.
The movement wasn't quick enough to shield his view of Drexler,
standing in the shadows of what was a dimly lit room.

There was an awkward pause. Hart cursed himself for coming
but it was too late to simply leave. "Look," he began, swallowing.
"I just wanted to say I'm sorry, okay? I . . . I was wrong to do
that. Without asking, I mean. And I don't intend to criticize. It's
Germany's expedition, your expedition. I'm just along for the
ride."

She blinked. "Oh. Yes." She seemed momentarily confused as
to what he was talking about and then, when she remembered,
struggling between having several things to say. Her mouth
opened but nothing came out.

It was obviously the wrong time. "Sorry to bother you." Hart felt foolish. She was silent, giving no encouragement but looking troubled. He turned and walked down the passageway. What a mess, he told himself. Stick to flying.

"Owen . . ." he heard her whisper.

But he kept going.

The expedition's turn toward disaster began with their return to the air. At first the flying was a relief. Hart welcomed the launching jolt and freezing air as a tonic to shock away his depression. The terrain was as Schmidt had remarked on the first beach: elemental. Simple. Without complication or attachment. This is what he'd come for, Hart thought, the opportunity to come to terms with a place that promised nothing. He had to concentrate on that.

The radio in *Boreas* had gone down and they were using that plane close to the ship, but the *Passat* was still flying wide surveys. They probed toward a barrier of mountains to the southwest, Hart dutifully leaning out to drop stakes like motes into a vast, white, unblinking eye. Then they headed north to the coast and out over the ice pack. Kauffman had decided to follow its edge back to the *Schwabenland*. As they swung east toward their ship Hart looked out at the bergs dotting the cold ocean. There was a darker shape among them and he hefted a pair of binoculars curiously. It was a ship! He focused and his initial impression was confirmed. It looked like a whaler. Hart jostled Kauffman on the shoulder and directed him to look. The pilot nodded and angled closer, peering.

"Damn," the German muttered. It looked like the *Aurora Australis*. "What are they doing this far south, so close to the ice?"

Hart swung the glasses around, searching. Then he pointed again. "Hunting." So wispy as to almost be missed, a tendril of spray puffed above the ocean and the waters roiled. Whales, midway between the Norwegians and Germans.

Kauffman aimed for the foreign ship, accelerating slightly. He roared over it barely above mast height, a couple of seamen instinctively ducking. "They're not supposed to be down this far,

Hart," the German growled. "They're trying to make a point, the bastards. Don't radio. We need to discuss this in private." The German set course for the *Schwabenland.*

Once on board they sprinted for the bridge. "The Norwegians are just fifty kilometers to the west," Kauffman reported. "Right down near the ice. There's a pod of whales between us and them. Icebergs all around. It's far below their normal hunting range."

Instead of commenting, Heiden turned to Drexler and waited. The political liaison frowned, pondering. "I don't care what that bearded Viking said," he told the captain. "He wouldn't risk the ice just to chase whales in this region. He's shadowing us. Making a point."

"Perhaps. Or looking for the *Bergen.*"

"Maybe he's just hunting," Hart offered.

"Hunting and posturing." Drexler turned to Feder. "Was our rendezvous before Christmas planned, do you think? Is he trying to track us?"

"No, it was fortuitous, coincidental. The ocean is vast, our timing uncertain. But he's smart, and curious. Do we know something he doesn't? Are whales down here? He trails us, he looks for whales: why not, if hunting elsewhere is as poor as he claims?"

"How many whales?" asked Greta, who had also come to the bridge. She looked at Hart. "What kind?"

"Does it matter?" Drexler asked.

"They must have swum this far south to feed," she said, excited. "It would be interesting to see what they're preying on— to sample for krill."

Drexler considered this. Then he looked at Heiden.

"We can't permit him to come after us, dropping flags, confusing dates of first claim, muddling our authority. You know that."

The captain nodded unhappily. "We can't but we must. We're not at war, Jürgen. The sea is unclaimed. He can prowl where he wishes."

"Nonsense. Take a German trawler to Norwegian fishing grounds and you'll not hear them braying such nonsense. They simply act to protect what is theirs. We must do the same if we're to fulfill our duty to the Reich."

Heiden looked wary. "What do you want to do?"

Drexler nodded toward Greta. "Sample krill," he said decisively. "At the pod."

"Krill?"

"Yes, krill. I want to cut him off." He looked at Greta, calculating. "He can't hunt if we're at the pod first, doing scientific research. We can save these whales for future breeding, help Greta do her research, and send a message that this is no longer a profitable whaling ground—all at the same time. This is ultimately why we came here, Konrad: to make our interests plain."

"Jesus," said Hart. "Cut him off? Did you get a look at that guy? I don't think he's the type to take interference lightly."

"Do you think *I* am?" Drexler said. He glanced again at Greta. "I'm not afraid of a bunch of damned fish eaters. I'm not afraid of accomplishing my mission."

Greta was watching them uncertainly. "What's your plan?"

"Simple enough. Our ship between theirs and the whales. You in a boat sampling krill, observing behavior, whatever you wish. We're here for science, yes?"

"It sounds risky," Hart objected.

"History's lesson is that it's inaction that is risky."

The pilot looked at Greta, waiting for her to say no. "I do want to see the whales," she said instead, hesitantly, looking at her fellow Germans.

Hart shook his head. "But what if the Norwegians—"

"I want our time down here to *mean* something," she said. "Jürgen is right."

Hart bit his lip, irritated at her choice but reminded by her manner that he was the foreigner. "All right. It's your expedition."

Drexler nodded. "Exactly." He turned to Heiden, assuming an air of command. "Set course now."

The captain gave a short, hesitant nod. "As you wish." He

barked some orders. The ship began to turn and pick up speed. Hart was surprised at the deference to the political liaison.

"It's best to hurry," Feder said. "The barometric pressure is dropping. A threat of bad weather."

"Jürgen, will we get there in time?" Greta asked.

"It's late in the day. I'll do my best." He laid a rule against the chart, then glanced up at the pilots. "Good eyes, Reinhard. And you too, Hart. But now I suggest you adjourn to the galley. We're going to be busy up here, making clear the new order of things."

The pair retreated down the companionway.

"A bit presumptive, isn't he?" asked Hart. "I thought he was an advisor. Suddenly he's acting like an admiral."

"This is an issue of *territory*, Owen," the German pilot replied. "When Reich politics are at stake, we turn to our major in the SS."

CHAPTER ELEVEN

The Norwegian whaler was leaking blood.

It was late in the day, the sun sinking into a chill haze and the wind slowly rising. The *Schwabenland* rolled uneasily in the growing swell, Hart feeling slightly ill as he stood at the rail and studied the carcass being towed behind the *Aurora Australis.* The whale's body had been pumped full of compressed air to keep it afloat and its tail rose and fell in the swells with a doleful wave, leaving a trail of scarlet. Jansen had struck at the pod. Now a boat was fastening a flag to the beast and the Norwegian was cutting the whale loose to drift for later recovery. His ship began to leave a broader wake as it accelerated, aiming for the survivors. Aiming toward Greta Heinz.

Hart had gone out on deck after another frustrating encounter on the bridge. The Norwegians and Germans had arrived at the whales at almost the same time, Jansen swinging away to hunt down a stray at the edge of the pod. As the Germans slowed to a drift while considering what to do, the Norwegian's harpoon had made a crack clearly audible across the icy sea. Drexler watched unhappily, mentally calculating how far he dared push the situation.

"Are we too late?" asked Feder.

In answer, the feeding whales swam past the German ship as if instinctively seeking shelter, water roiling when they surfaced. Suddenly the *Schwabenland* was interposed between hunter and hunted.

"It appears not," decided Drexler. He picked up the radio. "This is the *Schwabenland* calling *Aurora Australis.* We're conducting a scientific survey of this pod of whales and your hunting is disrupting our investigation. We request that you depart immediately."

"I'm sorry, my friends," Sigvald Jansen's voice crackled back. "We got here first."

Drexler considered a moment. "These are now German territorial waters by right of exploration and formal claim," he tried.

"The hell they are. We follow the rules of the Whaling Convention and no other. Haven't you heard of freedom of the seas?" Jansen clicked off, ignoring further calls.

The Germans looked at each other. "Greta, do you know what kind of biological study you want to conduct here?" Heiden asked.

"To sample for krill and observe the whales' behavior from the motor launch. Can some sailors get me close?"

"I think so."

Hart had come back up from the galley, uneasy at the idea of putting Greta out on the sea. "Let's think about this," he cautioned again. "You're going to put her out there in an open boat with this Sigvald Jansen firing his harpoon gun?"

"Only to establish that we're doing legitimate scientific research," Drexler said, a note of scorn in his voice. "There's no *danger,* Hart, if that's what has aroused your famed prudence. We're simply establishing our legitimate claim to this pod."

"I'm worried about *her,* not us. She's the one at risk."

"It's all right, Owen," Greta assured. "The whales are shy."

"That whaler isn't. What if we have a confrontation?"

"Then we'll win and the fish eaters will go home," Drexler said. He turned to Greta. "Don't listen to Hart. These whalers won't come near you or your whales. I suspect that with us on the scene they'll content themselves with their one kill and go back to their factory ship. If not, we'll warn them off with the *Schwabenland*. Our ship is twice their size."

"I still think this is a needless confrontation," the pilot insisted.

"And I think you were hired to provide technical advice, not opinions," Drexler retorted. He turned again to the biologist. "Greta? This is your decision."

She watched the whales, her face becoming determined. "I want to go. This is the kind of observation I came to Antarctica to make. I just don't want a fight."

"The whole point of this is to avoid future fights, by making clear our position."

"Greta, there's no need for this," Hart tried.

"We've been pinned to the coast, conducting your aerial exploration, Owen," she replied. "You've had your chance and this is mine." She turned to Drexler. "I'll go fetch my nets."

Hart unhappily watched her go. "Your bravado could put that woman in danger."

"Only if your timidity prevents my protecting her from that danger. Why don't you stay off the bridge if our course disturbs you?"

Now she and the launch were a speck following the ephemeral blowhole mist. And Sigvald Jansen, far from being satisfied with one whale, was pointing on the same course.

The *Schwabenland* began to pick up speed too, circling some icebergs as it tried to maintain a barrier. Hart found himself alone on deck. The mountaineering troops were staying out of sight and the crew was busy driving the ship. He was uneasy at the nearness of the icebergs, carved into baroque castles by sun and wind. Some were sharpened to points, others undercut by caves, still more constructed of arches and buttresses. In the growing overcast they looked opaque and dull, rocking on the sea with nodding menace.

Fritz came to the rail with a thermos and Hart scented coffee. "I see we've made a detour," the German said.

"More like a wrong turn." Hart accepted a cup. "Drexler wants to claim whales as well as a continent, so we're chasing fish. And if Norwegians are anything like Alaskans, all hell is going to break loose when we try to interpose the *Schwabenland* between Sigvald Jansen and his whales."

"Serve him right." It was unclear who Fritz meant.

"Meanwhile the only woman in a thousand miles is out there in an open boat, thanks to our crazy political liaison."

"*Is* he so crazy? Now the woman requires rescue."

Hart looked at the sailor sourly. "So this idiocy is a mating game?"

"Simply human nature at its baldest, Owen."

"Jesus." The pilot let the coffee steam play across his face. "Drexler's version is that Germany is just trying to get its rights back."

"Germany's just trying to get its balls back. Especially one German. You know, Owen, you shouldn't have embarrassed him in the plane. Not in front of Greta."

"He had it coming. If he wasn't so arrogant—like this little stunt here—he wouldn't get embarrassed."

Fritz gave Hart a long look. "Everyone, everywhere, trying to get their balls back. Right? There you have all of human history."

Hart laughed, even at himself. "Male history!"

Fritz shook his head. "Human history."

At first Jansen appeared to be turning away, either to leave or chase another whale at the periphery of the pod. Then, as if thinking better of it, he swung again and began throwing up an arcing bow wave as his whaler cut through glassy swells, a Norwegian sailor at the bow bracing himself against the shoulder struts of the harpoon. He was heading right for the heart of the pod. Straight for the motor launch with Greta.

"My God," said Feder on the bridge. "He's making for the woman."

"He thinks we'll back down and flee," Heiden assessed.

"A foolish assumption," said Drexler. "I'll be damned if I'm going to let him come close to Greta." He bent to the intercom that was connected to the engine room. "Full speed ahead! Full speed! We're going to push those arrogant sons of bitches all the way back to Norway!"

"Jürgen, you're going to risk collision?"

"No." The voice was cold. "*He* risked collision. And now he's going to be forced to turn away."

The final German surge sent an excited shudder through every rivet of the ship. Hart had gone to the bow to watch and the full powering of the engines made the deck tremble beneath his feet. Black smoke boiled out of the *Schwabenland*'s stack, and Greta and the sailors in the motor launch were steering hurriedly out of the way. Yet the charging whalers seemed oblivious to the approaching German seaplane tender.

Hart glanced back upward at the bridge. He could see Drexler up there against the glass, grimly determined, his eyes reflecting the mental calculation of his navigation. Heiden was less visible in the shadows, watching from his chair. Across the water, Greta's motor launch was abandoning the whales.

The pilot looked ahead again. One ship or the other would give way. Would *have* to. Norwegian sailors began appearing at the rails of their whaler, waving the Germans off or shaking their fists. Yet the *Schwabenland* didn't waver, thrusting forward like a Roman ram. Closer and closer the whaler loomed, the Norwegians becoming more and more distinct, their features distorted by anger or fear, the harpoonist looking anxiously first at a targeted whale and then at the racing research ship more than a hundred feet longer than his own vessel. The water separating the two shrank to a lake, a pond, a moat. Hart could see the streaks of rust on the *Aurora Australis,* a deck gutter stained with blood. "Jesussss . . ." He seized the deck's anchor chain for support.

Jansen finally swerved.

It was too late to avoid a collision but the blow was more glancing. The whaler swelled to fill everything Hart could see and then there was a great echoing boom and a howl of metal as the two hulls hit and ground against each other. Despite his grip the pilot was knocked sprawling back over the anchor chain. The growling screech went on and on, the bow of the whaler slithering along the side of the bigger research ship, the Norwegians being bulldozed off course. Then they were past, the *Aurora Australis* out of speed and bobbing in their wake, the harpoonist apparently knocked from his perch.

There were howls of triumph on the German bridge. The *Schwabenland* began to circle back to pick up Greta, who was waving frantically. The whaler appeared to be backing off.

Hart ran angrily up the outside ladder to the bridge.

Drexler was occupied on the radio but he glanced up at the American with irritation. The sound of Jansen's curses were crackling over the speaker, his voice a rage. "Fucking krauts!" the Norwegian roared. "Look what you've done to my ship, you Nazi bastards!" The Germans instinctively turned to see. The whaler's bow was slightly crumpled and its side hull was bruised, the plates showing a ripple in the dull light. Discoloration from the scraping ranged from bare metal to red undercoating to the *Schwabenland*'s own green hull paint.

"That was insane!" Hart shouted.

"Silence!" barked Heiden, in no mood for criticism. His Prussian features could have been carved out of stone, his voice forged in the cold of the polar plateau.

"But Captain, for God's sake—"

"Enough!"

Jansen was still apoplectic on the radio. "You sausage-headed lunatics!" he roared. "You'll pay for that, pay every damned pfennig, and Oslo will make sure your bosses have your hide! In twenty years at sea, that was the most outrageous, dangerous, arrogant—"

Drexler cut him off. "It was *your* bow that struck *our* side, Captain," he snapped. "A commercial vessel interfering with the mission of a scientific research ship, trying to force its way into our sample pod of whales—"

"A violation of every rule of safe navigation—"

"We will file a diplomatic complaint about your whaling in German territorial waters, offshore from a clear German claim you'd already been informed of—"

"Fuck you with a horse's dick." The radio went dead.

Drexler smiled in triumph. "Well. That little whale hunt was cut short." He looked out toward the stern. Greta's launch was being hoisted aboard. "And perhaps we've indeed learned what brings the creatures to these icy waters." He took a breath. "I trust our damage was not too severe."

Sailors had come to report. "We lost some paint," Heiden summarized.

Greta came hurrying breathlessly into the bridge in boots and oilskins. She looked alarmed. "I thought we were simply going to warn him off!"

"I tried," Drexler said. "He ignored me."

"My God, Jürgen, I thought you were going to sink both our ships!"

"There was never any danger and no need to break off your biological investigation. Everything is fine." He swung around to the pilot. "As for you, Hart, I must remind you again that you're a hired aerial consultant, an American national, and have no say, and no right to comment, on the operation of this ship. And I told you to stay off the bridge."

But Owen wasn't listening. He was staring out the bridge's side windows at the Norwegian whaler. "He isn't giving up," he said quietly.

Indeed, the *Aurora Australis* had renewed its course for the receding whales, its bow wave steadily climbing again. They could recognize Jansen on the wing of his bridge, making an obscene gesture.

"Unbelievable." Drexler frowned. "Ridiculous obstinacy. Well then. Full speed ahead!"

"Jürgen, no," Greta said. "We've made our point."

The political officer ignored her and picked up the engine room intercom. "Speed, dammit! I asked for speed!"

"Jürgen, you've made your gesture—"

"Quiet!" Too late he tried to bite it back. She looked stricken. He took a breath, laboring with his emotions. "Please, Greta. It's time to establish claim to these waters and fulfill what the Reich Minister sent us down here for. I'm not afraid of a few damned whalers. We'll have it out now, and then it will be over."

"Jürgen . . ." she pleaded.

"Captain, a course to intercept," he ordered. "Hart, get out."

The pilot went to the bow again, his jaw clenched. Everyone a damn fool, as Fritz had said. He didn't see the little sailor but the German pilots, Lambert and Kauffman, joined him as spectators. The ships were racing on more parallel courses this time, the *Schwabenland* angling toward the Norwegian whaler and the spume of the whales a gossamer lure to the surging vessels. The sky continued to darken and the horizon was shrinking. "Snow," Hart predicted to himself.

The German ship was straining to cut the *Aurora Australis* off. Again the gap of water narrowed between them, but more slowly this time. The harpoonist was back, Hart saw, and the side of the whaler that had sustained damage was facing away. Like a recurring nightmare, nothing seemed to have changed; the collision seemed doomed to happen all over again.

Then Jansen appeared on his bridge wing like a huge black crow, oilskins flapping in the wind. He lifted his hands in warning.

He had a gun, a rifle or shotgun.

Hart looked up at the bridge. Greta was gone. Drexler appeared calm, looking at the Norwegian with amused scorn.

The two ships came closer, the foamy black water between them like a rushing chute. They were going to collide again.

Jansen aimed.

"Get down!" Hart shouted, lunging for Kauffman. There was

a rattle like hail and a boom snatched away by the wind, the noise reaching them after the pellets had. The Norwegian had fired.

Lambert had fallen on top of them, howling. "Shit! Oh, damn! Damn, damn, damn!" He'd been hit. There were bright drops of blood on the deck and the pilot's parka was pierced by several dark shotgun holes, some welling red.

Hart jerked up. The gap between the ships was widening, the *Schwabenland* finally swerving away. The crazy Norwegian fired another blast, this time toward the bridge. Hart couldn't see anyone up there and supposed they'd ducked. More pellets rang against the steel.

"Jesus, it hurts," Lambert groaned.

Then there was a deeper report, and then several more. The SS mountaineers had emerged with semiautomatic carbines and were firing back. Now the Norwegians were scattering, Jansen ducking into his bridge and others sprawling on deck, either from being hit or in a scramble for cover. "Christ on a crutch," Hart breathed. Drexler and Jansen had started a war.

"Help me, Owen!" It was Kauffman. The German pilot wanted to carry his injured friend below. Nodding, the American took Lambert's legs as Kauffman did his shoulders and they carried him to a hatchway. They could hear heavier bullets striking the *Schwabenland:* more of the Norwegians were firing back, probably with hunting rifles. The two pilots accidentally slammed Lambert's shoulder into the hatch coaming as they were dragging him through and he yelped in pain.

"For God's sake, let me walk to the infirmary, you idiots! It's not that bad unless you finish me off."

They set him down. "Sorry, Siegfried," Kauffman said, gasping for breath. "We weren't prepared for this."

"Now I have to face that animal doctor Schmidt. Of all the luck . . ."

The companionway steps rang from pounding feet above and Drexler was on top of them, breathless and excited. "You two!" he shouted at Kauffman and Hart. "Get to the planes! The one with the working radio! We need to use the advantage we have; you're going to take some of my troops up with you and end this once and for all!"

"What?" Kauffman asked.

"We have some grenades, some explosives. We're going to attack from both air and sea and end this as quickly as we can, before more Germans are hurt!"

Hart groaned. "Jürgen, you're going to bomb them? For Christ's sake, let's break this off before someone gets—"

"Silence! Another word from you and I'll have you tossed overboard! If you don't want a part of this, coward, then get below!"

"I'll be damned if I'm going to bomb—"

"Fine. You're out of it. You!" He pointed at Kauffman. "Get the plane warmed up. That's an order."

Kauffman had paled. "Jürgen, Owen is right—"

"*Now,* dammit! They fired first. They're lunatics! Crazy men! Do you want more of your shipmates hit?"

Kauffman bit his lip, agonizing. "Is this an order?"

"On the authority of Hermann Göring and the SS!"

"I want it in writing."

"I'll carve it in stone! Now go!"

He nodded unhappily. "All right."

"Go back on the starboard side in case there's more gunfire. You'll be shielded."

"Yes, Major." He left for the plane. Drexler bounded back up to the bridge.

Hart helped Lambert walk down to the infirmary and then stood inside the ship, undecided. The *Schwabenland* tilted first one way, then another, swerving as it danced with the Norwegians. He was tired of being called a coward. He walked aft to where the seaplane catapults were. The propellers of *Passat* were beginning to spin and the *Aurora Australis* appeared headed for them again. Hart ran to the airplane's hatch and climbed inside. Looking down the dim fuselage he saw four of the mountaineers crouched there, sorting out hand grenades. One had a submachine gun. Everyone has gone mad, he thought. Kauffman was studying his instruments in the cockpit. "I'll co-pilot, Reinhard," the

American offered grimly. "It's wrong to stick you with this lunacy alone."

The German glanced back and shook his head. "No, get out of the plane, Owen. I appreciate the gesture but better that only one of us has to live with this. With any luck, I'll end this quickly and chase them away."

"If they shoot and hit you . . ."

"They won't. All they've got is a few rifles. Get out."

"I'm not leaving, dammit."

"Get out now! Now! Look, they're approaching, I need to get us off! Please!"

Hart looked. The whaler was looming closer again. Gunfire crackled. For God's sake, what was Jansen doing? He hesitated just a moment longer.

"All right." To hell with it. Let the Germans have their war.

Hart dropped out of the plane's belly and a sailor slammed the hatchway shut. The engine howled and the airplane shivered, ready to go. Hart backed away toward the *Boreas*. Kauffman glanced outside, grinning fiercely, and gave a thumbs-up. Beyond, the American could see the looming hull of the *Aurora Australis*. A crewman reached to fire the catapult.

Before he could launch, there was another bang and then an explosion.

The cockpit of the *Passat* disintegrated, pieces of metal skittering across the stern deck of the German ship. Hart was hit with a spatter of blood. Then the whaler was swerving steeply away, leaning, a line drawn from the shattered airplane cockpit to the Norwegian's bow.

"Jesus!" The flying boat had been hit with the whaler's explosive-tipped harpoon. Now the flanges of its head were buried in the remains of the cockpit, pulling at the Dornier. Reinhard Kauffman was dead, his remains hurled at Hart and the stunned sailors. The mountaineers inside were shouting as the plane began to tip. A soldier tumbled from its belly, then another.

The *Passat* tore free of its catapult, one wing dipping over the *Schwabenland*'s side. It caught for a moment, leaned precariously, and then lurched. The harpoon line snapped but the pressure had been enough. The airplane toppled into the sea with a crash.

"Men overboard!" The cry went up around the ship.

Sailors ran to fling life rings at the bobbing airplane. The *Schwabenland*'s engines slowed and the ship began a tight turn. The two remaining mountaineers popped up in the ocean next to their airplane and swam onto its wing.

"Lifeboat! Man the lifeboat!" The craft began to be lowered. The shattered seaplane was slowly filling, the mountaineers sinking with it, the wing shining blue as it was enveloped by cold water. The lifeboat hit the water with a splash and reached the mountaineers just as the airplane sunk out from under them, still looking as if it was trying to fly as it slid into the deep. The soldiers were hauled aboard half dead from the shock of the water, ice forming on their clothes.

Then with a whoosh and cloud of white steam, a crewman released the air pressure on the port catapult. Its usefulness was over.

CHAPTER TWELVE

The *Aurora Australis* was fleeing and Hart assumed the Germans would let it go. Drexler came running back to the stern after the Norwegian harpooning, wild with frustration. He stopped and stared in disbelief at the chaos.

"What happened?"

"They speared us," one of the sailors said.

Drexler looked at the red-stained stern of the retreating whaler. "Who was hurt?"

"Two of the soldiers almost drowned. Reinhard is dead." The sailor's voice was wooden, numbed by shock.

Drexler's eyes flitted around nervously. "What about the other plane?"

No one answered him.

"Who could fly the other plane?"

Again, no answer. His gaze jerked around, then settled on Hart.

The pilot stared menacingly back at him. It was a look that spoke volumes. There would be no more flying today.

"That murdering bastard," Drexler muttered. Then he turned and ran back toward the bridge.

As he watched the German leave, Hart realized he was trembling from reaction. Reinhard Kauffman had unwittingly saved his life by ordering him out of the plane. Yet, what kind of destiny did Hart confront now, with Drexler having created an international incident that was certain to overshadow whatever the expedition had accomplished?

From the ship's motion in the rising swells, the pilot could tell they were picking up speed again. The added wind was cold. He stood up to see. The stern was temporarily deserted but he noticed a commotion toward the bow. The SS troops were piling loose crates and gear to form a barricade and laying weapons behind it. Hart's chill increased. He stiffly climbed up on the catapult to get a better view ahead. They were steaming south at full speed into an archipelago of icebergs, still chasing the *Aurora Australis,* its stern a taunting lure. The horizon was shrinking as the wind grew. Feder's storm was coming.

Enough is enough. Hart began walking back to the bridge. Twice he saw bullet holes. Brass shell casings rolled and tinkled on the canting deck like strewn toys. Madness!

The bridge was a welcome pocket of heat but Drexler swung on him immediately.

"I told you to stay away!"

Hart ignored him, turning to Heiden. "Captain, as an expedition member with experience in Antarctic waters, I must protest our speed and course. The ice and weather make it entirely unsafe."

"Hart, I want you below!"

"Captain?"

Heiden was silent.

"Captain, you know I'm right. You've been in the Arctic. Or ask Feder. This is risky."

The gap between the two ships was slowly narrowing. A berg the size of a city block slid by on the port side, its underwater bulk like a swollen blue cheese.

"We're pursuing a criminal, Hart," Drexler said. "A ship which killed one of our company. Destroyed one of our planes."

"Captain Heiden, please."

Heiden finally swiveled in his chair to address the pilot. "We can't end it like this. Or we're finished anyway."

"That's better than sinking!"

"No it isn't." Heiden was resigned. "Things have gone too far, Hart. We'll close in half an hour."

"But what are we going to do if we catch them?"

"I don't know." He nodded toward Drexler.

The political liaison turned away, fixing his gaze on the stern of the whaling ship. An ice floe banged against the hull, ringing it like a bell.

"Barometer is still dropping," Feder said worriedly into the hush. "It's growing dark."

Hart glanced around. The Germans avoided his gaze. Ahead, the *Aurora Australis* was disappearing into a cold fog. Flakes of snow drifted down.

Drexler bent to the intercom. "I need more speed!"

"Jürgen, we're not going to be able to see," Feder warned.

The liaison nodded. "Two men out on the wings, listening for surf on the ice."

Heiden issued the order.

Hart noticed that the helmsman was sweating. "This is crazy," the pilot insisted.

No one answered. The atmosphere was one of controlled fury. Instead of losing his grip on the group, Drexler had strengthened it. Defeated, Hart clomped down the stairs toward the galley, feeling impotent.

Greta was there, a mug of tea in front of her, staring at the table. Hart hesitated a moment, then got some coffee and slumped into a chair across from her. The biologist's hair hung around her face like a curtain and her hands were splayed on the surface as if she were examining them for the first time.

Slowly she looked up. Her eyes were moist. Whatever had divided the pair was momentarily forgotten. "I didn't think our sampling would lead to *that*," she said, shaking her head in disbelief. "I didn't think men would go that far."

Hart let her words hang in the air. Then he said: "This voyage was always about politics, not science, wasn't it?"

She looked at him fiercely. "It was about *both*. You can't separate so neatly—it's naive to think you can. Everything we humans do is confused by human relationships. That's what made me so angry on the beach—that you recognized that element in regards to my own presence aboard. Of *course* Jürgen made a difference. Of course he's a reason I'm here, me instead of any of a hundred other biologists. That doesn't mean I know what to feel, how to behave, what standard I can use to judge myself. What role I've really played."

Hart inwardly winced. She was blaming herself. "Greta, you're not responsible for Jürgen Drexler. Or Sigvald Jansen."

"I'm responsible for me."

He reached out and placed his hand on hers. It was cold to his touch and his was larger, like a blanket. She didn't pull away. "We do our best and go on," he said. "The lucky ones know how to pray. I had a friend who believed angels sat on your shoulder."

She laughed at that. "Sounds like my nuns." For a moment her thoughts were far away and then the sadness came back. "But we don't look for magic any longer, it seems, we look for resources." The last word was bitter. "Owen, I don't want to help Germany hunt whales any longer."

He held her hand now, his fingers against her palm, marveling at her fineness. He nodded. "You won't have to. I think we're about done down here—"

But his sentence was cut off by an enormous boom, so loud it was as if they were suspended inside a drum. They were jerked off their chairs and hurled onto the deck amid a cascade of splintering crockery and clattering tableware. There was a long, grating, terrifying squeal of tortured metal. Then the lights went out.

She felt for him in the dark. "What happened?"

"Ice, I think. They gambled and lost." He could hear confused shouts, the pounding of feet, the slamming of hatches. Maybe gushing water too, or perhaps he was imagining that. He struggled to sit up, the deck tilt not too severe yet. "Are you all right?" Dim light, he noticed, still filtered through the galley portholes.

"I think so. It hurt, but I think so." She sat up too, holding on to his sweater. "I'm sorry. I'm frightened."

"So am I. We're a long ways from help." He was reluctant to leave her touch but he gently moved her hands to her lap for a moment and stood up. His feet slid on loose shards of dishes as he staggered to a porthole. A wall of ice filled his view. The ship groaned as it rose and fell in clumsy embrace with the berg as the ice leveraged a wider gash in the hull.

The pilot went back to Greta and boosted her up. Her hand in his was electric, sensual, like an act of sex. He could feel his pulse quickening. *Like a schoolboy,* he thought. "Let's try to get to the bridge."

He led up the companionway toward the bridge, listening to the creak of torn metal and the rattle of skittering debris as the ship rolled. Then the lights flickered, once, twice, and came back on. A sailor was above them and she dropped his hand as if it were hot. He noticed now the reassuring thud of the engine. It seemed to be shifting from forward to reverse in an effort to move the ship off the ice.

The expedition officers were clustered around the wheel. Sailors continued to shout, some of the voices pitched unnaturally high. The iceberg had slipped away and the *Schwabenland* was backing with a wallow, leaning to starboard where they had struck.

Drexler and Heiden wouldn't even look at him. "What went wrong?" he whispered to Feder.

"We heard the surf but not soon enough to stop; we were going too fast. The captain said the berg must have had a prong of ice that hit us below the steel reinforcing belt at the waterline; it's the lowest compartments that are flooded. Where the flotation drums are. We sealed the hatches but the drums are banging around down there. It's not good."

Hart listened. Even on the bridge he could hear a dull rhythmic drumming of the flotation devices shifting with each wave.

Schmidt had come up from the infirmary, anxious and agitated. "Do we send an SOS?"

Drexler laughed bitterly. "To who, down here?"

"The Norwegians, I suppose."

"They'd think it a trick. Besides, I won't ask those bastards for help until I'm neck-deep. We're not desperate yet. We're not sinking."

"But if they steam away . . ." Schmidt let the thought hang there.

"They steam away." Jürgen glanced at Greta and then looked down, realizing bravado had gone too far. She was struggling not to cry.

The pilot remained quiet. There was no need to say anything.

"Well, what's your plan then?" Schmidt's tone was insistent. The doctor was not going to be easily deflected.

Drexler was uncharacteristically silent.

Heiden spoke up. "If we can make the ship seaworthy we can steam for repairs. To Cape Town or Montevideo or even the Falklands. But it's almost impossible to do much at sea with ice all around. We need a quick harbor. The coast, an island: somewhere to work on a temporary patch. If we don't create one we risk having the hull unzip."

"Wonderful," Schmidt said caustically.

"Hamburg Bay," offered Feder. "The first one where we landed . . ."

"Too far," Heiden said. "And too far into the ice. The mainland if we must, but an island farther north would be less risky as the season grows late. Less ice."

Feder bent over a largely blank chart. "These waters are mostly unexplored . . ."

Greta had closed her eyes.

"The plane." It was Drexler.

"Yes?" Heiden said.

"The *Boreas.* We still have one airplane. We'll use it to find a refuge."

The captain shook his head. "We've got one pilot dead, another wounded. The barometer's still dropping. It's night. Even if we could get a plane off I don't know if it could fly in this weather or if we could recover it. Could it land amid this ice? In these seas? I doubt it."

There was a silence for a moment, the shouts of the sailors echoing up to the bridge.

"It could land in the harbor," Hart said, half wishing he'd stayed quiet.

Heiden turned to him. "What good would that do?"

"I'll find a harbor, let you know where it is, land there and wait for you."

"The radio is down."

"I'll drop directions, coordinates, to the ship. I've dropped things before."

Drexler studied him suspiciously.

"There's only one flaw in this plan," Schmidt said. "What if you don't find a harbor in this storm? Then you have to try to land out here amid the ice on the ocean. Maybe you'll make it, maybe not."

Hart nodded. "That's the flaw all right."

Greta looked at him worriedly. "There has to be a better way."

The pilot looked at Drexler. "Unfortunately, there isn't."

Heiden considered. "It's the best gamble, considering the welfare of the entire crew."

"How do we know you're not going to fly off to the Norwegians?" Drexler said.

Hart laughed. "They already harpooned one plane. You think I'm going to let them within range of the other? I was there when Reinhard died. It wasn't pretty." He looked hard at the German. "Besides, I have friends on board the *Schwabenland.*" He nodded toward Greta.

"You've emergency food," Heiden said. "Lines and anchor. But you need someone to help you search, drop the message, secure the plane. Your little friend Fritz perhaps."

Hart nodded. "If he volunteers."

"No." It was Drexler, taking a breath. "I'll go. I took the risk and lost. Now I need to try to get us out. I'll fly with Hart."

Heiden frowned. "We know you don't like to fly, Jürgen . . ."

"I don't. And Hart doesn't like to fly in this kind of weather. He's going because he must, and I'm going because I must. We'll hunt together. And survive or die together." He looked defiantly at the American.

Well, that would be one satisfaction, the pilot thought. Taking him with me.

"Together," Hart agreed aloud. "The brief summer dusk will start to lighten again in a couple hours. We'll launch as soon as we can see."

CHAPTER THIRTEEN

The *Schwabenland* was sluggish, weighted down with hundreds of tons of seawater. It had settled several feet, some of its portholes awash from passing swells. The ship's lean tilted the catapult: takeoff would be awkward. Hart told Heiden to put the stern in a slow arc once the flying boat's engines were at full power, giving him a choice of wind direction and ice conditions to launch into. He'd signal the catapult operator the best moment for release. No one had slept; tension was too high.

While the solstice was past, the long days of January still prevailed in the Southern Hemisphere. By three A.M. Hart judged it light enough to go. Heiden said he was going to slowly steam due north after launch to get clearer of the ice and the pilot nodded, saying he could find them again on that track. "Keep the running lights burning."

Drexler climbed stiffly into the seaplane without saying a word.

Hart glanced over at the empty catapult that had held the *Passat.* The deck had been swabbed of blood but there'd been no ceremony to mark Kauffman's passing. Now Drexler was uncharacteristically quiet. He sat firmly cinched in the co-pilot seat, staring out the canopy but no doubt seeing only the events of the last few hours.

Hart didn't want his new flying partner to freeze up. "Listen, Jürgen, I credit your courage for coming along," the pilot grudgingly offered as he checked his instruments. "I know you don't like airplanes and this isn't ideal flying. But the Dornier is a tough, tough craft. We should be fine."

There was a long silence and Hart thought maybe Drexler was paying no attention. Then the German finally replied. "Do you really think I care what happens to me right now? I only want to find shelter for *Schwabenland*. My fear, or lack of it, is inconsequential after my . . . error." He swallowed. "I tried and failed. All I have left is duty."

Just what we need, romantic fatalism, Hart thought. "Fine. But I still have *my* hide, and your duty is to help me keep it. So keep a lid on the German stoic crap, please, and try to help us survive." Drexler refused to turn to look at him. "And if you vomit, do it in the head. Or you can walk home."

The Nazi swung around then. "If you do any of your damned aerial acrobatics, I will make sure I vomit on *you.*"

Hart's mouth set into its characteristic half grin of tension. "I see we understand each other. Contact!" There was a barking cough and then a roar as the engine came to life. The pilot ran it to full power and gave a thumbs-up, answered by the catapult crew. The stern began to slowly pivot and the American spotted an ice-free lane in which they could put down if anything went wrong, the waves dangerously heaving. When they were almost centered his thumb went up again. There was the bang, the hiss, the jolt . . . and then they were off the ship, awkwardly tipped a moment because of the lean of the stern, dipping a wing toward black water. Then climbing, banking to skim past a massive iceberg.

The familiar feeling of liberated exhilaration came back. Hart wished he had fuel to fly all the way to America.

They'd decided to search eastward since the ship had yet to explore that way. The problem was visibility. Towers of cloud were everywhere, leaking snow from long black tendrils. A milky haze hung on the sea. Hart looked over at Drexler. His skin wasn't green but the German's hands still clutched the seat and cockpit rim. Hart rapped on the compass to get his attention. "Start counting!" If they were going to find the ship again the political liaison would have to keep scrupulous track of their direction, speed, and winds to allow them to dead-reckon where they were in relationship to the *Schwabenland.* Drexler swallowed hard, blinked, and then bent to get paper and stopwatch. He was sweating slightly but favored Hart with a wan expression of reassurance.

The plane hit an air pocket and sickeningly dropped. Drexler's hands dropped with it, seizing the seat and spilling his clipboard. Then the plane rose again, bouncing, and—his mouth set in a firm line of determination this time—the German picked up the clipboard and began writing. The pen shook slightly, but he did it.

They flew in silence for a while. Hart realized he was sweating too, despite the cold. There was a very real chance they'd find nothing and the Germans would have to try to limp across the stormiest waters in the world in a punctured ship. Worse, he and Drexler might be unable to get back aboard. He could see little but gray overcast. These were the conditions he always feared, a featureless blankness that swallowed planes whole. Drexler's needless showdown may already have doomed them.

"You don't like us very much, do you?"

It was startling to have the quiet broken. The German's voice was flat.

"Who?"

"Us. The Germans. National Socialists."

Hart considered a moment. "Maybe." He decided to be honest. "Maybe I just don't like *you.*"

"Yes, that's obvious. Many people don't, I know. I'm not popular. Respected, perhaps. But not popular. I'm serious, obsessed with my work, with the Party, with Germany. People . . . resent that. Don't understand it. They know I'm not like them—that I'm not content with competent mediocrity."

Hart looked over at him. "You just need to stop trying to carry the world on your shoulders, that's all."

Drexler smiled. "Of course. And yet at some point we all carry that which we might rather not, because it's become a part of us. Yes?"

Hart sighed. "We all struggle with who we are, Jürgen. But I don't think ramming a ship and starting a battle is excused by one's personality. Nor is it the best way to win friends and influence people. You know, a book on that subject came out recently, an American book. Maybe you should read it."

"Ha! Americans! Obsessed with friends. With popularity. So much that they write and read books about it. Yet I don't think you're popular either, Hart."

"Maybe I haven't read the book."

"No, I would guess not. One trick in this book, I suspect, is to figure out why people truly *don't* like you."

"You sound like you're trying to figure that out."

"Whether, in other words, it is really *me* they don't like, or something else. A jealousy. An envy. A desperate longing to belong."

"Belong to what?"

"A cause. A country. A purpose."

Now Hart gave a short laugh. "Envy of black shirts and skull insignia and silver daggers? The trouble with you Nazis is that you'd rather be feared than liked."

"There's no menace intended. You're referring to the uniform of our Hitler Guard, our *Schutzstaffel* mountaineers. It's simply an elite unit. Like your American marines."

"The marines don't dress like gangsters or pirates."

"That's naive. Every strong nation has its fierce traditions. Similar uniforms and insignia were worn by some of the elite Prussian regiments that fought Napoleon. The swastika is a medieval design. There's nothing sinister. Simply pride in the order and discipline that we stand for."

"Too much pride. That's why Kauffman's dead and our ship half sunk. *That's* why I don't like you, Jürgen. Nazi pride."

"No, Owen, it's something else and you know it. You envy my sense of purpose, of belonging. Even if you won't admit it to yourself."

The pilot didn't reply.

The island, when they found it, seemed so favorable in its geography that Hart would later have an eerie sense of predestination. It initially loomed like a cloud bank, so ill-defined that the pilot was inclined to dismiss it when Drexler first pointed hesitantly in that direction. As they neared, however, parts of the cloud took on rigid definition and what had seemed to be mist was suddenly revealed to be a hard ridge of snow. A mountain rose out of the cold gray sea, ice girdling its rocky coastline.

Hart flew cautiously, trying to discern the island's outline in its shroud of swirling cloud. He made a long circuit and identified two peaks a dozen miles apart, presumably connected, but the island's lower reaches were too fogged to be sure. Drexler was intently scanning the coastline, his unease in the air forgotten by the excitement of finding land. "I don't see a bay yet," he reported.

"I'm going to fly over the top to look for a break in the cloud. We might bump a couple of times." The overcast was thick enough that Hart was quickly blind. The plane jostled in the turbulent air and the pilot prayed he'd climbed high enough that they wouldn't slam into an unseen peak.

A strong updraft hit the Dornier and the pilot's nose tightened. "What's that?"

Drexler sniffed. "Sulfur." A moment's bewilderment gave way to understanding. "Volcano, I think. We're passing over it."

They came out of their own cloud and looked down at others. It was as if the island was in a cocoon. Then a curtain of overcast parted to reveal a curving knifelike ridge with a crest of dark rocks like stitching on the snow. The rim of another volcano? Beyond it the overcast thinned further. Water. Then snow again.

"What the hell?" Hart circled. Clouds teased them, swirling in and out, but slowly the terrain revealed itself like a series of snapshots. Part of the island was a crater, a volcanic crater filled with water. And at one point on the wall—there?—no, clouds again . . . yes! A slot led from the caldera to the sea. Torn apart at one side by a violent explosion, the old crater formed a bay of the Southern Ocean.

It was the snuggest harbor Hart had ever seen: a bowl with a gate, perfectly protected from storm. If the sea channel and lagoon were deep enough the *Schwabenland* could obtain ideal shelter. Drexler uncharacteristically whooped and pounded on Hart's shoulder. "We found it!"

Then it was gone again, shrouded by storm. Hart looked at the fuel gauge. They might just make it. "Can you find the ship again?"

The German nodded, newly determined. "Of course." With purpose the old confidence was returning. He studied his notes. "Steer west-northwest for two hundred and eleven kilometers." He peered down at the whitecaps on the ocean. "We still can't land, can we?"

Hart shook his head. "The wind would flip us like a toy before they could pick us up. We need to find the ship, drop instructions, and get back to that crater before we run out of fuel. I wish these planes had a spare radio."

Drexler nodded. "Already planned. For next year's expedition."

The galley had prepared three old flour sacks as aerial "bombs," filling them with dried peas for weight. Drexler calculated the island's direction and distance from the *Schwabenland,* copied it three times, and inserted each in a sack and tied it up.

Hart flew on through squalls, the seaplane rattling, fuel slowly eroding, always looking for the ship. At Drexler's calculated rendezvous point they were flying in milk. He dropped to three hundred feet to get below the ceiling. No such luck. He swung north.

"Christ!" It was the German. The tooth of a towering iceberg passed just beneath the belly of the plane. "Can't you pull up, Hart?"

"Not if we're going to find the ship."

Then they broke clear and there it was, tilted to starboard in a stormy sea streaked with foam, its lights blazing as requested. Waves were throwing spray across the catapult deck. "Get ready!" Hart said. "I'll pass over. Aim for the stack!"

Drexler nodded, crawling back to the hatch. There was a shriek of wind as he opened it. The American approached the ship from its starboard side, tiny figures waving. He shot by at two hundred feet, banked hard . . . and the first bomb whizzed briskly past the smokestack and made a neat splash in the sea. Damn. One fewer pot of pea soup on the way home.

Drexler crawled back up. "I missed."

"Let's try again! I'll come in lower, up the length of the ship!" He began to turn. The stern of the ship came into view again.

Come on, Hart breathed to himself. It worked with Ramona. "Let go just before we reach the stern!"

This time the pilot aimed his airplane directly for the stack, determined to just barely clear it as he flew the length of the ship. He roared over close enough that some of the sailors ducked . . . yes!

He circled. A group had clustered around the sack of dropped peas and then waved madly. The hatch shut and Drexler came back, his face raw with cold. "Perfect hit," he said, grinning. "One to spare." He held up the third message sack.

"Save it until we get to a post office."

Hart turned to the east again, glancing at the fuel gauge. One third left. The German handed him the course and coordinates, all business now, his fear of the airplane under control. "Good job, Jürgen." The partnership gave him new respect for the man.

"And good flying," the German allowed. "The message aboard, my stomach intact . . . maybe God's on our side after all."

"We'll know that when we put down inside that lagoon."

The island was not difficult to find on the return trip. The overcast was breaking up and the volcanic shape became more distinct as they neared. There were two main mountains, Hart saw: the crater with its harbor and behind it a higher, steeper, narrower volcano with a wispy plume of steam coming off the top. Ridges and valleys connected the two and glaciers stuck out from the flanks like tongues, feeding ice into the sea. The crater looked too deep and narrow to fly into from above so he dropped to fifty feet and aimed for the slot in the volcano's flank, skimming the wave tops. No second chances: the gas gauge was on empty. The pilot hoped winds wouldn't blow them into the cliffs.

Eruptions of spray were coming off rocks near the narrow entrance. The seaplane passed over a small flat berg, a sapphire in an otherwise monochrome world. The engine coughed and the plane dipped an instant, its propeller on fumes. Don't give up yet! Then they were in the slot through the side of the crater, water welling up from the ocean swells below to curdle with foam, wet basalt cliffs on either side, spray spattering the canopy . . . and on into the foggy caldera, its shorelines shrouded, the surface relatively calm. Hart dropped the seaplane quickly, the floats skidding with a hiss. They were safe, the *Boreas* at heel. Its nose slowly rotated, looking for a place to tie up.

"My God."

It was Drexler. He was looking back toward the caldera entrance. Hart turned too, the airplane slowly pivoting in that direction. The engine coughed again, then caught. "Come on baby, just a bit more . . ."

The pilot stared. There against the shore, its bow reaching vainly toward the harbor entrance, was a half-sunken, snow-encrusted ship, its stern underwater as if pulled down while trying to escape. Fog and flakes of snow whipped past its ice-coated superstructure. At its bow like a menacing figurehead was the muzzle of a harpoon, pointed to the cliff face above.

"I think we've found the missing *Bergen*," the German said. "The Norwegians never came off this island." ·

CHAPTER FOURTEEN

Hart taxied the plane toward the wrecked ship. "Jürgen, there's a line in the nose compartment. You're going to have to get out on the float, tie it to the plane, and then jump for the ship when I taxi over the sunken afterdeck. Be careful. Can you manage that?"

"I can manage the careful part. I can't swim." He bent to fetch a rope.

The derelict whaler actually proved ideal as a moorage point. The seaplane's pontoons slid shallowly over its half-drowned deck, a wing tip just clearing some stanchions. Drexler leaped nimbly, caught a railing, and braked the aircraft. Hart swiftly shut down the stuttering propeller, starved of fuel anyway. Then he came out the hatch grinning.

"I guess God showed up for us after all."

Pulling up their parka hoods and tugging on their mittens, the two men stood on the ship's slippery deck and looked around. The caldera was easily two miles across, Hart guessed, maybe more, the swirling mist revealing no other sign of human habitation. Yet their protection from the storm was complete. They were in a natural amphitheater in which the swells surging in from the caldera entrance quieted to a moderate chop. It was a perfect natural harbor.

"Hitler luck!" Drexler shouted, the sound echoing away. He sucked in the cold air, obviously delighted to be out of the stuffy airplane. His earlier gloom had evaporated. "What a supreme shelter for a base, not yet recorded on any maps!" Hart could imagine the man's sudden calculation of possibilities for rehabilitation. Heroic sea battle against foreign rivals, discovery of an ideal harbor, mapping of a continent, sighting of whales . . .

Assuming the *Schwabenland* followed to pick them up.

"I wonder what happened to this ship," the pilot said.

They looked up the sloping deck. One lifeboat still hung in its davits but its cover was off, its hull filled with snow. The other was missing. Uncoiled lines snaked down the deck, twisted and frozen. Icicles hung off the bridge. It looked like the whaler had been abandoned in a hurry.

"Let's check inside," Drexler said.

The first hatchway was so thoroughly rusted that the two of them together couldn't budge it. A second yielded with a squeal of metal. Hart peered through the opening. The interior was dim, illuminated only by pale light from ice-encrusted portholes. He stepped over the coaming. The deck was slick with frost. There was utter silence.

"This gives me the creeps."

"It's only a boat," Drexler replied. He pushed his way to the front, glad for a chance to reassert his leadership.

The cabin doors were closed and they were reluctant to try them, but there was a companionway up to the bridge. "This way," the German said. It was as cold inside as out, their breath steaming as they climbed, the ship's dying tilt making the stairs even steeper. The wooden door to the bridge was also closed but Drexler leaned, grunting, and it scraped open to push back a drift of powdery snow. A window had shattered and let the weather in. The German stepped through.

He was silent a moment. Then: "God in heaven."

Hart followed and saw what Drexler was staring at. There was a body in the captain's chair. It was leaning backward, mouth open, back curved, one leg straight out, caught in a rictus of pain. Something—a skua, maybe—had pecked out the eyes before the corpse had frozen solid. Now it was mummified by the dry cold, a cap gone to reveal a wisp of hair on a balding head. The skin had dried a deep brown, spotted by black boils on the face. The mouth, its lips pulled back to reveal yellow teeth, displayed the look of a man who'd died quickly but not quickly enough: in agony.

"Jesus," Hart murmured, his breath making a cloud to confirm his own continued vitality. "What happened to him?"

Drexler gingerly approached. "Some kind of disease, I suspect. But why is he here, on the bridge, and not in bed?" He looked around. Charts were still on a table, stained brown from a toppled mug of coffee and spotted with bird droppings. A wall calendar had stopped at December 29 of 1937, the Antarctic season before. Sea coats still hung on pegs. Pencils had spilled. He looked at the wheel. A brass nameplate, greenish now, read BERGEN. Everything was covered with a rime of ice. "Food poisoning? I don't know. It doesn't make sense."

"Whatever it is, I don't want to catch it."

"A boot." Drexler pointed. The German moved to the navigator's cubicle, leaving tracks in the snow. The cubicle was curtained so its light would not destroy the night vision of the helmsman and lookouts. Pushing the curtain aside they saw that a body was sprawled inside. Once again the mouth was yawning open, the eyes gone, the expression one of horror. The fingers were curved like claws as if trying to grasp what could no longer be grasped.

Next to it was a dead bird.

"Don't touch them," Drexler advised. "If they were sick, death and cold should have contained any germs, but there's no need to take chances. Certainly something bizarre happened here."

"And why the sinking? What happened to the *Bergen*?"

"Who knows? They could have hit one of those rocks when entering or trying to leave the harbor. Perhaps survivors were trying to scuttle her. Perhaps she was tied up and leaked after the crew died." He took a deep breath. "At least it doesn't smell. A benefit of Antarctica, yes?"

Hart wanted to go back to the airplane but Drexler's curiosity was obviously aroused. He insisted they explore further.

The galley was a tableau of shadows that wavered in watery light. Some dishes had slid off the tables and broken on the deck as the stern of the ship sank, but others still remained, bearing frozen leavings of half-eaten meals. Dirty pots were heaped in the sink. Cupboard doors hung open, one dribbling a leakage of flour from a mysteriously torn sack. There was another body in the pantry, reaching.

On the deck below, two cabins were empty but a third held a corpse. His spine was hideously bent, his frozen remains rigid, feet on his bunk and head on the floor. Whatever had struck the ship had been monstrous.

Farther aft, seawater lapped corridors leading to the hold and engine rooms. It was chill to the touch but apparently warm enough not to freeze over. Drexler nodded as if he somehow understood such calamity. "Amazing." He led the way back. There was a moment of anxiety when confusion led them to try the rusted door again to the outside deck and they couldn't budge it—a feeling of entrapment—but then they walked to the other hatchway and got out on deck again, breathing deeply.

"My God," Hart said. "A plague, you think?"

"Perhaps. But from where, in this icebox?" Drexler studied the snow-dusted pumice slopes of the crater. "No, Antarctica is far too cold, I think. Food poisoning, perhaps, something from a fish or whale . . . who knows? Maybe Schmidt or Greta will have an idea. But I think we should restrict access to this ship."

Hart nodded. He'd no desire to go back inside. The pilot would feel better when the *Schwabenland* showed up, damaged or not. The presence of the dead bodies made it seem even lonelier here, wind shrieking up on the crater rim. He watched tatters of cloud stream across and dive, dissolving in the caldera's relative warmth. And it *was* warmer here, Hart realized: not just shielded from the wind but slightly less bitter than the open sea or the continent to the south. He looked again at the mist on the far shore. Some was simply fog, he knew, but some . . . the beach was steaming. Yes, he was sure of it. Hot water. Well, it was an old volcano.

The *Boreas* provided a tube of shelter but the airplane's metal skin retained little heat. The men had brought blankets and wrapped themselves, suddenly realizing how tired they were. They hadn't slept for thirty-four hours. What a long, nightmarish day it had been!

The pair ate some cold sausage and bread. Hart was so exhausted he could hardly think. Still, the long day deserved comment.

"Weird, isn't it, Jürgen, to find a refuge and then make such a ghoulish discovery? Like finding life and death at the same time."

Drexler nodded wearily. "Fortune is curious."

The phrase jogged a memory. "That's what Otto Kohl told me when I met him in Alaska."

"Ah. Well, Otto is a survivor. It's the kind of thing he would say." Drexler lay back, his eyes on the ribbed fuselage ceiling. "The trick, Otto told *me,* is to recognize that every obstacle represents new opportunity. I try to remember that when things go wrong."

"Like now?"

Drexler looked at Hart with eyes unreadable in the shadows of the fuselage. "Exactly like now."

And sometimes disaster simply means the end, Hart thought, but he didn't say that. It wasn't helpful. As the pilot slipped into sleep he felt he was sinking into a well of bottomless water, azure and pure, a silver mirror above, inky darkness below. Sinking like the stern of the doomed *Bergen.* Or sinking like the harpooned *Passat,* flown into the abyss by the shattered body of Reinhard Kauffman.

CHAPTER FIFTEEN

Damn slop. I'm frozen above the knees and mired in quicksand below. You've combined the worst of two worlds, Owen: you've found a subzero bog. This is as much fun as a prostitute with cast-iron underwear."

"You speak from experience, Fritz?"

The little German dragged on a cigarette. "No, I can simply imagine the worst. It's a talent, like finding the only beach in Antarctica that's so warm you wallow in it. Jesus! Mud in an ice-box!"

Hart ignored the ribbing. He felt good. He'd slept and then wakened to find the *Schwabenland* anchored in the volcanic caldera. A boat fetched the two aerial scouts for a hot breakfast. Everyone was jubilant at having found a temporary safe harbor and Greta kissed both Owen and Jürgen on the cheek. The relief was quickly undercut by the report of corpses on the *Bergen,* of course, but the wrecked whaler was also a perverse reminder that the Germans weren't entirely alone in the world. "We may be able to salvage items we need for repair," Heiden said.

Safety was the first question. The expedition leaders, including

Greta, rowed over to the Norwegian ghost ship to investigate the mysterious tragedy. At Schmidt's insistence they went gloved and masked against possible disease. "Don't touch anything you don't have to," he warned.

Hart was content to watch them go, wanting no part of a return to the gloomy *Bergen.* Instead he volunteered to explore the island for other clues to the whalers' fate. Now he was off the cramped ship and on the crater beach with Fritz, who in truth seemed to relish the freedom as much as the pilot did. The sailor's complaint was understandable, however: the shore was as peculiar as the island's snug harbor. It steamed from a seep of hot mineral water that made the black volcanic sand mushy instead of frozen. Walking was laborious.

The weather had improved, the overcast breaking up. Hart preferred not risking the *Boreas* in a takeoff in the confined crater—it would be safer to wait for a catapult launch out at sea, he advised—but was willing to climb to the crater rim for a better look at where they were. Heiden had confirmed when arriving by ship that the island consisted of two major volcanic peaks and the usual mantle of snow and glaciers but knew little beyond that. "Perhaps our mishap will prove fortunate if this sheltered harbor can serve as a future base," the captain had mused at breakfast. "Look around with that in mind, Hart." It was the same benefit-from-adversity line spouted by Jürgen Drexler. Maybe the Germans taught it in school.

"Cheer up, Fritz," the pilot now said. "I'm going to take you out of this mud." He pointed to the crater rim, at least two thousand feet above them. "Should be good walking, once we get on top."

The little German let his head tilt back to study the snow-patched pumice slope. The sheltered caldera and its heat apparently prevented the heavy accumulation of snow normally encountered in Antarctica. "God in heaven." He took another drag on his cigarette. "Perhaps you've confused me with those mountain Nazis. I went to sea to stay out of the infantry, my friend."

"No confusion. I asked for you because you're the better conversationalist."

"Ha! A donkey's ass makes better conversation than those robots. As if I'll have breath to gasp a word anyway."

"Exactly. Every trial has its benefits. You Germans keep telling me that."

"If you're relying on Germans for advice you've been on the ship too long."

They started up. The mud ended immediately but the pumice was like climbing a sand dune. Their feet slid backward and puffs of ocher dust colored their trousers. They began aiming for patches of snow, preferring to kick-step their way up frozen crust. The ship's motor launch had landed them on the western, seaward side of the crater. Hart's plan was to climb to the top, follow the rim around to where it faced the other volcano—giving an interior view of the island—and then descend to the opposite eastern crater shore.

Climbing was hard, slogging work. They shed their parkas and paused frequently to rest, the ships shrinking to toys beneath them. The *Schwabenland* churned out a steady stream of water. The crew had wrapped its breach with canvas to let the pumps get ahead of the leakage, but a more permanent repair was required before they returned to sea.

Cold wind at the crater rim swiftly went from refreshing to chilling and they put their parkas back on. The ocean beyond the crater was indigo this day, dotted with icebergs and fractured platters of sea ice. Far to the south the mountains of the Antarctic mainland formed a serrated wall. Across the caldera lagoon the peak of the other volcano poked higher than their own, still gently steaming. The raw beauty, the wild emptiness, the crisp tug of the air: all were like an intoxicating drug to the pilot. For a moment life seemed scrubbed clean again. The horror of the *Bergen* and the insane battle with the *Aurora Australis* could be forgotten.

"Gorgeous, eh, Fritz?"

"Aye." The seaman was still breathing heavily. "Though it would be better with palm trees. And a stein of beer."

They started around the crater ridgeline of hardened lava and crusted snow. Looking down, Hart saw some of the troops carrying shrouded bodies out of the half-sunken whaler. They were ferrying them ashore by longboat.

The pair reached the opposite side of the rim at noon and sat down to eat and drink. The need to fight dehydration reminded Hart of the importance of fresh water to any future German base. Melting snow or glacial ice was laborious. Here, perhaps, the earth's heat would provide a more convenient source. Studying that portion of the crater lit by the low Antarctic sun, he indeed saw liquid water emerging from a point halfway up its inner slope. The stream sank back into the pumice before reaching the crater lagoon but the beach beneath steamed with heat. They'd take a closer look on the way back down, he decided.

A peculiar valley linked their truncated cone to the higher, steeper volcano that still steamed. Hart had heard talk of Antarctic dry valleys but this was the first one he'd seen: a long cleft between knifelike igneous ridges with a frozen lake at its bottom. The surrounding pumice slopes and basalt outcrops looked as barren as Mars. Unlike the rest of the island some combination of wind, heat, and low precipitation kept the valley almost entirely snow-free. It reminded Hart of deserts he'd visited in Arizona.

"I wonder what keeps the snow out."

"Elves." Fritz grunted, tired enough to have sprawled on the rocky ridge with his pack for a pillow and his face turned to the chilly sun. "Lava. A toll gate. Who cares?"

"You don't want to investigate?"

"I don't see any women down there, do you?"

"Where's your spirit of adventure, Fritz?"

"With my respect for your leadership. Lost in the first five hundred feet of that damned pumice slope."

They started back down the inside of the crater. Rather than aim for the beach where he intended to be picked up, Hart angled for the silvery cord of the emerging stream. It originated from shadow at the base of a rocky outcrop on the crater wall.

"A cave," he announced. The water emerged from a spring on the crater flank, steaming in the cold. Just behind the small pool was a dark, tunnel-like opening. "Lava tube, it looks like. I've seen them in the West. Magma runs through them and empties out, leaving a cave behind."

"So it goes into the mountain?" Fritz asked. "Stinks like it." There was a faint odor of sulfur.

"Maybe." Hart took out a tin drinking cup to dip some water, gingerly putting his finger in first. "Warm, but not too hot." Then he sniffed, making a slight face. "Minerals." He offered it to the German. "Smell it."

Fritz was hesitant but did so, crinkling his nose. "Bilgewater!" He looked at the American skeptically.

"We should have Greta here to investigate," Hart said.

"Yes. To keep you from poisoning us." Fritz pushed past him. "I'm more interested in the cave. Warmer, I suspect." He entered the opening. "It seems to go back a ways. Cozy despite the stink . . . ow! Damn rocks!"

Hart followed him and stopped to let his eyes adjust to the dimness. The sailor was rubbing his shin. A number of volcanic stones had been pyramided to build a cairn and Fritz had stumbled over it.

"Someone has been here before us," the pilot said. "They left a marker."

"Wonderful. In a place just dark enough that I could break my leg on it."

"No. They knew anyone coming to the island would eventually come here to look for water. This tube is sheltered from storms. A perfect place."

"For what?"

"To . . . mark something." He looked around at the walls of the cave but saw nothing. "Maybe to call attention to this tunnel. Or to bury something."

"From the *Bergen*?"

"Perhaps." He scratched with his knife at the soil.

"Treasure?" With new enthusiasm, Fritz began tossing the rocks to one side, dismantling the cairn.

"It was a whaler, Fritz, not a Spanish galleon."

"They cached their blubber right here."

Once the rocks were scattered they had to dig only a few inches before striking something metallic. It was a steel box a foot square: a simple food tin. The label was illegible. "Look at the rust," the pilot said. Antarctic air was usually so dry and cold that wood would not rot, metal would not rust, food would stay frozen. "You can tell it's warmer and wetter here."

"Science triumphs again. Of course I noticed that by putting my parka hood back, but then I'm just a simple sailor."

Hart pried at the box with his knife and it popped open easily. "No gold coins, I'm afraid." He lifted the object out. "A book." He flipped it open and saw handwriting, the pages brown with discoloration. "A notebook, or journal." He handed it to the German.

Fritz carried the book to the mouth of the cave where the light was better. "It's in Norwegian. From the *Bergen,* no doubt. A diary of some kind. See the dates?" Hart looked over his shoulder.

"Why would they bury a diary?" the pilot wondered. "And just our luck that we can't read it."

"I can," said Fritz. "Slowly. I learned when I fished with the Norwegians while Germany was in the Depression. It was the only way to scan the newspapers the supply tenders brought out. But I'm as rusty as that tin. A dictionary would help; I think I saw one in *Schwabenland*'s library. We did, after all, expect to meet Norwegians down here."

"Can you make anything out?"

The seaman flipped idly through. "I think it talks about the sickness they found here. The author was a last survivor." A piece of loose paper slipped from the book and Hart snatched it before it was carried away by the wind. It had just a few large words, scrawled in ink. He handed it to Fritz. "What does this say?"

The seaman studied it for a moment, then looked soberly up at the pilot. "It says, 'Get off the island.'"

"Our island needs a name, Alfred," Captain Heiden challenged. "What should we call it?"

The geographer sipped his tea moodily, studying the officers gathered after dinner in the *Schwabenland*'s mess. "'Destruction' has occurred to me," Feder said sourly. "Or 'Cataclysm.' They're appropriate for whatever explosion blew off the top of this volcano and created the fissure that let in the sea, not to mention the *Bergen* and out current plight."

"My goodness, Alfred," Drexler said. "Even the Vikings had the sense to name their discovery 'Greenland' in hopes others might follow. Can't we be more optimistic? How about 'Opportunity Island,' or at least 'Destination'? I swear the Fates mean us to be here."

"I would agree to 'Termination' if it means we can end this expedition and get back to Germany before we sink," Feder replied. "This harbor feels as snug as a trap to me, with that damn ghost ship so nearby."

"That's worse than your first two!" Heiden laughed. "You're in too bad a mood to name anything."

"All those bodies." Feder grimaced.

"Hart, you've been ashore," the captain said, turning to the pilot. Owen had already reported the warm beach, the view from the crater rim, the spring of mineral water, and the cave. He'd decided to keep news of the diary to himself for the moment. Fritz was trying to read it now in his cabin below. "Any suggestions?"

The pilot shook his head. "All we saw was pumice and snow. And let's face it, we don't know yet if this island will prove cozy or hostile."

The group was quiet a moment. All had been disturbed by the wrecked whaler.

"Surely the former," Heiden finally said. "As hideous as the fate of the *Bergen* appears to be, its presence means we should be able to salvage some of its bow plate for a temporary patch. The repair won't be perfectly watertight but should be good enough that our pumps can keep pace with it. Then we can go home."

Everyone nodded. Since the seaplane tender had been damaged and one plane lost, home seemed very far away indeed.

"All this is predicated on the *Bergen*'s being safe to work on," Heiden went on. "Clearly, something disastrous happened here and we don't want to repeat the experience. So let's set the naming aside a moment and turn to that. Dr. Schmidt?"

The German's hands were wrapped around a coffee mug for warmth and his thin frame was hunched even in the overheated mess. "It's freezing on that wreck," he observed. "But for us this is actually good. It makes unlikely any chance of our own contamination."

Heiden nodded.

"I've inspected some of the corpses," Schmidt went on. "The contortions of the bodies suggest some assault on the nerves or muscles. Their fluid-filled lungs suggest a pneumonic disease, something that can be spread by breathing or coughing. A truly ghastly contagion and extremely quick, judging from the place of death: many collapsed at their station. But violently virulent diseases tend to burn themselves out quickly. The bacteria or virus usually dies with those initially infected. If not, the cold should have killed or immobilized the microbes. So I think the chance of catching the disease is extremely slight, though it's best to remain masked and gloved. To be surer I'm having the bodies stacked on the beach and will burn them with aviation fuel. But with their removal and the confinement of our own sailors to the *Bergen*'s outer deck, I think the risks are acceptable. After all, we *do* have to repair *Schwabenland*." He glanced with irritation at Drexler, who ignored him.

"Good," said Heiden. "Greta? What has our biologist found?"

"Dr. Schmidt and I took tissue samples," she reported. "I've been examining them under the microscope. Unfortunately, it's a bit like trying to reconstruct a battle from a field of bones. There are signs of microscopic trauma, of bursting cell walls. Also remains of rodlike bacteria, a shape we call bacilli. Similar to plague virus."

"Bubonic plague?"

"I doubt it; the corpses don't quite match those symptoms. It seems more likely in this clime that the Norwegians encountered something new." She hesitated, taking a breath and glancing at Drexler. "Meanwhile I'm going to try to culture some of the samples."

"Meaning what?" Feder asked.

"Grow the remains on a nutrient, such as agar," she replied. "The human cells, of course, will not regenerate. They've been dead over a year. But one of the properties of some microscopic beings—from small worms to tiny bacteria—is that they can enter stasis, or a kind of suspended animation, when conditions are unfavorable. For example, when it's cold and dry, such as on the *Bergen.* Then they resuscitate when things improve, such as with the presence of liquid water."

"You mean come back to life?" Hart asked.

"In a way. These creatures don't really die or reproduce as we do; they divide themselves forever. Sometimes microorganisms are killed, of course, but they don't expire of old age. And sometimes they simply suspend all activity until their environment improves and then they begin growing again. It's possible the disease organisms will resuscitate in my petri dishes."

The men looked uneasy. "That sounds dangerous," Feder objected.

"It is if you're careless," Drexler said. "Greta is not." He smiled at her encouragingly.

"I really don't have proper laboratory facilities on board this ship," the biologist cautioned, glancing at Drexler. "But Jürgen and Dr. Schmidt think it would be prudent to study the pathogen. For science."

"Study it!" Hart exclaimed. "Didn't you look at the contortions of those corpses? It seems to me it would be wise to throw your corpse tissues into that other volcano!"

"Probably we will," Drexler said mildly. "After we understand it."

"This organism may be the expedition's most remarkable discovery yet," Greta argued.

"That's an understatement," Schmidt said. "Its fast-acting virulence is so . . . out of our experience—it could shed light on all kinds of interesting medical questions."

"And no one should have to die like that again," Greta added.

The group was quiet again for a moment.

"This culture, if it works—does it then become immortal in a sense?" Drexler asked. "Can we sustain it indefinitely? For research, I mean."

She nodded. "Perhaps. I must caution that bacteria aren't always easy to grow. Most don't survive a laboratory's hospitality. We don't know the right temperature or nutrient or moisture levels. I'm trying as many variables as I have dishes and equipment for, but it would help enormously if we knew its source in the natural world."

Drexler nodded. "Of course. We're going to try to learn that." He paused a moment. "You know, all this talk of laboratory resurrection gives me an idea for what to name this place. How about 'Restoration Island'?"

The group thought about it for a moment.

"Not bad," Heiden commented. "But is it tempting fate? After all, we haven't finished the repairs yet."

Drexler smiled. "Sailor's superstition, eh? Well, how about a name connected to fate: one of the Greek Fates, perhaps?"

"You remember their names?" said Feder.

"I forget very little. There were three, I recall, but Clotho and Lachesis have little poetry, by my ear. 'Atropos Island,' however, is a name I believe might work. It has a certain music, don't you agree?"

The others looked uncertain except for Schmidt, who smiled wryly. Heiden finally shrugged. "Why not? It's as good a name as any, and those who judge such things will think us literate. Ha!" Then he sobered. "Jürgen, you and your men have given the

Bergen a pretty good inspection. Can you tell us anything more about *its* fate?"

"Well. The ship's log ends in late December of last year without mention of the disease. It must have struck extremely swiftly—so swiftly that men died where they stood."

"If so, we're dealing with something unprecedented," said Schmidt.

"Exactly," said Drexler. "That's what intrigues me."

The meeting broke up and the doctor drew the political liaison aside. "I'm impressed by your classical education, Jürgen."

"At the time I thought that classroom mythology was useless."

"Yes. And your talk of the Fates sparked memories of my own."

"Then you might fully understand why I think my choice was appropriate, Max." Drexler poured himself a brandy.

Schmidt nodded. "Clotho, if I recall, spins the thread of life. Lachesis determines its length."

"Very good, Doctor. And Atropos cuts it off. Like our fascinating microbe."

Someone was knocking at Hart's cabin door. It was late, the sky dark, the ship quiet after an exhausting day, and the pilot had already fallen asleep. He awoke groggily and pulled the door half open. It was Fritz.

"Two survived."

Without asking for permission the seaman pushed past the pilot and closed the door. He was carrying the Norwegian diary and sat down heavily on Hart's unmade bunk. His eyes were red from reading. "Two lived, and they themselves weren't sure why. They took one of the lifeboats and sailed north. They knew their chances were slight but what option did they have?"

Hart sat on his cabin chair. "Did they know what had happened?"

Fritz shook his head. "The disease came quickly, after they'd been on the island for several days. These two, Henry Sandvik and Svein Jungvald, had been poking into the cave: quite deeply, apparently. Others had been exploring the island. They were excited about making a whaling base here because it's so far south and so well protected from the weather. Then the disease began to strike. The captain and crew panicked, tried to sail, hit a rock and began to sink. Henry and Svein were the only ones still healthy enough to man a lifeboat. They fled the ship and went to the cave to get out of the cold and wait for the end, but it never came. Neither got sick."

"Why?"

"They wondered if the source of the disease was contaminated food. They were afraid to go back to the ship and get any. The *Bergen* was wrecked and they were thousands of miles from help. They had the emergency food in the lifeboat, water from the spring, and a sail. They left the diary as a warning and a testimonial."

"Jesus. Two men, an open boat, minimal food? They couldn't have made it."

"No." Fritz shook his head. "Unless they capsized, their end may have been slower and more agonizing than the disease. It's not a pretty story, Owen."

Hart pondered. "It could've been food, I suppose. But the timing is coincidental with their arrival at the island. And these two, in the cave . . . maybe something blew onto the ship while they were underground?"

Fritz shrugged. "I don't know. The two Norwegians wondered that too. But this island makes me uneasy, my friend. The steam, the emptiness: do you realize we've not seen penguin or seabird colonies here? It's too damned quiet. I want to finish the repairs and get out of here."

"They'll try to finish tomorrow," said Hart. "That's the plan. I think everyone wants to leave as quickly as possible."

"It can't be too soon. This crater reminds me of an open grave."

"Everyone except Jürgen. And maybe Schmidt."

The sailor grinned wryly. "They could stay behind."

"No, they're just interested in the disease. Like a couple of damned Frankensteins. Medicine, my ass. I'm worried they'll keep us here until we catch it. And Greta's going along with it."

"She's a good German. Or, should I say, a practical one."

"Meaning what?"

"Meaning she's attracted to you, but her future is with him."

Hart was brought up short. "How do you know that?"

"She's ambitious, like any bright young scientist."

"No," Hart said impatiently, "how do you know she's attracted to *me?*"

Fritz laughed. "It's obvious every time she looks at you! My God, how did you ever get a pilot's license if you're so blind? What does she have to do, rip open her blouse? I wish you two would get it over with so the rest of us could relax."

Hart flushed. "I'm not trying to bed her, Fritz."

"That's exactly the problem."

Hart glowered at the sailor but Fritz seemed to pay him no mind, flipping idly through the diary.

"She would be *happier* with you, I think. But this is just Fritz talking. I'm on the lower deck, the dutiful seaman. I know nothing."

"Fuck you."

Fritz grinned, still reading.

The shadows in his cabin were dancing. An odd light was glimmering through the porthole. Hart stood to look. "Fire," he announced. "They're burning the bodies."

Fritz came over to join him and looked out at the pyre on the beach. Fueled by aviation gasoline, the flames roared skyward with greasy black smoke, the light shining on the water.

"Heiden must have decided to do it at night and get it out of the way before it could affect morale," Hart speculated. "I tell you, it makes *me* feel better to see their diseased bodies cremated like that."

"Yes," said Fritz. "And worse to know your girlfriend still has bits of them on board our ship here."

Hart ignored the sarcasm. "I want to know what they're doing with those cultures."

"Careful, my friend. It's when you know too much that you get into trouble in the Third Reich."

CHAPTER SIXTEEN

Hart brooded. The flames were dying down. The diary lay open on his bunk where Fritz had left it before retiring. *Two survived.* What did that mean? He didn't trust Jürgen Drexler. He wanted to talk to Greta.

What were the words Fritz had used to describe her? Yes, he remembered now: *your girlfriend.* Was his interest in Greta so transparent? Had he unwittingly entered into some competition with Drexler that he was destined to lose? Conflicting impulses tore at him. He realized he was beginning to lose his certainty about why he was here, about what his role was.

He slipped into the corridor. The ship was quiet, everyone exhausted from the events of the past three days. He made his way to Greta's cabin and rapped softly. "Greta?" There was no answer. Maybe she was asleep. Maybe she was ignoring him. He stood, undecided. Wasn't the diary's news important? He tried the knob.

Her cabin was empty. Guiltily, he glanced about. It was neat, impersonally so. There were no photographs, no decoration. A white nightgown hung on a closet hook, the room's sole concession to femininity. That, and its scent of perfume. The bed was made, its blanket displaying a military tautness. Hart swallowed. Was she with Drexler?

He eased the door shut again. Just go back to sleep, he told himself.

But answers might be in her laboratory. Maybe she was still working.

He moved quickly down a ladder and along a passageway. The laboratory had no lock but someone had posted a crude sign on the cabin door. ENTRY FORBIDDEN. There was a skull and cross-bones drawn above. Plain enough, Hart thought, but he knocked anyway. There was no answer. He tried the knob and it opened. The laboratory was dim, lit by two lamps on a center table. No one was there.

She's with Jürgen, he thought again.

The awful certainty of it made him reckless. To hell with German rules and secrets. He slipped inside, closed the door, and flicked on the main light. He wanted to *know*. Know as much as Jürgen Drexler did.

The laboratory was as neat as her cabin, but crowded. Two microscopes on a bench. Shelves with formaldehyde jars ranked like soldiers, filled with fresh organisms she'd netted from the sea. Notebooks similarly cased, and neatly labeled. A large storage locker beyond, stacked with nets and buckets and oilskins and rubber boots. And on a table in the center were rows of covered glass dishes. Petri dishes, she'd called them. Each half filled with a golden gelatin and labeled. Some on ice, some on a hot plate, some under the lamps, some covered by dark cloth. Her cultures. None of them looked like anything to him. Had she failed?

He heard voices and footsteps. Her feminine tone, so unique on the ship, and then Drexler's. Low and anxious. Both coming this way. He doused the main light and looked around in a panic of potential embarrassment. He quickly retreated to the shadow of the storage locker and slipped behind the hanging oilskins.

The door swung open and Drexler stalked in, looking impatient. Greta followed, her face tight. They were fully clothed,

Hart noticed immediately: in the same outfits they'd worn at the after-dinner meeting. Relief washed over him. She'd never gone to bed.

"I understand your concern, Greta," Drexler said tiredly, taking out a gauze mask from a box and handing it to her, then tying on one of his own. Both pulled on rubber gloves. "But the expedition is in crisis and the risk is acceptable. This is the kind of discovery that can make your career back in Germany. That can change your life. *Our* life."

"Or *end* it, Jürgen. I think we're playing with fire here."

"We have a chance to use this like fire, as a tool. For Germany. For advancement." He bent over the petri dishes. "It's encouraging they grew so fast. Which ones?"

She pointed, unenthusiastically. "There. And there and there."

He held one to the light. "Just white dots."

"Each speck is a colony. Enough, presumably, to kill us all."

"*If* you are careless."

"And it *is* me, isn't it, Jürgen? I who have to culture a plague. I who have to safeguard it. This isn't a proper laboratory. It's crazy, bringing this aboard."

"It's only temporary until we know what we're dealing with." He put the dish down and laid a hand on her shoulder. "Greta, listen to me. Norway will be breathing fire over that unfortunate . . . *incident* with the whaler. They'll be in full cry, demanding compensation, boldly asserting their claims. It was critical we find something that would offset that *irritation*—throw the expedition in a positive light. Now God has put that *something* in our grasp—an organism unlike any other, a bacterium that seems to kill with a speed and lethality that makes other plagues look like a common cold! And *you* are the key scientist. All of us are depending on *you*. You alone are going to know how to culture this thing, how to study it. The world's expert on . . . what? I don't know. Maybe we'll even name it after you."

"What an honor." Her voice was sarcastic.

"Or not, whatever you wish. My point is that to simply burn the corpses and sail away would be even crazier. Perhaps we can stop a future plague with our discovery. Make this island safe for a base. Understand a new polar biology. Greta, we're doing the right thing."

"Then why the spores? Why does Schmidt care about the spores?"

"He's a scientist, like you."

"No he isn't. He's a doctor and hardly even that—a quack pathologist—cracking open those Norwegians' chest cavities like a greedy coroner to look for spore coats. Why?"

"To understand the biology. To locate the source."

"I'm not stupid, Jürgen."

"To *learn,* Greta."

She shook her head. "I read the literature. I know what a government could do with the right plague bacteria . . ."

"Like the British in Scotland?"

"With a spore-coated microbe . . ."

"Like the British and anthrax? Their sly little experiments, on the possible eve of war?"

"You don't know that for sure . . ."

"I know far, far more about such matters than you'll ever know." He failed to keep a note of condescension out of his voice. "Greta, you're a good biologist, but you're as naive about politics as that ill-educated American. The Great Powers want to crush the Reich, darling. *Crush* it. Before it grows too strong. Because we represent the future. And if something like this can buy us time . . ."

"Don't talk about him like that."

"Who?"

"Owen. He's good at what he does and yet you always mock him, insult him."

"He's nosy and contentious. And *you* always flirt with him."

"That's a lie! You're so insecure . . ."

"I'm simply tired of that damned American and tired of you defending him. We should never have asked him aboard. Now I simply ask that we—you and I—focus on Germany."

"Don't patronize me with your Nazi patriotism! Schmidt doesn't want to buy time. He wants to build a weapon!"

"To counter *their* weapons, to make *their* evil unusable. Can't you see that? Schmidt thinks we've stumbled on a power never before seen. And Germany can use it to preserve a balance of power."

"Jürgen, I don't want to work on this," she said in frustration. "Not with that ghoul Schmidt. I saw him at that funeral pyre on the beach—he was completely in his element. Let's just go home, get on with our lives . . ."

"This *is* our life. And you *will* work on it!"

"*Listen* to me! These dishes could kill us! What if they break? I swear, I'll destroy the cultures!" Her warning sounded real.

He stared at her then with surprise, a surprise that swiftly evolved to barely contained outrage. His face was tight from lidded anger and his voice quieted with menace. "Now you listen to me, Greta Heinz. You *will* work on it as a loyal member of a Reich expedition—or by all the saints I'll not protect you from the consequences when we return! I'm not going to allow your childish and simplistic view of things to derail our future! *My* future."

She looked so shocked at his vehemence that her look halted him. He bit his lip, struggling to regain control of his emotions. His face twisted with the inner pain of self-betrayal. He took a deep breath. "What you don't understand is that I love you," he finally managed, more weakly. "I *love* you, Greta. And all I'm asking is that you do this one thing, work on this one discovery, for *us*. For us and for the Reich. For Germany. As the right thing to do."

Her face screwed up. "Jürgen, I can't!" she pleaded. "I'm frightened!"

"I'm frightened too. By the possibility of failure." He looked at her solemnly, his expression confessing his need. "You can't let that happen to me." He took off his mask and gloves and leaned stiffly to kiss her rigid cheek. Then he walked out.

Hart stood still, frozen. There was a small sound. Greta was weeping.

The tears were running into her mask and she lifted her rubbered hands up to try to brush them. The she angrily tore the gloves off, flinging them and the mask in a corner. "Damn it," she sobbed, "damn all men, damn these plates, I'm so afraid of these cultures—"

"It didn't kill everyone."

Her head jerked up. Hart felt he could hardly breathe.

"It didn't kill everyone," he repeated. He clumsily stepped out from the storage locker. She whirled.

"You!"

"We found a diary and—" He lifted a hand toward her.

Instantly, her anger fastened on him. "My God! How long have you been standing there? How *dare* you—"

"Greta, please, I'm sorry, I didn't mean to, I came to the lab to share this news but you weren't here and then I heard footsteps and, and . . ." It sounded lame, he knew.

Her face was shiny with tears. "What did you hear? How long were you there?"

He shrugged.

"You heard everything, didn't you?"

"Yes, but I wasn't trying—"

"Get *out,* leave here now!"

"Two survived the disease—"

"Get out, get out, get out! God, I hate *both* of you so *much!*"

He backed to the door, cringing from her rage, and then shut it behind him, leaning against it, his eyes closed.

Inside, he heard her wail. "God, how I wish I could get off this cursed ship!"

Hart couldn't sleep, his mind a tumult of emotions. Always a disaster, every time he went near her. Would she tell Drexler? He'd be lucky they didn't throw him overboard as a damned spy. Lord, he was tired . . .

Then there was a thump and he found himself stunned. He

realized he'd slept finally, and not just slept but descended into the drugged sleep of the exhausted. Now he had rolled out of his bunk. The deck was sharply canted and bright polar sunlight poured through his porthole. "What the hell?" Were they sinking again?

The pilot became aware of loud banging and clanging but realized groggily that it was the noise of purpose, not confusion. There was a deeper rumble of pumps. He looked at his watch. It was early afternoon; he'd slept a long time. Groaning, he stood unsteadily against the tilt, feeling gritty. The Norwegian diary had skittered across the floor and he picked it up and inserted it under his mattress, then dressed clumsily and made his way to the top deck.

The *Schwabenland* was moored against the half-sunken *Bergen,* sailors swarming over both. Cables from the higher German ship had been strung to winches on the Norwegian one. Some of the German cargo had been temporarily unloaded onto the *Bergen's* deck and more—the numbered crates that had puzzled him— were being ferried ashore. Selective flooding of compartments and winching had tilted the *Schwabenland* far enough to port to allow the breach in the hull to clear the water. Lifeboats had been tied alongside the long gash and sailors were beating, cutting, and riveting metal. At the raised bow of the Norwegian ship a section of plating was being cut away with a shower of sparks. Ropes had been strung to bar entry to the interior of the Norwegian whaler but even so, the sailors wore precautionary gauze masks. Heiden was stalking this way and that, closely observing and issuing orders.

Hart looked for Fritz and didn't spot him. He approached Heiden.

"Why are supplies going ashore? Are we staying?"

"No," Heiden replied. "Jürgen's idea. A cache for next year."

So the Germans planned to return. "Have you seen Fritz?"

The captain shook his head. "No. If you do, tell the lazy bastard to get to work."

"Do you know when we can leave?"

"When my ship is repaired." The tone was impatient and short.

The pilot backed off and went to the stern, looking morosely out across the cold lagoon. Once more, Antarctica had proved a disaster. Drexler despised him, despite their successful flight together. Greta apparently hated him. The clash with the whalers had probably eliminated any chance of cheerful publicity. Fritz had disappeared. He felt utterly alone.

And then she was at his elbow, the hood of her parka down, her red hair stealing softly across his shoulder as she leaned on the railing. He started, it was so sudden.

"*Who* survived?"

Her question was clinical, betraying nothing. She looked at him flatly. "Well? Who survived, Owen?"

"Two of the sailors," he half stammered. "The Norwegian whalers. They lived, and took a lifeboat, and sailed out of the lagoon. I doubt they finally made it."

She nodded, absorbing this. "How?"

"I don't know. They didn't know. They were exploring a cave, and they came out, and then the disease hit except that they didn't get it . . ."

"A cave? What cave?"

"The one Fritz and I found. I mentioned it last evening at the meeting. There, you can see it from here." He pointed across the caldera to the crater wall.

She followed his arm, then looked back again. Her tone was still peculiarly detached, as if she'd used up all her emotions the night before. "What was in the cave?"

"I don't know. They didn't say. We didn't explore. There's a hot spring and a sulfur smell—I think it's an old lava tube—and that's all I know. I thought you might know. That's why I came to your lab."

She thought a long time about this. "Do you know what the temperature of this harbor is?"

"No."

"One point eight degrees centigrade. Comfortably above freezing. Peculiar, no?"

"Is it?"

"The ocean outside the crater is below the freshwater freezing point; only salt and pressure prevent it from turning solid. But in here the water is warmer. There's no ice and the crater slopes have little snow: this is a warm place, yes?"

"It's a volcano, Greta."

She nodded. "Exactly. Alive with heat and energy." She looked across the water, studying the cave. "I remember you spent part of your childhood spelunking. Correct?"

He grinned uncertainly. "The best years of my life."

"Owen, I want a cure."

"A what?"

"An antidote to whatever killed the Norwegians. Do you think it could lie inside that cave?"

"That's what I came to ask *you*. Last night, I mean. I . . . I'm sorry I listened."

"You *should* be sorry." She smiled sadly. "Do you know why I don't always like you, Owen?"

He didn't answer.

"Because you always seem to know a little too much about me. Just like Jürgen."

He didn't know how to respond.

"Well, I have reproduced a microbe, and now I want a way to kill it. As a safety valve. As a way to retain control over whatever you crazy men try to do next. And I'm intrigued by this cave. Will you take me there?"

"Me? I thought you were angry."

"I *am* angry. But I'm also calm. I can't afford the luxury of my anger."

"So is this for Jürgen? Or for Germany?"

"You won't help me?"

"I didn't say that."

She bit her lip. "It's for science."

"Ah. Like this voyage."

"And for me."

He bowed his head in acknowledgment. "Then I'll do it."

"And for us."

"Which us?"

She didn't reply.

"You want to go now?"

She shook her head. "Tonight. When Jürgen can't see. He'd never let me go with you."

"We'll be looking for a cure?"

"We'll be looking for something to make all this madness worthwhile."

CHAPTER SEVENTEEN

I t looks dark."

"It's a cave, Greta."

They were standing by the spring. The brief night of late Antarctic summer was ending and the dome of brilliant stars above the crater rim was fading into a ceiling of faint blue. Across the dark caldera the lights of the *Schwabenland* illuminated its embrace with the crippled *Bergen*.

Up to this point, Greta had been bold and assertive: collecting exploration gear from hanging lockers, commandeering a row ashore from the night watch on the vague pretext of inspecting the ashes of the pyre, and shouldering a pack for the hike along the beach. She'd said little, determined to get away from the ship while the other officers were still asleep. Now that she and Owen were facing the mouth of the lava tube with its scent of sulfur, he could hear a note of hesitation in her voice. Going underground did that to people. Hell was imagined deep within the earth.

"Thousands of years ago people used caves for shelter," Hart said, trying to be reassuring. "And we'll have plenty of light." He snapped on a flashlight and led the way to where he and Fritz had unearthed the diary. Then a gas lantern was pumped and lit. They blinked in the glow, reassured by its steady hiss. "We'll go slowly. You pick the direction and I'll try to find the way." He gestured to the lengths of bright cloth hanging from his belt. "We'll tie a survey ribbon at every turn and junction. Like Hansel and Gretel leaving bread crumbs."

She smiled at that memory. "All right." He knew that despite her natural uneasiness she'd made up her mind to go in. Just like Drexler, he admitted. Another German who doesn't back off.

Unlike a limestone cavern there was nothing colorful about this volcanic one. The tube was like entering the encrusted circulatory system of a smoldering heart. The basalt was a dull black-red and there were no stalactites. In a few places water dripped.

For the first hundred yards the entry tunnel was fairly level and broad. A few openings branched out to tempt a detour but Hart's flashlight revealed that they ended quickly in collapses of rock. Slabs of basalt had also fallen off the ceiling of the central tunnel, periodically forcing the pair to squeeze around them. The pilot didn't reveal his uneasiness at the possibility of a cave-in but wondered how often eruptions or earthquakes occurred. Giving some reassurance was the occasional boot print. The Norwegians had come this way and nothing had disturbed their mark in the year since.

The tube dead-ended at a chimney, or at least that's what it seemed like to Hart. A large vertical tunnel hundreds of feet high and deep led upward and down into the mountain. He shined his light to where the beam was lost in the gloom, the fissure giving him a slight sense of vertigo.

"Here we are at the elevator shaft," Greta murmured, studying the cleft. "Where's a button to push?"

"This must have been a major lava corridor when the volcano was erupting." When Hart pointed the light downward it illuminated some boulders choking the shaft, dark openings indicating a way around them. There was a welter of boot prints on the shelf. "The Norwegians were as uncertain as we are, Fräulein Biologist. Which way should we go?"

She glanced around, thinking. Greta still had a remote, distracted air of cool professionalism. It was the first time Hart had spent this much time alone with her and yet she wasn't focused on him at all. He accepted this philosophically. He realized that for the moment he was a means to an end, a way to reassert her independence from Jürgen Drexler. Still, he was here and Drexler wasn't. He smiled at the thought of the German's reaction in the morning when the night watch reported the pair had gone ashore together and not come back.

Greta knelt, peering over the edge. "Down, I think. If you can get us back up."

He nodded. "We'll leave one of the lines tied here. I don't know how far these tubes go but most shouldn't be this steep. I hope."

"I want to go down because the waters from that hot spring must ultimately come from deeper in the mountain where the source of heat is. Life needs energy and heat, yes? So I think we should descend."

"Maybe the antidote, if there is one, isn't biological," Hart reasoned. "Could it be something chemical? Minerals in the water?"

"I don't think so. If the bacteria are indigenous to this island they should have adapted over the eons to the local chemistry. Yet who knows? Maybe these two sailors simply missed the initial infection, or had a natural immunity, or didn't develop symptoms until they escaped by boat. This may be a hopeless quest. But what I'm looking for are two forms of life in uneasy coexistence: the disease bacteria, and something toxic to it, evolved in self-defense. A biological stalemate, if you will. Something that can keep that terrible plague in check."

"You're the scientist. Down it is."

He tied a line on an outcropping of rock and let it uncoil into the darkness. Another line, doubled, lowered their packs. "I'm not really a climber, or even much of an amateur cave rat, but I know enough to go slow," he advised. "Move only one hand, or one foot, at a time. And don't hug the rock, it makes your foot

want to slip off its hold. Lean out a bit so your body is vertical."
He tipped his hand to show her.

"All right." She looked uncertain but determined. "After you."

He went first, guiding her progress with the flashlight. In
truth, Hart admitted, she was as good at the descent as he was:
not as strong, perhaps, but balanced, lithe. If she was afraid she
didn't show it. They climbed down a hundred feet to a point
where a boulder had jammed in the tube. She arrived breathless
but elated. "Goodness!" She laughed. "I know I can go down, but
can I get back up?"

"The way you're going, you'll be carrying me." He led the way
down again.

There was a squeeze around the boulder, then a drop of another
twenty feet. From there the tube descended at more of an angle,
its floor jumbled rock. It was slow, rugged going. The cave continued to warm as they explored deeper and soon they shed all but
trousers and shirts. The bitter chill of Antarctica seemed far away.

The floor smoothed but the ceiling continued to get lower.
Suddenly Hart paused. He'd felt a tremor. From somewhere there
was the distant echo of falling or shifting rock, like the groan of
something disturbed.

"What was that?" Her elation had disappeared.

"Earthquake, I think. A small one."

"My God."

"This is dangerous, Greta. I have to warn you of that. We're in
a volcano, after all. Do you want to go back?"

There was a silence as she considered. "No. I have to know."

"All right."

He led on. Soon they were stooping, then on all fours. Finally
it narrowed ahead to a belly-crawl. "Owen, are we going the right
way?"

"I don't know. Wait here." Hart crept ahead, then came back.
"I hear water."

"But are we at an end?"

"Not necessarily. There were tight places in the caves in
Montana, and then you'd squeeze through and find a big room.

Maybe this will be the same. But we can also squeeze and get stuck, or, if we're not careful, pop through to another elevator shaft. So I'm going to tie a rope around my waist and you're going to play out the line—I'll show you how—while I explore with the flashlight. Can you do that?"

"Of course."

He wriggled forward as the ceiling pressed down. His beam of light continued to be lost in the dark vacuum ahead, an encouraging sign. The rough rock began scraping on his pack and so he shrugged that off, leaving it for a moment. A final tight spot . . . and then his arms and head were jutting into empty space and he could hear the sound of a river echoing off rock walls. He shone the light around. He had found a grotto. The beam danced on flowing water.

"Owen, what do you see?" Her call seemed faint behind him.

"Maybe what we're looking for!"

He climbed out of the tunnel and dragged out his pack, lowering it to the floor below. On his instructions Greta doused her lantern and shoved her gear ahead as he slowly reeled in the rope.

Her head poked through and he grasped her under the arms and pulled. She slithered out and instinctively grasped him as she landed and he held her a moment longer than he needed to, his face in her hair, imagining he could feel the rush of her heart. Then she gently pulled away. "I think we should light the lantern," she said.

The grotto was a rock chamber about two hundred feet long and thirty feet high. It was split by a stream that emerged from a different dark opening and disappeared down a chute at the far end. A jumble of boulders occupied most of the floor but the water had deposited a sandy bar in the middle, dry and soft. A hot spring bubbled nearby and its water joined the main flow. The cave was pleasantly warm. Rocks near the spring radiated like heaters.

"We should eat," Greta said. "I'm famished."

They sat in the lantern's pool of light. Each had brought a

blanket in case their stay became extended and they unfolded these now on the sand. There were tins of ham and cheese and a rich brown bread from the *Schwabenland*'s ovens. Owen pulled out a bottle of wine. "I liberated this from Heiden's stock in the galley," he confessed.

She smiled. "It's cozy here. Warm. Almost like a little restaurant. I'm getting used to the dark."

"And do you think we're near what we're looking for?"

"I don't know. I'll look at the water after I eat. It's so strange being down here: they didn't teach us about caves at the university. I have no idea what to expect." She took a swig of the wine; there were no glasses. She used her fingers to dab at the corner of her mouth.

The biologist sat then looking at the sand, lost in thought. She's so pretty, Hart mused, admiring the facial sculpture of highlight and shadow in the gaslight. Some hair had come loose from where she'd bound it in a ponytail and it trailed across her cheeks. So alluring, yet so remote. What drove her to risk penetrating this dark hole?

"Greta," he said, "why are we here?"

"What? To explore—to search for an antidote, of course."

"Yes, but why the sudden urgency? And why the turnabout? You didn't seem to mind making the lab cultures at first. Not at the meeting. But then something happened with Schmidt. Last night you talked about spores. Why are they so important?"

"Oh. Him." She shook her head as if dismissing her other thoughts and took a bite of bread. "Everything has happened very fast, Owen. The Norwegians. The iceberg. This island. The *Bergen*. It made sense to me to try to find out what happened to those poor men, if for no other reason than to protect ourselves. That's why I agreed to do the cultures. But Schmidt was ahead of me, I think. And Jürgen. They wanted to understand where a disease came from in such a sterile environment. And so he searched the lungs and respiratory tracts for spore coats."

"Which are . . . ?"

"A casing. A bit like a seed coat or an eggshell. Some microbes develop them when displaced from their preferred environment. They're like a cocoon and the organism is in stasis within, waiting for favorable conditions when it can break out and multiply. Schmidt thinks this could explain the infection. The spores were on the island from an unknown source. Somehow the Norwegians got into them and breathed some in. The body's enzymes cracked them open, like a Trojan horse, and they began doubling every twenty to thirty minutes: first two, then four, then eight—in a single day you can have billions. People begin coughing and sneezing. Finally the muscles seize, the nerves burn like fire, the organs dissolve . . . and you're dead."

"So you're afraid these spores could strike again?"

She nodded. "Yes. That's a possibility. But I'm more worried by Jürgen's talk of creating a lethal new weapon."

"Is that really possible?"

"With most diseases, I'd say possible but not practical. After all, how do you store them? How can you prevent being exposed yourself? The complications are many. But diseases that develop spore coats are ideal. The coating solves many of the problems."

"And neither Schmidt nor Jürgen care about the morality of it all?"

She laughed bitterly. "Schmidt, he's as amoral as they come. Jürgen, he's relentlessly moralistic. And it's a circle, you see—at the two extremes the means to achieve an end come together. He and Schmidt concur."

"He said last night that he loved you."

"Yes. I know he does. He means it."

"And do you love him?"

She smiled, her eyes still downcast. "Ah, we're back to an earlier conversation, I think." Greta considered as if the question had never occurred to her. "No. Well . . . Yes. I do." There was a note of doubt in her voice. "But not in the same way, perhaps, as . . . I'm *fond* of him, when he relaxes. He can be affectionate, you know. I admire him, his sense of purpose—his moralism, if you will. His certainty. He's a strong man. Intelligent. He intrigues me."

"You're talking yourself into it, Greta."

She looked troubled. "I don't know, Owen. He also frightens me sometimes with his intensity. The fight with the whalers. I don't know what I feel or what I'm supposed to feel. This love. It confuses me."

She waited. There was just the sound of the river, the hissing of the lantern.

"Me too." It sounded inadequate, yet he was uncertain what else to say.

She nodded solemnly, swallowing. "And that's good, I think. Easier." Her voice caught a bit. "Because I want to do what we came down here to do. Explore this cave." She briskly thrust the remains of their meal back into the pack and stood up. She was all business again. "So. You come with the lantern while I study this stream."

"Greta . . ." Hart stood. He was struggling for the right balance, afraid of being too bold and startling her into bolting, like a deer in a meadow.

She put a finger to his open lips, quieting him. "Owen, it's better for the work to let things be."

They explored along the water. The main stream was clear and cold: her measurement showed it was 6.3 degrees centigrade. The hot spring tributary, in contrast, was forty degrees, hot to the touch. It was crusted with minerals and a kind of slime. "Owen, look at that," the biologist said with a touch of wonder. "No light and yet something lives, fueled by this underground heat, perhaps. I wish I had my microscope."

She found more slime on rocks downstream from the confluence which warmed the river. And then at the end of the grotto there was a chute and the stream splashed toward darkness below. Her flashlight played across its surface and something undulated in the current like luxuriant hair.

"A plant?" Hart asked.

"Not down here. No sunlight. But a growth of something primitive, an odd algae that gets its energy from something other than photosynthesis, or maybe an animal colony like a sponge or a coral. Maybe what the Norwegians found. Let me get a sample . . ."

"Better wait until I can rope us up."

But she was already wading ahead and unable to hear him. She reached down to seize the wispy organism, grasping it just as her boots slipped on the slime of the underwater rocks.

"Greta!"

And then with a cry she was gone.

"Are we catching a train? Is that it? Is there a railroad track at the end of this valley that I don't know about? Because that, I suppose, could explain this frantic hurrying, this wheezing for breath that I'm enduring. Perhaps I can understand it if there's an express to Munich. Or if you've spied the lights of a beer hall."

"Shut your mouth, you whining weasel," SS sergeant Gunther Schultz growled at Fritz, with no confidence his order would have any effect. Christ, what a complainer: why had Drexler saddled them with this hobbling slacker? The political liaison had sent them off the ship and into the mysterious dry valley at dawn the previous day, Jürgen sleepless and sour and nagging from who knew what setback. Probably the damned woman, the SS troopers whispered. By late morning the soldiers were over the crater rim and they camped that evening in the valley bottom, cut off from the ship: the field radio didn't work unless they climbed up a side slope to communicate. The soldiers weren't happy. Schmidt had assured them there was no risk but they weren't stupid: they'd carried the bodies out of the *Bergen*, sweating under their gauze masks. And so, instead of their usual delight at being able to stretch their legs, they were no happier being so far from the ship than Fritz was. "This is a dead place, a death place," one of the soldiers had told Schultz while gazing down the arid frozen valley. "I just want to get back on the boat and go home." But Drexler wanted the island scouted for some clue to the disease, and the assumption was that nothing was to be found on the island's shroud of ice. So they would look here in the depths of the valley, eating wind-blown dust.

Fritz had been a last-minute addition. The political liaison had obviously decided to penalize the sailor for his tiresome sarcasm, calling him a damned communist before assigning him as a "guide" because of his previous trip ashore with the American. Fritz of course knew not a thing about where they were going except that he had no desire to go there. "I've seen that valley from the rim and it has all the charm of a gravel pit," he'd warned them before they left the ship. "A sewage ditch is more inviting."

"Of course if there *is* no train, then it might be possible to take a rest right here," Fritz now went on. "We *are* next to a lake here, albeit a frozen one. Have some lunch, order a stein, talk about gardening . . ."

"Fine," Schultz said in exasperation. "I'm sick of your moaning. You stay with the gear while we push to the end of the valley. We'll be back before dark."

"You're leaving me alone?"

"And good riddance," one of the soldiers said.

"Oh. You know, I've felt safer in a Hamburg back alley."

"If you don't stay here and shut up, you'll never see Hamburg."

The mountaineers trudged on, Schultz looking sourly at the enclosing hills of red pumice. It looked like pictures of another planet, the sergeant thought. The ice of the lake was old, never thawing, and sculpted into uneven frozen waves by sun and scouring winds.

They nursed their water. Dr. Schmidt had warned them not to risk drinking anything that could be a source of disease. Now they saw there were hot springs ahead at the base of the second volcano, the pools steaming placidly in the cold air. The mineral water spilled down a series of terraces stained yellow and ocher, the hot trickles melting a thin wedge of ice at the end of the frozen lake. Upslope a glacier from the second volcano had bulldozed to a halt, its ice and snout of gravel debris hanging over the springs.

Schultz climbed up to the pools to look about. Some had dried, leaving behind a residue of brownish dust carried up from inside the earth. But no sign of prior Norwegians, nor clues to the disaster. A gust of wind caught some of the dust and a plume of grit blew over the squad of mountaineers, forcing them to squint against it.

"Jesus, what a damnable place," the sergeant muttered. "And we haven't found a thing that is useful."

A soldier nodded in wan agreement.

Then he sneezed.

CHAPTER EIGHTEEN

G reta!"

Hart had crept as close to the lip of the chute as he dared, wild with despair and hopelessness.

Then in the blackness below he heard it, faint against the roar of the falls. "Owennnnn! Oh my God, Owen! I'm in the water! Please help me!"

Her voice was like an electric shock to his system. "I'm coming!" he shouted hoarsely. "Hang on!"

The pilot scrambled back to the packs, grabbed a line and the lantern, and hurried back, splashing down the middle of the stream. He set the lantern on an overhanging boulder where it would serve as a beacon, tied off the rope, and cast it down the falls. Seizing the rough hemp, he began lowering himself backward, cold water foaming over his thighs. A flashlight tucked downward in his belt offered meager illumination. She'd slipped down the chute as if carried on a log flume.

"Owen, I see you!" she called. "I'm in a pool, a lake!"

The chute grew steeper as he went down, bending until it was vertical. The chimney the water fell down opened into a much vaster space. Hart leaned out. He could see light reflecting on black water and could hear her down there, pleading with him to hurry. His own arms ached from the effort and his heart hammered. Down, down . . .

He was out of rope.

He hesitated only a moment. There really was no alternative, was there? He would rescue her or he would die trying. Because the alternative was unacceptable.

He let go and plunged.

He was braced for a shock of cold water, the kind that sucks away air and threatens to stop the heart. Instead he hit a black pool that was surprisingly warm. When he surfaced, spitting out water that had a brackish taste, she was on him, sobbing joyfully, clinging to him in a warm dark lake underneath a frozen, fiery mountain.

They were alive.

He kissed her, fiercely, possessively, and she kissed him back this time, as greedy as he. They sank while holding each other in a hug of reunion and then broke apart to struggle up, laughing and coughing.

"Drowning in a volcano and we think it's funny," he sputtered.

She was treading water, the light so dim she was only a silhouette. "It *is* funny, Owen. I was terrified when I fell, certain I was about to smash onto the rocks. But now you're here and the water is warm. It's like nothing is real anymore."

They swam back to the base of the cliff where the stream poured down, grasping a wet ledge to rest. Far above, Hart could see the lighthouse-like beacon of the lantern. And across the black water was a blue glow. He pointed to it. "What's that?"

She looked, blinking away the water. "Ice, it looks like. So strange. A glacier? I don't know."

"Stay here and rest."

He swam out toward the glow, noticing as he did so the play of warm and cold currents across his body and a swirl of matlike organisms against his arms and legs. A diaphanous fuzz that seemed to dissolve when he tried to grasp it. The rock ceiling gave way to ice above, he finally saw, an arching vault of frozen water spangled with millions of tiny crystal icicles fed from the pool's condensing steam. The ceiling of ice seemed to dip down to the water somewhere in the gloom beyond. Pale blue light from a remote sun seeped dimly through what must be an immensely thick lid. The lake was under some kind of ice cap: perhaps it was the frozen lake of the valley he and Fritz had observed. And in the juncture between hot underground volcanic springs and frozen overhead ice was this tepid netherworld, dusky and secret, laden with some kind of strange growth.

He swam back to Greta. She was plopping handfuls of the organic mats on the ledge by the waterfall, creating a pile of brown goo.

"This is weird," he said in her ear above the rush of water.

She nodded. "I suspect we have a kind of loop, meltwater descending, heating, rising, carrying minerals from the depths of the island. And these primitive growths fed by . . . what? Chemical energy? Can life thrive underground? It is *amazing*."

"If it doesn't kill us."

"If it does I've at least lived to see this." Her head kept rotating to take it in, excited as a child. "And maybe something like this vegetation will *save* us."

"That goo there?" he said doubtfully.

"Have you heard of penicillin?" she asked, smiling mischievously. "It comes from mold. Or lysozyme? It comes from the stuff in your nose."

"The joy of slime. Remind me to stay away from biologists."

She laughed, splashing him. He splashed back.

"Stop, I'm wet enough!"

He reached out more tenderly and brushed beads of water from her forehead. Combed watery jewels from her hair. She shivered but didn't shy from his touch.

Then she turned abruptly and scooped another palmful of living fuzz and slapped it onto her cache. "And how am I going to get this back?" She looked at the sloppy organic mess instead of him, all science again.

"Here." Hart shed his wool shirt, leaving a sleeveless white undershirt. He scooped the organism onto it and tied the sleeves. "You're going to owe me a cleaning, Miss Heinz."

"If you can get me back to a laundry, I'll clean it." She shivered again, from cold this time. They'd been in the water too long and were beginning to feel chilled despite its heat. "Owen, how are we going to get up that chute?"

He looked at the distant beacon of the lantern. "The rope isn't too far above, maybe twenty feet." He pointed. "The stream comes out of a tunnel, or chimney. If we can climb to that we can wedge ourselves, our back to one side and our feet on the other, and then climb."

She looked up doubtfully. "I don't know if I can."

"You will because you must. Come on, before we get so cold we can't function."

With a thrust of his arms he boosted himself to a sitting position on the ledge, Greta watching the play of muscles in his shoulders. He took off his boots and tied them around his neck, instructing her to do the same. "For a better grip on this wet rock." He ran his belt through the makeshift sack of algae and awkwardly stood, leaning away from the falls to search for handholds. The basalt was rough enough that they were plentiful, but the plunge of cold water seemed to want to pry them off the cliff. Greta seemed stuck, incapable of climbing up farther. "Wait!" Hart said.

He scrambled up by himself, shouldering through the water until he could brace himself in the chimney and reach the rope. He jammed the shirt with its algal cargo into a crevice and dragged off his pants. No time for modesty, and hell, it was dark anyway. He tied one leg to the rope and let the other drop. Another four feet, at least. He looked down to where Greta was clinging. She nodded, then let herself go and fell into the lake. Treading water, she shed her shirt and pants as well. Swimming back to the cliff face, she flung them up. He added them to the rope and pulled to test. It seemed strong enough. He let himself down, felt her reaching arms on his leg, seized one of her wrists . . . and slowly she began climbing. He let her scramble up him and clutch his chest and shoulders for reassurance. Greta was panting, her skin goose-bumped by the cold.

"Are you all right?"

She nodded.

"Try to climb up past me."

Greta took a deep breath and continued, pushing against him. She reached the rock tunnel and wedged herself, grasping the rope and resting a moment. Hart climbed up next to her and brought the bottom of the rope up, untying her shirt. "Here, or you'll scrape your back." She braced her wet skin against his as she pulled it back on. She was slick, cold. Now that they were closer to the lantern he could see the tiny shadow of erect nipples in her wet bra as she buttoned. He wanted to touch them. *You'll make us both fall, you ass.* If she noticed his look she gave no sign.

"That was the worst. We're going to make it, Greta."

Wordlessly she turned her head and kissed him again, her expression solemn. Then she grasped the rope with both hands.

"Try not to be late." As she climbed past him he noticed her bare legs were bruised from the fall. Rivulets of water ran down her thighs.

He wanted her so much.

She was standing in the stream and breathing heavily when he hauled himself over the lip of the water chute. He was clad only in his underwear with the bag of algae belted to his waist, and felt faintly ridiculous. But she looked beautiful in the lantern light, wet and gleaming. Her shirt, still half unbuttoned, ended at her thighs. Her hair was a wild tangle. Hart knew his own desire was all too apparent as he looked at her. He didn't care.

Without speaking she turned and waded back upstream toward the sandy bar. The pilot coiled the rope, untied their clothes from its end, took the lantern, and followed.

She was waiting, pale and perfect. She had unbuttoned the shirt and it hung open, letting him see the rise of her breasts above her bra. Her neck was high, its line and the clavicles of her shoulder making an arabesque of curves echoed in her waist, her hips, her thighs. He ached to possess her.

"We must dry these," she said, all business except that her voice caught a bit. She reached for the soggy bundle of clothes and turned away to climb up to the hot rocks around the steaming spring, draping the clothes on them. He watched the delicate architecture of her back as she worked, the play of bone and muscle. Then she stepped down and stood to face him again, shaking her head to get wet hair away from her shoulders. He could see the aureole of her nipples through her soaked bra. They looked like twin dark moons. The triangle under her wet panties was a shadowy gate. And yet she was hesitant. She crossed her arms to hug herself, still cold, her thighs pressed together.

He stepped toward her.

"We didn't plan this," she said softly.

"No, we didn't." The tips of his fingers touched her cheek and he brushed away a drop of water. Or was it a tear?

"Hold me, Owen. I'm so cold."

His arms enclosed her and she huddled inside them. He leaned to nuzzle her ear, her neck. She was shivering again.

"I love you, Greta."

"Please don't say that." The plea was unconvincing.

"I love you more than I thought it was possible to love anyone. I've loved you since I saw you beside the fire at Karinhall but didn't fully admit it myself until you fell and for a terrible moment I thought I'd lost you forever. I love you and would rather die than not have you. I'd *half died* before I met you. I'd gone numb after Antarctica." He kissed, finding her neck, her cheek, her lips, the tip of her tongue. "And you made me alive again . . ."

"Owen, please, I'm still confused, I think this may be wrong . . ."

"You know it isn't wrong."

"It must be. Jürgen, the expedition . . ." But then she kissed him, hard and hungry, aching, unfolding her arms to grasp his shoulders. She broke away to gasp. "This is so irrational, so emotional . . ."

"You know how right this feels." He kissed her again.

"So unscientific . . ."

"To hell with science."

Her eyes were wet, luminous, her breath coming in quick gasps. She blinked them shut. "I think I love you too, and it makes me afraid. That I love you so much."

He stroked her back, the wet cotton on her rump, and she arched under his hand, sighing. "You'll catch a chill unless you get all these things off," he whispered in her ear, his voice thick.

Greta bit her lower lip and nodded. She broke free and turned, presenting her back. He unfastened her bra and she let it drop, the white straps slipping down her white arms. Hart could see the ripe swell of her breasts at her sides. Then she tugged her panties down too, wiggling a bit to get them off her hips, her bottom round and firm. Bending, she laid her underwear on the rocks, carefully smoothing. Then she turned to face him, naked, trembling. She held out her hand.

"Your laundry, Mr. Hart?"

He peeled off his undershirt and shorts and gave them to her. He was erect and rock hard, his blood pounding in his ears. He was shaking too. How long? he thought. How long since he'd been with a woman he truly loved?

She tossed his things on the rocks.

And then they were together again, she melting against him this time, clutching desperately, opening her mouth to his kisses, hungry for them, and an exultant roaring filled his head that blotted out the sound of the river. His hands ran down her back, slipped over her buttocks, felt her soaking wetness, and his penis was nuzzled by her damp fur as she pressed hard against him. He cradled a breast.

And as he bent to kiss her stiff nipples her hair enclosed their faces for a moment like a tent to create an intimacy. "My God, Owen, I have felt so *alone* . . ."

He carried her to the blankets then, she curled in his arms with her face pressed into his neck. He knelt to lay her down gently. And then he held and stroked and kissed her for a long time, she unfolding to him, stretching, their bodies growing heated. And eventually her cries echoed in the grotto. Unheard by anyone but them.

CHAPTER NINETEEN

Something was wrong. The *Schwabenland* was still coupled to the *Bergen* and the seaplane tender had righted itself, the repairs to its torn hull apparently done. Yet crewmen were running along its decks in seeming panic. Sailors were shouting orders and hoisting cargo back into the Germans' hold and the ship's stack was already smoking. The seaplane tender was preparing to get underway, some of its supply crates still scattered on the beach. Meanwhile, clouds were mounding over the crater. The weather was turning bad again.

The two spelunkers had been dirty but happy after their climb out of the cave. "Light!" Greta exclaimed with relief at the mouth of the lava tube. She hugged Hart and he kissed her again, grinning, and they marched along the crater shore in a contented mood of new partnership. But when the motor launch came to ferry the couple back to the ship they awkwardly reverted to a pose of proper distance. Out on the *Schwabenland* they saw the figure of Jürgen Drexler on the wing of the bridge, watching them stiffly.

"Let me talk to him," Greta whispered.

They left their gear on deck, the biologist removing one bottle from her pack and slipping it into her pocket. Schmidt met them on their way to the bridge.

"Did you go into the valley?"

They shook their heads.

He appraised them warily. "Come on, then. It should be safe."

"I'd like to see Jürgen alone," Greta said.

"No time for that now."

Ordinary seamen had been dismissed from the bridge but Heiden, Feder, and Drexler were there. There was an uncomfortable silence as the Germans studied the couple, trying to assess how much had happened. Greta let her gaze drift to the ship's wheel. Owen stared back evenly. Jürgen stood rigid, his humiliation at her recent absence plain. The political liaison couldn't keep his eyes from flickering from one to the other.

Finally Heiden spoke. "We thought you were dead."

"We went to Owen's cave," Greta said, now glancing at Drexler. He stonily looked back. "At my request. To study the underground biology of the island."

"You left the ship without permission," the captain complained. "You were absent without leave. That's tantamount to desertion."

"We're not in the navy, for Christ's sake," Hart replied.

"You go overnight and leave no word?" Drexler's voice was tight. "We were frantic with worry." He looked at Greta. "I thought you'd caught the disease."

She shook her head. "No, we left to investigate a scientific hypothesis. To explore."

"And did you find what you were looking for?" Feder asked slyly. He looked from the couple to Drexler, striving to keep a straight face.

Greta ignored him.

Drexler's gaze fixed on Hart. "That was irresponsible and in violation of every safety procedure and you know it. You could have killed her."

"That's ripe, coming from a guy who's had her culturing plague viruses. She's here, isn't she?"

"Looking like you dragged her behind a truck!"

"Listen, why don't you—"

"Enough!" The roar was Heiden's. He pointed at them as Drexler had, his finger accusatory. "You both know you broke every commonsense safety rule of this ship. Leaving like that was irresponsible, and caves are dangerous." He shook his head in disgust. "You're lucky you returned when you did or we might have left you behind. We're departing as soon as possible."

"Leaving?" Greta protested.

"Some of the men are sick. With the *Bergen's* disease, we think. It's time to flee before more die."

"Oh my God!"

"Who?" said Hart.

"A squad of the mountaineers. They were exploring that dry valley. Schultz, some others."

"How many?"

"Five. No, six. The mountaineers and Eckermann."

"What!"

"I thought it was time Fritz exercised his legs as well as his mouth," Drexler said grimly. "Now his wit has gotten him into trouble."

"Jesus Christ. Are they in the infirmary?"

"No, ashore."

"You'd better tell us what happened," Greta said worriedly, looking at Drexler with dismay.

"We don't really know," said Heiden. "Eckermann radioed from near the crater rim this morning. He reported they'd entered the valley the day before and by yesterday evening some of the men began developing symptoms. He said he still felt fine and was going back to help. The source of the contagion remains unclear, though he babbled about dust. In any event we can't take chances and jeopardize the expedition. They haven't radioed again and we've no sign of them. We're going to leave before someone comes down with the disease here."

"You're just going to *abandon* them?" Hart asked, incredulous.

"Under the circumstances we have no choice. We don't know where they are and can't help them medically if we did. Even if we could get them back aboard they might turn this ship into another *Bergen*. It's time to leave this cursed place. It was a mistake to send them, perhaps, but what's done is done. The crew is near panic."

"You're not going to catch anything out in this lagoon," objected Hart.

"And how do you know that, given that we have a ghost ship of a whaler tied to our side?" countered Drexler. "You don't know how or where that disease will strike."

"If there's a chance that those people are alive—"

"Gentlemen!" It was Schmidt, sounding impatient. "It seems to me that we have a more immediate question: whether to quarantine our two AWOL explorers."

"We're not a risk," said Greta.

"You don't know that."

"Maybe I do," said Greta. She turned to Drexler and Heiden. "The reason we went ashore is that Owen and Fritz found documentary evidence—a diary—that some Norwegians survived. They'd been in the cave; Owen and I went there to learn why. We . . . thought it would be quicker to just go without telling anyone." She glanced apologetically at Drexler. "We weren't trying to alarm you."

He looked at her gloomily.

She took a breath. "We found an interesting organism there, an algae or spongelike animal colony, tied to a subterranean heat source and possibly independent of the need for sunlight. My hypothesis is that this organic growth may have evolved toxins to stave off the bacterium. That's common enough in nature. Perhaps the Norwegians who lived drank cave water. We fell into an underground lake and inadvertently swallowed some of the water, so far without ill effect. And before we left the ship I filled this small bottle with a culture of the disease from my laboratory."

She brought it out of her pocket and held it up.

"At that time the solution was a cloudy white from the explosive growth of the bacteria. So I added some of the cave organism. As you can see, it has turned perfectly clear."

The Germans looked confused. Schmidt took the bottle curiously.

"What does this mean?" Heiden asked slowly.

"That there might be an antidote to this disease," Greta explained. "A naturally produced antibiotic. And if it kills this bacteria, perhaps it will kill others. Just like Fleming's penicillin."

"That British research was a failure," Schmidt objected. "Fleming couldn't find a way to efficiently grow, purify, or store his mold. He gave up. That's why German laboratories have developed a chemical alternative, prontosil."

"Yes, but penicillin worked better than chemicals in the tiny amounts Fleming could isolate," Greta countered. "His mold didn't damage healthy tissue. And this may work too, at least for an emergency." She turned to Drexler. "Can't you see, Jürgen? This could be far more important and exciting than a ghastly new microbe. Infection killed millions in the Great War. What if we had a way to battle it? We can't leave on the verge of such a discovery."

Drexler studied her, considering. Hart almost felt sorry for the man, his wound so obvious. Clearly, the political officer was still deeply in love with Greta and to have to listen as she lamely defended her leave-taking while standing next to the man she'd gone away with—well, it must have been tough.

And yet, the pilot could see Jürgen mentally squelching the pain, compartmentalizing it, as he thought furiously of the broader picture. Greta's betrayal, the risk of disease, a new microbe, the chance for the expedition to become a medical success, led to this island by . . . Jürgen Drexler. The German swung his gaze to Hart.

"What you say is intriguing," Drexler said carefully. "But all we have at this moment is a bottle of clear liquid and two people still alive after crawling through a hole in the ground." He considered. "And an opportunity for an immediate test." He nodded toward the captain.

"Yes," said Heiden cautiously. "It's obvious. See if this slime you found helps those soldiers."

"And Fritz," Hart amended.

"Exactly," Drexler agreed. "God has given us a chance to try for a miracle, perhaps. *If* you're right. And *if* we can find them."

"I'll find them," Hart said.

"Owen!" Greta touched his sleeve, Jürgen's eye following her hand. "No."

Hart looked at Drexler. "I'm not leaving live men behind. I'll find them from *Boreas*. If they're alive, I'll land to either distribute the drug or ferry them out."

"Then I'll go with him," Greta announced.

"Out of the question," snapped Drexler.

"It's my discovery, Jürgen!"

"No. I'm not risking you again and you've neglected your cultures long enough. If you want to study this cave slime, the best place is your lab."

She looked frustrated.

"Hart, on the other hand, is our last fit pilot. Lambert is still bandaged up. And he's right, the airplane is the fastest way to locate the squad. Then we can decide what to do next."

Greta knew better than to protest further. She flashed a pained look at Hart.

The pilot met her gaze, then turned to Heiden. "This bowl is too narrow for takeoff. We need to launch and recover from outside the crater. Is the ship seaworthy enough to do that?"

"I hope so. That's been the point of our repairs."

"The plane's radio is still out. I'll fly, find them, and return. I want the skis attached to the bottom of the pontoons in case I have to land on snow."

"Will you need a man to come with you again?" Feder asked.

Drexler scowled.

"No," Hart decided. "It's senseless to risk more lives than necessary. Let me check on their condition and we'll proceed from there."

"What if you don't come back?" Schmidt asked.

He shrugged. "Sail without me."

"No!" Greta cried. "That's crazy!"

"I'll be back." He turned and took the biologist by her shoulders. "Greta, I'll eat the organisms myself and go with a mask. We can't wait to test this drug further, we have to bet on it *now*. Lives are at stake. I trust your judgment. Will this stuff help Fritz and those men? Will it keep me alive?"

"My God, Owen, I can't promise that for raw . . . pond scum, based on a single bottled experiment. Even drugs that work well for one person don't always work for another. Maybe the organism loses its effectiveness as it dries, or with time. And those men may already be dead. This is an incredible risk." Her eyes were troubled. "Please, don't go alone. *Please.*"

"A short flight, a check on their situation, and I'm back." He turned to Schmidt. "If they're alive, if they're not too far gone, we can quarantine them on the aft deck where *Passat* was tethered. You can isolate me too."

"So, how long before you get back?" Feder asked.

Hart shrugged. "The valley is too dry for the skis so I'll have to find an ice field upslope to land. Four hours?"

"Six," demanded Greta.

"No!" said Feder. "The barometer is dropping again and this patched tub is going to be out on an ocean awash with icebergs. It must be quicker!"

"Eight," said Drexler. "Or more." He looked at Greta. "I'm not abandoning anybody either."

Hart launched as planned from the open ocean, climbed around the flank of the harbor volcano, and squeezed over the valley ridge beyond, flying below a thickening ceiling of dark cloud.

The valley was like a brown trough with the white platter of frozen lake running up its center, its eroded ice far too rumpled to land on. Despite the landscape's sterility the pilot flew to the second volcano without seeing anything: the beleaguered squad was surprisingly hard to spot from the air. He turned and dropped in elevation, going back the way he'd come. Still nothing.

Then a rock sprang to life and began waving frantically.

Hart waggled his wings and circled, studying the barren pumice slope to finally pick out the forms of still humans. The mountaineers were sprawled like scattered sticks. One stood apart, dancing energetically.

It looked like Fritz! Owen began looking for a place to land.

Glaciers nosed into the valley but were too steep and broken to serve as a safe runway. Hart flew over the enclosing ridgeline again and scouted the smoother slopes on the seaward side. There was a promising plateau of snow near the flank of the volcano that formed the island's snug harbor. The pilot put down there and climbed out, squinting at the darkening sky.

The wind was rising so he ran lines from the wings and tied them to metal swastika stakes he found in the back of the plane. "The first practical use of these damned things the whole trip," he muttered to himself, driving the stakes into the hard snow. He wrapped a tarp around the engine cowling and another around the cockpit bubble and set out with his backpack and the drug. The empty panorama was intimidating but the pilot admitted he actually liked being alone again for a moment. It reminded him of his independence in Alaska.

The most direct route led down the face of a glacier cut by crevasses, but he decided it would be safer to circle to the flank of the volcano and descend its smoother slope into the valley. The hiking was uncomfortable. His feet slipped on snow patches and loose rock and the gauze disease mask warmed his face but also tended to ice up. When he reached the frozen lake at the bottom he confirmed that its ice was as strange as the rest of Antarctica. Pockets of dust had melted into its thick covering at a faster rate than more reflective places, producing a labyrinth of waist-high undulations or frozen waves.

He hurried on. As he neared the site where he'd spotted the

sprawled SS soldiers Fritz skittered down a pumice slope to meet him, waving his arms to get Owen to stop short. The sailor was masked with a handkerchief like a bandit. They paused at a cautious distance.

"Don't come any closer, Owen, as much as I'd love to give you a hug, my friend! Your airplane made me happier than a lingerie merchant in a heated harem!"

"Don't be too enthused. Before you get to fly away you have to walk to the Dornier, Fritz. Several miles."

"Better than sitting here! I was about to freeze stiffer than Nazi protocol!"

Hart smiled. "Well, your tongue is still working, at least. Is the rest of you sick?"

He nodded. "I thought maybe I'd escaped but I'm beginning to ache. The truth is, I'm frightened. I'm babbling because I've seen what the disease does to others. It's *monstrous*."

The pilot threw him a canteen. "Drink this. It may save your life."

Fritz lifted the bottom of his mask and took a swig. "Ach!" He sputtered and coughed. "What is it? Penguin pee?"

"Medicine. I know it's vile. I've had some myself."

"So of course you want to share." He cautiously drank again.

"Greta thinks it may be an antidote, an antibiotic, that fights the plague microbes. It's terrible but you've got to drink as much as you can. We found it in that cave."

Fritz drank some more and grimaced. "Marched, diseased, now poisoned: I've had better cruises. Still, if this doesn't help I'm going to die, my friend." His eyes were somber.

"The others?"

"Gone already. Horrible pain. Some of them contorted like pretzels."

"Yet you're too unsociable even for microbes?"

"No, just for Schultz, God rest his soul. He was so tired of my complaining that he left me not far from here while the rest went to the end of the valley. By the time they got back a couple were already coughing. I put on a mask and moved away—you can imagine how popular that was—but it's the only reason I'm still alive. I took the radio up the slope to alert the *Schwabenland* and then came back to try to get the survivors moving before this storm hits. It was too late. Schultz was the last, and he died two hours ago."

"My God."

"We're in hell, Owen. A cold hell."

Hart hoisted his own canteen and drank, wincing. "You're probably contagious. We'll have to share the drug and then be quarantined on the deck of the *Schwabenland*."

Fritz nodded. "Drexler's been dreaming of that the whole voyage, I suspect. Though the best reason to live is to see his face when he realizes I'm the only survivor." He took another mouthful. "But that assumes you can get us out of here." Some snowflakes were beginning to fall. "I suggest we hurry to your plane."

CHAPTER TWENTY

Why hasn't he returned?"

Greta stared out at a darkening world. Atropos Island was gray, fogged by increasing snow, and the sea was growing rougher. They could see spray hurling skyward at the caldera entrance as the swells built, the *Schwabenland* wallowing miserably as it crept to maintain station in case *Boreas* came back. Icebergs drifted by like dreadnoughts, Heiden periodically snapping orders to change course slightly to stay out of their way. Yet there was no sign of Owen Hart. Nor had the field radio taken by the mountaineers issued any more calls. The crew was anxious. Even high on their bridge the officers could hear the labor of pumps keeping thudding pace with the slow leakage around the iceberg patch in the hull. The leak was still manageable but as the swells had mounded and the ship creaked, the invasion of cold seawater had grown worse.

"I told you it was madness to let him go," Feder fretted. "And madness to stay here waiting when we should be making for a proper port. We seem determined to compound one mistake with another."

"How can you say we shouldn't wait when he may just be pinned down by weather?" Greta demanded.

"Because if we wait too long we may be pinned as well!"

"That's quite enough, Alfred," Heiden growled. "We're in no danger of sinking. And if you two hens want to cackle at each other, do it off the bridge."

Feder scowled. "I just want it on record that I pointed out the dangerous weather the *first* time we got into trouble out here."

"Recorded. Now, silence!"

Drexler saw an opportunity and moved close to Greta, careful not to try touching her yet. "I know how fond you've become of Hart," he offered quietly. "I understand your worry. But he's a resourceful outdoorsman. I'm sure he's all right."

She sighed. "It's just so frustrating to have him all alone out there so soon after—" She stopped. "It's just so hard to wait, Jürgen. And what if I was wrong about the cave organism? What if he trusted me and flew off to his death from the disease?"

"That's nonsense. You acted on the best knowledge you had. We're all struggling. You, Hart, myself. And didn't you try it in your bottle? It must do some kind of good."

"I just wish I was sure."

"Could you try it on the cultures?"

"Owen took all the antidote." She hesitated. "And besides, the cultures are gone."

"What?"

"I destroyed them, Jürgen. I warned you I would. We've had enough death."

He looked at her in shock. *Careful*, he thought. *Control your emotions or you'll lose her. She'll run away.*

"Are you angry?"

He swallowed. "Surprised," he managed. "It seems . . . unscientific."

She looked away.

"Well." His face twisted in dismay. "I'd hoped to bring something back to Germany, but . . ." *Preserve what you have*, some instinct told him. He tried a different tack: "You and I have had some differences, Greta. But that hasn't changed my . . . my feelings for you. Whatever has happened, please remember: I'm *still* your friend."

She nodded, looking relieved. "Thank you. I value that, Jürgen."

He turned away to hide his wince.

The hike to the plane exhausted Fritz. The *Boreas* was behind a ridge on the opposite side of the lake from where the mountaineers had died and the little sailor insisted on minimizing the distance by cutting across its frozen surface. But as Hart warned, the eroded frozen waves proved a slippery nightmare difficult to scramble over. They both fell several times. Worse, their subsequent direction up the valley wall in the growing snow drifted off course and they got themselves onto the snowy crust of a glacier. They trudged mindlessly up its gloomy slope until there was a crack and Fritz almost dropped out of sight.

"My God!" he cried, scrambling away. "Now the island is trying to devour me!"

Hart cautiously crept to the edge of the crevasse and peered into its blue twilight. From its depths he felt an even deeper chill, from walls as hard as steel. "You're lucky."

"And your guiding skills have not improved."

"Conceded. Are you all right?"

Fritz sighed. "I ache, Owen. It's . . . frightening." The pilot gave him more of the drug. The supply was already nearly gone.

Hart carefully led their way back off the glacier and up a snow-dusted pumice slope. Eventually, breathing hard, they gained the ridge and came out on the plateau. The wind was shrieking. The seaplane was still there, snow drifting against its ski-converted floats and its wing tugging against the anchored swastika stakes. The ocean beyond was a blur of gray streaked with white. The *Schwabenland* couldn't be seen because it was around the flank of the volcano. Hart was conscious of time draining away. Surely the Germans would realize he couldn't fly back in a storm?

"Can we take off in this wind, Owen?"

"Maybe. And maybe fly in it. Maybe even find our way back to the ship. But landing on the sea, with that scudding ice . . ."

Fritz shivered. They were cold, dangerously so.

"Should we wait it out in the plane?"

"If we have to. But the skin has no insulation and the fuselage will be freezing." Hart looked around.

"Where else then?"

The pilot pointed. "Inside the mountain, maybe. It's warmer there."

The sailor followed his finger. There was a dark opening in the snow like a lidded eye.

"I noticed that on my hike down and the snow hasn't covered it up. That means it might be an overhang or a cave. If the latter, it's better than the plane."

"And if not?"

"Climbing will keep you warm. Can you manage the pain?"

Fritz paused to take internal inventory. "Actually, I'm beginning to feel better. Maybe that piss of Greta's really works."

They slowly plowed toward the distant eye, breathing hard, their goal lost at times through blowing snow. The wind howled harder as they worked higher, gusts snapping the ends of their parkas. The cold stung their lungs and rasped their throats. Hart's feet and hands were growing numb and he knew the little sailor must be far worse. It hurt to live.

Then they reached a chest-high wall of lava rock, part of an outcrop on the volcano's snowy flank. There was a shelf on top and then the small cave. Owen lifted the weary sailor up onto the ledge and pushed him ahead.

The entry tunnel was tight, forcing them to crawl on hands and knees, but there was a living-room-sized chamber beyond that was floored with sand. They sprawled gratefully. The sound of the wind had abruptly dropped and the temperature had soared.

"I think we're going to make it," Owen said. "Do you want some food?"

The sailor looked at him wearily. "Like your canteen? Yes, book

paste and paint thinner, please. I can't get enough of your cooking."

Hart's promised four-hour absence went by. Greta's six hours.
Drexler's eight. Still no sign of the pilot. Night came and the
Schwabenland uneasily maintained its rocking station at sea, the
crew grumbling nervously as large bergs swept by and smaller
floes clanked and skittered along the damaged hull. Snow coated
the decks before finally stopping at a gauzy dawn. Greta was
sleepless, her eyes red. The mood on the bridge was somber.

"It's time to consider our situation," said Schmidt. "We should
either reenter the shelter of the harbor or consider going back
north. With the season growing to a close the weather can only
grow worse."

"Owen asked us to remain out here," Greta said.

There was silence.

"Well, I've said what *I* have to say and I'm not saying it again,"
Feder reminded.

Heiden drummed his fingers, looking out the bridge windows.
"The entrance to the caldera is still stormy." They could all see
the spray. "I don't want to risk the fate of the *Bergen* and hit a
rock. Now that we're outside I prefer to stay outside until the
weather calms."

"And how long do you propose to stay?" Schmidt asked. "The
leak has gotten worse again."

"Slightly worse." The captain looked unhappy.

"There can't be any surprise at the pilot's absence," the doctor
insisted. "We've all seen what that disease can do."

"We don't know that!" Greta protested.

"We know that every man who has ventured into that valley
has failed to return."

Greta looked at the officers imploringly. Most shifted their
gaze away. Drexler didn't.

"Listen," he said. "I've been thinking. Our problem is lack of
information, not lack of will. We all want to do what's best for

the American and the mountaineers but we've no word from any of them so we can't act. Let me try to rectify that."

"What do you propose?" said Heiden.

"Take the motor launch back into the caldera. That way we risk a boat, not the ship."

"You can't even swim!"

"Swimming is pointless in this cold water," he dismissed. "And I don't want it said I abandoned the American." He glanced at Greta. She cast her eyes down.

"Your plan?" asked Schmidt.

"I'll ask for volunteers, we'll go ashore, and climb up to the crater rim. No farther! Hart and Eckermann did it safely when we first arrived so we should be able to as well. I'll see if I can spot any sign of the men or the plane. If we do . . . we can plan from there."

"And if we don't?"

"Then the best thing is to leave." He heard Greta take a sharp breath. "I'm sorry, but we can't indefinitely endanger the many for the few. Our primary duty to Germany is to return and report our claims."

They waited.

"It's a reasonable course of action," Heiden told her. "Maybe he'll even fly back while Jürgen is scouting."

She nodded miserably.

"This trip will also let me accomplish another task," Drexler said. "I think we should blow up the *Bergen*."

"Why?" asked Feder.

"Two reasons. One, the hull could retain traces of the disease despite our cremation of the corpses. There's no reason to endanger future explorers. And second, its removal would eliminate any competing Norwegian claims to this island. With the bodies burned and the ship gone, no one will know the whalers ever got here. It could still make a splendid German base, once we understand the disease. The cached supplies mark our claim."

"You'd come *back* here?" Greta gasped.

"With proper expertise and equipment. In fact, if the Reich allows, I'll come next season. But first things first. Do I hear volunteers?"

Feder smiled grimly. "I'll go if it will speed our getting out of here."

"When am I going to learn not to follow your lead? Great God in heaven."

"It's just a tremor, Fritz. At this point, this is the fastest way out."

They were suspended in the cave like flies on a wall. Ironically, their present precarious situation had only been made possible because of Fritz's improving health. The remaining drug organism, food, and the warmth of the cave had done wonders in restoring the sailor's strength. Consequently, he'd been persuaded to help explore the cave while they waited for the storm to abate. Hart's pack still had the lantern and flashlight and candles he'd used on his trip with Greta and they wound down a steep tunnel toward the interior of the mountain. But just when Fritz believed they'd reached the point of necessary return, the pilot had instead become enormously excited. Far from turning back, the crazy American wanted to go on.

"It's the elevator shaft!" Hart had cried.

"The what?"

"Greta and I followed this downward to the lake where we found the drug that seems to be saving your life! We entered it halfway up, while this tunnel breaks into its top. The two cave entrances are connected!"

"Wonderful. By a pit so deep we can't even see the bottom."

Hart had shone his light around. "The chimney is hundreds of feet deep, but not bottomless. And look, it has ledges and handholds. Halfway down is the horizontal tunnel Greta and I entered before. This shaft can lead us back through the mountain to the caldera. While we're there I can even return to the lake and get some of the drug—now that we know it works."

"You want *me* to climb down *there*?"

"Only halfway. If the Germans have any sense they brought the

Schwabenland back into the lagoon once they realized the serious-ness of the storm. We'll walk out and meet them."

"And if they don't have any sense, which is my judgment of this entire expedition?"

"Then you wait by the spring while I climb back over the rim of the volcano to get the airplane. In the meantime you'll have more medicine."

"Why am I letting you talk me into climbing a sheer cliff?"

"Because that direction is all downhill." He clapped Fritz on the back. "Don't worry, we'll rope up."

"Ah. We can fall together."

Fritz actually did fine until the small volcanic earthquake came. Then the cave wall shuddered and a few loosened fragments of rock cut through the air past them, exploding into stony shrap-nel somewhere far below. Now the sailor was trembling. "I don't like caves!"

"We're almost out of this one, Fritz." The pilot shone his flash-light. "See? There's the ledge we're making for. Much closer than trying to go back. The cave is unstable, but we won't be here long."

"Christ. I'm never getting off the ship again. I don't care what Pig-Head orders."

"You'll already be a hero. You won't have to."

Hart drove a final piton into the rock and threaded the rope through it, then led Fritz down its double length. On the sandy ledge where he and Greta had hesitated—it seemed like centuries ago—he reeled in the line. The pilot was cheerful. He'd be seeing her again soon.

The pair walked to the entrance of the crater's cave, blinking in the gray light of a new dawn. The storm was dying but wind still whistled up on the crater rim and spray pounded the caldera entrance. There was no sign of the *Schwabenland*, which was wor-risome. But if Drexler was as patient as promised, it should still be waiting at sea. At least Hart hoped so. "I'll go quickly down to the lake to get you enough of the organic mats. If they still haven't returned by the time I get back I'll get the airplane. The storm should be completely over by then. Then I'll find the ship. Meanwhile, just get some sleep."

Fritz looked out tiredly, utterly spent. "You know, Owen, we're not the two most popular members of this cruise. Do you really think they'll wait?"

"Of course. Greta will make them wait."

Later that morning Jürgen Drexler and his volunteers sailed the frost-coated motor launch through the heaving swells of the caldera entrance, the open boat surprisingly stable as it surfed the breaking waves into the choppy lagoon. Except for the scattered crates of abandoned supplies onshore that formed a mournful monument to a seemingly thwarted mission, the crater was empty: Hart was deep in the heart of the mountain and Fritz was asleep. Drexler used his binoculars to scan the crater rim. No one waved or shouted.

The political liaison was put on shore with Feder to climb up the crater wall while the remaining volunteers motored to the *Bergen* to ready it with explosives. The two Germans hiked steadily to the top, the geographer panting hard, and came tentatively over the crest. Feder's urge to cringe from an imaginary assault of germs was dampened by a stiff wind that blew from their backs, sweeping the mysterious menace of the dry valley away from them. Even so, both wore a gauze mask, sticky on the inside and frosted on its surface.

The valley was desolate and deserted: as deserted as Drexler had secretly hoped. As the hours had ticked by on the ship, the idea that the annoying American might not be coming back had filled the political liaison with rising excitement. It would solve so many problems! Still, he hiked along the rim to make sure. He had to know, for both Greta and himself. After a quarter mile he found the radio that Fritz had hauled up from the valley bottom, snow-crusted and abandoned a hundred yards below the rim.

"I'm not going near it," Feder said.

"Then wait here. We must check." Drexler slid down the outer slope, sweating at even this tentative descent into the valley of death, but he made himself do it. A try revealed that the radio's batteries had died in the cold; he couldn't reach the ship. Otherwise there was no sign of Fritz, Hart, or the mountaineers. Drexler considered a moment, then climbed back and pointed along the rim.

"We hike on."

Feder unconsciously had backed a foot away from him, as if he might already be contaminated. "For God's sake, Jürgen, they're gone! Lost!"

"No. I want a view along the ridgeline of the valley."

Drexler's heart initially sank when they spied the flying boat. So, the pilot hadn't crashed. The Germans could see it tethered on the snow far below and studied it carefully for a sign of life. It was a quiet relief that they saw none. The plane was crusted with snow, its surroundings trackless. Hart had obviously left before the storm and not come back.

"Do you see anything?" Drexler asked, lowering his binoculars.

"Only an abandoned airplane. My God, wouldn't Hart have returned by now if he's still alive? He said four hours and it's been a day!"

The political liaison nodded, glad to have a witness. "Perhaps we should climb down and inspect," he offered carefully.

"No! The launch might leave *us*! Do you want us all to die, one by one, looking for each other? I'm going no nearer that pestilence than right here. It's time to go back!"

Drexler made a show of reluctance, looking out across the island with binoculars. Then, "You're right, Alfred. Even Hart advocated prudence." It was obvious, he told himself. The American had landed, descended into the valley, and died from the microbe or exposure. As much as he would like fresh tissue samples of the disease, it would be suicide to search for the bodies. It was over. His rival was dead.

He exhaled, realizing how tensely he had been holding his body. "So. We saw the plane abandoned and no sign of life. Agreed?"

"I *told* him not to come."

"We'd better return to the launch. They'll be wondering what happened to us."

"Finally. I'm freezing." When they turned the wind was bitter in their faces. Jürgen led the way back, brooding as he turned events over in his mind. The whole episode was a tragedy, yes. He was willing to admit that. But who could have foreseen that a simple scouting expedition would lead to so many deaths? And they'd learned valuable lessons to prepare them for return: his men hadn't died in vain. The disaster demonstrated the power of this strange new microbe, potentially an awesome new weapon!

He continued to muse as he and Feder picked their way down the slope. Atropos Island: the Fate that scheduled death, the Fate that was going to resurrect his career once he restored the cultures by returning next year. Too, by consigning Hart to some unknown end, Fate had resurrected his relationship with Greta. After reviewing the chain of events, his conscience was clear. Everyone had done the right thing as best they were able. *Everyone*.

As the pair neared the bottom of the crater, they saw the motor launch pulling away from the derelict whaler to meet them for the trip back to the *Schwabenland*. Suddenly, there was a flash of light and they abruptly halted their descent, watching the whaler's bridge explode. The demolition had begun! Then another explosion, and another. The whaler was being ripped apart, smoke and water spewing skyward. Drexler could feel the sound and pressure in his bones as the energy punched across the volcanic bowl. Then the column of smoke began to dissipate, black caldera water smoothing over the wreck site. The Germans in the boat below cheered.

Suddenly there was a new rumble and Drexler turned to the noise. The explosion had triggered a snow and rock avalanche on the crater wall, he saw, at a point right above Hart's damnable cave. Jürgen couldn't help grinning at the spectacle. A cloud of debris was sliding over the entrance in a great plume of dust, helping to erase bitter memory. The cavern of betrayal was history.

"My God, an awesome detonation," Feder breathed. "I'd no idea we had that much explosive aboard."

"As I told Hart, we Germans like to be thorough." Drexler watched the plume of dust dissipate in the wind. The cave entrance had disappeared. *Yes.*

Suddenly exhilarated, he began bounding down the slope toward the approaching boat as the geographer clumsily followed, the pair's shoes kicking up gouts of pumice dust.

It was time to look to the future, not to the past.

It was time to comfort Greta.

Fritz was jerked awake by a roar. He'd been sleeping in the cave and was disoriented by darkness; only after a second or two did his eyes swing toward the light of the cave's entrance as the source of the noise. There was a whole series of thuds outside and he staggered toward the cave mouth to see what was going on.

The whaler had erupted in a plume of spray and debris, he saw, fragments still raining down into the lagoon. Groggily, he realized the *Schwabenland*'s motor launch was also in the harbor. For rescue! He lifted an arm to wave.

Then there was a deeper, nearer roar and the lava cave began to tremble. Rocks crashed across the tube entrance and then a sluice of dirt and snow began pouring down to blot out his view. Jesus Christ! Dust billowed in at him and he began to cough. What had the fucking Nazis done now?

The sailor began a stumbling run back into the tube to get away from the avalanche at the entrance, confused by this calamity. Suddenly there was a splintering crack and a huge slab from the ceiling thudded down behind him. Cave-in! The floor shuddered and the air quaked and as more pieces hinged down he was running madly, the noise growing . . . and then he was swatted down and time stopped. Blackness.

He woke to a hand shaking his shoulder. A voice was saying his name. It seemed a cruel thing to do. He felt not so much pain as leakage, his life force draining away. Why call him back?

"Fritz!"

It was Owen. Still alive? That was something . . .

"Fritz! What happened?"

The sailor spoke. Or tried to. It came as a croak. He was frustrated that he couldn't do better than a fucking croak. That he wouldn't get back to the ship to surprise Pig-Head.

"What?" The pilot bent closer.

Fritz managed a hoarse whisper. "Get back to her, Owen." He spoke in a swoon of pain. "Don't give up again."

And then the last of him drained away.

Sky. The ice-dotted ocean. As vast and brilliant as the cave had been close and dark. Now Hart was flying in its terrifying emptiness with a leaden cargo of sudden, devastating loss. It seemed he was utterly alone in the world. The cave destroyed, Fritz dead, the ship disappeared, Greta gone. He was too late. As he'd instructed, they'd sailed without him.

The pilot watched the fuel gauge measure the sinking of his hope. At the very end he planned to dive steeply into the sea; the crash would be quicker than frigid water. But he'd hunt until the last drop of petrol. He'd already come so far.

He'd been halfway to the lake when the cave-in occurred, the deeper mountain quaking ominously with a guttural rumble. What in hell? Pondering the mystery, he decided on a quick retreat. When he scrambled back to the chimney it was full of choking dust. Alarmed, he climbed up the shaft to a lava tube suddenly littered with broken rock. He found his little friend at the inner boundary of complete collapse, half buried and bleeding. Great God, why a cave-in *then*? The timing was monstrously bitter. And as Fritz slipped away Owen spent precious time grieving, giving way to self-pity at life's unfairness. He numbly gathered purpose only by remembering Greta, and then began the long, lonely climb toward the cave's back door, praying that it had not been sealed as well. One by one his lights had died; first the flashlight, then the lantern, and then the candles. He crawled the last hour in utter darkness, guided only by his knowledge that there *was* a way out and it lay somewhere at the top of this labyrinth of tunnels. Twice he hit dead ends, backtracked, and tried a different tunnel. Three times he almost gave up, lying in the dark with only the sound of his own breathing, drops of melt-water eventually prodding him to climb on. Yet finally he was on the snowy shelf again, dazzled by polar light, blood pounding, the cold an electric shock, taking in great shuddering breaths of frigid air. Groaning at the inexorable drainage of time. How long would they wait?

He'd eventually hiked wearily to the plane, dug it out, un-leashed its wings, unwrapped the tarps, and laboriously warmed its engine. He was slow, clumsy, tired, and it took forever. Forever! Always he was conscious of the minutes and hours tick-ing by, the dying light, the diminishing chances. And yet when he finally brought the engine to a roar, skidding down the snowy plateau and lifting away at last from the cursed island, he still had hope. That he could catch them. That he could reach *her*.

The crater lagoon was empty, even of the *Bergen*. So was the sea.

He swung his head in anxious search until his neck ached and saw nothing. He flew over an ocean so lifeless that perhaps he *had* died, and now was in a cold heaven or endless hell.

He was so damned tired. His head was nodding. His body ached. His heart was a stone of sorrow. How could life be so briefly sweet, and then turn so quickly and frustratingly wrong again? Why had he left her at all?

God, he hated Antarctica.

And then from the corner of his eye he spotted a dark point amid the shards of icy white. As he flew closer he realized it was extruding a tendril of smoke.

He glanced down. The gas gauge was past empty.

And here was a ship.

Realization slowly penetrated. A ship! It was Greta! He'd made it!

Elmer's angel.

He wept as he put *Boreas* in a long, flat, gliding dive to stretch his fuel, leaning forward, pushing the Dornier by sheer will.

And then as he landed the plane on the sea a final time, clipping the wave tops, he finally saw the name on the hull he was chasing.

It was the Norwegian whaler, the *Aurora Australis*. Turning slowly toward him.

PART TWO

1939–44

CHAPTER TWENTY-ONE

Pain subsides, but memory just roots deeper. Greta was burned into Hart's brain like the after-dazzle of flash powder: her face framed by fur as she watched icebergs the color of her eyes, her body bathed by lantern light in the womblike grotto of the cave, her fingers touching his sleeve as she asked him not to leave the ship—not to leave *her*. And that bright remembrance was shadowed by the darker tumor of Jürgen Drexler. Other mental images were etched by acid and sun fire: the bite of polar wind, the disease-contorted bodies, the tantalizing crack of light that made him crawl for the surface when muscle and will seemed utterly expended, the ominous disappearance of *Schwabenland* and the *Bergen*. Antarctica was a song so exquisite and so vile that he could not get it—could not get *her*—out of his head. And because of that he couldn't forget her, nor replace her, nor move past her. He'd lost her and yet somehow it wasn't over, he knew. It couldn't be over until they met again.

Initially he simply gave way to despair as he lay on a musty cotton mattress in a storeroom of the *Aurora Australis*, confined by the distrust of Sigvald Jansen. Lit by a caged bulb, the steel chamber mercifully prevented much contact with the Norwegian sailors, still furious about their confrontation with the Germans. "Murderer," one muttered at the pilot as he slid food through the doorway. One of the whalers had been killed in the gun battle and two wounded, Hart learned.

For a while the whalers waited grimly for him to exhibit symptoms of the dread new disease he talked wildly about, waited in both anticipation and fear. But no symptoms appeared. So he existed for a while outside of normal time, in a debilitating fog of grief and longing and regret. The sudden loss of Greta and Fritz was torment so great that at first he didn't think he could live, that he would ever again want to live. And yet he did live: numbly, automatically. And slowly—it was as if he was on a rack that was being ratcheted down day by agonizing day—the loss became more bearable. His choices became inevitabilities, never to be reversed, and his defeats a bitter peace. The alternative was madness. And as days turned to weeks—while the whaler finished its interminable season and then slowly steamed home—the hole in his heart began to scab over. The future began to replace the past and determination eclipsed despair. Even if the expedition had become a tragic fiasco—even if he'd been given up for dead— couldn't he get back into Greta's life? That must be his goal.

The Norwegians, who'd been so thirsty for revenge that they gleefully rammed the *Boreas* and sent the empty flying boat to the ocean's bottom, were puzzled. Was Hart a German spy, deserter, or the refugee he claimed? Nothing he said could be verified. The American claimed to have escaped from a new plague but had no sign of it. He claimed to have found the *Bergen* but had no proof: in fact, he claimed there *was* no proof, that the missing ship had mysteriously disappeared from the caldera of a mysterious island, its lagoon empty the last time he flew over. So in the end Jansen simply locked the American away and brooded about the strange clash with the Nazis, keeping Hart confined all the way to Norway. The pilot promised Jansen that a woman, some German biologist, could confirm his strange story, and he even confided to Sigvald his fantasies about reunion and rehabilitation. He would describe to authorities the forbidding island, he said. Then Norwegian scientists could return next year, armed and cautious.

But the pilot's hopes came to nothing.

The American was a diplomatic and legal conundrum and so was confined in Oslo while the Norwegians considered what to do. Hart had not a shred of evidence. And Norway was reluctant to challenge Nazi Germany over such a baffling and, in the context of recent developments, *trivial* incident. Greta Heinz? Not only did Hart have no address, there was no mention in the German press of her. Nor of the expedition, for that matter, or of the return of the *Schwabenland*. Had the crippled ship gone down? It was very odd.

Hart pondered. "It's the disease," he suggested. "They want to keep their microbe secret. Their very silence proves what I've been saying."

Of course. And did Hart have papers or passport?

All left on the ship, he explained.

Of course.

As the weeks and months passed, the Germans made no announcement of discovery of a new island and no complaint of a Norwegian whaler interfering with Reich biological sampling. The Norwegians, in turn, saw no reason to reveal to the Germans the survival of the *Aurora Australis*, the rescue and confinement of Owen Hart, or his report on the fate of the *Bergen*. The Nazis would learn all that when they returned to the island one day to find a Norwegian flag fluttering in the harbor ahead of them—assuming it even existed.

The pilot was freed in September by the turn of events. Poland had been invaded by Germany, and France and England had declared war. Brought to a hearing room, Hart was informed he was no longer wanted in Norway but had limited options. If he tried to make his claims public, the government would be forced to respond to rumors of a tragic Antarctic confrontation and the logical action would be to try Hart—the only member of the *Schwabenland* in custody—for the murder of the Norwegian whaler who'd died. Promised silence, however, would enable his release.

"Then let me go back to Germany," Hart pleaded. "I need to learn what happened. I need to find Greta Heinz."

"I'm afraid it's too late for that," a minister said. "The Reich has closed its borders. We've arranged with the American embassy to issue new papers and a ticket out of Norway if you'll sign these forms absolving all parties of liability and agreeing to confidentiality about regrettable incidents in polar waters. We prefer not to complicate our relations with Germany at this time."

Hart asked to be sent to England. He'd look for Greta from there. London absorbed him readily enough in its mammoth anonymity, but contacting expedition members proved impossible. If they were alive they'd been swallowed by the Reich, as remote as if on another planet. The vacuum of information was maddening: it was as if Hart had dreamed the entire voyage. He realized how little he knew about Greta. The sound and smell and touch of her was as vivid as his remembrance of what she looked like, but her past was opaque. He wrote letters, unsigned and with only a London post box as a return address (he assumed the letters would be steamed open and read by the German police), to the Reich Interior, Air Force, Forest, and Hunt ministries. Anything remotely connected to Göring.

Dear Greta. If you can read this, thank God you're alive. So am I, in London. Can you join me?

They were cryptic, he knew. He wasn't a writer and besides, he had no idea if she was alive or dead, married or alone. Had she returned? Did she think him dead? What was her situation? What was her mood? There was no reply. At times he thought the uncertainty would kill him. But of course it didn't kill him, and day simply followed day.

Nothing was getting in and out of Germany that the Nazis didn't wish. Like a hornet's nest being wrapped in ever-deeper layers of paper, the Third Reich was being sealed up. The political exodus of Jews and intellectuals from Germany was increasing and Hart held unrealistic hopes that Greta would materialize in

the locomotive steam of a London train station, expelled and
ready to make a new life. Aimlessly, gripped in depression, he
went to the platforms a few times and threaded through the
crowds, looking for her face in an exercise he knew was patently
ridiculous. Other avenues proved a dead end. The German embassy had closed. The Red Cross had no record on its refugee lists.
His vigil was hopeless, he was told. And yet he had no interest in
returning to America and being an ocean away from Germany.
No interest in other women. No interest in the larger world.

While World War II walled off Germany, it also proved a psy-
chological salvation for Hart. Suddenly he was not alone in his in-
ability to control events; millions were being swept along a great
dark river. And he found refuge in work. The American became a
flight instructor for the Royal Air Force, throwing himself into
the task with grim purpose. The pilots were so young! Many confided they hoped a glamorous skill might keep them out of the
trenches of this new war. Their escape became his own. He lost
himself in the air.

The training field's RAF flight captain slowly befriended the
quiet, remote American, once expressing curiosity at Hart's reluctance to take advantage of wartime opportunities with women.
The pilot confided his despair over Greta. "In love with a Jerry!"
the man marveled. "Best to keep a lid on that little secret, old
chap. And better to give her up and get on with your life. If she's
alive, she's entombed in a bloody madhouse."

"She's the only reason I *want* a life," Owen responded. "She's
the one who let me come back to life."

"Don't let her rob you of it now."

Yugoslavia, Greece, North Africa, Russia. A drumbeat of defeat. If Greta was still alive she was caught in a web of monstrous
dimension, a new empire that stretched from Normandy to the
Caucasus and from the Arctic Circle to the Sahara. Then came
Pearl Harbor. With America's entry into the war, Hart joined the
U.S. Army Air Corps in England and was tapped for reconnaissance and intelligence because of his fluency in German. Hart's
superiors did not appreciate his opinion that the Germans were

no more likely to crack under strategic bombing than the British had, but they acknowledged his skill at interrogating captured enemy pilots.

On a few occasions Hart volunteered for reconnaissance flights over Europe. His planes were pounded by flak and hounded by fighter planes and yet he found the experience oddly dispassionate. His emotional shell—his spore coat, he thought wryly—had grown so necessarily thick that it was like watching his own peril from a distance. Even if he could still fear the long agonizing minutes it would take to plunge from twenty thousand feet, death itself promised a certain peace. His emotions were further confused by the realization that in an indirect way he could be helping to kill Greta; he sometimes looked at the great fires raging below and imagined her trapped within them. And yet when he was honest with himself he did not think she was dead, or likely to die. He felt he would know instantly if that happened—that the whole fabric of the universe would seem to come undone—and moreover, that destiny had more in store for them.

For Owen Hart, then, most of World War II was a period of endless waiting, waiting so prolonged and dreadful that time itself seemed to have been repealed. Yet finally it was the fall of 1944, the Allied forces had liberated most of France, and the pilot experienced one of those encounters that suggest fate rules life: a meeting that replaced five years of despair with a thread of hope, enough hope to fuel desperation. A prisoner was asking for Owen Hart and his name was Otto Kohl.

American military policemen saluted smartly as Major Hart strode down the gloomy corridor of a former mental hospital, his boots echoing on hardwood floors that neglect had robbed of any sheen. The pilot's face was a mask, struggling to hide rising excitement. Kohl! Owen had occasionally searched the ballooning lists of German prisoners for some connection to the past but had known it was as futile as elbowing the crowds of London train stations. And yet here was Otto, popping up out of nowhere, asking for him! One of countless Germans who'd been swept up after the

fall of Paris, his fleeing Mercedes reportedly found overheated and
sprung out from the weight of wine cases, gilt picture frames, a
hoard of jewelry, and a Gallic mistress thirty years his junior. The
French woman had been seized by nearby villagers and shaved
bald. The German, however, was whisked away for an interrogation in which he boasted of high-ranking connections. The self-
importance had won him temporary confinement in a political
prison established at the abandoned mental institution. During
the Occupation its regular inmates had mysteriously disappeared.

The war had left its dreary mark. The steel bars were past-due
for painting. The elevator cage was grounded, heavy with dust.
The green of the walls had darkened from restful to sick. A gur-
ney had been abandoned in one corner, its gray sheet stained with
gray blood. The small office used for interrogation was barren except for a table and two chairs. Late-autumn sun made a geomet-
ric pattern on the walls from the wire mesh on the windows; the
temperature was cold. And there at the table was Otto Kohl,
dressed in prison fatigues with his ankles manacled. The German
blinked and tentatively smiled as Hart came in, looking almost
shy. He stood awkwardly.

"Owen!" Kohl greeted hoarsely. "Back from the dead!"

Hart sat down and Kohl hesitantly followed. The German
looked older, his hair grayer, and yet the war seemed not to have
treated him badly. Well fed. "Just back from Antarctica, Otto.
The ship didn't wait."

Kohl bobbed his head anxiously. "Yes. Obviously not. But then
the report was that you'd died in a heroic aerial rescue attempt.
It's a miracle—my finding you alive like this. Fortune is curious,
no?"

"Not half as curious as I am." So, the ship *had* definitely survived. He stared at Kohl, remembering the dinner at Karinhall,
Greta in the firelight. "What in hell are you doing here?"

Kohl nodded excitedly. "Exactly! Exactly the right question!
I've been telling my captors for weeks that I have no military connections, that I'm simply a businessman, a government facilitator, a minor functionary! I don't belong in a cage. I should be

employed in reconstruction, in reconciliation, where I can help people. It's a tragic waste, my being here."

Hart appeared to consider this. Then he opened his folder. "It says here you looted half the Loire Valley."

"That's an outrageous interpretation! I simply served as an import-export link to Germany."

"That you had a château there and a town house in Paris. That you cut a social swath in Occupation and Vichy circles. That you wore a swastika in your lapel by day and haunted the cabarets at night. That you were a black market profiteer. A womanizer. That you arranged the transshipment of slave labor."

"No!" Kohl shook his head vigorously, anxiously. "No, no, no. Reports spread by the jealous, by my enemies, by captives anxious to save their own skin by spreading false stories—all with no basis in fact. I was simply directed to help with the economic integration of Germany and France. When my presence in Washington became impossible."

Hart said nothing.

"I've tried to explain to your supervisors that I'm a man of business, Owen. A man of vision. A man of science. I cited the Antarctica expedition. That was the true Otto Kohl! Organizing expeditions to explore the natural world! I'd even included an American, I said. An international effort! And then one of your interrogators, a Colonel Cathcart, mentioned you. He said that you'd referred to such an expedition and that you were here, alive, in France. And it was electric, revelatory! A bolt of lightning! I couldn't believe it! And so of course I asked for you: Owen Hart, my old friend, the man who could identify me for what I really am!"

Hart studied the German dubiously. "I could learn nothing about the expedition after its return."

"Yes, it was kept confidential."

"Not even word of my own fate. It was as if I'd vanished. No mention. No credit. No reward."

"Do you think that didn't trouble me? To have recruited you and then such a cruel illness: it was a tragedy. And we wanted, of course, to send your back pay but there were no relatives, no address—"

"How did you know that?"

"But then the entire Antarctic expedition had gone seriously awry and—"

"How did you *know* that, Otto?"

He stopped. "Know what?"

"That I died of an illness? Earlier you said I died in a heroic aerial rescue attempt."

He frowned. "Did I say that? Did I say illness? I meant that was my assumption, our assumption, it was the natural—"

"We were in Antarctica, not Panama. There are no illnesses there—except perhaps frostbite. So: what *did* they tell you of my death?"

Kohl appeared to be doing an inner calculus, weighing what Owen wanted to hear. "Well, there was talk of a discovery—a dread new disease. You were one of the casualties. People felt very bad about your death. Drexler declared his intention to return the following season to perform more cutting-edge research. Except . . ."

"Except?"

"The war. The British navy was blocking the way."

Hart stood, restless, and paced around the small room, Kohl's eyes nervously following. Five years of questions were bubbling in the pilot's mind. He stopped and studied the German narrowly. "So you know of no weapons program arising from the expedition?"

"Absolutely not. I simply met the ship and learned you were missing along with some other crew members. Heiden told me they'd escaped from this disease and crazy whalers, there was damage . . . it was very bewildering."

"Other crew members? Who else was missing?"

"Well . . . no one, really. That I knew. Soldiers, I guess. Certainly, the important people were all there: Heiden, Drexler . . ."

"Greta?"

There was a pause. Kohl gave his interrogator a careful look. "No . . ."

Hart's spirits sank.

"Not at *first*, not at the docking. But she came up afterward with Drexler. She seemed quiet, subdued. Hustled off to the station rather quickly. Probably couldn't wait to get off the ship."

Hart leaned forward. "Where did she go?"

Kohl bit his lip, considering. "Don't get me wrong, Owen. I'm hesitating only because of what I heard. There was talk on the ship that . . . that you and Greta were more than simply colleagues. More than friends. Is this true?"

"Where did she go, dammit?"

"So you *were* lovers?"

Hart was quiet, looking at the calculating Kohl. Then he leaned slowly forward again, his voice tight. "Why ask questions when you know the answers?"

Kohl leaned away from the American. He was sweating despite the room's chill, and wiped his forehead with his sleeve. "It's funny how our positions have reversed, isn't it, Owen?"

"Why did you want to see me, Otto?"

Kohl automatically glanced about—Fritz's German glance, instinctive after more than a decade in the Third Reich—and leaned forward himself. His own voice fell to a whisper. "I can help you."

Hart sat back. "That's rich. How can *you* help me?"

"I have information you want."

"Always the salesman," Hart said, making no effort to hide his contempt. "So, what are your wares?"

"I can help you get Greta out."

Hart went rigid. "What?"

"Get her out. Of the Reich. Germany is losing the war, Owen. Everyone can see that. The noose is tightening. But you—*we*—could get her out. You and me. Before it's too late."

Hart felt unsteady. "Why?" he managed. "Why would we do that?"

"Because, even though she believes you're dead, she's never

stopped loving you. She *would* escape with you. I'm sure of it. My idea . . . well, my *plan* is that you and I will contact her, and then you'll fly us both to safety. *That's* why I asked for you."

"You can find her?"

"Oh, yes."

"Why should I believe you?"

"Believe it. I know the exact address."

"No. The part about her still loving me. Why would she confide such feelings to *you?*"

"Because Greta Heinz is my daughter," Kohl said.

Hart jerked, as if struck.

"And," he continued, "Jürgen Drexler is my son-in-law."

CHAPTER TWENTY-TWO

Like a wilderness lit by lightning, Germany was a dark, flickering void at night. The necessary wartime blackout robbed it of the illumination of civilization, turning its nocturnal hours as opaque as those of the Middle Ages. From the air where Hart and Kohl flew in a light plane, only far horizons blinked. Artillery and antiaircraft fire, distant flames, the searchlights of probing air defenses—these were the signs that the Third Reich remained inhabited. Somewhere in the abyss below Greta still lived.

Hart had simply left. It was a necessity. The American air force would never permit him to go behind enemy lines to look for a woman. So he'd taken a plane and risked the loss of one empty life in a gamble for another.

Kohl had thought their scheme through. The pair commandeered a jeep, telling Hart's superiors that the wily German was going to lead Owen to a cache of stolen art near Paris in return for the American's plea for leniency. But instead of hunting for Impressionist loot, Hart accompanied Kohl to a forger who supplied them with Reich papers in return for all the dollars he could extort from the American's savings. This was followed by the borrowing of a light plane to allegedly fly the informant Otto Kohl, reputed vessel of critical strategic information, to Third Army headquarters.

"It will work if we move quickly enough," Kohl promised. And it had. Once the fugitives were aloft they turned and streaked low in the night for Berlin, skimming treetops to stay off radar screens. "They'll presume you're shot down and missing," Kohl explained. "If it soothes your conscience, you can play the spy. Your superiors would gladly give up a light plane to get a ground observation of conditions in Berlin."

"How do we get back?"

Kohl exuded confidence. "I have a farm on the outskirts of the capital. We hide the airplane there, contact Greta, then fly to Switzerland. I have access to money—enough to grease the proper palms. The Swiss will help us invent new lives, and we'll go on to wherever we want to go."

"And Greta will come with us?"

"That's up to you, of course."

Hart had gambled everything she would. And yet, he couldn't help wondering about her marriage to Drexler. Should he believe Otto's assurances that it was a loveless union, that Greta carried a torch for her so-far-as-*she*-knew dead American pilot? *Was* the relationship that of two people leading parallel but separate lives? He questioned the German more closely. "I never quite understood the hold Jürgen seemed to have on her," he said. "What is the basis of it?"

Kohl stared somberly out the cockpit window, seeming to pluck memories from the inky darkness. "Even before Jürgen," he began, "there was a man. A husband, in fact. An older German biologist at the University of Hamburg. In retrospect, the attraction wasn't entirely surprising: Greta's mother had died in childbirth, and I . . . well, I was abroad a lot. The girl was raised in convent and boarding schools."

Kohl shook his head wearily. "Her childhood was lonely, Owen. That was my fault, of course."

He went on to explain that the awkward union abruptly ended

when Professor Heinz died in an automobile accident. For Greta, it was a crushing blow, and not just because of the loss of his security. She'd curtailed her own studies for the marriage. Its end meant her career as an unproven female biologist in a male-dominated profession suddenly held meager promise. Both her mentor and her academic momentum were gone.

Kohl had come back to Germany from Washington, D.C., to help his daughter decide her future and improve his own connections to the Reich government. He quickly decided she must find a new husband: some bright young official likely to emerge at the top of the new regime, a man who would prove as useful to him as to her.

And so he'd cultivated Drexler, the poster-boy Nazi, who in turn saw Kohl as a quick-witted advisor with friends and connections.

Kohl took Greta to a party celebrating the Führer's birthday and persuaded Drexler to be there too. The young Nazi was clearly smitten; a moth to a flame. Yet she was hesitant. Yes, he was handsome, bright, and ambitious. Yes, his vision of Germany's future was heady, even thrilling. And he campaigned for her doggedly: it was flattering. Women thought him gorgeous.

"He's just a bit cold, Papa," she confided. "I mean preoccupied. I suspect he's already married—to his career."

"All successful men have the mistress of their work! That man could be your future. *Our* future! He'll open doors for you."

She sighed. "I know. He's an . . . amazing person. But he doesn't always seem to see what I see, care for what I care for. Sometimes we run out of things to talk about. He's actually a bit awkward."

"With women, perhaps. Not with the people in power."

Then Drexler let slip the coming Antarctic expedition, boasting that he'd been picked to represent its political side. Göring himself was the power behind it! Those who accompanied it would become heroes. And the science team for the voyage was being assembled.

For Kohl, the expedition was an answer to a prayer. It just so happened that he had a brilliant young biologist to suggest for the ship's company. And while her presence as a woman was unusual for a Reich sea voyage, it would give Drexler the time to really get to know her.

Greta was uncertain. What if she and Jürgen fell out? But she was also thrilled. Antarctica! She'd be the first German woman to visit the place. It was heady, momentous. The biologist felt her abilities merited a second chance to establish her professional reputation. She asked the young Nazi if he was recruiting her as a capable scientist or as a woman.

"I'm recruiting the best person I can find," Drexler replied.

The memory of the day Greta received confirmation she'd been accepted for the expedition came back to Kohl now as a gust of wind buffeted the plane. "You should have been there, Owen," the German said. "She was delirious. Never had I seen her so radiant." Suddenly, his face darkened. "The exact opposite of the girl who was returned to me three months later when the *Schwabenland* tied up at the Hamburg docks."

Hart continued staring straight ahead, though his fingers were beginning to feel moist and clammy on the controls. "She told you about . . . about *us*?"

Kohl nodded. "Through her tears. After her narration of the events leading . . . well, to your death, she went back to being numb. I wasn't sure quite how to deal with her, what to say. But Jürgen was—what's your American term? Johnny-on-the-spot. He made it his mission to distract Greta from her grief. I tell you, the man was a force of nature. He would not be denied. And in time, Greta relented. She had no momentum of her own, no direction. And Jürgen, he *is* direction." Kohl smiled bitterly. "Myself, I thought: this is the best thing for her."

"But it wasn't?" said Hart. His eyes lowered to check the compass heading. Still on course.

"Jürgen is very complex. Admirable in so many ways, but also, I've come to realize, *undeveloped*. He is like a child who battles for a toy, only to tire of it once it ceases to be an object of contention. I have no doubt that, were someone to try to wrest away his plunder, he would show his claws, but it is *not* because he derives much enjoyment from it. My daughter's loneliness is profound."

The dull ache that had resided in Hart's chest since returning from Antarctica now filled him completely, but he said nothing. Germany—dark, wounded—continued to unreel beneath them.

Their plan was hopeless in its sheer simple audacity, the pilot knew. Somehow get into Berlin. Somehow find Greta. Somehow persuade her to abandon her husband. Somehow avoid Drexler's claws. Somehow escape to Switzerland. Somehow make a new life.

Somehow. It was the clearest plan Hart had had in six years.

They flew on and the sky began to lighten. Fires glowed on the horizon and by Hart's dead reckoning they were about twenty miles from Berlin. Soon they'd cross the flak batteries. To be aloft at daylight would be suicide. "Where's that farm of yours?"

"Swing that way. We cross the Autobahn, and then several miles beyond . . ."

Hart was nervous. Their plane had American markings. "We have to get out of the sky soon or we're going to be jumped by a prowling fighter."

"If we don't get the plane hidden we'll be trapped in Germany. Be patient."

They flew in anxious silence for several more minutes. Then Kohl pointed. "All right. Werder's in that direction. And I recognize my buildings. Beautiful, from the air. You can put down in that pasture."

They bumped down in the dawn light and taxied up to the barn, climbing out stiff and weary. Somewhere a rooster crowed.

"It looks like the Germany I remember," Hart said, glancing about. "Tidy."

"Caretakers come. But not for a few days. Here, help me push this plane into the barn." They rolled it forward, the wings sliding over empty stalls. Another vehicle was already inside under a tarp and Hart peeked. A Mercedes.

"No petrol," Kohl explained. "And a vehicle invites inspection. We'll bicycle. It's several hours into the city."

Hart nodded. "I didn't know you were so athletic, Otto."

"I'm not. Merely cautious. We're in the heart of Nazi Germany."

There were only occasional signs of the war at Berlin's edge. A bomber's burned-out husk had skidded to the edge of a school yard. Silvery strings of chaff dropped by Allied planes to confuse radar were draped on autumn trees like Christmas tinsel. A line of water-filled bomb craters marched across a field to record an Allied miss. As they pedaled into the suburbs they found a checkerboard of normalcy and destruction: here a street retained an aura of prewar order, there a stick of bombs had fallen to splinter four houses and a park. At Berlin's core the ruin became more complete. They passed whole neighborhoods that had been reduced to ridges of shattered masonry, blocks and streets undulating like a series of sand dunes. Rising above this manmade talus were the ghostly ruins of gutted buildings that had not yet completely collapsed, empty window openings lighting apartments that no longer existed.

Kohl wobbled his bicycle around a litter of broken glass and stopped to pant.

"Are you all right, Otto?"

"Not my tailbone. I may never walk again."

The pause made Hart nervous. Passing Germans barely glanced at them but half the men he saw were in uniform. A word from Kohl and he was betrayed. What reassured him was the devastation. Kohl wouldn't wish to stay here, and Owen Hart was his only exit.

"Is she nearby?"

"She was." Grimacing, he hoisted himself back onto the seat. "Pray that your airplanes haven't gotten to her neighborhood." They pedaled on.

Jürgen and Greta had been lucky. The town houses on their tree-lined avenue stood ranked and redoubtable with prewar confidence. A milk wagon trundled reassuringly down the pavement. Normalcy. Kohl pointed. "That one."

It was four stories, as fashionable as a New York brownstone.

Jürgen Drexler had done well, it seemed. Confronted by the man's intact home, Hart suddenly felt doubt. It was the kind of house he'd never had and perhaps never would have: strong, secure, stylish. The kind of home a woman would like.

"I can't visit her in his house."

"No, of course not," Kohl said. "That would be dangerous. They have servants and maybe even a security guard, who knows? Jürgen is a *Standartenführer* now, a colonel, in the civilian branch of the SS. He moves in the highest circles, which means his telephone is probably tapped. But I'll approach briefly. Any staff present should take only casual note even if I'm recognized: they may assume I escaped France and am on routine travels. I'll explain the situation and then leave to do some business, I have some money to assemble in Berlin before we go. Now, as for you. There's a statue of Frederick the Great opposite the Bebelplatz, not far from the Hotel Adlon where you once stayed. Do you remember it? About a mile east of here?"

Hart nodded uncertainly.

"Meet her there in an hour. Understood?"

"Yes, but what if she doesn't—"

Kohl held his hand up, looking back at the imposing town house. Hart noticed now that its windows were blank, covered with blackout coverings. It would be dim inside.

"She'll come."

CHAPTER TWENTY-THREE

King Frederick was another casualty of war. His tricornered hat had been chipped by shrapnel and one of his eyes had become an empty socket. Some of the buildings surrounding the Bebelplatz remained intact but others had folded in on themselves, debris spilling from their pulverized interiors like an avalanche chute. Hart arrived early and, too anxious to sit, paced around the plaza, stepping around fragments of masonry and keeping an eye on Frederick's mounted figure. Passing Germans ignored him, hurrying by on missions of their own. No one had checked his forged papers—the robotic bureaucracy of the Third Reich was beginning to corrode from the prospect of defeat—but his anxiety at meeting Greta had grown. Almost six years! She'd been twenty-eight and unmarried then. He braced himself for a betrayal of memory.

And yet betrayal didn't come. As she approached through the square he recognized her instantly: the walk, the plume of glorious red hair, even the upright bearing of her head when so many faces seemed cast downward. He sucked in his breath. She was as lovely as he remembered and much more stylishly dressed; her erect carriage reflected the assurance of high station. She strode past the ruins in a long wool coat trimmed in fur and in fashionable boots, her heels clicking on the paving stones. A string of pearls was at her neck. Drexler, Hart admitted, was a good provider.

Yet when she slowed and then stopped several feet short of him, looking without expression, Hart noticed something more: a new gravity in her face. A tautness from emotions held in check. Her gaze was so objective—so analytical—he feared for a moment that whatever hold he'd once had on her was gone, erased by time.

She blinked in wonder. "So. It *is* really you." Her tone revealed nothing.

"Hello, Greta," he said, swallowing. "I told you I'd come back."

Her eyes roamed his face, taking it in. "I thought you dead. And yet here you stand, in the middle of Berlin." She judged him clinically. "You've hardly changed."

"You're prettier, I think."

She gave no reaction to the compliment, looking at him as if he was a phantom. Her detachment disturbed him.

He swallowed and reached into his coat pocket. "I had this made in London in 1939. I've been waiting a long time to give it to you." He put out his hand. Draped on his fingers was a gold chain with a locket. "Please, take it."

After a moment's hesitation she did so. Their fingers touched and she gave a little jerk as if she'd been shocked. Then she held the jewelry, looking at it as if in a trance.

"Open it."

The locket was gold and shaped like a penguin. She clicked it open. There was a word engraved inside: *hope*. And a dull pebble.

"The pebble is from the cave. I found it in my boot. It's a gift. Like the penguins give."

She looked at the pebble for a long time as if she'd never seen a stone before. He waited, watching her sway slightly in a rush of memory. Then she began to tremble, lifting eyes that were mist-

ing with tears. She'd allowed herself, finally, to believe. Her
mouth opened. "Oh, Owen." Her voice caught. "It's really you . . ."
And then the space between them seemed to dissolve of its own
accord and he was holding her, clutching her through the rich
wool of her coat, his face buried in her hair and inhaling her wonderful scent.

"I thought you were *dead!*" she exclaimed. "I thought I'd killed
you, that I'd failed you . . ."

She wore perfume, he marveled. She dressed up, for me.

And then her cry was stifled as he kissed her, tasting the salt of
her tears—kissed her heedless of who was watching, kissed her
with the urgent longing of six missing years.

She kissed back with desperate need, aching, and then pushed
him away. "Owen, my God. Do you know how many times I've
dreamed of such a moment? But not here. Not now. Please."

He glanced around, grinning in triumph. An old woman with
a string bag scowled but a younger one smiled in passing, wistfully.

He held Greta by the shoulders, unwilling to let go. "I tried to
write," he explained, "tried to reach you, but nothing seemed to
get through . . ."

The tears were running freely down her cheeks. "I thought
you'd died!" she repeated. "All these years, not a word, not a
whisper! And yet here you are, come back to life, come back to
this earthly hell of Berlin." She was taking deep gulping breaths,
her breasts rising against his chest, her eyes still wide with wonder. "Come back to *me*." And then she threw back her head and
gave a shout of laughter, suddenly, shockingly, gaily. "And now,
at last, for just this one instant I am so *happy!* My whole life, and
all its pain, made worthwhile by this single moment!" She
smiled, her face glistening.

Hart tenderly stroked her wet cheek. "Whoa, whoa," he said
with a grin. "It's just a pebble. No wonder the male penguins find
it so effective."

She shook her head. "Such a different world, such an age ago.

Antarctica has seemed like a dream. And a nightmare. And yet here you are, resurrected. How? Why? My God, the questions . . ."

"Your organism *worked*, Greta. It worked on me, it even worked on Fritz, but then . . . We captured your father, and flew . . . It's a long story."

She nodded uncertainly, bewildered but excited. "It worked?"

"It cured Fritz. I know it did. Then he was killed in the cave. The entrance collapsed."

"My God." Her gaze turned serious, brooding. "We should have tested it more thoroughly. Have you heard that the Allies finally succeeded with penicillin? How many Germans could we have saved in this war?" She shook her head. "Always regret! So many regrets. Well." She looked at the locket she was still holding, deciding, and then looked at him shyly. "Will you put this on me?"

He glanced around with amusement. "Do you dare? Would it raise questions?"

She looked out at the ruined buildings, immensely sad for a moment. "Yes. Of course it would raise questions. But right now I want to feel its weight on my neck. I'll wear it inside my dress and take it off later."

He took the chain and locket and she turned, pulling her hair up to reveal the ivory of her neck. He fastened it. She fingered the penguin a moment, smiling shyly now, and then slipped it down the front of her dress. She shivered. "It makes my heart beat faster."

He smiled. "Greta, I've come to get you out. From Germany and the war."

She was sober. "That's impossible."

"No it isn't. I have a plane. Your father has money and papers."

"Owen, things have changed so much . . ."

"Otto told me about the marriage. He also said you still loved me. That's why I *came*, Greta."

Her head lowered. "It's a marriage in name more than practice," she admitted. "I thought I could change him, teach him

happiness. He thought he could win me, give me purpose. But
. . . too much had happened in Antarctica."

"So you don't love him?"

"I do . . . in a way." Her voice was very small. "He was there for
me, Owen, when you weren't. Just not in the same way."

He touched her cheek. "I've never stopped loving you, Greta.
Never for a moment. I thought I'd have to wait to search for you
after the war but then Otto appeared like a miracle and I came in
an instant. I've left my unit. I've thrown my old life away. And
now I want you to come away with me. You *know* Germany is finished. The Nazis have made a mess of the world. Your father and
I want to fly you to Switzerland. To a new life."

She shook her head, trembling. "Owen, it isn't that simple.
There are vows. Duty. Country."

"Greta, if you stay here with Jürgen you'll be killed. Berlin is
going to become a battlefield. We can have happiness if we have
the courage to grasp it."

She closed her eyes. "I married Jürgen, Owen. *Married* him. If
you'd come back with us, it might have been different, but you
didn't. Did you know he even went ashore in the rough seas at the
end of the storm to look for you? He said there was no sign—"

"My airplane was *there*, I was in the cave, there was a collapse . . ."

Greta shook her head. "I don't know about all that. It was a
painful subject for both of us. I didn't want to remember." She
glanced around. "My God, leave everything? My work, my home,
my husband—"

"For *happiness*, Greta. You owe yourself that."

She looked torn. "All this is so sudden, so . . . bewildering.
Papa appearing at my door, you back from the dead. I feel dazed."
She shivered, collecting herself, then looked at him with fierce
hope. "I *want* to start over, Owen. You must know that. I want to
start over far from Germany and far from Antarctica."

"As far as we can get."

She nodded. "But I don't want to hurt Jürgen. I accepted his
comfort. I must think about all this."

"Greta, you're all I've ever wanted. I couldn't bear to lose you again."

She sighed, torn. "When would we leave?"

"*Now*. We'll walk to your house for your things. Then we disappear before Jürgen even knows I'm alive." He put his hand out, fingered the chain of her locket.

"No," she said, shaking her head. "I must think." She held him away. "Think for *myself* instead of for the men in my life: you and Jürgen and Papa." She took a deep breath. "I'll give you my answer tomorrow, Owen. Here, at noon. I'll bring what I need to escape if I've decided to come with you. But you have to wait until then. Hide in the ruins and speak to no one."

"Greta, please! Life doesn't give many chances. We have to go now, before it's too late!"

She seemed to waver, then clenched her fists in resolve. "Are you going to meet my father?"

"Later." It was a groan.

"Tell him noon tomorrow." She put her finger to his lips. "Give me time, Owen. Time to listen to my head and to my heart."

CHAPTER TWENTY-FOUR

Greta wandered the city's battered streets alone for a while, trying to reassert control over her emotions. She didn't expect happiness anymore. Not after losing her first husband, and then Owen, and then in a different way Jürgen: a man who'd taken her back and then come to regard their soulless union as his own fitting self-punishment, refusing to give her up and taking some kind of perverse strength from the pain of their proximity. She'd traded happiness for the surface accomplishments of home and career, traded hope for resignation, and dully moved through a succession of days. She waited, she supposed, for a bomb to take her.

Now she'd been shocked back into life. Shocked back to longing, to desire, and, yes, to betrayal. The impact of seeing Owen again was enough for her to consider leaving her husband, her home, her country, and the dry possessions of an empty existence. She could almost taste the promised freedom.

Her finger traced the golden chain around her neck, the penguin locket warmed by the skin of her breast. Jürgen had given her gift after gift and become frustrated that his presents didn't help but rather hurt, seeming to add to her self-imposed burden of sin at having let Owen die. She'd hated herself for hating Jürgen's effort. Now everything was turned upside down, her husband again a victim of her romantic confusion. She dreaded going back to their home to face him, dreaded having to decide whether to betray him once again. But autumn dusk was falling on an increasingly dangerous city and her town house beckoned as the only sensible destination. At its steps, she unfastened the locket and slipped it into a pocket of her dress.

"Frau Drexler! It's late, we were worried. Are you all right?"

"Yes, Ingrid." Greta pulled off her coat and handed it to the maid, who slung it over her arm. "I had to walk and think and lost track of time. Is Jürgen home?"

"No, not yet." *Of course* not yet. As the war deepened Drexler's days had grown longer. He often missed dinner, pleading work. Greta suspected a mistress, or at least the periodic whore, and was secretly relieved at not feeling guilt over that aspect of their estrangement as well. While polite and companionable in public, they slept in separate bedrooms in the too-large, echoing town house, rattling about while tens of thousands remained homeless from the bombing. The house's size allowed them to avoid their marriage.

"I won't be requiring a formal dinner tonight, Ingrid. I'm feeling a bit under the weather, and will just take a bite in my room. Tell Herr Drexler I retired early."

"As you wish. Today's caller, he—"

"Disturbed me, Ingrid. A face from the past. Please don't mention the visitor to my husband."

"As you wish." She bit her lip.

Ingrid confided that instruction to Arnold, the cook, as she collected a light dinner. "I think the Führer would say a German wife doesn't keep secrets," she commented disapprovingly.

"I think the Führer would say the German servant does what she is told," he responded.

Greta distractedly paced her suite, struggling with her emotions. Why hadn't she just run away with Owen? Why come back here to torture herself? Because she *did* retain some feelings for

Jürgen, she told herself. For his loyalty, and for the pain of his disappointment when he realized she'd never love him as he loved her.

She sat on her bed and stared numbly at her open wardrobes. What would she take if she left? Practical clothes. Some money, but not all of it: she couldn't do that to Jürgen. Not much more than a shoulder bag to keep from arousing suspicion. The resulting narrow choice was daunting and yet it was odd how little the clothes meant to her now that she contemplated giving them up. They seemed like an anchor she could finally cut loose from. The problem was deciding to take *anything* of this past. She lay back on the bed, thinking of Owen, wishing she'd kissed him longer, wishing he were beside her now, wishing they'd never met and she didn't have this monstrous choice . . .

She awoke with a start. She'd fallen asleep. It was dark, the house quiet. Groggily she sat up and turned on a light. After midnight. There was a tray of untouched food that Ingrid had left on the night stand. Her bag and clothes were strewn next to her on the bed. She got up, went to the door, and opened it quietly. Downstairs was dark, the house filled with shadow. Everyone must be asleep. She closed the door again, restless, her mind churning. Perhaps she should draw a bath to relax.

She shed her clothes on the cold tile and waited impatiently for the tub to fill. Idly, she stooped to retrieve the locket from her dress pocket. The penguin would go in her shoulder bag until she and Owen were safely away. She opened the piece again and looked at the pebble, smiling to herself in remembrance: her fear of the cave, the frightening and strange lake, their lovemaking on the rough woolen blankets. Impulsively she closed the locket and slipped it on, looking at herself in the bathroom mirror. It hung just above her breasts as if nesting between two hills, its glow fueled by her own warmth. She studied herself critically, turning to look at her back, the swell of her hips. Would Owen still think her attractive? He'd told her she was pretty. She'd liked that. No one had told her that in a long time.

She went to the tub, shut off the taps, and carefully stepped in.

The water was hot, her feet tingling after the chill of the tile floor. She stood a moment in pleasure as steam rose to dew on her hair, the down of the soft delta between her thighs curling slightly. Then she lowered herself, gasping gratefully, and lay back, floating in the heat. She felt herself calm as the warmth crept inside her. She looked down. Her breasts floated like twin icebergs, the penguin swimming between them, and the image brought a smile. Meeting Owen already seemed like a dream except that here was tangible evidence, smooth and hard. For nearly six years he'd carried this jewelry! It was an amazing thought.

She soaped a sponge and squeezed. A glacier of suds slid down from her neck to melt into the Southern Ocean. Greta, the white continent! She let her knees break clear of the water. Atropos Island! Her lap was the volcanic caldera and the cave, well, she knew where that was . . . She felt herself there. It was as if her body was awakening from a long slumber. Faintly embarrassed, she pulled her fingers away.

Her mind had hibernated as well, she realized. Owen's reported death had destroyed her interest in Antarctica. She'd published no papers and written no reports from the voyage, which was veiled in official secrecy anyway. It was beginning to come back to her now: the whales, the krill, her microscope, the hideous petri dishes and their spawn . . .

She hugged herself. Think of *Owen*, she told herself. Think of his strong hands, his mouth on your throat.

The whales! The war had severely curtailed research of the natural world. Her university supervisors remained condescending and opportunities to collect new specimens had been shut off. It had become impossible even to keep up with developments in biology. And after the inevitable German defeat, what then? It would not be easy for the country's scientists. In America, however, science would explode. Could she reconstruct a career? The possibility intrigued her.

She was going to leave with Owen, she realized. The decision had been made. She was planning a future, something she hadn't done in a long time.

Then the lights went out.

Startled, she sat upright. It wasn't unusual to have the power fail during the raids. And yes, there it was, the mournful wail of an air raid siren prodding at the sleeping city in the night. Damn. She'd never been caught in the bath before, and it was disorienting. She stood, water streaming off her. Doors were slamming as Arnold and Ingrid and Jürgen hurried downstairs.

She was so tired of retreating to the cellar in the night. But then that was the point of the raids, wasn't it? To make Jerry tired.

She lifted one foot out of the tub, put her weight on it, and slipped, coming down with a crash. Water sloshed out with her, spilling across the floor. "Clumsy, Greta." She fumbled in the dark for towels. It felt comical to be mopping naked on her hands and knees in the dark. The siren droned on.

She stood finally, sore, and felt her way to the bathroom door. Her bedroom was just as dark. She groped toward the end table with her arms outstretched, scolding herself, planning to find the oil lamp and matches so she could have light to get dressed.

Then the door burst open.

"Greta!"

It was Jürgen. He was dressed in hastily pulled on trousers and a sleeveless undershirt, holding a lamp. Instinctively she used her hands to cover what she could of herself and they both froze a moment in surprise.

He hadn't seen her nude in years. He stared, his intended statement choked off.

"What are you doing here?" she managed. "You should be in the cellar."

"So should you." He closed the door behind him and stepped forward, emboldened by their words. "I was worried when you didn't come. I thought perhaps you hadn't awakened with the sirens." His voice was hoarse. His eyes roamed her.

She didn't like it. She turned and briskly lifted her bed's comforter, heedlessly spilling her bag and clothes on the floor. She pulled it around her, standing straighter. "This is my room. You never come to my room."

He set the lamp on a table, aroused now, irked at her covering. "*Our* room. We're married, remember?"

"*My* room. You know you keep to your own, that was *your* decision as much as mine. My goodness, you frightened me, storming in like that. The bombers caught me in the bath. I nearly broke a leg."

He was looking at her hungrily, sadly. She looked away. It made her uncomfortable. Guilty. "We'd better get to the cellar." She limped to a dresser and pulled out a nightgown. "Please don't watch." Surprisingly, he obeyed. She dropped the comforter and swiftly pulled the bedclothes over herself while his eyes cast impatiently about the room. They came to the heap by the bed. A look of doubt appeared. When she tried to move past him he caught her arm.

"Wait." He pointed to the clothes and bag. "What's that? Are you going somewhere?"

She looked at the heap as if surprised it was there. "I'm simply sorting clothes."

"In the middle of the night?"

"Jürgen, I fell asleep!" They could begin to hear the stuttering pop of antiaircraft guns. "Hurry, we must go." She pulled but his grip tightened.

"A bath too, in the middle of the night?"

"To help me get back to sleep! Stop holding me!"

He seized her then by both shoulders, yanking her close. "I'll hold you all I wish. I'm your husband, dammit!"

"Jürgen!" She twisted in his grasp. She couldn't stand this intimacy, not now, not this night. "If you don't let us get down to the cellar we're both going to be killed!"

He bent then to kiss her, roughly, angrily, and she turned her face away. "Stop it!" Pulling one arm free, she slapped him, the impact stinging her palm. "Get control of yourself!"

For a fraction of a second he looked shocked. Then he instinctively shoved. She went flying backward, slamming down on her bed with a whoof.

They glared at each other, panting. Somewhere they heard the dull concussion of falling bombs. Finally he nodded, sneering. "Fine. Find your own way to the cellar. Live alone, frigid. Like an ice queen." He picked up the lamp and moved toward the door, stopping to contemplate her. "You know, I've given you everything, Greta. In return for nothing."

"No," she said without thinking. "I lost everything."

"Bitch." He seized the handle to go out. Then he stopped, hesitated and swung about again. "What did you say?"

She was silent.

"What do you mean you lost everything? When? What are you referring to?"

"Jürgen, just go."

He was suspicious now. He raised the lamp, peering at her. "What's that?"

Her heart began to accelerate. "What's what?"

"That thing. On your neck." He walked into the room again, striding toward the bed.

Instinctively her hand went up to her throat. She'd forgotten she was still wearing the locket. "Just some jewelry." She grasped it in protection. "Leave it alone."

His hand fastened over hers, the powerful fingers prying hers open. Then he grabbed the locket and yanked, the chain snapping. He held it up. The golden penguin swung rhythmically in the dim light.

She stared at it dumbly.

"A penguin." He said this flatly, considering. "Shades of Antarctica. An odd choice, given our history. I don't recall giving you this."

She was flushed, her skin prickling. She hoped he couldn't notice in the lamplight. "I found it myself. In a shop two Christmases ago, when we went to Bavaria."

"Really?" He snapped it open. "*Hope*," he read. "Now there's an appropriate sentiment for this stage of the war." He turned the locket over and the small pebble fell into his palm. "And a piece of grit left inside! Sloppy, no?" He tossed it onto the carpet where it was lost in the dark, watching the frantic flicker of her eyes. "Yet I don't remember this piece. And I remember everything."

The thud of bombs was growing in volume. She closed her eyes. "Jürgen, please, let's go to the cellar where it's safe."

"This wouldn't have caught my attention except for the visitor you had today. Some mysterious older man. And then you put on your outdoor coat and disappear in a hurry, not returning until dark. Why was that, Greta?"

"I think you're mistaken."

"Not according to Ingrid." He smiled thinly. "Ingrid, who knows better than to keep secrets from me."

"Ingrid is a silly gossip who exaggerates."

He laughed. "I think it's called telling the truth, my dear."

"If she is talking behind my back I want her fired!"

"When you have no power, Greta, everyone betrays you. Everyone." He dangled the penguin in front of her face. "A mysterious visitor, a new bauble, the disorder of packing. My darling wife, what *is* going on?"

Another bomb, closer this time. The window rattled.

"How dare you pry into my private business!"

"How dare you keep things from me." He swung the penguin again from his fingers, studying her carefully. She watched as if hypnotized, thinking desperately. She dared not betray Owen.

"It . . . it's from my father," she finally stammered. "He came today. A quick visit as he passes through." Ingrid, she knew, might have passed on a description that Jürgen would recognize as fitting Kohl.

"Ah." He flipped the piece up and bunched it in his fist, then looked hard at her. "Otto in Berlin? How surprising. I thought he'd disappeared in France."

"He just showed up. I was startled. He gave the locket to me. He said he got it in . . . Paris. That it reminded him of me, of the expedition. He's worried about the bombing and invited me to

. . . to accompany him on a trip. A business trip. I was going to ask you about it at breakfast."

Drexler's face was impassive. "I see."

"There's no secret, Jürgen . . ."

"Ingrid thought there was."

"You know how she jumps to conclusions—"

"Silence!" He probed. "And were you going to come back from this trip?"

She looked at him then a long time, summoning her courage. This was the point of no return, wasn't it? This was the time to finally tell the truth, to him and to herself. "No. I'm leaving you, Jürgen." She tried to keep her voice steady, but it caught. He still thinks Owen is dead, she reminded herself.

"So." His face betrayed the hollowness that Antarctica had left in their relationship. "You're leaving me. Here, now, at a time when Germany is in such crisis."

"I don't love you anymore." Her voice was a whisper but she realized suddenly that the statement was true. "I never learned to love you as a wife should and I want to get out from under the threat of the bombs. There's nothing in our marriage to hold me here. Papa knows that. He's known for a long time."

Drexler looked as if he was in physical pain. "When? When will you leave?"

"Tomorrow, I think."

"My God. How long have you been planning this?"

"I haven't planned it. It . . . just . . . happened. I'm sorry, Jürgen. You should leave Berlin too. But not with me."

"I can't abandon the Reich." His tone was still stunned. "I'll never abandon the Reich. You know that."

She nodded. "I know. And I won't sacrifice my life for it. Not anymore. I want my life *back*, Jürgen. I want *me* back. We each thought we could change the other and we failed."

His eyes roamed the room as if looking for a clue. "But I still love you." It was plaintive. There was another boom and the window rattled nervously. The bombs were getting closer.

"I'm sorry, Jürgen. Please, let's go to the cellar. If that window shatters we could be hurt."

He nodded but didn't move. "Is this why Otto sneaked back? To get you?"

She shrugged.

He was thinking aloud. "Yet why would a coward like Otto Kohl risk coming back to Berlin? To fetch a daughter he's ignored his whole life? Somehow I doubt it. To fetch some ill-gotten money? His war profiteering? That, I could understand."

"Jürgen, the bombs . . ." There was another explosion, nearer, and the window rattled again.

"And how did he get here?"

"Jürgen, I don't know. Please . . ."

"And he buys you jewelry . . . ?" He looked at the penguin, puzzled. Then he slipped it in his pocket. "Well. Would you have informed me at all if we hadn't had this little confrontation? I doubt it. Left even a note? Probably not."

She cast her eyes downward.

"I might have followed, you know."

"Jürgen, please. This is hard. I don't want to hurt you. Just let me go."

"Ah, of course. Just say goodbye to six years of marriage. Poof! Well. It's charming, this little reunion of yours with Papa, but I feel left out—as I'm sure you can see. Otto Kohl magically materializes? Very odd. I think I want Otto to come for dinner tomorrow night. My curiosity has been aroused. We'll discuss the future then, yes?"

Greta swallowed and nodded. She'd be gone by then.

"And you'll let me go?"

Another bomb went off, and he stood. "I've never wanted a woman who doesn't want me." His voice was strained as he said it. "Hurry then! Let's go to the cellar."

The next morning there was a stranger in Greta's kitchen. He wore a black SS uniform and was reading the newspaper as if he owned the place. His chair was positioned near the rear door.

"Who's this?" Greta demanded.

The security policeman gave no answer. Ingrid, making an elaborate show of polishing the teapot, glanced at the man as if noticing him for the first time. "Your husband invited him here for your security," she said. She avoided Greta's eye.

"I need no special security."

"Herr Drexler said you do." Now the maid looked at her smugly, as if this had been just what she expected. Greta could have strangled her.

"Oh really? And where is Herr Drexler?"

"He's gone out."

"Then I'm going out too." She marched to the front foyer to fetch her coat. There was a second SS man there, his chair by the door. He watched her impassively as she put the coat on, saying nothing. When she moved toward the door he stood politely, braced.

"I'm sorry, Frau Drexler. Your husband has deemed it unsafe to go outside today. We've been asked to ensure your protection in this house."

"Nonsense. I have an appointment. Get out of the way."

"I'm sorry, Frau Drexler."

She hesitated. "Am I a prisoner in my own home?"

"I'm sorry, Frau Drexler. May I take your coat?"

She stood in the foyer, frightened and furious. The night had been dreadful and she was tired. Jürgen had said nothing more during the air raid but appeared to be brooding. Instead of going to his bed after the bombing he'd gone to his study and began working the telephone, searching for intact lines. She'd been furious with him for keeping her locket but feared that an argument over the jewelry might betray Owen. So she'd gone to her own room but couldn't sleep, worrying how much he'd guessed. Their own telephone had rung early in the morning and Jürgen answered immediately. Now he was gone.

If she missed the noon rendezvous, Papa and Owen might dare come here . . .

Did Jürgen really think her so hapless?

She surrendered her coat to the sentry. "Well. In that case." Greta retreated to the dining room and ate breakfast alone. What did Jürgen know? What would Jürgen do? She went to the study to check the cache of Reichsmarks and gold coin they'd stored for an emergency. It was gone, of course.

She had to act before he did.

"If I am to be a *prisoner* in my own house," she announced loudly in the kitchen, "then I'm going to take a nap. I barely slept last night." Ingrid and Arnold avoided her defiant gaze. They knew something was seriously wrong. "You two," she said, pointing at them, "had better dust and polish thoroughly for once. My father is coming tonight." Arnold shot Ingrid a sour look. "I'll check on your progress at noon."

She packed hurriedly, her mind set and her indecision gone. Underwear, a pair of trousers, a sweater. She wore a wool dress and the boots from yesterday, plus her strand of pearls. Maybe they could be hocked if the couple needed money. She found the pebble on her bedroom carpet, wrapped it in a fragment of ribbon, and slipped it inside her bra. "Hope," she whispered to herself, touching the bump.

She glanced about her room but felt no nostalgia. It had been a cell long before this morning. Shouldering her bag, she slipped out of the bedroom and locked the door behind her. Then she climbed to the fourth-floor servants' quarters and went to the attic hatchway, reaching up to pull. A ladder descended. "Goodbye, Jürgen," she whispered. She climbed and closed the hatchway behind her.

The attic was dark, illuminated only by the small portholes of round dormer windows on the slanting slate roof. Unlike the rest of the house they weren't covered with blackout coverings because there were no electric lights. The floorboards were thick with dust and littered by mouse droppings. She'd seen workmen use the attic to reach the roof for repairs.

She went to the small dormer windows. The front one appeared to be painted shut but the rear had a latch, she saw. She moved the lock open and pushed. The window didn't budge. She shoved

harder. Did she need some kind of a tool? She felt foolish in her
ignorance; what if she'd had to escape this way someday because
of a fire? She considered, then put her shoulder bag to her shoulder and ran against the window. It popped open with a bang.

She waited a moment. No sound from below.

She looked out. The overcast was breaking up, the air cold. The
slate roofing tiles looked steep and slick. She was on the rear side
of the town house and beyond the lead gutter was a dizzying drop
of three and a half stories to the small garden below. Pulling herself out a bit, she looked up. The peak of the roof was about a
body's length away and led to the flatter roof of the Haupsteds'
next door.

She could hear the faint sound of the telephone shrilling. What
if it was for her?

There really was no alternative.

Using her arms she boosted herself out through the window
and balanced awkwardly on the sill, facing the roof. Leaning
against the slate without looking down, she stepped precariously
up onto the top of the small dormer roof. Slowly she stretched upright, her hands sliding up the tiles of the main roof, the pebble
between her breast and the slippery slate. Not quite far enough.
She pushed up on the balls of her feet, feeling her toes begin to
slip as she stretched frantically. Finally her fingers closed over the
ridge. Yes! She pulled, scrabbling with her knees, and got her
torso and then a leg over the ridge. Then she was straddling the
roof, breathing hard.

She looked down at the street. The tree branches were a lacy
net. A municipal worker was sawing one off, his obscuring hat
like a saucer. He would black market the wood as fuel, she suspected.

She hiked herself along the roof peak until she reached the
Haupsteds', where she could shakily walk on the flat crown of
their mansard roof. There were four roofs to the corner, two
ridged like her own. One by one she mastered them, moving as
quickly as she could, remembering her climbing in the cave. At
the end of her block was an iron ladder leading to a balcony

below. She waited until the residential street was empty of traffic, climbed down, and then dropped from the balcony, hitting the street cobbles and slightly twisting an ankle. She glanced about. No one seemed to be peering through the curtains of the surrounding houses. At the corner she looked again. There was only the wood thief on her own street. She would have confronted him if she had time. Instead, she took a deep breath. Freedom! Limping slightly, she headed for the Frederick statue. Just once did she look back at her home.

She smiled at the thought of the SS sentries sitting arrogantly in her entry.

As she walked away the tree trimmer straightened to watch her disappearing form, then dropped his saw, climbed down, and ran lightly up to her front door, giving a quick knock. It swung open and an SS sentry looked out.

"You can tell Colonel Drexler she's on her way," he said. "Gunther will pick up the tail on the avenue."

The man nodded. "He's already arrested his father-in-law and found an airplane with American markings. Amazing what one learns about one's relatives, no? Kohl is beginning to talk."

The SS agent threw off his hat and began peeling the coat and baggy pants that concealed his uniform. "Foolish woman."

"She doesn't appreciate how lucky she is, married to a powerful *Standartenführer*."

"Yes. And if she's married to Colonel Drexler, she should know there's no escape from the Reich."

CHAPTER TWENTY-FIVE

Greta arrived at the statue first and hunched on a bench in the Bebelplatz. She was wary of the people passing by but no one seemed to take notice of her. She glanced over the damaged buildings at a sky that seemed to promise escape. Smoke was hanging on the horizon from the previous night's raid but pale sunlight shone above it. An autumn sun, low, like Antarctica's. It was quiet in late morning. Birds had disappeared from Berlin's plazas as completely as cars and trolleys had left its streets. They'd flown away as she planned to do. For a moment she smiled, remembering the world as it had been. Still, it was difficult to relax. A policeman strutted aimlessly near some chipped steps. "Hurry, hurry," she whispered.

And then Owen came as promised, striding across the plaza with an open, swinging gate that advertised him as an American to anyone with reason to suspect. The walk was reckless; she would have to teach him circumspection. Yet it made her chest ache with fondness to see that easy freedom. It was the manner of the place they were going to, she hoped. He looked grimy and unshaven but triumphant at seeing her again, knowing that her bag announced her decision. So she jumped up and hurried to him, her cheeks flush from the cold. They kissed quickly, Greta instinctively glancing around.

Hart laughed at her. "The German glance, Fritz called that."

"If you lived here, Owen, you too would learn to look over your shoulder. It's a good habit to get into." She hesitated, embarrassed. "Besides, there's danger. I told Jürgen I was leaving with my father. He sent soldiers to keep me at home and I had to escape across the rooftops."

"Jesus Christ. Were you followed?"

"I don't think so. But one can never be sure."

Hart looked worriedly around the plaza. "You're right. I'm learning the German glance." Then a thought grabbed him. "Where's Otto? He met me last night and promised to be here. Do you think Jürgen has had him picked up?"

"Anything is possible," she said, frowning. "What if he doesn't appear?"

"Then we'll have to fly without him."

Her eyes scanned the people passing to and fro, looking for some glimpse of Kohl. "I wouldn't like to leave my father in this city. Not with the enemy approaching. Not with my husband."

"Does Jürgen know about Otto's farm?"

"I don't know. We've never visited. I think we should go to the plane."

Hart considered. "I trust your instincts . . ."

The thought was cut short by a rising, mournful wail. The people around them stopped in mid-step and squinted at the sky, then broke into a hurried trot. Another air raid.

"Damn," Hart said. "Bombing weather."

They could see nothing yet. The American bombers flew so high.

"We'd better go to a shelter, Owen. It doesn't make sense to risk the raid. Maybe my father will find us down in the U-Bahn."

Hart shook his head with amazement. "Now I'll be able to say I was bombed by both sides."

A Friedrichstrasse subway station was nearby. They joined a

stream of people clattering down the steps and complaining in a babel of languages swept up from across the Nazi empire. The city was full of slave laborers, mistresses, collaborators, and opportunists: Slavs in padded jackets, blond Danes, smartly dressed French women, dark and thin Italians who looked cold and miserable in their doomed embrace with Germany. Despite the variety everyone looked gray and tired. The station was gloomily lit and crowded, smelling of sweat and fear. The sirens went on and on.

Hart pulled Greta into a corner of the waiting platform and they sat on the concrete, hugging each other. "How long do these last?"

She shrugged. "An hour. Sometimes more. You get past caring. Time loses its meaning."

"I wish your father would come."

He held her in silence for a while, stroking her hair. Her eyes shut and she leaned into him. They began to hear the distant bang of antiaircraft guns and then the heavy tread of bombs. The lights in the tunnel began blinking. A few people moaned and a baby began to cry. Its mother's anxious lullaby echoed in the enclosure. The baby cried harder.

The bombs came closer, a giant walking, and the shelter quaked. Dust filtered down from the ceiling. A light popped, casting the enclosure into half gloom.

She opened her eyes and looked at him. They were shining. "In nearly six years I've never been so happy," she whispered. A bomb hit close and a few women screamed. Greta reached up to touch his face and then kissed him again, long and deep this time. It was a kiss with hunger in it. He kissed her back with urgency and wished irritably that they were already alone.

Then she curled into him, nesting. "I've been lonely, Owen. Empty. Somehow my husband never became my friend."

He hugged her closer. "Was he cruel?"

She sighed. "No. He struck me once at the beginning, when he was frustrated, and then stopped in embarrassment. Later he treated me like a piece of china. We could never achieve the right tone with each other and that was partly my fault, I think: in my sorrow after Antarctica I let him be the solution to my future without caring what kind of future it was. He knew he'd won me, or captured as much of me as he ever could. And decided, apparently, that that was enough."

"For God's sake, why did he marry you?"

"I don't know." She closed her eyes. "He desired me. He hoped I could give him what he needed, even though neither of us ever understood what that was. And he simply can't stand to lose. There's something wrong with him, some fundamental insecurity. Once I agreed to marry him he seemed strangely satiated: as if marriage for him was not the beginning but the end. The relationship itself was inconsequential."

"Jesus."

They were silent for a while. "Did you ask for a divorce?"

"I asked if he wanted one. He told me fate had brought us together and that the future would reveal our purpose for Germany. It's insane! Always for Germany!"

"So what did you do all day?"

"I continued marine research but it was increasingly difficult. Biology was engulfed by the war and my colleagues made me uncomfortable: the Reich wants its women at home. So I made a domestic effort as well: socialized with the other empty wives, read, thought of you. I waited for life to play itself out."

Hart looked pained. "I'm sorry I didn't get back. The storm came, we sought shelter in the cave, and then part of it collapsed. Something triggered an earthquake. Fritz died, and by the time I got out the island was empty. The *Schwabenland* was gone and we couldn't find it. Even the *Bergen* was gone."

"Jürgen blew it up."

"What? Why?"

"To pretend Germans got to the island first. To rewrite history." She thought for a moment. "We could hear the roar of the explosion even outside the crater. Could it have been powerful enough to have caused your cave-in?"

He looked surprised. "I'd never guessed that. Maybe that explains it." He shook his head. "Fritz told me to come back to you, you know. He told me not to give up."

She swallowed. "It's so strange how our lives have intersected. Sometimes I wonder why God brought the three of us together. So much pain, so much lost time . . . And I'm not surprised you didn't find the *Schwabenland*. Did you know that we went east before we went north?"

"Still exploring, despite that hull patch?"

"Because of it. Captain Heiden said he wanted a following sea while he improved his repair. After a day we turned north. The leak was so well under control by then that we didn't stop until we got back to Germany."

"Do you think Jürgen . . . ?"

"Went that way to avoid you? I don't know. Subconsciously, perhaps. By that time I think we were all acting more than thinking, and reacting more than acting."

"God, what a mess." He was quiet for a while, remembering events in his mind. "Will you miss him?"

She leaned back against the tile wall of the station platform. "I'll think about him. I can't help that. And while it will be a relief to escape his fervor, I can't help but respect his commitment. So few people have that."

"Look at the horror outside. He's committed to the wrong things."

She closed her eyes. "I know that. But he was also committed to me."

"I'm sorry."

"Don't be sorry for what none of us could avoid."

He kissed her then, aching to be alone with her, imagining her enveloping him. The bombs marched this way and that, rattling their shelter.

Then he became dimly aware that there was a commotion in the crowd, that people were complaining. He straightened to glance around. A group of men were trying to walk across the densely packed platform, stepping or stumbling on huddled bodies to cries of pain and anger. "Sit down, sit down!" some of the shelter dwellers yelled.

One of the trench-coated figures flashed some identification and the complainers grew quiet. The intruders' eyes were sweeping the crowd like radar. Then one pointed at the couple. The finger was accusatory.

"Police," Hart said quietly, standing up. "Gestapo, maybe." He glanced around the station. "The bombing could actually give us cover to get away if we can reach the surface. Do you want to risk it?"

"Of course. I'm not going to be trapped down here."

He grabbed her hand and they started for the southern U-Bahn entrance, away from the one used by the approaching police. It was like wading in deep water. Someone grabbed Greta's leg by the ankle and she turned and stomped on the man's hand, setting off a howl of pain. Then they lurched ahead again.

Hart looked back over his shoulder. "I think we can beat them."

They were nearing the exit when there was a clatter on the tile stairway and a flurry of black boots came into view, descending the south entrance like pumping pistons. An SS detachment was cutting them off. There was a civilian in their midst.

"Damn," Hart said. "It's your father."

Kohl looked pale. As the soldiers reached the platform he was pushed toward the couple, his face bruised and his suit jacket torn. An SS man pointed and Otto nodded miserably. "I'm sorry, Greta."

Hart swung around. The police were still coming from the other direction, the crowd parting from the authorities like a biblical sea. Greta pulled at Owen. "The tunnel! The trains are dead with the electricity cut. If we can reach the tracks we can run to the next station."

The Germans were fanning out to block them. Pistols were being drawn and someone began screaming. The squeeze of the crowd was like being mired in quicksand.

Then Otto whirled, turning in a circle like a dervish with one hand thrown out. Paper spouted from his fingertips and the crowd erupted into frenzy.

It was money! Some of the Reichsmarks that Kohl had collected! "Run!" the German shouted. The SS leader savagely struck Greta's father across the face and he went down in the tumult. "Run!"

The couple bulldozed toward the edge of the platform. The air was filled with fluttering bills, confused oaths, and people springing to catch the notes. The police were shoved this way and that like boats in a storm, their leader howling in frustration.

The platform ended at a brink of darkness that hid even the tracks.

"Always with you it is some cave," Greta said wryly.

"Only because I enjoyed the last one."

"Halt!" There was a bang and something hot and angry buzzed near their heads, whining off tile on the far side of the tunnel. They crouched.

"Do you have a gun?"

"Yes." He glanced backward. "In France."

She gripped his hand and launched them into the blackness. When they sprawled on the cinders something squealed and Greta lurched up and kicked out. A tunnel rat scuttled away. A German mark fluttered down past them.

There was another shot and again a bullet bounced off the tunnel.

"Greta, come on!"

"Wait." She stooped, picked up a handful of rock cinders, cocked her arm, and threw. The aim was imperfect but the effect was like hitting a wasp's nest. Several people yelped and a fight broke out. The platform crowd became even more agitated with shoving people. The police were stuck in greed and anger as if gripped in tar.

"You throw like a girl," Hart judged. "Perfectly."

They began trotting past the stunned faces of Berliners peering down at them, uncertain what to make of the excitement. The rumble of bombs overhead added to the confusion; none of the shouts could be clearly heard above the background thunder. Then they were in the tunnel and it was black. She kicked out again.

"Are you all right?"

"Except for the damned rats. They've gotten fat and bold with the war. Don't stop." She pulled at his hand, her palm slick.

The air was dusty. In the lulls between explosions they heard hurrying boot steps and the confused shouts of their pursuers. Jutting his arm out blindly like a football player to avoid a collision with an unexpected wall, Hart broke into a trot, Greta following.

Suddenly there was a series of pistol shots and the pair fell flat for a moment. A riot of bullets pinged around them.

"Stop it, you fool!" someone yelled, the sound echoing. "You'll hit the police coming from the other end!"

"Are you hit?" Hart asked anxiously.

"No, but I'm scared."

"Me too."

They got up again and staggered on. The pilot looked for an emergency exit but could see nothing. Slowly he noticed light glowing from the next station ahead and saw blocking figures on the track, silhouetted against the illumination. "Damn." The pair of fugitives were still hidden by the dark but appeared to be trapped. Hart let go of Greta's hand for a moment to grope in the gloom. "We've got to find another way out," he said desperately, feeling along the ribs of the wall. "A door, a ladder."

As if in response there was a roar and the tunnel air cuffed them, knocking them down. Hart managed to roll on top of Greta as a blast of heat pulsed by, followed by a spray of rocks and dirt. Smoke choked the air and yet the blackness had given way to a brighter light. The pilot blinked. An American bomb had hit a weak point and punched into the tunnel where it joined the next station, replacing the waiting police with an avalanche slope of new rubble. The escarpment led upward toward a smoky sky.

"Come on!" Greta grunted, shoving Owen off herself and getting to her knees. "We can get out that way!" They both were shrouded in dust, her fine coat torn, her strand of pearls spilled like tears along the tracks. A trickle of blood ran down his forehead.

"God, I love you," he breathed.

"I love you too."

They began clambering up the collapsed tunnel ceiling toward the light, her hand in his. The noise of the air raid was much louder with the ceiling gone, an arrhythmic pounding that seemed to reverberate in their bones. As they emerged he saw the sky far above was freckled with black puffs of flak. There was an unnerving rattle as spent bits of metal from antiaircraft fire rained down on the city like hail.

They clambered out, the crater separating them from the shelter they'd nearly been trapped in. They just needed to run the other way. An apartment building adjacent to the gaping bomb crater had caught fire, its smoke serving as a screen.

"My ankle," Greta gasped. She was limping. Hart draped one arm across her shoulder and they began staggering, passing by two bodies sprawled on the cobblestones. He soon decided she was too slow and scooped her up in his arms to begin a stumbling run. He could see little and was terrified that all he was going to accomplish by coming to Berlin was getting Greta killed. Was the frequency of explosions lessening? He emerged from the smoke . . .

And slowed, then came to a stop. "Hell." Striding from the entrance of the next station was Jürgen Drexler, holding a pistol. Greta saw him and then clutched Owen's neck and buried her face in his chest.

Hart turned to go back the other way but SS men were emerging from the crater, smoke blowing through their blond hair. They had guns too.

It was over.

Drexler stopped a dozen feet away and lowered his automatic a moment, staring at Hart in amazement. "You're *alive* . . ." He blinked twice, as if not believing his senses. "But how?" A moment passed, then: "Ah, now I'm beginning to understand at least part of this."

Hart gently put Greta down. He didn't want her to get hurt.

"Jürgen, *please*," she entreated, still leaning on Owen. "Just let us go."

"You lied to me, Greta. You lied about the locket. You lied about running away."

"You told me Owen was dead," she countered. "Said his plane was missing."

"I truly thought he didn't make it, and was quietly glad. But it appears the joke is on me. How long have you known he was alive?"

"A day."

"And that quickly you decide to leave me?"

She looked at him unhappily. "I never had you, Jürgen. That's been the problem. You never let *anyone* have you. You never let anyone get inside . . . your spore coat."

He started at her choice of words and examined Hart more curiously then. "You knew what I was like," he objected, obviously thinking about more than that. Clearly, the wheels were turning. He looked Hart up and down. "How did you survive the disease?"

"The antibiotic worked," Owen said, shrugging. "Greta was right. You should have had more faith, Jürgen. You might have saved all of us a lot of pain."

Jürgen nodded thoughtfully. That calculation again. "Perhaps I can learn from my mistakes." He looked at Greta. "That slime was effective then?"

"Evidently," Greta said, impatient with the discussion. What did any of that matter now?

"And this organism. Could it have been reproduced? Manufactured?"

Greta seemed puzzled by his intensity. "We'll never know."

Hart glanced about. The bombing had stopped and the sirens were sounding an all-clear. Emergency workers were spraying water into the burning apartment building and Berliners were emerging from the underground stations. "Look at this mess,

Jürgen," he said. "Berlin is a charnel house. Why don't you just put that pistol down and come with us? I'll fly you out too. It's time for everyone to start over."

Drexler looked at him with amazement. "Fly away with the adulterers?"

"We're not adulterers!" Greta protested. "We just—"

"Shut up!" Drexler roared. "Shut up, shut up, shut up!"

Greta looked like she had been slapped.

"Do you think I'm an *idiot?*" he hissed, struggling to control the volume of his voice so his men could not hear. "Do you think I don't know your dreams have been filled with this ghost come back to life? And now I'm to go *with* you? Abandon my country and my career, shake hands and let this man steal my *wife?*" He shook his head. "Listen to me, Greta. You've betrayed me. *Betrayed* me. If not physically then mentally: many, many times. As a result, the days of my being the proper husband are over. Over! Understand? From this moment we have a new relationship, a relationship defined by the needs of the state. Both of you are in my power now. The Reich's power. Your only chance—your *only* chance—is to obey every command I give you."

There was a momentary silence while Hart shot Greta a look. It said: *stay calm.*

Drexler drew a few steps closer to the couple. "So . . . now that we understand each other, I have a question for you, Hart."

"Only one?"

"If you were *well,*" the SS colonel said, scowling, "why didn't you fly back to the *Schwabenland?* Why didn't you come off the island?"

"I was trapped in the damn cave. By a cave-in probably caused by your erasure of the *Bergen*. By the time I got out, you'd left. I flew, and stumbled on the Norwegians."

Drexler looked at him with genuine surprise. "You were in the *cave* when that avalanche occurred?"

"And so was Fritz. He died. And if you triggered the collapse, then you killed him."

"That's absurd. I had no idea anyone was in the cave to begin with. You can't blame that on me. And what the devil were you doing there?"

"Getting out of the storm."

"My God." Drexler shook his head. "The ironies of history. And now the cave is sealed, cutting off the source of the wonder drug. Pity." Suddenly his eyes narrowed. "But there's a problem with your story, Hart. You're here, *after* the avalanche. How did you get out of the cave?"

The pilot started to answer and then stopped. Now it was his turn to calculate. "Indeed. How *did* I get out, Jürgen?"

Drexler studied the pair speculatively. More police were arriving. With them was a bleeding and wincing Otto Kohl. His complexion was gray.

"Ah, the man who betrayed his daughter," Drexler greeted. His gaze swung to the agents. "We're discussing a matter of state security," he addressed them. "Leave him here a moment. I'll be with you shortly." Reluctantly, the men backed away.

Kohl looked at the ground. "I'm sorry, Greta. They made me tell them where you'd be." His voice was subdued. "They went to the farm and found the plane."

"It's all right, Papa." A tear ran down her cheek. "Jürgen learned that you were in Berlin from me. You did your best in the shelter."

"Throwing away money." A wry grin. "That was hard, for me."

"How touching," Drexler interrupted. "Otto, we were just discussing the fate of your family. The question, it seems, is whether I should put all of you up against that wall, hand you over to the Gestapo, or find a use for you."

"You'll do what you wish. We all know that."

"Exactly. That's why you've always been useful, Otto. You're a man who grasps reality."

"And the reality is that the war is lost. Everyone knows that. So take me if you must but let those two go. Let someone salvage something."

"That's where you're wrong, Otto. Victory can still be ours, I'm beginning to think. *If* you help."

He looked suspicious. "What do you mean?"

"You remain, I believe, a close personal associate of *Reichsmarschall* Göring, isn't that correct?" The title reflected Göring's military promotion.

"Our formal relationship has been in abeyance . . ."

"And your informal one?"

Kohl bit his lip.

"Don't think I'm unaware my father-in-law was a key facilitator in Göring's shopping expeditions in Occupied France. Two patriots, united by greed. And because of that, Otto, you may still be of some use to me. Because I need your help to see the *Reichsmarschall* again. Now. An emergency. He'll listen to you?"

"Possibly."

"You can get me to him?"

"I don't know. You remember he was less than satisfied with our expedition. But that was a long time ago. Why should he see you now?"

"Because the expedition he was disappointed in may turn out to have held promise after all. Promise at a critical juncture of the war."

Kohl looked skeptical. "And what do I get for this help?"

"Your life."

He barked a bitter laugh. "My life? Here? To do what, learn Russian?"

Drexler gave a thin smile. "And an exit. You can leave as you wished."

"With my savings, of course."

"No, that part is gone. Your property is now the property of the state."

"What! That money is mine! I'm an honest German businessman—"

"Nonsense!"

"That's my life's work, Jürgen. My life's work! I'm not going to surrender that now. I'd rather be shot."

"You may not have the luxury of being shot!"

"You may not have the luxury of getting to Hermann Göring."

They stared at each other, Drexler heated, Kohl implacable.

Finally Jürgen grimaced. "All right. You can have back what we seized. *If* everyone cooperates. Including your daughter."

"Cooperates with what?"

"That's what we're going to talk to Göring about." He raised his voice to speak to the nearby soldiers. "Johann! A holding cell for each of these!" He pointed to Owen and Greta. "And Abel!" The man came over quietly and Drexler bent to whisper to him. "Get me in touch with Maximilian Schmidt."

Hart looked at him curiously. "What are you up to now, Jürgen?"

"Why, Owen! Didn't I tell you once that from crisis comes opportunity?"

CHAPTER TWENTY-SIX

Karinhall seemed to have crawled under a blanket, hiding from the sky. Its gingerbread rooftops were tented by camouflage netting, the disguise supported by stripped firs and a spiderweb of cables like the rigging of a circus tent. Hermann Göring's aerial armada had been dissipated in a thousand far-flung battles and now the onetime lord of the air had to pretend his castle had sunk into the ground, lest Allied warplanes find it. The lawns around the great house had been torn up by the treads of military vehicles and its trees shaded a protective camp. Antiaircraft guns nested in sandbag emplacements, barrels jutting upward. With this humiliation had come the evaporation of much of the *Reichsmarschall*'s influence in Nazi Germany. Hitler's designated successor was only rarely summoned to councils of war.

As Germany's fortunes worsened, Göring's mind had escaped to a habit of mindless acquisition as distracting as drugs. Accordingly, it wasn't that difficult for one of his mercantile agents, Otto Kohl, to get through to the *Reichsmarschall* once again. Otto, back from oblivion! The reminder of heady plundering in France! And so the German facilitator once more came to the estate at dusk, Karinhall's lights hidden now behind blackout paper. Drexler and Schmidt shared the rear of the staff car attired in full-dress SS uniforms. Kohl was in a business suit retrieved from his farm outside Berlin, his forehead still bandaged from the scuffle in the air raid shelter. The promise of his eventual escape from Germany was shadowed by fear that Drexler would somehow betray him once they saw Göring. He was trying desperately to guess Jürgen's game, displaying a bluff heartiness he didn't feel.

"So here we are again!" Kohl exclaimed as the staff car grated to a stop in the gravel outside the entrance, the door flanked this time by sandbagged sentry posts with machine guns. "It brings back memories of a happier time."

Drexler looked out at the huge dim house. "It brings back memories of how far we've fallen, Otto," he replied. He was in no mood to reassure his father-in-law. "We're in desperate times. So you're going to have to charm desperately: for your daughter's sake."

"If it was up to me she'd be out of Germany and safe by now."

"If it was up to you I'd be cuckolded by an American flyboy living on the loot you plan to pirate out of Germany!"

Kohl sulked. "A fine mood you're in on this critical evening."

"The eve of *Götterdämmerung*," interjected Schmidt to break off the squabbling. "The Twilight of the Gods. Time for the unsheathing of the sword."

Kohl looked skeptically at this somber companion. "I'd no idea you were a man of literary allusion, Max."

"I'm not a man of literature, Otto." The doctor extinguished his cigarette before stepping out of the car. "I'm a man of will."

Guard dogs produced a volley of ferocious barking as the men stepped from the vehicle, prompting the trio to hesitate at the bottom of the steps. Then a harsh command silenced the animals and a Luftwaffe captain trotted down the granite to greet them. They were escorted into Karinhall's shadowy foyer where sentries briskly checked for weapons. There was no apology. The bomb attempt on Hitler's life the previous summer had tightened security procedures throughout Germany.

"This way, gentlemen," the Luftwaffe captain directed.

The large banquet table was covered by white sheets, suggesting it hadn't been used for some time. Oil paintings and tapestries had been taken down from the walls, leaving ghostly imprints. The pictures were stacked next to wooden crates for shipping to underground safety. All of Germany was burrowing.

The library was less changed, its books no more read now than they'd been six years before. A fire burned and they could see a figure in a high-backed chair, his back to them. "Your guests, *Reichsmarschall*."

Göring waved over the top of the chair. "Yes, bring them in." He sounded slightly impatient. "Come, come, gentlemen. No ceremony here."

They stood before him. Göring was in a silk dressing gown, one slippered leg up on an ottoman. "The damn gout." He'd aged, his face lined and pale, his eyes sunken, and he appeared to have lost some weight. His presence had shrunk as well; he no longer seemed to automatically dominate the room, let alone an empire. Still, the *Reichsmarschall*'s gaze retained a cold gleam of calculation. He studied his guests with a half smile, taking in the uniforms and the folder under Drexler's arm. "Very military." He gestured to three chairs arranged in a semicircle in front of his own. "Please, please, be seated. Memories of '38, no?"

"I'm honored you remember, sir." Drexler bowed.

"Oh, I remember. How we had to put a lid on the entire affair."

Drexler hesitated. "And now may be the opportune time to unwrap it."

They sat.

"It's good to see you well and safe, *Reichsmarschall*," Kohl offered.

"Yes, and you too, Otto." He grinned impishly at his old friend. "And what have you brought me this time?"

"Just myself, I'm afraid. I narrowly escaped from France. Just me and my . . . friends, here. With their interesting proposition."

Göring grunted his acceptance. "Well, you did splendidly in France for as long as you could. This champagne," he said, pointing out the bottle to the two others, "was in a shipment Otto shopped for me. The man has extraordinary taste." An orderly stepped forward and began pouring. They sipped. "Do you agree?"

"Otto has always known how to live," Drexler noted. "Who to know. And how to please them."

"Indeed! And now instead of Impressionist paintings or vintages from Bordeaux, he brings me you two. And I do remember our little mission to the bottom of the world. What an opportunity you had!" He shook his head. "Ah, the promise of that time, now lost. It's tragic, no?"

Hesitantly, his visitors nodded.

"What depresses me about the march of events is that I am at heart a builder, not a destroyer. A builder! What dreams we had of what we would build in our new world! Now I have to hide under that vast damned blanket overhead and bear insults and complaints from oafish idiots like that bunker worm Bormann. Even the Führer mocks me! Well. It wasn't I who decided to take on the entire world at once." He sipped again.

"Do you still believe in victory, *Reichsmarschall?*" Drexler finally asked.

Göring regarded the SS officer with small, dark eyes. "Of course, Colonel Drexler. My belief in the Führer and his destiny is unshaken. The superweapons, our secret plans. It's only a matter of time. God will not desert us in the end, no?" It was a rote affirmation.

"Perhaps he's already sent us a miracle."

"Really?" Göring drained his glass.

"Yes. Which is why we're here, *Reichsmarschall.* Why we asked our friend Otto—my father-in-law—to expedite our visit."

"You're related!"

"Yes. I'm married to Otto's daughter, Greta, the woman who accompanied us to Antarctica."

"Ah. I remember her. Lovely girl. I always remember the

women!" He barked a laugh, stopping when no one joined him. "Then I heard nothing more. But of course, you'd claimed her and hid her away! Well, here's to happy marriage!"

Drexler smiled thinly and lifted his glass. "Indeed."

Kohl studied the fire.

"And your miracle?"

Drexler leaned forward. "From an unlikely source we suspect we've found a potential key to victory. It's a long shot, I admit, far from assured. But desperate times deserve desperate remedies, no?"

Göring looked skeptical. "Not if they drain away valuable resources."

"One submarine," Drexler said. "*One* submarine and I—we— can win this war. Or at least force a favorable armistice. But we need your backing to do it, *Reichsmarschall*. And if we succeed you'll be the leader who saved Germany."

Göring laughed. "You're going to win the war with one boat? It's too bad you didn't join the navy in '39 and save Admiral Dönitz a lot of trouble!"

Drexler smiled. "We only need the U-boat for transport. To return to Antarctica and fetch something potentially powerful enough to reverse our fortunes."

"Ah. You're referring to your microbe again."

"Yes, *Reichsmarschall*. You remember our discovery. A weapon so powerful, so swift, so deadly, that it will force our enemies to sue for peace. A weapon easy to multiply and easy to deliver in these difficult times."

"But we knew of this weapon in 1939 and didn't return for it. As I recall, it was deemed far too hazardous to fool with. Plus, the war intervened."

"Correct. But circumstances may have changed in our favor." Drexler turned to Schmidt. "Doctor, can you review for the *Reichsmarschall* exactly what this microbe is capable of."

The Nazi doctor sat straighter at this cue. "First, it appears to be highly contagious, needing no third organism like a rat or a flea or mosquito for transmittal. It develops in the lungs and is spread by coughing, sneezing, even breathing. Second, in its dormant state it's extremely stable. It encases itself in a coating, or shell, that allows it to survive extremes of temperature, humidity—even a disturbance such as the detonation of a shell or bomb. This hardiness makes it easily deliverable. Third, it can kill with unprecedented swiftness. In as little as twelve hours from infection, individuals become incapacitated. Death of virtually one hundred percent of those exposed follows in a couple days. It's far more lethal than the more familiar bubonic or pneumonic plagues or anthrax. In all my years as a doctor I've never seen anything like it."

Göring pursed his lips in consideration and then slowly shook his head. "Which is why trying to harness it would be opening a Pandora's box. When you play with a witches' brew like plague, it can bounce back at you." He nodded significantly at Drexler. "As those mountaineer troops of yours learned too late."

Drexler put up his hand. "Conceded. But I discovered something *else* on that island, *Reichsmarschall*. An underground organism which some on the science team speculated might neutralize the microbe's effects."

"How is that significant?"

"Because when opening Pandora's box, one must possess immunity from its effects, as the Spaniards did from the European diseases that destroyed the Aztec and Inca empires."

"Obviously," Göring said impatiently. "So if you found a cure, why didn't you bring it back with you?"

"The expedition was in crisis. Men were dying, the ship in danger. The antibiotic's effectiveness on humans had not been fully demonstrated. After a futile effort to reach the SS squad during which our small supply of the antibiotic was depleted, the cave where the substance was found was blocked by a cave-in. For safety reasons we had to destroy the microbe as well; with the limited containment equipment we had, there was no way to ensure nonexposure. But now—"

"How has anything changed?" Göring said, tired of Drexler's obliqueness.

The SS colonel played his card. "Sir, just two days ago we made a remarkable capture that set our thinking on an entirely new course. Do you remember the American pilot, Owen Hart? He was here, at Karinhall."

"I remember the name, from the reports. Not the face."

"He was one of the mission's casualties—we *thought*. But it turns out he survived the microbe after all. Not forty-eight hours ago, he made a secret flight to Berlin to contact my wife. Once in custody, he admitted he'd survived the disease after ingesting the antibiotic. He's living proof a cure exists."

Göring frowned, idly twisting one of the rings on his left hand. "Contacted your wife?"

"Yes. You see it's Greta, my wife, who did much of the pioneering work on these discoveries in Antarctica. Hart, now an officer in American Intelligence, was apparently given a mission by his superiors to abduct Greta and force her to use this biology against us. Fortunately, her loyalty to the Reich allowed me to foil such a plot." He glanced sideways at Kohl. The German businessman swallowed and nodded in faint support.

"My point," Drexler went on, "is that we may be in a biological arms race. And the fortuitous arrest of Hart gives us the upper hand. If we could return to Atropos Island, we could collect enough disease spores to culture and grow the microbe. We could also collect the antibiotic organism and begin reproducing that as well. We then destroy the source of both, strike before the Americans, and force an end to the war."

"Your wife will help with this?"

"Of course. Her loyalty to the Reich and myself is beyond question." The other two sat as if made of stone.

Göring folded his hands and rested his chin on them. "Infection, plague—this isn't the kind of war I like to fight. How many millions do you intend to kill?"

"How many tens of millions have already died?" Schmidt responded. "The nation that can force a successful conclusion to this war before the last, greatest battles will have performed a humanitarian deed. We will have *saved* lives."

Göring tapped his fingers, considering. "This is fraught with difficulties."

"And it seems foolhardy to involve my daughter in this dangerous scheme," Kohl interjected worriedly.

"She's necessary," Drexler said with irritation. "The risk is acceptable to save Germany."

"You want to take your wife with you?" the *Reichsmarschall* asked. "She'll go?"

"If I explain the need."

"Well. Remarkable woman. Still, Otto is right. This is an extreme gamble."

"At this point it seems a gamble Germany must make."

"Yes." Göring thought, then pointed to a clock. "The key problem, of course, is time."

Schmidt nodded. "Time to get to the island, time to get these organisms, time to mass-produce them. With the Allies pressing, it will be difficult."

"But here, gentlemen, I have information that may make your task less hopeless than it seems." Göring paused, considering, then winked. He enjoyed demonstrating that he still occasionally played a part in the Reich's inner councils. "This is most secret, of course, but Germany is not as finished as the enemy believes. The Fatherland is going to strike back this winter, hitting the Americans and British where they least expect it. The Führer is confident this will bring victory. I'm less so but *am* confident our offensive will prolong the war. Enough perhaps to enable you to deliver us some kind of a miracle." He pondered. "This will require just a single submarine?"

"To win the war," Drexler promised. "When we return we'll need biological facilities to mass-produce both the disease and its antidote. A laboratory—perhaps located in a mine—should suffice. Germs are far cheaper than tanks or airplanes."

Göring laughed. "Our mines are getting crowded, so much has been moved there! Still, it would be nice to be in control of events again. Well." He seemed to have regained some of his old energy. He boosted himself to his feet, grunting a bit in pain. "Let's discuss the details of this further over dinner, Jürgen. I agree with Otto that the odds are stacked against us, but the idea of having an option of last resort intrigues me. We'll determine if this is truly feasible and you can tell me more about Antarctica."

"I'd be delighted, *Reichsmarschall*."

"Open it."

Drexler stood before the steel door in immaculate uniform, his jackboots shining and his pistol freshly oiled. With a clank the steel door was unlocked and hauled open by a thick, brutish SS guard, his arms roped with muscle and his head jutting forward. An animal set to guard animals. Drexler stepped through, the guard throwing on the light from an outside switch.

Greta jerked awake. She was on a bunk, huddled for warmth. The cell was otherwise bare except for a steel bucket. Drexler carried in a camp chair and sat. "Hello, Greta."

She sat up, blinking in the harsh light. She looked disheveled, exhausted, and very small. It was painful to see her in such surroundings. Humiliating. *Yet it's necessary*, he reminded himself. Necessary for her to understand how desperate their situation really was. Show no emotion, Drexler told himself. *Feel* no emotion. Every time you've surrendered to your heart, you've regretted it. Still, he found it difficult to begin.

It was Greta who finally spoke. "So, you've come to look? Does this please you? What you've done to keep me in Germany?"

Her sarcasm shattered his hesitation. It was he who was in control. "Do you think I *enjoy* seeing you like this? My wife jailed for trying to run away with an American Intelligence officer? The Gestapo is actually becoming suspicious you may have revealed key information to the enemy. I've spent all my political capital keeping this arrest quiet to protect both our reputations. Your impulsive selfishness has nearly destroyed me, Greta. Ruined me."

"All I wanted was to be let go."

"You know the Reich can't do that. The only debate your keepers have is how slowly you both should die. This is the reality of war, Greta: this cell is your situation without my protection, without my fine home, without my life and career and connections. Wake up! Because what can happen in a place like this is indescribable. All that stands between you and that is me."

She closed her eyes. "Where's Owen?"

"Waiting for your decision. Waiting for *you* to rescue *him*."

"What decision?"

"I ask you to look at your situation." He leaned toward her. "An American Intelligence officer in the heart of Berlin. A spy, by any nation's definition. A German woman consorting with him. Both of you could be shot, certainly. In fact, I've been working very hard to keep you from being shot."

"It would be a relief to have it over."

"I'm sorry to hear you say that. For Hart, though, it won't go so quickly. The Gestapo will have questions for an American spy. Inquiries that will take *days* to complete. By the end, he'll be *begging* for a bullet."

She looked him up and down, as if seeing him for the first time. "You came here to tell me this?"

"No, of course not. I *am* your husband, Greta. Our relationship has of course changed: I'm hurt, I'm angry. But despite your betrayal I still came here to help you. So you can help me."

She looked wary.

"I *need* your help, Greta." He nodded solemnly. "Germany needs your help. No, I don't want to see you dead. I might like to kill Hart but I can't afford to see him dead either. Because somehow he found his way out of that sealed cave, which means he can find a way back in. Accordingly, I want to offer you both a chance at redemption. A chance for us to work together again for a common good."

"What chance?" Her tone was skeptical.

"To return to Antarctica."

She had a sharp intake of breath. "No! That's where all this started!"

"To develop your *cure*, Greta. I didn't think it a real possibility until I saw Hart. And the need was not entirely apparent to me when we first visited Atropos Island. But the war has brought it home. What if we had a new antibiotic? It would make all the difference in our hospitals."

"Jürgen, there's a war on! We can't get back to Antarctica."

"But we *can*. On a submarine. The Reich is willing to make one available."

"But the time, it's so late in the war . . ."

"This war may go on longer than you think."

Her eyes became skeptical. "No. You're going for the microbe."

He shook his head, considering his words carefully. "I'm afraid Dr. Schmidt was one step ahead of both of us, Greta." He kept his gaze dead level with hers, trying to communicate the utmost sincerity. "I assumed all the cultures were destroyed, as you said, but it turns out Schmidt quietly created some of his own cultures, borrowing from your dishes."

"What?"

"He brought the disease back to Germany and it's been tested in the camps," Drexler lied. "The Reich is desperate, and may be forced to use it. All this came as a complete shock to me. Göring shares my fear but there is growing pressure coming from the Führer's headquarters: Bormann, maybe other advisors, I don't know. So the *Reichsmarschall* wants us to return to Antarctica to get an antidote as a safety valve. To get *your* antibiotic. To save lives, not take them." He watched her closely to see if she saw through him.

"You just want the drug?"

"Yes."

She looked confused, tired, hopeful. "If I helped you'd let Owen live?"

"I *need* Hart, to help get us back into the cave quickly. I can't risk the chance he'd lie in directing us on such a dangerous trip: I need him there to *show* us. And I need you to persuade him. I need you to help gather and culture the compound. I need you both. Just as you now need me. A partnership."

She shook her head in wonder. "The three of us returning again?"

"Greta, we're all in desperate straits. Do you think this is what I want, you in a prison cell? That's no victory. But Hart's appearance perversely means we can do something together to produce a *good* in this war. In partnership with my wife, even if she no longer loves me. We've all made mistakes, Greta, great and terrible and bitter ones. And I thought Hart's return was the worst mistake of all. Then I realized he's a sign of new opportunity, a chance to try again. It's late, very late. But not too late, perhaps."

"Jürgen . . ." It was a groan as she tried to sort out his motive.

He took a breath. "The war will end someday, in victory or defeat or stalemate: who knows? And then there'll be an accounting of what was done on all sides. I want that accounting to include a miracle new drug. A drug that *we* discovered. This is our chance to salvage something from catastrophe, Greta, regardless of what happens between you and me. Something that will be remembered in the postwar world. So come with me to Antarctica to do the expedition over, more completely this time. To correct the mistakes of the past. To succeed instead of fail."

"And afterward? You and me and Owen?"

"Your heart is your own. I've learned that. To be honest, I still hope to change your mind. But go where you will, with him if you must. My mission is for Germany. Do it and we'll all be saved."

She closed her eyes. "What do I have to do?"

"*Convince* him, Greta. Convince him he must cooperate."

"To save his life?"

"To save his. To save your father's. And to save yours."

She looked at her husband, her eyes sad, contemplating a return to the island. Finally she nodded. "I'll talk to him."

CHAPTER TWENTY-SEVEN

Greta inhaled the night air of the harbor. Northwestern Spain was cool in November but still warmer than Germany, its sky ablaze with stars. Smells both sweet and odorous wafted from the port of Vigo, the scent of sea and forest and fishing quay a heady reminder of better times. For two weeks she and Owen had been locked in a sterile world without windows: a succession of cells, paneled trucks, and then an airplane, its viewing ports taped over with blackout paper. They'd been kept more than twenty-four hours at opposite ends of a frigid metal hangar in Switzerland, sleepless and cramped on its hard concrete floor. Now, still stiff from the long journey, she had a moment's respite on the edge of the Atlantic in a nation that still granted refuge to Nazi ships.

A few lights twinkled on the water and music drifted from the whitewashed buildings stacked around Vigo's natural amphitheater. *This is what life is like without war,* she remembered. It was only a glimpse. Stone steps slick with seaweed led to a landing being approached by a motor launch. Across the bay was the low dark shadow of a U-boat. An impatient Schmidt was already down the steps, his gaunt silhouette identified by the glow of his cigarette. He'd not so much as glanced at the beauty of the harbor.

Despite being within fifty feet of her husband and her father and the man she loved, Greta felt helplessly alone. Jürgen had been warily polite, Otto had been kept separate, and any contact with Owen was prevented by the squad of granite-faced SS troopers that had flown with them out of Germany. The isolation hurt. She didn't think she'd survive to stand on a temperate shore again, and before being sealed into the submarine she wanted to share this final moment with the man she loved. For just that reason Drexler wouldn't allow it. While he needed both Owen and Greta to accomplish his plan, he didn't need them together. Not yet.

The pair's last conversation in Berlin had been hasty and anguished. Drexler had reluctantly agreed to allow his wife to go into Owen's cell alone to persuade the pilot to come on the new expedition. But the SS colonel was hammering on the door and hollering "Time!" long before they'd said all they needed to say. Greta had presented the cruel choice—Antarctica or a painful death—quickly, never doubting that Hart would agree to come. "It's all right," he'd assured her. "I know I'm not done with that place yet. Or this war. And I have an idea." But she wept when he agreed, hating herself for asking him to come and yet enormously relieved that he'd do so.

Now Owen remained caged inside a Spanish truck, waiting for transfer to the submarine. Her father stood morosely next to a decrepit warehouse, watched over by a yellow-haired giant named Hans. And Jürgen was brisk and confident, reanimated by what he clearly saw as a second chance to make his mark in the Reich and work together with Greta.

He still wore his formal black uniform to emphasize his authority. Now he watched the motor launch from the U-boat putter to the stone steps of the quay. The submarine commander who climbed out of the boat declined to return Drexler's Hitler salute, instead coming wearily up the quay steps in worn sweater and stained officer's cap and offering a brief nod at the top. He looked tired, his eyes red from long hours. "Colonel Drexler? Captain Joachim Freiwald, commander of the *U-4501*."

"Greetings, Captain. You're the skipper of a very new submarine, I understand."

"So new I would swear the paint is still drying. I'm sorry for not being on shore to meet you but the timing of your arrival was unclear. And our orders were quite sudden. We ran the Atlantic gauntlet from the shipyards at Kiel and have been scrambling to provision since our arrival in Spain. All for an ultimate destination we've yet to be informed of." He looked at Jürgen quizzically.

"I'll inform you of our mission once we're at sea, Captain. The haste is necessary, I'm afraid. The war is at a critical stage and we're under a tight deadline."

Freiwald looked uncomfortable. "My orders from U-boat Command are less than clear. Only to take on an unusually large number of added personnel for an unusually long voyage. I've radioed for clarification of my instructions."

"There's no need. I take *my* orders from Berlin." He pointed to his SS contingent. "These men take their orders from me. And so do you, as these papers will make clear." An orderly handed over a folder. "We can't afford to waste time with jurisdictional confusion so I had these orders drawn up making clear my authority. And I'm in a hurry. I want us underway before dawn, Captain."

Freiwald looked surprised. "I understood our departure date as tomorrow night, Colonel. Some of my men are in town on leave."

"Your directive has just changed. Your men's shore leave must be canceled. Our success depends upon speed."

"Colonel, we've been working ceaselessly to commission and then provision here in Spain. My men haven't had any rest since—"

"*Tonight,* Captain. Time is of the essence. They can go ashore after we win the war."

Freiwald pursed his lips and opened the folder. There was enough illumination from a warehouse floodlight to make out the signatures and stamps. He closed it, his face a mask. "Yes, Colonel. Departure at 0300 hours."

"You can reassemble your crew?"

He shrugged. "I know where to find them. The amusements of Vigo are limited."

"Good. Next, the biologist accompanying us is a woman. My wife, as a matter of fact, though that is irrelevant to your treatment of her. Her expertise is critical to this mission and as a woman she'll need a private cabin. You'll arrange this, please."

The skipper blinked. "Submarines are cramped, Colonel, even our new Type XXI. I have a cabin, and there's the first officer's compartment. It has only a single bunk—"

"That will be satisfactory. I won't be sharing her quarters. My apologies to the first officer but I'm sure he'll understand. Now, I also want a compartment reserved for my nine *Schutzstaffel* soldiers and myself: perhaps the forward torpedo room. You'll reassign your crew accordingly."

"But—"

"And the laboratory space, it's been cleared?"

"That necessity has made storage tight and those cages—"

"The heavy weather gear has arrived?"

"Yes—"

"And we also have a prisoner. An American Intelligence officer, with critical information for our success. Where can we confine him?"

Freiwald looked even more confused. "Nowhere, Colonel. A submarine has no brig."

"Then just lock him somewhere. To a pipe or bunk."

The captain frowned. "Is he a threat?"

"Potentially."

"Colonel, that won't work. Not on a long sea voyage. He'll be in the way if chained to one place and it won't be good for morale. Submarines are more . . . casual than what you're accustomed to in Berlin."

"What do you suggest, Captain?"

"Where can he go? What can he do? Believe me, he'll never be alone in the confines of a submarine, especially with so many extra soldiers on board. We simply watch him."

There was a dissatisfied grunt. "Very well. Just keep him away from the woman. My wife, I mean. He's not to talk with her."

Freiwald looked more baffled than ever.

"That will be all for now. You can begin transporting my men and their gear to your ship."

"It's called a boat, Colonel."

But Drexler was already walking away.

Otto Kohl watched the submarine commander's discomfiture from a distance, secretly amused at the obvious friction. The U-boat chief had just been given a short course in the way Drexler briskly arranged the world to fit his own designs. Kohl had expected to be allowed to stay in Switzerland but Jürgen had ordered him to continue on to Spain. For a while Kohl had feared being impressed into the submarine as well, but there was no sign of that. Instead he had to stand like a penitent schoolboy in the shadow of a gigantic SS goon, watching his only child standing alone nearby, depressed and probably afraid. Her isolation shamed him.

Drexler, in contrast, looked positively jaunty, as if embarking on a pleasure cruise. It occurred to Kohl that his son-in-law had quite possibly snapped. The Nazi strode up.

"This is where we say goodbye, Otto." He kept his hands clasped behind his back. "You're a lucky man to wait out the war here."

"Simply a sensible one." Deciding to try one last time, Kohl gestured toward the hills of Spain. "It could end for all of us, Jürgen. You're beyond the reach of the dying Reich. Make a separate peace and just go. You've done enough."

"You still don't understand people like myself, do you, Otto?" Jürgen's voice had the disdain of pity. "That some things are more important than one's own brief spark of existence. That there are such things as country and duty and honor. That sometimes the individual sacrifices for the many."

"In the right cause."

"Your Fatherland's cause is the right cause. Always. You no more choose your Fatherland than you choose your family. And you no more abandon your Fatherland than you abandon your family."

Kohl was quiet. He was abandoning both.

"Destiny has put me at this harbor," Drexler went on. "Destiny has given me the chance to reverse the tide of war. God led me to that island as surely as if he'd erected signposts, and you and Owen Hart fell out of the sky like trumpeting angels. I thought it a nightmare, at first. Then I realized it was the solution to all my problems."

God, what a grandiose, self-important fool. "No one knows what God intends," Kohl warned quietly. "If you must take this risk, then do so, Jürgen, but *please* . . . I beg of you. Leave my daughter behind. You don't need her."

"Ah, but I do. Do you think Hart would help me without Greta as leverage? Besides, your daughter is a remarkably intuitive scientist. Time is of the essence with the Allies knocking on the West Wall. I'm counting on her ingenuity to give us a head start on our plans. And besides, I need her for one more reason."

"What's that?"

"You."

"What do you mean?"

"Do you really think I trust either one of you? That I'm relaxed about turning Otto Kohl loose to run around Spain while I carry out a secret mission to Antarctica? No, she's my guarantee, dear father-in-law. You won't do anything foolish because if you did, it would endanger her: if we fail, she'll be the first to suffer the consequences."

"You can't make Greta hostage to my behavior! That's not our agreement!"

"Exactly. I agreed only to let you go, but we said nothing beyond that. Now I've filled in the blanks."

"Filled it with blackmail!"

"I learned from the master."

Kohl fumed. "It's not as if I was going to talk anyway. I'm no traitor."

"Then you should welcome this arrangement. We're allies."

Kohl wished he'd never met Jürgen Drexler. "When do you return?"

"In less than two months, I hope. By that time you should know Vigo like a native."

"I'm not about to sit waiting in *this* runt of a port. Barcelona, perhaps. Or over to Lisbon, in Portugal. I have the money to go where I wish now." He gestured toward the two leather satchels on the dirt near the truck, watched by an SS guard. They were stuffed with currency, gold, and bank certificates that Kohl had assembled in Switzerland after they flew there from Berlin to refuel. "If I have to waste my time for two months, it shall be in some comfort," said Otto. He moved to pick up the satchels.

Drexler put a hand on his arm. "No, Otto. There's one other amendment to our agreement."

"What's that?"

"You'll get your money, as I promised. But not *until* our safe return. Just one more reason for you to wish us a bon voyage. It goes on the submarine with me."

"What!"

"You'll be issued enough pesetas to keep you at Vigo's finest for two months. And to light a lamp for our homecoming. But you go nowhere else if you care about the fate of your daughter. Early in the new year we'll have a family reunion. Then you'll be a rich man and I a powerful one. Not before."

"That's outrageous! That money is mine!"

"Think of me as your banker."

"Jürgen, you son of a bitch . . ."

"There, there, Otto," Drexler said, smiling. "We mustn't have acrimony among family members." He nodded toward Greta. "Now, say goodbye to your daughter. Tell her how important her cooperation is. Kiss her cheek, for me." He was in a good mood.

Kohl struggled to master his composure. He watched Jürgen nod to a guard, who hoisted the satchels and carried them down the quay steps for transport to the submarine. Then, resigned to the loss, Kohl went to speak briefly to Greta. She touched his hand before an SS guard escorted her to the launch as well. Next came Hart, his hands cuffed. The boat pulled away with this first load.

Drexler came back beside Kohl. "Was it a warm send-off?"

"She told me she didn't expect to come back."

"Ah. Well. She always underestimates me."

"And you me," Kohl said. "I'm not your puppet, Jürgen. I refuse to be any man's puppet anymore."

"Of course not, Otto. You're lord of Vigo. The newest Spanish don. And with patience, you'll have your new life."

They watched the motor launch aim for the waiting submarine. They could see Greta looking back at them, her expression invisible. Then she melted into the dark and Drexler put his arm around Kohl's shoulder and guided him to a waiting car. The German sulkily got in and Drexler bent to the open window.

"Your daughter and your money are safe with me. I think the stars promise luck for us, don't you agree?"

Kohl looked straight ahead. "Goodbye, Jürgen." When he said nothing more, Drexler shrugged and the car pulled away.

Otto half expected a detour and a quick bullet on the drive into town but it didn't come. A mistake, he thought. If you knocked down a person, you finished him. He suspected Jürgen didn't quite have the stomach required for his schemes.

Kohl was escorted to a hotel room with a view of the dark harbor. "Your accommodations have been paid for," he was informed. From the balcony of his room he could see the light of the motor launch as it ferried back and forth. The submarine was too low and dark to be visible.

Kohl sighed, sat on his sagging bed, and contemplated the ruins of his life. Then he took out the object Greta had pressed into his hand. "Keep this safe for me," she'd whispered.

It was a scrap of soiled white ribbon. He unwound it to find a pebble inside, dull and brown. He supposed it had something to do with Owen. With it was a scrap of paper, carefully inked.

The issue is greater than us, Papa. You must stop this boat.

Kohl lay down on his bed. For the first time in many years, tears fogged his eyes. He was frightened at such sentiment.

For reassurance he felt the lining of his jacket where he'd sewn some currency inside. Then he considered what to do.

PART THREE

1944

CHAPTER TWENTY-EIGHT

The *U-4501* was one of a new class of U-boat that was years ahead of its time. Its displacement was more than twice that of the standard German U-boat and it was thirty feet longer, giving the necessary range and cargo area to reach Antarctica. A new "schnorkel" provided the breathing capability to stay underwater long enough to escape the coast of Europe. Even its appearance was futuristic, with a streamlined conning tower that reminded Hart of a fancy prewar DeSoto. The submarine boasted interior amenities that earlier U-boats lacked: a freezer, a single shower, and a hydraulic system for faster reloading of its torpedoes. It could dive to six hundred and fifty feet. Yet despite all this it remained a claustrophobic tube, noisy and damp.

The vessel was crammed. Counting himself and Greta, Owen, Schmidt, and the soldiers, Drexler had brought thirteen extra people on board—unlucky thirteen, some of the sailors muttered—to add to the normal crew of fifty-seven. Bunks had to be shared, one sailor crawling into the heat and smell of the prior occupant as watches changed. Additionally, making space for a crude laboratory and Antarctic supplies meant provisions were stuffed into every available space. The sailors walked on tins of food in the torpedo compartments and one head was temporarily occupied by smoked meats and sausages. The boat was so tightly packed that the sailors joked that they had to lose weight in order to squeeze through to fetch their food.

To Hart, who loved the expansiveness of sky and sea, the cylinder was grimly oppressive. From his assigned bunk in the aft torpedo compartment, he listened with disquiet to the rumble of pumps and gush of water as the U-boat dove after clearing Vigo's breakwater, imagining the ocean's dark squeeze as they began their long underwater run.

He was still lying there when Drexler suddenly appeared. It was the first time they'd been so close since Berlin. The German had exchanged his uniform coat for a navy sweater. He also wore an expression of distaste.

"Already seasick, Jürgen?" Hart needled.

"Simply sick of your proximity," said Drexler. "And I'll chain you up again if I have to. But I've refrained for now. I'd rather we put aside our personal differences and form the necessary professional partnership to complete our mission. The result may save many lives. Can I trust you to behave correctly?"

Hart pretended to consider this. "As much as I trust you."

"I saved you from the Gestapo: saved a man who planned to abscond with my wife. I did so on her promise that you'd be of use to us. Now I want *your* promise."

"You can't always have what you want."

"Ah, but I can, and now I do." He reached into his breast pocket and pulled out something golden, then let it dangle from his hand. "Remember?"

It was the penguin locket, and Hart started despite himself. He looked at the tiny bird swinging back and forth with growing anger. "That's Greta's, you son of a bitch. You stole that from Greta."

"Like you stole her from me."

Owen lifted himself onto his elbows in warning. "You know,

Jürgen, I *could* become a dangerous man. If I were you I *would* get out the handcuffs. Who knows what I might do?"

"You're the least of my fears," Drexler said, sneering. "I'm only trying to smooth our voyage. But if you make trouble, *you* have reason to be afraid of *me*." With that, he turned and walked away.

The encounter left the pilot depressed, confirming his feeling of impotence. He felt as guilty for rushing to Berlin and endangering Greta as he knew she felt guilty for allowing them to be caught. Chains or no chains, he'd never felt so helpless.

He lay thinking for a long time, the German sailors glancing at him curiously as they passed: the enemy at last given a face. Then he suddenly swung out of his bunk. He couldn't allow paralysis. He had to be ready to act if opportunity came. He decided to explore and, if possible, talk to Greta.

At first no one addressed him as he moved through the hatchways. Still a ghost, thought Owen. But word of his movement went ahead of him and Captain Freiwald swung around the periscope to block him in the control room. His look was not unfriendly, only assessing.

"The American stirs," he said.

Hart swung his gaze around the control room. "Just admiring this latest example of German engineering. Too bad it's too late to affect the war."

"Colonel Drexler doesn't think so."

"Colonel Drexler is a danger to himself and to others."

Freiwald paused at that. "And what are we to make of you?"

"I'm a little uncertain of that myself, Captain." Owen glanced around at the half dozen crew members manning instruments. They regarded the American curiously. "I'm an American officer who left my unit without permission to try to rescue a German woman from this crazy war. I'm your enemy and yet I agreed to lend my spelunking expertise to this mission. But only after I was given a choice between this boat and a Gestapo basement, as was Frau Drexler." He paused a moment to let Freiwald digest this, noticing the German officer glancing toward a curtained cubicle where he assumed Greta had been assigned.

"There's a connection between you and our biologist?"

"We knew each other before the war."

"And yet she is married to Colonel Drexler, who forces you on this voyage?"

Hart nodded. "Life gets complicated."

"And what cave does the colonel wish you to explore?"

"Hasn't Jürgen told you where we're going yet?"

"No."

"Believe me, you're happier not knowing. I doubt we'll be coming back."

Freiwald frowned. "Is that a threat?"

"No, simply a prophecy. But there's a solution." He raised his voice slightly. "I'll accept your surrender now and we can sail for Norfolk. The war is over, Captain."

Freiwald laughed. "Unfortunately it isn't. Not for you or for me. And my loyalty remains with my country, so I think I'll decline your terms." He scrutinized the American, his curiosity not satisfied. "My crew informs me that, in talking to Colonel Drexler just a few minutes ago, you used the adjective 'dangerous' to describe yourself."

Hart shrugged. "Any man is dangerous when pushed into a corner. Yet I'm not as dangerous to you as Jürgen, I promise."

"Just don't threaten my boat, Hart. I have a fondness for the *U-4501.*"

"I respect a man's fondness for the things he loves." Then he stepped around the captain and moved on.

"Greta?" He stopped outside her curtained cubicle.

"Owen?"

"Are you all right?"

One of the SS men suddenly filled the passageway. He was thickly muscled and his face was mapped with a relief of scar tissue. Wounds from the front, Hart guessed. The man's iron-gray hair was in a stubby crew cut: Bristle-Head, the pilot mentally dubbed him.

"You're not to talk to Frau Drexler."

"She may be ill. She gets seasick. I need to check on her."

"We're submerged. There is little roll."

"She may be sick anyway."

Bristle-Head leaned into his face. "You're not to talk with Frau Drexler. Stay away from her. Away from this part of the boat. You've no business with the colonel's wife."

"I like this part of the boat."

"If you try to stay I'll tie you up in the engine room."

Hart considered. Then the yellow-haired giant Hans came through a hatchway as well, towering over them both. The pilot studied their faces. "In America, this is called an ugly situation." He turned. "Greta," he called softly. "There's something I haven't told you about the island. Something that will give us a chance."

Then he looked defiantly at the SS men and retreated.

While the new submarine could cruise for days underwater, progress was still swiftest on the surface. As they came abreast of Africa the Germans elected to risk surfacing at night. With the swells came motion as the submarine's sausage shape rolled. Word filtered through the boat that the woman, who'd kept closely to her cabin, was queasy.

Drexler had been uncomfortable approaching her ever since she'd tried to escape with Hart. Now he used her seasickness as an excuse to look in on her. "Are you ill?"

"I'm all right. I have a bucket."

"I can have Schmidt look at you."

"God no. Please leave me alone."

He considered. "Perhaps it would help if you were more active."

"Jürgen . . ."

"Come with me." It was not a request. He pulled Greta out of her cabin and led her to ladders that descended two decks to the boat's lowest level.

She looked down sulkily. "What's there?"

"Our future."

The compartment at the bottom had a clearance of only six feet and was shaped like a trough, the bulkheads curving inward toward a narrow deck above the keel. "I had them set this storage compartment aside for you," he said encouragingly. "As your laboratory."

She glanced around. There were two metal cabinets and a number of wooden crates on the floor, but no sink or workbench. Pipes and cables snaked over the surfaces. It was cold this low in the boat. The light was clinical and harsh near the ladder, shadowy and inadequate in the recesses. They could feel the throb of the engines just astern in the soles of their feet.

"Cozy," she said without enthusiasm. Something moved in the dark and she peered closer. Caged animals, she realized with a start, recognizing their smell. She went to inspect. "You brought animals? Is this an ark?"

"To test your drug. I didn't think humans would readily volunteer."

"I had no idea they were on board."

"We've kept them out of the way so as not to make the sailors uneasy. One of the men, Jacob, looks after them. So. Will all this work?"

"For what? To win the war?"

"Greta, I'm trying to help you. Will this satisfy your needs?"

She bit her lip. "It's impossibly cramped and inadequate. But . . . perhaps, with modifications. We need a bench, a drain."

He nodded, encouraged. He went to a crate and lifted a lid. "Your old biology books. I had them brought along to help." He lifted the one on top. It was the text on whales he'd given her on the *Schwabenland.*

The memory startled her. It had been so long. She looked around again. "It's actually like a refuge down here," she acknowledged. "Less crowded."

"The roll is less too, near the keel."

She even laughed at that. "Convince my stomach."

"In an emergency you're to come here. This is your battle station. The hatch will be sealed and you'll be isolated, but out of the way and as safe as any of us."

She shrugged.

He reached out then to tentatively touch her shoulder but she pulled away. "Greta, I'm sorry things came to this. That everything's so awkward. But now, in the end, maybe we still have a chance to do some good. Together."

She was in no mood to reply to this and they stood, in separated silence. "When do we get to Antarctica?" she finally said, in order to say something.

"Two weeks, perhaps less."

"And when do we get back?"

"That depends on you, doesn't it?"

She summoned her courage. "Are you going to—" She couldn't bring herself to utter the word *kill*. "Are you going to *leave* us down there, Jürgen?"

Drexler was taken aback. He swallowed. "No." He shook his head. "At first I wanted to leave *him*. But what would be the point? You're about to help me achieve what I want. And eliminating him won't win you back. So if you cooperate I'll set him free. Possibly I'll put him in a life raft off some port of refuge. Port Stanley in the Falklands, perhaps, or Ushuaia in Argentina. Even Cape Town."

"And what about me?"

"That'll be your choice. I can't stop you from joining him."

She looked incredulous.

"I *won't* stop you from joining him—if that's still what you want."

He saw the look of new hope on her face and realized he may have been *too* soothing. "Of course, this promise is contingent on both of you doing your jobs properly."

"So you can play with disease."

"No! To combat it!" He grimaced, frustrated. "Listen, I know you hate me right now, but this trip isn't as awful as you think. When the time is right I'll explain my plan in full and you may see our mission—and me—in a different light. And then you can choose between us."

"Jürgen, I've chosen. Why can't you accept that?"

"I think I have, as much as could be expected. He *is* on this boat, after all."

"Then let me talk to him."

"No!"

"Look at this clutter. Let him help me down here."

"No. I trust you, but not him. If you wish to talk, talk to me. If you need some help, come to *me.*"

"Sailors and soldiers of the Third Reich!" Drexler's voice crackled over the intercom. As many men as possible had crammed into the control room where he was speaking because it was easier to hear him in person than over the crude intercom system. Others cocked their heads toward the loudspeakers. All were curious about their fate.

"I bring you greetings from our Führer, Adolf Hitler. And from his designated successor, *Reichsmarschall* Göring. We have set out on a long voyage to a distant destination. All of you, of course, are wondering about our mission. And you men of the navy must wonder about so many new faces here on board. I apologize about the added crowding. These soldiers, I assure you, are vital to our success."

Hart was lying on his bunk, frowning at the Nazi squawking. Next to his bunk an engineer had his head tilted up, listening.

"Our destination is . . . Antarctica." Drexler paused for dramatic emphasis. There was a murmur of excited comment throughout the boat. The engineer frowned. "A cold place, but not as dreadful as you might think. Our northern winter is Antarctica's summer and we hope to find tolerable weather as we go south. With strength, endurance, and will, we should be able to accomplish our task rapidly and go home." Greta stood in the passageway by her cubicle, looking somberly at her husband.

"And what is that task? The chance to change history is given to few men. To us of the *U-4501*, that opportunity has been granted! We are setting out for the distant continent to retrieve a new drug, an underground organism significant enough to affect the tide of the war. Security prevents me from explaining fully the purpose of this compound, but clearly, Berlin and U-boat Command wouldn't risk one of Germany's best submarines on such a distant mission unless it was vitally important."

Heads nodded.

"This isn't a combat mission. With luck, we'll never encounter the enemy. We're like a silent cat, stealing stealthily across and under the sea. Yet if we do meet opposition we must battle to the last ounce of human will. Because what we're attempting to accomplish on this mission could truly save the lives of our loved ones in the Reich."

Drexler looked at Freiwald. "There are rumors of Allied superweapons. Clearly, Germany requires superweapons of its own to defend the Fatherland. This is our mission, to obtain the key to a superweapon, and you men are the agents of deliverance. We're journeying to an Antarctic island and should be back home early in the year, as heroes and saviors. For a while our purpose will remain a military secret. But when it's finally revealed the world will gasp at your achievement."

He nodded, confident. "I believe divine providence has made this voyage possible. I put my faith in his will, and the will of our Führer."

Drexler let his gaze sweep the control room, then lifted his arm. "Heil Hitler." And, rising like a phalanx of spears, the other arms in the room came up. "Heil Hitler!" came the roar through the boat. Hart pressed his hands over his ears.

Otto Kohl was tired, sore, and broke. His escape from Vigo had cost him all he had, buying him miserable truck, donkey, and cart rides across dusty mountains. His suit was filthy and torn, his feet blistered, his assurance and authority gone.

But the American Intelligence officer had come out of the embassy in Lisbon to meet him anyway. Now the German nervously licked his lips, considering for the thousandth time what he was about to do. Maybe he *had* been corrupted, as Drexler had claimed.

Or saved.

"Yes?" the attaché said, a bit impatiently.

"My name is Otto Kohl," he began. "Your records will show I escaped from American army custody in France. I've been to Germany. And I have the most extraordinary story to tell you . . ."

CHAPTER TWENTY-NINE

Alarm! Alaaarm! Dive! Dive! Dive!"

The klaxon blasted through the boat, setting off a tumult of cursing, frantic, hurtling men. Water roared into the submarine's ballast tanks and the vessel began to nose downward. Hatches slammed and valves were cranked. Anything unsecured began to tip onto the floor.

"My laboratory!" Greta caught her coffee mug as it began sliding off the edge of the tiny mess table and plunged into the torrent of sailors hurrying to their battle stations, shoulders cuffing her side as she struggled to the midships ladder.

"Dive! Hurry, dammit! Dive, dive!" Captain Freiwald came sliding down the conning tower ladder and banged onto the control room deck with his binoculars swinging and his cap knocked sideways.

"What is it?" shouted Lieutenant Erich Kluge, the first officer.

"Airplanes. Carrier patrol, probably." Freiwald looked up toward the tower that the sea was now enveloping as if he could see the sky. "Damn! We're already south of the equator! How did they pick us up?"

Greta noticed Kluge's accusing look as she rushed past. The first officer had pointedly avoided her since she'd displaced him in his cabin and now clearly viewed her as bad luck. Resigned, she descended the ladder in a half fall and, once at the bottom, seized the lab's hatch and banged it down after herself as she'd been instructed, turning the wheel. Locked in. She dropped to the steel flooring. A box was sliding with the tilt of the deck and she put out her foot to stop it. The klaxon switched off.

"Battle stations report!" the intercom squawked. One by one the submarine's compartments complied.

"Laboratory secure!" she shouted at her turn, her voice breaking from the tension.

Then she sat on the box, heart pounding, one hand on the ladder to brace herself against the slope of the diving boat. She could hear the nervous rustling of the rabbits.

"Hi."

She jumped. He was sitting in the shadows at the rear of the compartment, half hidden by boxes.

"Owen! You're not supposed to be down here!" Her tone was delighted.

"By my reckoning I'm not supposed to be on this boat at all, yet I can't seem to get off it. The attack seemed a good opportunity to let people forget about me for a moment. So I decided to drop in."

She shoved off the ladder to grasp him. "Thank God!" They hugged fiercely. "I've been so lonely . . ." She buried her face in his chest.

"I know," he said, meaning it.

They kissed for the first time since the air raid in Berlin. For a blessed instant they could forget where they were.

The tilt of the boat continued to steepen. There was a thud from the first depth charge, and the hull lurched. "They're going to get closer," he warned. "Hold on!"

She nodded grimly, grasping a pipe, and watched his lips move as he counted the seconds. There was a second detonation, a throbbing boom this time, that jerked the submarine as if it had been rammed. She felt the shock punch her body and was thrown violently sideways, hitting the curved bulkhead hard enough to have the wind knocked out of her.

"Jesus . . ." Hart groaned. He too had been tossed. "They're right on top of us."

Another explosion rang the plunging submarine like a gong, rolling it sideways. A cabinet popped open and vomited a spray of supplies. The lights blinked and went out.

"Owen?" It was a pained gasp. The tilt of the deck was increasing.

"Greta, are you all right?"

"I think so, just stunned . . ."

The boat bucked again, shuddering, and then again. They could hear shouts from the sailors on the decks above. Yet these explosions were slightly less violent than before. Less close.

She found him in the dark and clutched at his clothing, crawling up his length so they could hold each other again.

"We've got to stop meeting like this," he whispered, more lightly than he felt.

They waited in the dark as time ticked by with agonizing slowness. They could hear a gush of water but didn't know what it meant. The hull creaked.

"We're going deep," she observed.

Two more blows, more distant now. The airplanes were depth-charging blind. The slope of the deck kept increasing and the ruins of Greta's laboratory cabinet slithered along the floor. The laboratory rabbits were scrabbling at their wire mesh. There seemed no end to the dive. "Owen, are we going down?"

He couldn't answer. The sailors above had fallen silent and the steel in the hull was groaning. There was a sharp report somewhere in the submarine, like the bang of a gun, and then another.

"What's that?"

"Something giving way, I think. Bolts, valves. How deep is the ocean here?" he asked worriedly.

She hugged him harder. "I don't know. Three kilometers?"

"Deep enough."

More explosions, but distant enough that they just echoed through the hull, making it quake. The submarine hull squealed.

"It sounds like a whale," she whispered.

Then the tilt began to lessen. It was as if Freiwald was hauling on the reins of a horse, bringing its head up. The leveling was agonizingly slow, but it was happening. The boat creaked like a complaining hinge. They were sweating, waiting for it.

Finally the keel was even.

"I think we've stopped sinking." He whispered as if a noise would point them down again. They sagged in relief.

"Now what?"

"We hide."

Suddenly blue emergency lighting came on. The glow was eerie. The chaos was not as bad as it had sounded while things broke in the dark, but the floor was littered with debris. They examined each other. "Your arm is cut," he said, pointing. She nodded numbly. He tore a scrap of clean rag and bound it and they began boxing what they could.

"It's stuffy. Can we open that hatch?"

He shook his head. "Not until we're safe. The air will get worse before it gets better." He used a folder to shovel up shattered laboratory glassware, then found a storage tarp to lay on the deck and protect them from remnants. The submarine, on battery power, was quiet now, the crew trying not to make a sound. The Germans were trying to creep away.

Having secured what they could, Owen and Greta sat companionably side by side. There was nothing to do but wait.

"Do you think they've given up?"

"No. They'll be orbiting overhead, waiting for us to surface. And calling for destroyers with sonar. They won't give up easily."

"How long?"

"Hours, I suspect. Hours and hours."

She leaned against him. "Good."

They were quiet for a while, slowly recovering their equanimity in the calm, then their conversation started up again, drifting lightly from topic to topic. They'd almost succeeded in blocking out the seriousness of their situation when, suddenly, they heard a ghostly far-off echo:

Ping.

"Uh-oh."

Ping.

"What's that?"

"My navy. We're still being hunted."

They listened, her head on his chest. She could hear the thud of his heart.

Ping . . . ping . . . ping.

"They're getting closer." He pushed her upright. "Grab the ladder again. Brace yourself."

She pulled away reluctantly. "If they hit us, will it be quick?"

"Yes." In truth, he didn't know.

Ping, ping, ping, ping . . . They could hear the screws of the destroyer.

The submarine trembled slightly. Freiwald was trying to accelerate and turn away.

Wham! A wrenching concussion as powerful as the first one, and then another, and then a third. The light went out again and Greta gave a short sob, involuntarily, as the U-boat heeled. Their bodies lurched sideways, feet kicking, hanging on with their arms.

"Owennn . . ." she moaned.

The deck began tilting again.

"God. He's trying to go deeper."

Ping, ping, ping, ping . . .

"Hang on!"

Twin thuds, shaking the submarine to its core. The power of the explosions throbbed through their bodies and Hart felt he was clenching his jaw to keep his teeth from rattling. There were more bangs and they could hear oaths on the deck above and a roaring hiss of water. The *U-4501* was groaning, the depth squeezing it in on itself.

She crawled to him in the dark. "I'm going to hang on to you," she whispered.

Ping . . . ping . . . ping . . .

"We're pulling away from them, I think . . ."

Wham! The boat shook, not quite as hard this time.

"Maybe it would be best just to end it like this," she whispered. "In each other's arms. Easier."

"No. We're going to beat him." He did not mean the destroyer.

More explosions, farther away this time. Sluggishly, as if water-logged, the deck once more leveled.

"I wonder how deep we are now." He could sense the sea pressing like a vise. Tons of dark water. It was oppressive.

Slowly the depth-charging receded. The gush of water and the cries slowed, then stopped. The boat was quiet again, a crypt.

He sank his face in her hair. She sighed, reaching up to stroke his head.

"Jürgen told me he's going to let us go."

"Oh really?"

"I asked him if he was going to leave us in Antarctica, abandon us. The question embarrassed him. He said if we do what he wants he'll put us off the submarine in a raft, near a foreign port."

"And you believe that?"

"I don't know what to believe. He seems unpredictable. I think he still loves me in a way. But I no longer know him."

"Greta, he *can't* let us go."

"Why not, if he gets what he wants?"

"Because he thinks he's going to win the war with a secret we know. Because we're sitting in Germany's newest submarine. Because he needs your expertise to manufacture what he's after. I'm an American Intelligence officer, Greta. Do you think he's going to collect this drug for a plague and then put us ashore to talk about it? The only way he'll put me in a raft is if I'm already dead."

They were silent for a while. "Is he evil, Owen? Is *Germany* evil?"

He smiled wryly. "I think we're supposed to call it moral confusion. Besides, you told me he's simply dedicated."

"No." She shook her head. "He wants to destroy what he can't possess. That's wrong."

They lay waiting, listening. The sonar had grown more distant. Like confused dogs, the destroyers and airplanes were circling.

Somewhat feebly, the blue emergency light flicked on again.

Hart let go of the ladder and slid down on the tarp, holding Greta. "He'll be angry I sneaked down here, you know."

"Don't worry," she said, kissing him. "He can't get too vindictive just yet. He *needs* us."

"Yes, but I wonder how much. Those soldiers of his would find the cave entrance eventually. And someone—Schmidt maybe—can find and collect the goo."

The image made Greta laugh. "Somehow I don't see Dr. Schmidt as a swashbuckling spelunker."

But her lightheartedness was cut short.

Ping.

"Damn."

They waited.

Ping . . . The interval was longer. The sonar had lost them again.

"I'm hot," she finally complained, suddenly restless. "Sweaty." Without ventilation, the temperature in the submarine was rising. "I feel like I'm buried. Like I'm dying, buried alive."

"Me too."

She sat up, shaking her head. "No, I can feel you. You're alive. You're hard. Down there." She pointed.

"Greta!"

"It's hot and we're in danger and I want to take my clothes off. Take them off before I die. Please take them off me, Owen. I want to make you harder."

He swallowed and glanced at the hatch. "If we surface . . ."

"That's what makes it exciting." She hauled off her sweater. "I'm tired of dying. I've been dying for six years." She unfastened her bra and tossed it aside. Then she bent, her breasts brushing him, and worked at his buttons. "I've been dying and losing my life and now I have this one moment and no longer care about the next one, or what anyone thinks. So hurry. Hurry! Before the destroyers come back. I'm very sweaty, and very wet."

"Jesus." He yanked at his clothing and then hers, frantic with desire and uncertain what to pull off first. It didn't seem to matter as they kissed and tugged. Soon she pushed him onto his back and was astride him, her eyes dilated, her mouth partly opened.

"I want you more than anything in the world," she whispered.

And then she enveloped him like liquid fire, arching her own back, his hands on her nipples, their bodies slick with sweat and heat, their breath short and gasping in the increasing closeness of the chamber as she rocked up and down. Before he could control himself he exploded inside her, Greta giving a stifled cry as he bucked.

Then she leaned over him to let him suck a breast, her whisper hot and urgent in his ear. "I hope the destroyer keeps hunting. Because we're not done, you know."

Ping.

They were spent.

The couple lay breathing shallowly, half unconscious and drifting in troubled dreams from the lack of oxygen. After their lovemaking the destroyers had come again, hammering on the boat with remorseless fury. They'd hung grimly to the ladder and to each other, jaws clenched as the explosions wrenched them again and again and again. The light died once more. Then a pipe had burst with a spray of water like cold needles and Owen had hauled himself up to grope in the dark for the shaken valve to shut it off.

"Leak secured!" Greta had gasped to the intercom in reply to Freiwald's anxious question. The hatch remained shut.

They slumped, their lungs starved, waiting for another pass from the warships above. It didn't come. Time crawled. The eerie blue light came on again, like the glow from an Antarctic ice cave.

She sighed. "Now would be a time to end it, after we've made love."

"No." He stirred. "Greta, listen. We do have one chance. It's a desperate one, probably a crazy one, but it's the one reason I agreed we should come along. Before I escaped from the island last time I found something I could use to try to escape. The chance is too slim for you to attempt it but if I'm gone again Jürgen will probably let you live. Go back with him on the submarine to Germany. If I make it, I'll find you there."

"No! I'm not leaving you again!"

He touched her cheek, the side of her face. "Listen. He's going to kill me—*kill* me—once I show him the way back into that volcano. Unless I can escape. This is my best chance. *Your* best chance is to stay put and try to keep Jürgen and the others from hunting me down."

She looked doubtful. "What is it?"

"When I crawled out of the cave I found a cove . . ."

He whispered to her for some time. She lay there, deep in thought. "But how will you get that chance?"

"I don't know."

She rested her head on his shoulder. "I suspect it will be up to me to make it."

He could say nothing to that. Eventually, they slept.

The roar and shudder of the boat woke them. Hart looked at his watch. Sixteen hours. The ballast tanks were finally being blown and the submarine slowly rising. It was like being lifted from molasses. They groped hurriedly for their clothes, hauling them on.

"You stay behind for a moment," Greta said. "Try to sneak back in the excitement. Perhaps no one will notice where you were."

"I *want* him to know where I was. Exactly where I was. So there's no confusion."

"No. You have to survive, Owen. Survive until your chance. Don't lose your head."

They could hear a rising excitement from the decks above and when the schnorkel broke the surface a cheer rang out. The diesel engines rumbled into life and a cool breath of air came from the vent like a spring in a desert.

"So it's not over after all." She sounded almost sad. "We must go on."

"For a while. Someday this is going to be over and we're going to be together. Someday we're going to have time."

"Yes. Someday. Just remember to stay away from Jürgen."

She hugged him and moved toward the hatch. The handle was turning. She hoped to go up before anyone spotted Owen.

But when the hatch clanged open she had to jerk her head back from the fall of a pair of boots. Drexler thumped to the deck, looking concerned. "Greta, are you all right? I was worried about you!" Then he froze.

It was the damned American.

Greta had backed to stand with Hart. Fresher air was pouring in through the hatch and the couple took deep, shuddering breaths, holding each other in support. Jürgen himself looked haggard, his face lined with sleeplessness and his shirt soaked with sweat. He stared at the pilot in disbelief.

"I told you to stay away from her!" he said hoarsely.

"Yes, you did."

"God damn you!" Drexler's movement was swift. He yanked Greta away, shoving her against the bulkhead, and then whirled at his rival.

The pilot's fist struck him square in the face and the Nazi flew backward, slamming into the ladder with a grunt. He toppled, stunned, onto the deck. Hart clutched his fist, wincing. "Get up, you son of a bitch."

"Owen, don't! They'll kill you!"

There was a riot of shouts above and more booted bodies fell from the hatchway, filling the crowded laboratory. It was the storm troopers, Drexler's goons. Hart hauled his fist back to strike again but Hans lashed out expertly with a leg and the pilot went down with a bang, the wind whooshing out of him. Greta screamed and sprang, scratching, and was cuffed aside. As Hart boosted himself off the deck a boot caught him in the midsection and he dropped like a bag of sand. Another struck his head. He blacked out.

Greta was sobbing. Bristle-Head loomed over her, waiting.

"Leave her alone." It was Drexler, the words slurred by a bleeding mouth. He stood up stiffly, humiliated. His body shook as he strove to contain his emotion.

He pointed to Hart. "I want him chained this time. Until we get to the island." The SS men nodded.

Then he pointed to Greta. "And her I want alone. Down here. With me."

They dragged the unconscious American up through the hatch and it clanged shut. She stood stiffly, trembling. Drexler turned his face a moment to spit some blood, then licked his lips as he stared at her. His chest rose and fell, his eyes wounded.

"You *did* it with him, didn't you?" The tone was of utter disbelief. "Did it with him right here on the goddamned boat. Right in front of seventy men. My God."

She closed her eyes, a tear sliding down. "Please don't hurt him. Hurt me, but not him."

"Hurt you?" His voice filled with wonder. "Hurt *you?* My God, what could I possibly do to you that would remotely approach what you've done to me? You've *destroyed* me. You've obliterated any scrap of pride I had left. You've buried me with shame. You've made me a laughingstock. Hurt *you?* What a joke!"

"I told you!" she shouted, her eyes bright and wet. "I *told* you and you wouldn't listen! I told you I loved him and not you! So you put the three of us together on this damned submarine like a crazy man, babbling about working together—what did you *think* was going to happen?"

He looked defeated. "A last measure of . . . civility."

Tears were running freely down both cheeks. "Don't you see? It's too late for that."

He nodded dully. "Indeed."

She waited but he made no move. "So what are you going to do, Jürgen?"

He turned back to the ladder. "Save Germany."

CHAPTER THIRTY

Hart woke slowly. He was woozy, his body sore. When he turned there was a rattle and he blearily opened his eyes. He had a manacle on his wrist, surprisingly heavy. A chain led to a stanchion supporting his bunk. The submarine was rolling, he dimly noted, its diesels drumming a steady rumble that pounded in his head. They were on the surface and moving fast.

"Well, hell." He tugged feebly on the chain, slowly remembering what had happened. It was a wonder Drexler hadn't killed him. Apparently, he really was needed.

"Wake up. You need to eat." The pilot opened his eyes again. It was a sailor who bunked near him. Jacob, his name was, holding a mug of soup. "You should stay away from women. They're bad luck."

Hart sat up painfully and sipped. The broth seemed like it was flowing directly into his veins. "My luck is due to change."

"Not on this mission, I suspect."

Hart sipped again. "We're past the destroyers? Running on the surface?"

Jacob nodded. "For now. But we had to release some fuel to

make them think they scored a hit and we're rapidly burning what's left."

"I want to get out of this coffin."

"So does every man in the U-boat arm. Don't expect any sympathy from me."

Hart drained the cup.

"Good," Jacob said. "Now you go see the captain."

"I don't want to see the captain."

"That doesn't matter. He wants to see you."

The pilot lifted his manacled arm.

The sailor took out a key to unlock the chain. "The captain said to release you. If the colonel objects, he can take it up with Freiwald."

Groaning, Hart swung out of his bunk and followed Jacob to the control room. "Up there," the engineer pointed. Hart looked questioningly at the ladder. "The captain's on the conning tower. Here, take this coat and hat."

The tower well was shockingly cold after the long confinement in the submarine—cold enough to almost take his breath away. Then he inhaled deeply, sucking in clean air, and felt light-headed, almost intoxicated. It was glorious.

"Shut the damn hatch."

The pilot stood next to the captain. It was night. The U-boat was racing furiously through the swells, rocking with an easy gait as water foamed in a glittering rapid down the narrow foredeck. Hart hadn't realized how far south they'd come. The Germans were in a realm of lunar light so intense that icebergs glowed like the white mountains of the moon. The Milky Way was as palpable as a silk ribbon, stars and moon so reflective in the sea that there was an illusion they were sailing into the sky, or sailing upside down. They'd entered the Southern Ocean and he could pick out the Southern Cross. Antarctica lay somewhere ahead.

Hart pulled up his hood. Freiwald was leaning forward on the conning tower bulkhead to watch for ice while a sailor kept watch from the antiaircraft gun mount behind, too far to hear what the pair said. Out here it seemed as if they were the only people on the planet.

"We've made good time, Captain."

"These boats are incredibly swift underwater. And incredibly strong. We've just broken a depth record: that's why you're alive right now. If we had enough of them we could control the Atlantic." He shook his head. "But we don't. We in the navy knew this war was madness in 1939. Dönitz told us to be prepared to fight for seven years. We'll be lucky if we last that long."

"Jacob said you fooled them with a release of an oil slick."

"Confused them at least. Our satisfaction may only be temporary. We no longer have enough fuel to get back and so I've had to radio for a milch cow—a supply submarine—to rendezvous on our homeward voyage. It was a risk to make the call. U-boat Command claims it's scientifically impossible to break our codes—and yet why are all my friends on the bottom? I prefer to stay off the radio."

"What are our chances then?"

"Perhaps you know better than I?" the captain said, searchingly.

The pilot laughed. "*My* chances are lousy. I make a hash of things in Antarctica even in peacetime."

"And now you're doing no better in war."

His irritated tone sobered the pilot. "Meaning?"

"I called you up here because it's time I learned what's going on between you and the Drexlers. I don't tolerate fighting on my boat. I don't like my thirteen new passengers. I don't like arrogant SS pricks pretending to command my submarine, I don't like women showing up where they don't belong, and I don't like my insubordinate American prisoner. I want to hear a reason why I shouldn't throw all three of you overboard before you cause more trouble."

"Well." Hart considered. "You can't toss me because I'm the only one who knows how to get into a mountain to fetch what Germany wants. You can't toss Greta because she's the only one who knows how to process the drug we're going to find. You *could* toss Jürgen. I can't see that he's any use at all."

Freiwald scowled. "Why did you go to the laboratory during the attack? You knew that wasn't your station."

"I didn't see how it mattered where I was. I have no combat duties on board."

"Dammit, answer my question! Why did you insist on seeing the woman after you were told not to?"

Hart hesitated only a second. "I'm in love with Greta, Captain. And she's in love with me. She's married to Jürgen Drexler in name only. We fell in love before the war on a prior expedition to the island we're going to. I was delayed returning to the ship, Drexler reported I was dead, and eventually he persuaded Greta to marry him. When I learned she was still alive I stole a plane, flew to Berlin, and convinced her to run away with me. As you can imagine, this has produced some tension among the three of us."

"God in heaven." Freiwald frowned. "Does the High Command know about this?"

"Of course not. If they knew the truth, Drexler would be in an asylum. But then so would half the High Command."

Freiwald threw him a sour glance but didn't dispute the point. "And you. Why do you go along with this mission? You feel no loyalty to your country, to its cause?"

"Quite the contrary," Hart said grimly. He paused, wondering how much he should say. Finally, he decided he had nothing to lose by being frank. "Captain, there's a famous proverb about a peasant who angers a great king, sufficient to have the king order his death. Just as he's about to lose his neck, the peasant yells out to the sovereign, 'Wait, if you give me an additional year to live, I'll teach your horse to talk.' The king thinks it over and, deciding he has nothing to lose, grants the temporary reprieve. Afterward, a friend of the peasant approaches him and asks why he's struck a bargain he obviously can't deliver on. The peasant replies: 'A lot can happen in a year. I could die. The king could die. Even better, the king's horse could teach *himself* to talk.'"

Freiwald smiled at the punch line. "You're amusing, Hart. Amusing and, I think, very much a wild card in this whole thing. You make me nervous."

"I guess I have to hone my relationship skills."

Freiwald shifted slightly to put his back to the wind. "This drug everyone keeps referring to—tell me about it."

"A drug to control a new plague. The worst disease you've ever seen. Jürgen Drexler wants to unleash it on the world. And he needs your help to do it."

"And you think this is wrong."

"I think it's evil."

"To obtain an antibiotic?"

"A cure is the only safe way to unleash the disease. Surely you've figured that out by now."

"Jürgen says there's more to his plan."

"Has he told you what it is?"

"No."

"Nor me. Captain, you mustn't help him with this."

Freiwald looked out at the icebergs drifting across the sea. "Have you ever been to Hamburg, Hart?"

"Yes. The earlier expedition left from Hamburg."

"Have you ever seen a firestorm? Its effect?"

He swallowed. "No."

"The British caused a firestorm in Hamburg. A city burning so hot that it sucks oxygen toward its center like a whirlpool. Winds so powerful they can sweep up little children. Did you know that in one night more people died in Hamburg than in your American battle of Gettysburg? Not soldiers! Women. Children. Old people."

"I saw the London Blitz, Captain. You're describing modern war."

"Exactly. And that's why Jürgen Drexler is no monster. He's simply a modern man. A modern warrior. Religion has been replaced with ideology. The centurions of morality are gone, the walls of order breached. We live in a barbaric age."

"Captain, if you follow Drexler to the bitter end I swear he'll kill you. His cause is disaster. Don't risk death for this man."

"I don't risk death for *this* man, whose mind and character I find dubious at best. I don't risk death even for our Führer. But I do risk death for the Fatherland. I do risk it to save Germany. And I don't fear death. Do you know why?"

"No. Why?"

"Because I've already died, and the man you see standing before you is a ghost. You see, my family was in Hamburg that night, and they were roasted in that firestorm, and all the good in me died with them." He nodded. "So you *will* help us, Hart, because in the modern world terror must be met with terror."

"Somewhere it has to end, Captain."

"And Jürgen Drexler promises he can end it. So. Now you'll go below so Jacob can lock you to your bunk again."

CHAPTER THIRTY-ONE

Atropos Island loomed on the horizon like a thunderous cloud, towering and shadowy. The white of its glaciers evaporated into mist that billowed to form fantastic canyons of creamy vapor, the confection topped by the darker syrup of a volcanic plume from the second peak. The increase in eruptive activity did not appear to be threatening enough to prevent their reentering the caldera anchorage, but the drift of ash added to the unease of the German soldiers and sailors on deck. As they approached the island the sea was a flat calm, the submarine threading slowly through dark water between rafts of pack ice. The temperature was below freezing and the conning tower was frosted. The sky overhead was a patchwork: an occasional squall would send a brief snow flurry across the boat, followed a few minutes later by pale polar sun. As they rounded the flank of the island some of the flakes were grayer and grittier. Volcanic ash, the sailors were told. They held up their mittens in wonder.

Even Hart was allowed to come up on deck. He watched the tail of volcanic smoke with disquiet, wondering what this change meant for descending underground. And yet when the *U-4501* nosed through the caldera entrance the harbor seemed not to have changed at all in six years. There was still the same pinto pattern of pumice and snow, still the absence of any bird or animal life, still the lonely beaches that steamed in the cold. Even the crates of supplies left by the *Schwabenland* remained undisturbed. He shivered, but not from the temperature. The familiarity of it after so many years seemed chilling. The bodies of the mountaineers, he assumed, still lay where they fell, stained a coffee color and mummified by the dry freeze of time.

Freiwald anchored not far from the underwater wreck of the *Bergen*, and the U-boat men on deck began assembly of a prefabricated motor launch. Antarctic clothing was dragged out of storage and ropes, buckets, lanterns, lamps, and packs were readied. Despite the smoking volcano, there was an air of excitement aboard now that they'd survived the attack and reached Antarctica. Here would be a tale to tell one's grandchildren about.

Hart was issued a parka, boots, a backpack, lights, food, and climbing gear that included an ice ax. He joined five other SS men on the foredeck. Last to emerge were Jürgen and Greta. It was the first time the pilot had seen her since the depth charge attack and she granted him a brief, reassuring smile but didn't attempt to speak. She was solemn as she looked at the island. Owen was relieved that her face was unmarked.

Drexler seemed subdued but determined. "Here's where you earn your keep, Hart," he growled, keeping between the pilot and Greta. "I could blast and dig my way into the mountain the old way but it would take time and we have no timbers to shore up the ceiling. The alternative you found will prove more expedient, I hope."

"It might be a tight squeeze for some of your gorillas, Jürgen. Those boys afraid of the dark?"

The storm troopers looked scornfully at the pilot.

"My men aren't afraid of anything but failure. Which is the only thing you should fear as well. We'll get what we came for one way or another. But if you and my wife assist as promised, things will be easier for everyone."

Hart looked evenly at the soldiers. "Looking forward to their company. Especially Hans there, the one with the big boot."

The yellow-haired giant grinned at him.

They clambered into the launch, motored ashore, and the party shouldered their packs. The pilot led off, switchbacking up the slope of the crater. Soon they were sweating in the cold, the submarine shrinking in the lagoon below. As they neared the rim Hart noticed the launch had returned to the submarine and another party was boarding. The pilot thought he recognized among them the cadaverous, hunched figure of Schmidt. Where was *he* going?

They moved on up to the crest and out of sight of the submarine, Drexler bringing up the rear with Greta. It was clear he wasn't anxious for the American to talk to her, but the German maintained his own stiff distance from her as well. Whatever their exchange after the depth charge attack, it hadn't been a friendly one. Owen decided to be patient. Despite the situation his spirits had revived somewhat with his escape from the confines of the *U-4501*. Even the dour SS men brightened. The air was sharp and cold and exquisitely clean. The unaccustomed walking brought an almost welcome tightness to their muscles. Hart paused frequently. "Drink lots of water," he kept admonishing. "It's arid here, despite the snow."

They circuited the crest in a window of brilliant sunshine, Hart looking down the dry valley where he knew the husks of the dead Germans still lay scattered. Was that where Schmidt was aiming? To get the bodies or the spores? The pilot decided against pointing out the deadly vale to his group of Germans. Like it or not, they all needed each other to descend safely into the mountain. Panic wouldn't help.

Beyond the valley he could see the other volcano, exhausting unevenly. Sometimes the plume would be dark with ash and other times it would lighten with steam. The snow around its top had been stained charcoal. He wondered what Elmer would make of this. "The island doesn't want you to be here," the old Eskimo would have said. "I don't want to be here either," Hart would have replied.

When they'd hiked the rim to the seaward side of the crater Hart abruptly turned off the crest. Below was a panoramic view. To his left was the sea, the island skirted by a fractured maze of pack ice. Directly ahead was the snowy plateau where he'd landed the *Boreas,* bordered by the adjacent jagged ridge of rock that linked the two volcanoes. Behind, to his right, was the valley. Without a word he led them skittering downward on the snow of the volcano's outer flank. They stopped on the shelf of bare basalt that extruded from the mountain a third of the way down its slope.

Hart looked back up. "It's tough going back over the rim of the volcano," he told the soldiers. "You're going to get a workout packing our cargo to the submarine."

"We're not afraid to work," Hans said.

Hart nodded. "Of course we *did* have a tube leading right through the mountain, right out to the caldera, but Colonel Drexler demolished that one. Back in 1939. You can ask him about it on the way back up."

"It was an accidental collapse, Hart. And keep your tiresome history to yourself."

"Yes, my commander." He gave a mock salute and pointed with the tip of his ax. "The exit I found is right there."

Still looking like a sleepy eye, a dark slit of a hole looked out at the ocean and its mosaic of ice. "We're crawling in there?" Rudolf, the man Hart knew as Bristle-Head, asked doubtfully.

"It's bigger inside."

They paused to get out the ropes and lights, including miner's helmets with headlamps. As the others finished preparing to enter the cave, Hart looked intently down the volcano's flank at the small, relatively ice-free bay far below. His eye swept its shoreline as if searching for something. Then, while Drexler was bent over his pack, he moved quickly to Greta.

"It's still there," he whispered.

She looked down the slope quickly, not seeing what he'd spotted, and then glanced at the sea. "The ocean's so vast," she worried.

"But possible."

She stole a touch of his gloved hand.

"Hart, are you ready?" Drexler snapped. He was following their gaze with suspicion, obviously irritated at the whispering but not wanting to make a scene. The SS men looked at the trio with interest.

"I'm ready."

"Then do your job and lead."

The initial crawl led to the sandy room near the entrance. Then the tube became tight again as it led down into the mountain. Hart explained that he'd leave a colored flag every ten meters or so to mark the convoluted route. The cave would temporarily widen when they reached the long vertical chimney—the elevator shaft—that he and Fritz had descended so long ago. Then narrow once again before the grotto. They'd fix climbing ropes along the route.

The group worked slowly, bracing themselves against a sudden fall. Periodically a rock would break loose and roll down through the spelunkers, banging its way ahead of them into the pits below.

"Dammit! This is worse than that midget-designed submarine," Hans complained after sliding through a tight spot on his back, dragging his pack behind him.

"At least it's warmer in here than outside," Bristle-Head responded.

"It's warmer anywhere than outside."

Hart had to pause several times, occasionally backtracking. The lava tubes were a labyrinth; it'd been a miracle he'd found his way back out in the dark. Now he deliberately took a periodic wrong turn, trying to develop a mental picture of where all the alternate routes led. The rest of the party rested gratefully while he explored. "I nearly died in here once and I don't want to make a wrong turn again," he explained.

The chimney remained the most daunting. The lava tube descended to its roof with the dangerous pitch of a children's slide, then opened to a vertical well hundreds of feet deep. Owen cautiously let himself down on a rope to that junction and, letting his legs dangle in space, dropped a rock to emphasize the need for caution. It fell into the blackness without a sound for what seemed like an eternity of time, finally banging and bouncing somewhere far below. Its echoes drifted up to them.

"Jesus," one of the SS men said. "This dung hole is virtually bottomless. We're climbing down there?"

"Not only that," said Hart, "but you're going to have to climb back out. With a heavier pack than you have now."

"I hate this fucking war."

"Finally, we agree."

The pilot unreeled a rope into the darkness and started down, pausing periodically to drive climbing pitons to anchor the line. Gingerly, the others followed.

At the shelf where the tube from the old entrance joined the chimney, Hart paused until the group reassembled. Everyone was breathing hard. He glanced at Greta. She'd been compliant but silent, freezing the Nazis out, and the soldiers tended to keep a wary distance. Drexler stayed nearer, always between his wife and Hart, and yet avoided looking at her.

She was gazing down the chimney to where they'd descended before, lost in memory, when Hart jerked his head down the horizontal tube and said, "This way." Greta's mouth opened in surprise and then closed. They walked as if exiting the mountain from the tube that had collapsed.

"Jürgen!" Hart called. "Can you come up to the front? I want to show you something."

Drexler pushed ahead. The beam from his headlamp picked out a wall of cascading rock from the cave-in, and it was obvious that Hart had led them to another dead end. He was impatient with the frequent detours but had refrained from complaining: he still needed the American. "What is it?" he asked grumpily.

"The result of German purpose." Hart was searching with the beam from his own helmet. "There." He pointed.

Greta gasped. Bones. Lying broken in a heap of rubble was a body, decay far advanced in the relative warmth of the cave. The skull still had a few leathery scraps. A buckle, buttons, and a pocketknife were ensnarled on the web of tendrils clinging to the skeletal ribs. Rocks still obscured the mashed legs.

Drexler had gone rigid.

"Why it's Fritz, Jürgen!" Hart said. "Lying right where that cave-in you started crushed the life out of him."

There was a murmur of unease among the SS men. "This is bad luck," one muttered.

Drexler looked balefully at Hart. "What's this got to do with our mission?"

"Just underscores your deep concern for the men who serve under you."

"Spare me the finger pointing, Hart. Smart-mouthed communist or not, Eckermann was not someone I wished dead. He simply was in the wrong place at the right time."

"Well, we're going to bury him."

"We don't have time for this maudlin pity!"

Hart crossed his arms. "We're staying here until he's covered with rocks and a prayer said over his grave."

No one wanted to spend more time arguing in the depth of the cave. The little German was swiftly covered with stones and Hart led the others in the Lord's Prayer, a couple of the SS men stumbling over the words. Then he turned to the others. "This was one man. Before we go farther on this mission, I want you to imagine burying a million others: the victims of a new plague."

"We're all tired of your moral pretensions, Hart," Drexler added. "There's a war on. And we're down here to *save* lives, not kill them: to get a cure, not a disease. I suggest the first life you should worry about is your own. So. Lead on."

Owen looked at them sadly. "Very well." He pointed. "We go back to the shaft." The men moved off, anxious to get away from the body. Drexler led this time.

The pilot caught up to Greta, looking at her with concern. "Are you all right?"

She nodded. "Yes. We only quarreled."

"It worries me to leave you alone with him."

"I'm not afraid of Jürgen."

"I am."

The American Intelligence officer sat on the embassy terrace in Lisbon, the contents of a folder spilled across the table. It was evening, the night cool but not unpleasant. The naval attaché had called them there.

"Maybe the kraut isn't a liar after all," he told them.

"Come on, Sam," the OSS man scoffed. "He doesn't have a shred of evidence for his wild story. And how do we know he didn't just murder Hart? The German is either a plant or a psychotic."

"I thought that too." The attaché pointed to the papers. "Except that his story is beginning to check out."

"What do you mean?"

"Six days ago an escort carrier task force transiting to the Indian Ocean put up a routine air patrol and encountered a German submarine in the South Atlantic, far away from any convoy route or the normal battlefields. A big boat, the pilots thought, and their guess was that it was heading for Japan on some kind of swap mission. They depth-charged and got a slick. They couldn't confirm the kill, however."

"So?"

"Two days later we intercepted a coded radio message from a sub even farther south. It said the pig-boat was short on fuel and needed resupply to get back to Germany. Asked for a future rendezvous with a milch cow, but not immediately: it was going somewhere first. The timing is odd. Not enough time to get to Japan, certainly. South America, possibly. Or . . . Antarctica."

The OSS man frowned.

"Think about it, Phil," the naval attaché reasoned. "This man Kohl shows up raving about a secret mission and then we independently find a submarine about where he predicted it would be.

Besides, why would this Kohl come here when he's an escapee from France?"

"Because he wants us to divert resources way the hell down into Antarctica. It's a Nazi ploy."

"Maybe. But what if he's right? What if he's really changing sides? An opportunist like him, this late in the war . . ."

"Sam . . ."

"We've got a destroyer at Punta Arenas. We've got the biggest damn navy in the world, Hitler is on the ropes . . ."

"Tell that to the guys getting pasted in the Bulge!"

". . . and we can afford to divert one ship. Dammit, Phil, what if he's right?"

"Or what if the krauts are building some kind of secret hide-out down there?" the deputy ambassador interjected quietly. "To hole up after the war. I think Sam is right. I think we should ask the navy to check this out."

"I don't know if we can convince Washington."

"We can if we promise them a sub to bag," the attaché said.

"And we can put that damned oily Nazi on board," the deputy ambassador suggested. "To either help us find this sub or be left down there for causing us the trouble."

CHAPTER THIRTY-TWO

Greta felt violated. The grotto in the cave had been a secret place, a sweet memory she'd clung to during all the dark years of the war. Now Jürgen's SS ruffians occupied it like lords, their coarse laughter a despoiling sacrilege. It was as if fate was determined to ruin all she held dear. She loathed Jürgen for coming here. Even if he didn't know what had happened on the blankets then perhaps he could guess, and if he guessed it was like an invasion of her deepest privacy, her fondest moment. The memory had become stained.

Owen was wet and shivering: the Germans were using him as a slave. They'd rigged a rope down the chute of water that led to the underground lake and sent him down with small steel buckets, hoisting up his harvest of the mysterious drug organism. The lake was as warm as ever, Owen had reported, but the constant soaking and the exhausting climb left him weary and chilled. Now he'd been allowed a respite to throw his soaked clothes on the hot rocks and wrap himself in a blanket. He looked frustrated and helpless. Sometimes Greta caught him looking at her sadly and she had to look away, not wanting to reveal her own despair.

As she squatted on the banks of the underground river, the biologist's own muscles ached as she sieved the slime into a concentration that would be packed to the surface. Two of the SS men had already departed with a load. Now Jürgen came over and gazed downward at her. His gloom had metamorphosed into nervous excitement now that the work had begun.

"Is this what we want?" he asked. "Is this going to cure the disease?"

She put down her sieve and tiredly rocked back on her heels. "I don't know, Jürgen. Yes, this is what Owen and I found, but who knows if it can be grown in mass quantities? This is such an unusual place, a dark cavern, its water full of unknown microscopic life and chemicals. It may take a long time to duplicate in a laboratory."

"We don't have a long time. We barely have even a short time. That's why it's imperative to start experimenting now, in the submarine. I want to know what's necessary for success before we leave this island. If we have to pump some of this water to propagate this organism, we'll do it."

She wearily wiped her forehead with her arm. "So Germany can unleash your microbe?"

"No! So I can end this war."

She looked up skeptically. "Jürgen, can't you see how insane this is?"

"Why do you insist on seeing me as a monster?"

"Maybe because I'm a captive?" She stood stiffly, her hands at the small of her back. "Maybe because you named this island after the Greek Fate who ends life?"

He scowled.

"Yes, I looked it up."

"Listen, I don't *want* a captive," he said impatiently. "I want a partner. I wouldn't have had to confine you if you'd exhibited the loyalty and faith of a proper German wife."

"And when have you ever behaved like a proper German husband? When have you ever let love compete with ambition?"

He half raised his hand at that and the SS men looked their way with interest. Then his hand dropped. "For God's sake, let's stop this silly quarreling," he hissed. "Six years of marriage and still you don't know me, still you don't understand me."

"I understand that unless we move cautiously, nothing good can come of this."

He looked impatient. "And that's where you're wrong. Only speed can win success." He considered a moment. "You're right, our motives are more complex than what I revealed in Berlin. But not in the way you think. I told you I had more to reveal about my plans and now is the time, I think. Time to comprehend what we're doing here. Time you learned the true Jürgen Drexler." He turned to the American. "Hart! Come over here!" Then he turned back to Greta. "I'll tell you both, and then you'll understand why we've come back this long, hard way."

The trio moved out of earshot of the remaining three SS men and Drexler stood, thinking about what he was going to say. Their triangle looked bedraggled. Hart was wet, his eyes tired, and Greta and Jürgen were grimy. No one had slept properly in weeks.

"Listen," Drexler finally began. "Do you think I'd be down in this dank asshole of the earth, processing scum, if not for a great purpose? I mean, my God! This is hell, I think!" He waved at the grotto.

"Interesting that you claim to know, Jürgen," Hart said.

Drexler scowled. "Shut up for once, you uneducated buffoon. I'm tired of mockery from a man who has accomplished nothing with his life except the theft of my wife." He let that hang. "Has it penetrated your dim brain yet that I don't need you anymore now that you've led us back into the mountain? That you've become superfluous to our expedition? One more sneering comment and I'll shoot you myself!"

The pilot opened his mouth, then thought better of it.

Drexler took a deep breath. "All right. Good. Now. It's true that when we came to this island the first time, my initial interest was solely in the disease. A tool for German defense, I thought, or at least for research. But then my men got sick and died and it seemed over, at least until we could return."

"So why not leave it be?" she asked.

"I'm coming to that. Will you please *listen?*" He looked at her with frustration. "We reported what we'd found, of course, but Reich strategists pointed out such a disease was too dangerous for us to use unless our own troops were immune. And then the war began, our victories were stunning, Antarctica was far away, and the matter receded from my mind. But as the Reich's fortunes darkened my thoughts returned to this island. I remembered Greta's excitement after your exploration of this cave and wondered if I'd been too hasty. And then *you* appeared, Hart! A personal disaster, yes. But also a revelation. An inspiration! Because I realized that in our personal problems was a key to success. Not to destroy, but to end the destruction. To force an armistice to this war."

"Jürgen, the war's ending soon anyway," Hart objected. "Maybe by Christmas."

"That's where you're wrong. That's what you don't understand. Even as we speak Germany is launching a great new offensive in the West that will take the Allies totally by surprise. And this is only the beginning of what our Führer promises. This remarkable new submarine that saved your life is merely one of hundreds being built that will soon reverse the tide of the naval war. The Reich has developed a new kind of airplane with a revolutionary jet engine. And Germany is building rockets capable of reaching America. The war is not nearly finished, Hart. It could go on for years. Years and years. Unless *we* act. Unless we succeed."

And you wouldn't disclose all these secrets unless I'm about to be sacrificed, the pilot thought gloomily.

"And so the idea that came to me is to use this microbe not as an instrument of mass murder but of mass salvation. To put an end to this war once and for all. To bring the world to its senses. Because with your antibiotic, Greta, suddenly we're not threatening death. We're offering life."

"What?"

"Look. Even if we could unleash this plague and perfectly protect our own people, Germany's peril would not be over. The other side would still seek to retaliate. There are rumors the Americans are working on a superweapon of their own: some new kind of bomb. German scientists think such a bomb is years away, but who knows? What if we escalated the war and the United States replied in turn? Killing begets killing. That's been the lesson of this century. But what if we offered *life?* What if we offered the Allies the opportunity to *cure* a terrible plague, in return for agreeing to an armistice? What if we could achieve a cease-fire on our terms? Yes, peace! By an emergency effort of German doctors and nurses to end a pestilence in Washington or London or Moscow."

The couple looked confused. "But, Jürgen," Greta objected, "how would such a plague get started?"

"By rocket," he answered matter-of-factly. "Or plane or submarine or even truck. We'd have to deliver the spores. The swiftest would be a V-2 air burst at night. Whole cities could be held hostage to the germ, the clock ticking. But no one would have to die if the Allies agreed quickly enough to German help in return for peace. And then the war could end."

"You'd infect a whole city?"

"Yes. And then save it. To end the war, you see. To balance terror with mercy, and thus bring peace. In the final accounting we'll be heroes." He looked at them expectantly.

"But women? Children?" Greta objected. "People will flee, the problems with distributing an antibiotic—"

"Those are *details.* It will work. It will work! If we *make* it work. And it begins here, in this cave. So you see, I'm *not* a monster, Greta. I'm a man of vision. The one man who can clearly see how to end this war on German terms."

She looked at him with dismay.

Hart spoke up. "Well, I quit."

Drexler sighed. "Hart, you can't quit—until I say so." The threat was clear.

"Jürgen," Greta said despairingly, "just let the war end by it-self—"

"No! I refuse to be a victim of events when I have the oppor-tunity to direct them. What we have here is a dazzling opportu-nity, far more dazzling than what we hoped for when we first came to Antarctica. This is what I've been waiting to tell you. This is what I've been waiting to share with you. Will you help?"

Greta studied her husband for a long time. Then, slowly, sadly, she nodded. "I'll do what I have to do, Jürgen."

"Are the charges ready?" Schmidt asked mildly, hunching in the cold wind of the dry valley. His voice was muffled behind the visor of his gas mask.

"Yes, Doctor. It should be quite a show." The SS man was splic-ing the wires to the detonator.

Schmidt looked sourly at the smoking volcano above them, the vista blurred by the scratched eyepieces of his mask. The plume of ash had made him nervous the whole time they were collecting spores at the upper end of the frozen lake and he wanted to get back to the submarine before the damned woman did: she might become irrational if she knew he was collecting more than a few spores to test the antidote—if she realized they'd come to stock-pile the disease as well as the cure. That was not the only reason for his impatience: he hated the outdoors and couldn't wait to get back to the controlled environment of the U-boat. He also hated the clammy rubber of the mask but knew it was all that was keep-ing him alive until Greta returned with the antidote. The mum-mified bodies they'd passed in the valley had been warning enough. He dared not breathe a spore.

It was obvious the bacteria were carried to the surface in hot springs, spores drying on the surface and then carried by wind across the island. It might be impossible to permanently shut off the source but it seemed feasible to hide it at least until the end of the war, lest the Allies come here. The Reich had enough spores now to begin mass propagation in laboratories. At the rapid rate of bacterial growth there'd be plenty of plague within weeks. Their flowering would coincide with the readying of the rockets.

Schmidt thought Drexler's elaborate scheme to hold Allied capitals hostage to peace was absurd. Too complicated. Better to kill as many of the enemy as possible while waiting for additional German superweapons to reach the field. War was about killing, not psychology. But Drexler was most energetic when allowed his naive dreams, so the doctor let him prattle. And the question was moot until both disease and cure were in hand. Schmidt was content to leave the final strategy to others: as a man of science he preferred the purity of research.

He longed for a cigarette and wished he could tear off the mask to light one. Well. At least the first step was done. Time to start back home.

"Detonation," he ordered calmly. The soldier twisted the crank.

A boom thundered on the glacier that hung over the end of the valley and a geyser of snow and dirty till erupted into the air, cracks racing away on the ice. Then another and another and another, on and on, some explosions quite high on the frozen snout. Their crack was counterpointed by a deeper rumble of avalanche. A slurry of snow, chunks of ice, and glacial rock debris started down, pushing a billowing white cloud before it.

"Splendid!" The mask made Schmidt look like a gigantic insect. Behind it his eyes glowed as he watched the mantle of the mountain slide down. The SS squad faced away as a shock wave of air hit and staggered them, a momentary blizzard of snow and dust blowing by. Then the avalanche clattered to a stop and it was quiet again, the hot springs covered with a rubble of rocks, dirt, and chunks of ice. Wisps of steam curled upward.

The SS men cheered, the sound muffled behind their masks. The doctor studied their handiwork. There'd be some melt but the terrain was covered enough to discourage others from collecting. The secret was sealed.

"Gentlemen, the Reich now holds a monopoly on the trump card of history," he told them. "Let's take our prize back to the boat."

CHAPTER THIRTY-THREE

Greta was exhausted, slumped on a crate in the submarine's makeshift laboratory after almost thirty hours of nonstop work. She was alone. Schmidt, having succeeded in multiplying the microbe so they could test the antidote, had finally pleaded the weariness of age and staggered off. Now she sat breathing through a gauze mask, her hands rubbered, staring at the cages with a sense of ashen victory. Four of the rabbits were dead, their bodies elongated as if tormented on a rack. She could see the small white teeth of their final grimace. It was clear that the cave organism didn't immunize against the disease: giving it to the animals *before* they were injected with plague had done no good at all. The rest of the animals had survived, however, after being infected first by the microbe and then treated with antibiotic. They'd sickened briefly, some writhing in their cage, and then recovered. As a cure, the stuff worked.

She hated killing the laboratory animals. But maybe she had a bizarre tool now to save human lives and stop a greater madness, as Jürgen suggested. Had she done the right thing? Or was she making the unleashing of the microbe even more likely by combating it? In her weariness she felt she'd lost her moral compass and suddenly envied the certainty of the nuns she'd grown up with. But then what dilemmas did they ever face, the sheltered sisters? She wished she had Owen to talk to.

The biologist stretched, desperately tired and yet too tense to sleep. Conditions were so crude. A single water pipe and a crude drain. An alcohol stove. Planks had been set to make a workbench for Schmidt's microbial cultures, the originating spores harvested from the dry valley. The doctor hadn't wanted to draw on Germany's safely guarded microbe supply, he said, because of the risk involved in taking the cultures aboard ship sans antidote. Better, he explained to her, to wait until they arrived at Atropos to bring spore samples aboard. The cultures were lined under lamps now, petri platters of disease. Next to them were other cultures of more mild diseases, which they *had* felt safe bringing along. So far, the antibiotic seemed equally effective against them.

Greta intended to recommend destroying all the disease cultures before the U-boat sailed. Their usefulness had pretty much ended, and what was the point of taking chances?

The experiments suggested the expedition would be a success. Early tests in a vat showed promise that the drug organism could be grown and multiplied in Germany. Greta's experiment at reducing the scum to a more stable, storable, and usable dry powder with heat and evaporation had also succeeded: rabbits injected with it had recovered as rapidly as those given the compound raw. So the antibiotic worked, at least on animals or when swabbed or dripped into a lab dish. Admittedly, drugs were so mysterious and variable that the organism's true value couldn't be determined before clinical human tests at home. Still, they had the drug and that meant Jürgen must keep his promise: Owen would be released from the cave and would come to her again here in the submarine. Wouldn't he?

Unexpectedly, the idea depressed her. Owen's return would mean he would then attempt his escape, and even if he succeeded—which he admitted was unlikely—they'd be separated again at least until the end of the war. With Owen gone, the submarine would be sealed again for its long voyage home and she'd once more be imprisoned in a microcosm of the Reich she'd come to despise. Locked together again with Jürgen Drexler. She longed to run away with Owen but knew that if she did the alarm might be raised more quickly and their chances cut to zero. Aboard, she might delay or confuse any pursuit. To save him, she had to give him up. That was their plan.

The necessity was terrible.

With a sense of grim purpose, she reached into a drawer for the backpack she'd pilfered and set out for the ship's galley, where she hoped to steal enough food to keep a man alive on the open sea for—dare she think it?—several weeks.

Hart groaned. Hans was awakening him again by jabbing him with the tip of a boot. It was "morning," or what passed for morning in the sunless dungeon of the grotto. The pilot was still sore from his tantrum the evening before. The Nazi's arrogance had finally prompted Hart to take a tired, wild swing at the yellow-haired bastard and Owen had found himself expertly flipped onto his back, the Nazi's knees on his chest.

"You're too easy, Hart. I like to fight but you don't even make it fun." Hans had slapped him, almost casually, but enough to cut his lip. "You should learn to fight. It's part of being a man."

Hart spat at him and was cuffed so hard that his head rang. Then he lay still, defeated.

"He's a pussy," Hans said to Rudolf.

Hart was also tired from the increasingly long swims into the lake to gather the diaphanous organism. The SS men wouldn't help him, sitting instead at the top of the waterfall to haul up his harvest and playing cards in the lantern light. He knew they were trying to sap his energy as carefully as he was trying to conserve his strength. He was a slave and when the gathering was done his life would be over as well. No opportunity for escape had yet presented itself. As if to remind him of that, there was a clanking as he shifted his leg to get up. Each night Hans shackled him with a manacle to a cluster of cooking pots that served as a crude alarm.

"Like the bell of a goat," the storm trooper had said.

Now a new SS man named Oscar had descended for breakfast, unshouldering his heavy pack with a relieved grunt. The pans were unlocked from Hart's leg, rinsed quickly, and a small camp stove was turned on to heat water. Hart limped over to accept some bread. They didn't give him enough to eat for the work he was doing. When he'd complained, Bristle-Head had kicked his soup into the sand.

"You're in luck, American," the Nazi now growled. "We've got nearly as much as we can carry out of this hole. One more day! You're tired of swimming, no?"

"I'm tired of swimming."

"Yes, and you should learn to be tired of women." He waggled a spoon at the pilot. "They bring nothing but trouble. Look at you." The SS men laughed.

"Look at me." Hart chewed morosely then, thinking. "Oscar," he finally ventured, "that's a big pack you brought in if all we're doing is climbing out."

"Heavy, yes. But I get to leave it here."

"Leave it?"

The men looked at each other. Hans shrugged.

"Explosives," Bristle-Head explained. "To finish what the colonel started back in 1939. Seal this place up so that only Germany has this drug. Ka-boom!" He spread his hands, smiling. Then he squinted in mock suspicion. "You don't have other exits up your sleeve, do you?"

"Do you think I'd tell you?"

He sneered. "You'd tell me anything if I wanted you to."

"Well, the answer is no, but I think this place is going to blow anyway. Have you felt those tremors? That other volcano? Like the cave-in before."

Hans and Oscar looked uneasy but Bristle-Head nodded. "Good. We'll give Mother Nature a hand." He brought his hands together with a crash. "Now. Enough dawdling. Time to go swimming, Hart."

The pilot wearily stood and shed his boots and outer garments, stuffing them under a rock near his blanket. Then he trudged to the lip of the water chute and grasped the fixed rope, wincing as he stepped into the cold of the underground river. If he was going to escape he'd have to give those thick-headed bastards the slip on the climb out of the cave. First the shadowy lake, however. "I could use more help," he called.

"We have to pack out your damn scum," said Oscar. "That's help enough."

The morning watch had begun and Schmidt had risen with the sailors, unshaven and with his gray hair matted and tangled. Up on deck he took a drag on a cigarette and stared thoughtfully across the lagoon, reflecting on how splendidly the mission seemed to be coming together. He'd already cached a plentiful supply of the spores in a sealed container, and the last of the antidote organism was due to be gathered today. Assuming Frau Drexler's testing still showed it was effective, they were home free. The next step was to process the remaining cave sludge before more came aboard. He descended to the laboratory.

Greta was already there, peering uneasily at his microbial cultures on the lab bench. "Ah, I see your appetite for the work has you up early too," Schmidt said.

She glanced up. "I'm not used to such enthusiasm so early in the morning, Doctor. Why the good cheer?"

"Why not?" Reflexively, his hands went for another cigarette but then he remembered the injunction against smoking belowdecks. "We're about to set sail for the Reich, where the High Command is bound to be delighted at the gifts we'll be bearing. I assume your data still suggests one hundred percent efficiency when the drug is reduced to a powder?"

"There are no guarantees until we administer it to human subjects. I just hope the antibiotic is effective against a broad array of bacteria. If, as I suspect, this substance is many times more effective than penicillin, there are many sick people we'll be able to help."

"Yes, of course." He gazed at her with wonder. Did she really think they were here to cure a flu?

Greta noticed his look. "Not that *you* care. I know you and Jürgen have a different goal."

"Do you now?" Schmidt looked amused.

She leaned back wearily. "I can halfway understand Jürgen's point of view. He's a soldier. He wants to win. But you're a doctor, Schmidt. You swore an oath—"

"The only vow I took was a personal one. To follow knowledge's path wherever it led me. These organisms you and I have harvested these past few days—our respective contributions to the Reich—they are a higher form of efficiency, a purer biology. Only the ignorant walk away from knowledge—especially knowledge that can be used in defense of the homeland."

Greta looked at him sadly. "You lied to me, didn't you? You never had the microbe in Germany. You collected the spores not just for these tests but to take back home."

"If you figured that out, Frau Drexler, you're the last one on the boat to do so. The collection is necessary only because you threw your indignant fit in 1939 and destroyed your cultures, betraying science."

"So if I hadn't agreed to come back here this time to save Owen, there wouldn't be a threat of plague." Her tone was hollow.

"Don't exaggerate your importance. I would have come for the bacteria anyway. Still, I'll concede you've been useful. Now you have your drug and I have my microbe. We've gathered more than enough spore material for our purposes. And if the enemy retraces our steps, they'll find nothing."

"What are you talking about?"

"Do you think we're reckless enough to let other nations follow our example? We set explosives to bury the springs where the spores emerge. Let the Allies poke where they will, *if* they come.

They'll find rubble. And by March the Reich will have cultured enough to wipe out all our enemies."

Greta looked at him in dismay. Yet her heart began to beat faster, a flicker of excitement pushing aside her weariness. "Then what we have on this submarine are now the *only* microbes and spores?" she clarified.

"More precious than gold," Schmidt enthused. He gave Greta a wary look. "And I suppose you're about to volunteer to help me safeguard our stash: protect them as you did on the *Schwabenland*. Well, you needn't bother. The microbe has become a matter of state security and I've found a spot aboard for the remaining spores that I alone know about."

She looked at him with disquiet. "That's dangerous, Max. What if a sailor stumbles on them? What if Freiwald finds out what you've tucked around his U-boat?"

"Safer than putting them in *your* custody. Safer than leaving them in this lab."

She had no comeback for that.

Schmidt turned to go. "The spores are mine, the drug is yours. My advice: keep your mind on the drug. Since your purification process appears to work, I suggest you concentrate some more of this cave slime to make room. An additional load will be coming on board from the cave soon."

CHAPTER THIRTY-FOUR

The gloom of the underground lake abruptly deepened.

Hart stopped, treading water. It wasn't completely dark because there was still a faint blue glow from the ice roof, but the reflected light that came from the lantern at the upper end of the cave waterfall had gone out. He waited a minute for the storm troopers to restore it but nothing happened. The pilot shouted. There was no answer. He could just make out the pale glimmer of the falls and he began breast-stroking toward it. The light didn't come back on.

He reached the rock shelf at the base of the waterfall, rested a moment, and then boosted himself up. With growing apprehension he side-stepped along the ledge to the waterfall and groped in its spray for the climbing line. The rope had disappeared.

"Hans!" he yelled. "Rudolf!"

Silence.

They'd abandoned him.

So much for Drexler's promise. Greta must have succeeded with the drug and the couple's usefulness was at an end. Worriedly, he wondered if Drexler would harm her.

Hart had expected them to wait until the last of the lake growth had been delivered to the sub. His escape plan—it was more a desperate *hope* than a plan—had always called for Greta's assistance. She'd organize a distraction of some sort, make sure he had at least some supplies—enough to attempt the unthinkable.

By simply leaving him in this dark hole, though, Drexler seemed to have foreclosed that possibility. He tried to think. They must be satisfied he couldn't follow even though he'd mentioned his climb out in the dark before. How could they be so sure? What were they counting on?

Of course. Rudolf had said it. They were going to blow up the cave.

"My God."

He shivered. *Don't panic! If you panic you'll never get back to Greta.*

He realized he had one chance. They must have allowed time for themselves to get clear of the grotto: Fritz's skeleton had forcibly demonstrated how unstable the tubes were during a nearby explosion. The lantern hadn't been extinguished that long. It was plain: he'd have to catch them before the timer went off.

He clenched the cliff. He *would* catch them.

He'd climbed this waterfall and chimney so frequently along the rope, learning hand- and footholds, that he should be able to do it blind without one. Now that would be tested. Reaching up in the cold water he groped for a familiar handhold, found it, and pulled, placing his foot next. Yes. Just as he remembered. Think! Go slow enough to think.

When would the explosion go off?

He pushed himself up as the water beat on him in the dark, leaning out to gasp for breath. *Damn them!* But anger spoiled concentration. So. Carefully. Three points on the rock at all time. Reach only with one hand or one foot. Up . . .

It was disorienting in the dark, but he climbed until echoes told him he'd reached the point where the water fell out of its pipelike chute toward the lake. He reached in back of himself and his palm slapped rock. Yes! He pushed off, his back slamming against the other side of the chimney to wedge himself. Now he could ascend with more confidence.

How many minutes had passed? How long would the timer be set for?

Progress was painful: at one point the chute widened so much that he had to brace with his arms instead of his back, trembling from the strain. Then he was past it and sound and touch told him he was finally near the chute's upper lip. Bending and bracing, he brought himself around to a point where he could lunge face-first into the rushing river above the edge of the falls, frantically grabbing for slimy handholds to prevent himself from being swept back down into the lake. Then he kicked and pulled furiously until he was up, kneeling in the level stream, chest heaving, one hand around a vine for support.

A vine?

He dropped it as if shocked. It had to be the wire of the demolition charge.

"Jesus Christ." He stood, swaying as he caught his breath. It was pitch black. He carefully shuffled forward against the current until his shin brushed the wire and elaborately stepped over it. A thought occurred to him. If the Germans had bothered to set explosives on the downstream end of the grotto, where the river would eventually cut a new path anyway, they'd certainly wire the upstream end as well. He'd have to watch for explosives there too.

How much time?

He counted his steps upstream, trying to visualize the grotto. One chance, one chance, he kept telling himself.

By his calculation he was near his sleeping spot. There wasn't even a spark of illumination. It was blacker than night, as black as a tomb. But if they'd been hasty . . . He crawled out of the river and groped in the sand, the mineral smell of the hot spring giving him a crude compass. Yes! The wool of his blanket! He scrambled across it, banged painfully into a rock, felt its underside . . . Thank God. They'd left what he'd stored there: his parka, boots, and helmet. The miner's helmet. The bastards had been too arrogant or too lazy to pack his gear out. Too stupid. He sobbed a prayer of relief.

He found the battery and flicked on the light, its modest glow seeming brilliant. Hastily he hauled on clothes and boots and sprang up with the helmet on his head, the beam stabbing wildly around the lip of the falls. He spotted a drooping wire connecting two charges on either side of the water. A box, a clock. He inspected. The timer hand had stalled at the zero point! Had the demolition failed? He bent closer, peering, and realized there was an audible ticking. The timer hand was simply close. Very close. Two minutes to go?

He didn't have a clue what would happen if he tried to disconnect the wire.

He began running upstream, water spraying and the beam of his helmet bouncing madly. Ahead was the dark hole of the tunnel that led out of the grotto. He jumped, wedging his arms into the tunnel, and kicked upward. Another wire caught on his coat. Damnation! Gently he lifted the parka free and humped over it like a worm, losing the thread of seconds he'd been counting in his brain. His boot snagged and he tensed for an explosion that didn't come. Then he was past the wire and crawling furiously through the narrow tunnel, his sphincter tightening at the thought of the charge about to go off at his back. He came to the tight squeeze he and Greta had found and wriggled through it like a madman, his clothes a smear of dirt. Then on and on, each yard a measure of safety . . .

Something kicked him hard from behind and a roar clapped his ears. The explosion actually lifted and shoved him forward, hot as hell, the roar blasting his helmet off and sending it sailing ahead of him until the battery wire yanked taut. Then he came down with an oof and a gout of heat and smoke and gritty debris rattled past him, choking his throat with dust. Somewhere he could hear the crash of immensely heavy rock falling.

Crawl, dammit! Crawl!

He was clawing now, the helmet jammed back on his head, wriggling forward until he could rise to his hands and knees, then to a crouch, staggering as fast as he could with his bent back scraping rock. Air kept pummeling him as the ceiling gave way behind, each collapse triggering another in a chain reaction. He managed a stooped run just as the roof of the low tunnel gave way with a roar.

Something heavy clipped him like the swipe of a claw . . . and then he was beyond the cave-in, coughing painfully in a swirling cloud of dust and smoke, his head ringing and the miraculously shining beam of his headlamp knocked awry.

For the moment, at least, he was alive.

He stood a minute, dazed. Then he dimly remembered he didn't have time to rest: the storm troopers were well ahead of him, no doubt readying another explosion at the outer entrance. He stumbled on, finding the haze beginning to clear as he climbed up the slope of broken basalt boulders. Ahead was the vertical chimney that led out of the mountain. He climbed to the plug that choked the chimney's base.

Anxiety plagued him. Had they blown the outer entrance? No, not yet. Of course not yet: the Germans hadn't had time to climb out themselves. Get a grip! Panting, he worked around the jam of rock to where he could see up the immense chimney, flicking off his headlamp.

Far, far above was the bob of lamps like his own, as remote as stars, as elusive as fairy lights. It was them. The storm troopers. They were still hoisting themselves and their packs of lake organism out of the cave, slowly inching up the chimney toward the tunnel that led to his alternate exit. The lights were like a taunting beacon.

Somehow he'd have to outrun them. He groped along the wall. Yes! They were packing out so much cargo they'd failed to carry out all the ropes. And why bother? With the initial explosion the American was certainly already dead, the cave useless. So they'd left in place the climbing line that followed the first pitch up the vertical shaft. He grasped it and pulled as hard as he could with grim satisfaction. Should have cut it, Bristle-Head. Should have stopped to make sure. Too cocky. Too lazy. He put up a foot to climb.

The cave quivered then and he put out a hand to brace himself. Another explosion? No, a tremor from the sister volcano. A sympathetic echo to the manmade bomb. He heard cries of alarm from the Germans far above, and behind him there was a growl of settling rock. Shards rattled down the chimney and he crouched, listening to them whine and shatter. Christ, what a hellhole he'd found!

Then the cave quieted again. The shouts echoed away. Both Hart and the Germans resumed climbing, the pilot going as hard as he could while watching the lights above. At least he wasn't burdened with a damn pack. He was gaining.

Twenty feet. Fifty. Seventy. All by feel up the rope. The cave so dark it was as if he was climbing in space. It became a kind of rhythm, his trance broken only by another falling rock, this time dislodged by someone above. He hugged the chimney wall as it sizzled past with terrifying energy, its fragments clicking like angry insects when they ricocheted back up the shaft around him. The rock had to be an accident, he told himself. There was no way the Germans could be throwing at him. No way they could see unlit Owen Hart, the stalking ghost.

He reached the tunnel shelf where he and Greta had first entered the cave and risked a quick blink of light. Another climbing line was still in place. He grasped it.

"What was that?" The voice came from far above.

"What?"

"I thought I saw a light!"

He waited. The headlamps above had paused.

"I don't see anything."

"You're spooked," someone growled. "Come on, let's get out of this pit." It was Hans, the pilot guessed. "I'd feel safer on the Russian Front." The lights began moving again, Hart following as he heard them shouting instructions to each other to belay their heavy packs.

Finally the lamps began to wink out: the Germans had reached the steep tunnel at the top of the chimney that would take them to the outside and were slowly climbing into it. He waited a moment until the last one disappeared and then gratefully flicked his own headlamp on, momentarily half blinded. One more rope to go! He still had a chance! The damn Nazis would have to pause at the top exit to set further charges. He'd catch them there.

With his light on he could move faster. He'd never worked so hard in his life, lungs aching, muscle fiber screaming. Up, up, up. The dread of being trapped in the mountain electrified him. Somehow, he would get to Greta, take the food, say goodbye . . .

"Goddamn!"

The oath made Hart jerk in alarm. There was a bang and a bullet whined off the face of the shaft, the pilot instinctively ducking his head. Then another, closer this time. He switched off his lamp.

"What is it?"

"The American! He's following us up the rope!" Another shot.

"What! Impossible! Cut the line, cut the line!"

"No, wait! I think I can hit him . . ."

Another bullet slammed inches above the pilot's head. Owen planted his boots on a ledge and hugged the cliff face, trying to melt into it. More shots, wilder this time in the dark. Then a headlamp beam was dancing as it tried to find him.

"There he is!"

Hart froze in the illumination.

"I've got him . . ."

The rope went slack.

"No!"

Hart clutched the cliff.

"Jesussss . . . !" The cry above dissolved into a scream and the headlamp beam began revolving. One of the Germans had cut the line while the shooter was still hanging on it. The rope slithered down past Hart, its end slapping him in the face, and the gunman hurtled by at the same time, his body cleaving the air, his wild screams echoing and reechoing as his light tumbled down into the pit. There was a sickening thud, far below, and the lamp went out.

"God in heaven! What happened?"

"It was Oscar! He went back down the rope, you fucking idiot!"

A moment of silence. Then, "Where's Hart?"

"How the hell do I know?"

"If you'd just shot him at the bottom like I told you—"

"Shut up. I'm going back down to look for him."

"No! There's no rope!" A pause. "He can't follow us."

"Maybe. Come here." The voices grew quieter. Were they climbing again?

Hart was trembling, afraid his fear would shiver him right off the cliff. There was nothing to do for it but struggle upward. He risked his light, tensing for a gunshot, and then, when no bullet came, picked out handholds he'd used before. Amazing what the brain remembered! So he climbed like a man possessed, his gaze fixed on the tunnel hole at the ceiling. His lamp was growing faint, his muscles trembling, his mind screaming at itself not to think about the hundreds of feet of yawning blackness below. And then at last he was at the tunnel too, jamming his exhausted arms and kicking his way upward, his breath coming in gasps, sweat stinging his eyes. He switched off his lamp to disguise his success and crawled hard up the lava tunnel. Time. Time! Soon they'd be setting the last charges. As he crawled upward, sometimes banging painfully into unyielding rock, he tried to listen for sounds of the Germans ahead. Silence. Were they simply outrunning him?

Suddenly light blazed and he was squinting into the glare of a headlamp. Hans was filling the tunnel ahead with his giant's body, his head uphill, grinning at Hart over the cocked readiness of his upraised knees. "Now we fight one last time, yes?" the German greeted. Then he lashed out with his boots.

Hart reared back, the leather missing his nose by the width of a sole. The pilot skidded downward into safer shadows, braced, and yelled. "Too slow, you Nazi gorilla!"

"Come here, Hart! Fight like a man, you coward!"

Owen reviewed his mental map of where they were. Switching on his lamp for an instant he spied a side tunnel. He turned the light off and writhed into it.

"You kick like a girl, Hans! You fight like your mother!"

Cursing, the German fired. A pistol bullet whined off the rocks. Then more shots, an angry fusillade more to vent anger than hit anything. He heard the click of a fresh clip being slipped into the gun. "Hart!" The pilot was silent. Hans worked down the tunnel after him. Owen waited.

"Hart?"

There was silence.

"Hart, where are you?"

Cautious now, his gun out, the German slid past the side tunnel, dropping toward the junction of tube and chimney.

"Hart? Did I get you, yellow man?"

The pilot pushed off into the main tube and dropped toward the German. Hans twisted with a curse, trying to bring his gun around in the restricting tube, but before he could get his arm free Owen struck with his own boot, catching the storm trooper on the nose. The man howled and slipped toward the abyss, his vision blurred by his own blood. The gun skittered out from under him.

"Boots hurt, don't they?" the American growled.

Hans had jammed himself into the tube at the lip of the chimney, his legs kicking in empty air as he arrested his fall. "You *bastard!*" he roared. "I'm going to *choke* the life out of you! I'm going to squeeze until you *beg!*"

"Fuck you, Hans." Owen braced himself uphill from the German and pulled on a loose rock, yanking it free and shoving it downward as hard as he could. The exertion cost him his own grip and he slid after the small boulder as it banged down toward the storm trooper. Hans instinctively put out his arms to protect his face, a fatal error. He lost his grip on the tunnel.

"Shit!"

There was a thud as the boulder hit, a howl of outrage, and a rattle of loosened rocks. Then Hans's light disappeared. He was gone.

Hart thrust out his own arms and legs to brake himself at the edge of the chimney and skidded to a stop, listening in horrified fascination to the long, trailing scream. Then it stopped abruptly, the sound dying in its own echoes.

Two down, one to go. Panting, the pilot began climbing again, yanking away the route-marking ribbons he'd left on their initial descent.

When he neared the surface he switched off his light and crept ahead cautiously. Had the remaining Nazi simply set the charges and fled? Hart almost hoped so. He was too exhausted for a fight. He debated, sweating.

Then he risked a shout. "Rudolf!" The yell echoed through the cave.

"Hart?" The voice was wary.

Owen tightened his voice as if he was in pain. "It's Hans. Hart hurt me, but I got him! Help!"

"Hans?"

"Help me, dammit! I can't climb out! I lost my light!"

There was an uneasy silence. Then a scraping as the German began to slowly descend. "I'm coming!" He added a cautious warning. "I have a gun!"

"For God's sake don't shoot!" Hart slipped down into a side tunnel he'd explored earlier. "Help me! I'm bleeding!"

"Try to climb up, Hans! We have to hurry! The timers are set!"

"Please! It hurts!"

"Fuck." The German scrabbled lower. His light began to glow on the tube walls.

Hart retreated into the side tunnel. "In here!"

There was a splash of light. Bristle-Head followed, swearing. "It's too tight! What are you doing in here?"

"I'm lost!" Hart groaned. "Hurry!"

Then he dropped quickly and silently to the main tube and began to double back toward the surface.

"Hans! Where are you? Hans?"

Quickly now, very quickly.

"Christ! The markers are all gone! Hans?" Silence. "Where the hell are you?"

Time. How much time?

Realization dawned. "Hart! Hart, you son of a bitch!" Bristle-Head began to climb back. "A dead end! Where are the damn markers? Hart, you sneaking bastard . . ."

Owen switched his lamp on to hurry. Bristle-Head must have seen its receding glow because another shot rang out far below him, its energy consumed by ricochet.

"Hart . . . !"

The pilot staggered into the small, sandy-floored room at the cave mouth. His battery was nearly exhausted, its light duller than a candle. In the feeble gleam and the pale light from the nearby entrance he saw explosives wired as before. Behind and below he could hear the German swearing furiously as he tried to find his way up the cave. The pilot looked at the timers. Eleven minutes. Too long. Taking a breath, he shoved the minute hand on the dial to one, praying he hadn't disrupted its mechanism. "Time's up, Rudolf," he whispered.

He hurtled forward on hands and knees toward the low slit of the cave opening, clawing for its brightness. His head popped out into the shock of Antarctic cold and he rolled out onto the shelf and over its lip to the snow below, landing with a thud and digging in with fingers and toes to arrest his slide. Then he pressed his face into the slush and waited.

The flank of the mountain heaved.

There was a roar and a fountain of rock debris made an arcing plume from the cave entrance. The fragments sailed over the pilot's head and spattered onto the cone far below Hart's position. He could hear the grinding collapse of rock inside the mountain.

Was it over?

Then there was an ominous rumble, outside this time. He lifted his head. Beyond the haze of smoke and dust at the collapsed tube's mouth, farther upslope, a slice of snow had sheared away and was avalanching downward like an advancing wave. Hart staggered upward to the basalt outcrop and threw himself at its toe. Thundering snow blasted over his head and crashed onto the slope where he'd lain moments before, churning like a threshing machine, eating space. He pressed himself into the outcrop. Then the avalanche guttered out on the slopes below and the mountain's quivering stopped. Sound growled away.

Numb, he stood up. The cave was gone, erased by a smear of rock. He was alone and the world was still.

Turning, he looked out over the immensity of Antarctica. A clean sharp wind snapped at his filthy clothes. The cove far below still beckoned.

He took a deep breath. It was time to get back to Greta.

CHAPTER THIRTY-FIVE

The *U-4501* was quiet again, most of its crew asleep. It was dark outside and the submarine rocked slightly in a rising wind, waves splashing against the side of the boat. Greta sat on her bunk, impatient and angry. Owen should be back by now with the men from the cave. Had Jürgen betrayed them? She felt with her heels under her bed. Instead of one crammed pack there were now two, filled with food she'd quietly stolen from the Antarctic stores, as well as some rope and twine.

She'd made a decision. If God granted her wish and she saw Owen again, she was going to go with him. She'd begun seeing her situation with unusual clarity since that morning's conversation with Schmidt. She now knew—if, indeed, she'd ever doubted it—that she lived in a dark world of betrayal. If she remained in the sub, sailed home with Jürgen, the darkness would only deepen. Jürgen would continue his power over her, keep her around as a witness to his bizarre schemes. So hopeless. So crazy. The unspeakable misery they'd cause.

Contemplating her future, the only light she saw was Owen. She was enough of a realist to realize the light would be brief, that two people couldn't survive the small-boat ocean crossing he hoped to attempt. But at the moment of her death, there would be a certain satisfaction. She would know that, even if she hadn't *lived* her life well, she'd *ended* it well, with the man she loved.

To hide her preparation she'd been snarling at anyone who so much as bumped her cubicle curtain, claiming a right of privacy as a female. It had the desired effect, the sailors giving her a wide berth. Now she could only wait. Where *was* he? Restless, she got up to confront her husband.

Schmidt met her in the corridor before she could reach a ladder, carrying a sturdy metal tank the size of a large sausage.

"Another safe for your microbes, Max?" she asked caustically.

"For your antibiotic, actually. The drug powder should fit in this gas cylinder, the toughest container I could find. In case we're attacked again on the way home."

"Ah. Well, in that case the lab cultures you made from the spores need to be boxed or destroyed too. We can't risk them breaking."

"Yes, but I'm experimenting with growth variables. One colony is really exploding! I should be able to use these findings to accelerate production when we reach Germany. I want to give them as much time as I can. Don't worry. I'll see to the cultures before departure."

She looked at him doubtfully. "You've already hidden your spores from me. Don't take foolish risks with the ones you've hatched and grown."

"No risk, Frau Drexler. We doctors respect disease."

She bit her lip at that and gestured down the corridor. "Is Jürgen in his quarters?"

"No, on deck, preparing to go ashore. The last soldiers haven't returned from the cave. He's leading a search party."

She started, looking dismayed. "Did something go wrong?"

"Who knows?" Schmidt smiled at her weakness for the pilot. "That's what he's checking."

Greta put on her parka and climbed to the deck. It was very dark and the strength of the wind caught her by surprise. She had so little sense of the elements inside the submarine. The sky was like a tattered sail, streamers of cloud blowing past the stars. A storm was building and the realization dismayed her. Would nothing favor them?

The motor launch was alongside, bumping against the hull as Jürgen's search party of storm troopers boarded by the illumination of flashlights. She walked along the wet deck, whipped by spray.

"Going for more microbe spores?"

He jumped at her bitter voice. "What are you doing up here?"

"What are *you* doing? Hunting for fresh diseases like the good doctor?"

He squinted at her sourly, irritated at her complaint of betrayal. "Safeguarding our mission."

"You lied to me again."

He shrugged. "Does it matter anymore?"

The indifference hurt. "No. Not anymore." She looked at the boatload of men. "So. Where are you going?"

He considered his reply. "If you must know, I'm looking for your damned pilot."

"Why isn't he back yet?"

Drexler looked out at the walls of the crater. "That's what we're going to find out. Hans and Rudolf and Oscar haven't returned either. It's a dreadful night and I don't want them getting lost in a storm."

"You won't leave without him this time?"

He looked at her resentfully. "Not if he's alive."

"What does that mean?"

"Nothing! For God's sake, can you stop mooning for one moment over Owen Hart? Go below and get some sleep. You need it."

She stood, frustrated. Part of her wanted him to assure her, to promise Owen's safety. But what were Jürgen's promises worth anymore? *Nothing.* This time she'd have to trust in God.

Saying a prayer to herself, she turned and went below.

*   *   *

Hart watched the lights of the launch pull away from the submarine with quiet satisfaction. Finally! He felt savagely energized despite his cold and hunger. He was alive and his tormentors, some of them at least, vanquished. He felt a powerful freedom he hadn't enjoyed since his capture in Berlin.

After the explosion he'd slid down to the snug little cove visible from the lava outcrop and checked again on his discovery from six years before, satisfying himself that his desperate plan was not entirely impossible. Then he'd wearily climbed back to the volcano rim and sat, catching his breath and looking down at the submarine in the caldera like a raptor eyeing prey. When dusk fell he'd descended into the crater and sheltered at the mouth of the lava tube he and Fritz had found so long before. Enough of an overhang remained after the cave-in to shield him from the wind. For hours the U-boat remained stubbornly impregnable, anchored in its cold lagoon with the motor launch tied alongside. Yet he knew that the disappearance of the SS men would sooner or later raise questions. Now the Nazis were coming to answer them, giving him a chance to get to Greta.

The last stars were gone and a few snowflakes were beginning to fall. Perfect: the storm would obscure his tracks. Confident that the dark hid him from view, he left the cave and loped down the slope to the crater beach, then hiked along the shoreline toward the point the running lights appeared aimed at. The grumble of the launch engine faded and the lights went out, suggesting the boat had reached shore. After a few minutes new lights switched on and he watched them swing as the storm troopers began moving up the crater slope. Lanterns for the search.

Then there was a bang and a red star went wavering up into the night. Flare! Hart fell flat. The illumination was poor in the growing snow and he knew the light was more to attract the lost SS men than to actually spot them. Still, it revealed to him that one man had stayed with the boat. A sentry. When the wavering red glow flickered out, the pilot sat up, removed a boot, and methodically filled one sock with beach gravel. The thought of what he was about to do didn't give him pause at all. Then he put his boot back on and walked ahead.

He dropped as a second flare arched skyward. Ten-minute intervals, he guessed. When the night darkened again he hurried forward, then sank to a crouch and crept the last several yards.

The sentry was hunched over with his back to the wind, a glow showing that he was drawing on a cigarette. Hart's feet crunched on gravel. The sentry turned, fumbling with a submachine gun caught under his parka. "Who's there?"

"Oscar," Hart replied.

"Thank God! We feared you'd—"

The pilot swung and the sock exploded on the storm trooper's temple, gravel spraying. The man sprawled and Hart was on top of him in an instant. He'd salvaged a sharp steel climbing piton from the cave, hard enough to be hammered into cracks of rock. Now he felt under the dazed man's parka hood with it, thrust, and cut. The squirt of blood splattered Owen despite his instinctive lurch back. Grimly, he let the sentry's head flop down.

There was another bang, and a lurid glow of red. Hart stood quickly to become the sentry to anyone watching from the submarine or above. The snow was thickening. As the flare died he watched the chain of bobbing lights climb up and over the crater rim. No alarm had been raised.

Owen could still hear the sentry's dying gurgle. He felt nothing except relief. That was four of the bastards! He yanked the submachine gun out from under the dead man, wiped it on the soldier's parka, and threw it into the boat. Pockets yielded a flashlight, dagger, an extra clip, and some papers. Hart took an envelope, emptied it, crouched, and slipped a pebble inside. Then he dragged the dead Nazi into the cold water, looping a mooring line around his torso. The pilot shoved the boat off the beach, jumped aboard, and pressed the button to start the engine, remembering the procedure the Germans had used. Backing out, he turned and headed toward the U-boat. At the halfway point he slowed and cut the mooring line. The towed body sank from sight.

When he banged inexpertly against the submarine a sailor on watch caught the boat. "Where are the others?" the seaman asked.

"Still searching." Hart prayed the man wouldn't recognize his voice. "The colonel sent a message for the woman." He handed over the envelope. "She's assembling additional supplies. She's to come up and confer with me." Hart dared not venture into the submarine with his recognizable face and his parka spattered with blood. The man hesitated. "I'll stand watch. Hurry, dammit! It's fucking cold!" The sailor disappeared down the hatch.

Hart hauled the submachine gun onto his lap and studied it. He'd never fired one before. He found the apparent safety but dared not squeeze the trigger to confirm his discovery, simply setting it aside where it would be ready. Then he bent to the emergency sailing rigging stored in the bottom of the launch and began taking it apart, fumbling in the snow and cold. The sail and its lines he set aside.

He looked restlessly about, hoping to see Greta, dreading their imminent goodbye. The necessity for her to ride home with the Germans, her only realistic chance, twisted his stomach. He wanted her. Needed her. Yet it was madness to go with him . . .

The hatch banged open and a pack emerged, falling over on the deck. Then a second. The sailor came out and then bent to offer his hand to Greta. And there she was, a slim silhouette, dragging the packs down the ash-and snow-crusted deck and heaving them into the motor launch. Hart started the engine, not knowing what to expect.

She jumped aboard. "Thank God you're here."

"Should I report anything to the captain?" the sailor asked from the deck.

"Only that you should have been quicker," Hart growled. "Get back on watch." He hoped he'd mustered the right tone of SS arrogance. The sailor hesitated a moment, resentful, then spat into the water and backed to the conning tower.

"Did something happen in the cave?" Greta whispered. "When that sailor told me the motor launch had returned I feared it was

Jürgen to tell me of your death. And then when I opened that envelope I almost screamed for joy!"

Hart smiled. The pebble had scored again. "The soldiers tried to leave me in the lake and wired the cave with explosives. I got out just before the detonation. *They* didn't."

"So Jürgen lied about letting you go." She stiffened with resolve. "Owen, I've decided to come with you. We can just take this boat and flee. Jürgen's on shore. We'll maroon him there."

Touched, the pilot shook his head. "Greta, you *can't*. I'm going to try to cross the stormiest ocean in the world. It's impossible."

"Even *more* impossible to try alone."

"No. It's foolish for us both to die. Besides, they'd raise the alarm too soon if we took this launch. I'm going over the volcano, as we planned, and you stay on the submarine."

She shook her head. "Owen, I can't watch you leave me again. I *won't*. Whatever our fate is, *please*, let's face it together."

"*No*." He didn't want to kill her and had to dissuade her. "If you flee, they'll come after us."

"It's a big ocean, Owen, and, if Jürgen thinks I'm sulking and huddled in my cabin, there's a possibility I won't be missed for hours."

He looked at Greta's face. The certainty of staying together—even if it risked death—trumped the possibility of permanent separation. She wasn't going to take no for an answer.

"All right," he said finally, swallowing. His eyes were moist. "It's crazy, but all right. If we die, I'll still have you."

She nodded.

"We still have to leave this boat on the beach so they won't hunt for it with the submarine," he pointed out. "We still have to hike to the cove."

"I understand. So hurry, let's . . . wait." She sat straighter. "Wait, wait. You told me the cave was blown up. What happened to the last batch of lake organism?"

"Sealed with the Nazis, I suppose."

"My God." She seized his parka. "We can *stop* them!"

"What?"

"Don't you see? The only lake organism left is on the submarine and Schmidt hasn't locked that away yet; he's still expecting more from underground when Jürgen returns. If we destroy it they can't reproduce any in Germany! They'll have the disease but no cure, and unless they're totally insane they won't dare unleash it! We *can* beat them, Owen! If we hurry!"

"Go back inside? They'll recognize me, Greta. They'll ask too many questions."

"I know. I'll do it. It's late, people are asleep. I'll hurry."

"What if someone notices what you're doing?"

"I'll do it quickly, quietly."

"No, it's too risky . . ."

"Trust me, Owen." And then before he could grab her she was springing back on deck and trotting to the hatch. She yanked it open and disappeared inside.

The sailor came clambering down from the conning tower. The pilot's hand drifted to the submachine gun and he waited, tensely.

"I thought she was going with you?" The question was troubled, suspicious, the sailor's features invisible in the dark.

Hart shrugged. "She is. But she forgot something." He spat. "You know. Women."

CHAPTER THIRTY-SIX

Greta climbed down to the main deck and listened. The submarine hummed with the ceaseless, oil-scented drone of a warship, but was otherwise still. The desultory sailor on watch in the control room barely nodded as she slipped down the midships ladder to her laboratory, her pulse hammering. She opened the hatch cautiously. Empty. She closed it after her.

Despite her abortive efforts at straightening the lab, clutter remained. Schmidt's tank of drug was in plain view on a crate used as a makeshift table, the drug storage tubes he'd emptied into it scattered around. Remaining canisters of the organic sludge sat on the deck along one bulkhead. The workbench with its bacterial cultures of disease was on the other. Beakers and flasks and pots remained crusted with paste. The surviving rabbits skittered in their cages at her entrance, no doubt afraid of another needle. She'd thought she was done with this claustrophobic warren and yet here she was again.

She moved decisively. A sampling of the drug sludge went into a bottle slipped into her pocket. Then she lifted the heavy canister it came from and began pouring the remainder into their drain pipe. The unprocessed organism would go into the U-boat's waste system and overboard. It glugged with glacial slowness but at last emptied. She let the canister drop to the deck and picked up another. She was sweating in her heavy outdoor gear.

There was a click and a bump as the hatch opened again. She started, but kept pouring. Probably Jacob, the animal tender, and she could outbluff any sailor. It would be enough to point to the disease. Get out, go away! It's dangerous down here!

Boots thumped onto the deck. She prepared to turn suddenly in irritation.

"What do you think you're doing?"

She jumped. It was Schmidt! She looked at him in guilty surprise as he watched her pour. He seemed confused and haggard.

"Max! I thought you were asleep."

"Having coffee." His expression began to narrow. "Sleep has tended to elude me of late, and a chance mention by the watch of your being down here got me curious." His look became grim. "I shudder to think what might have happened had I not decided to investigate. Put that damn container down. Now."

Reluctantly, she did so. "I only—"

"Only what? Only wanted to destroy everything we worked for. Back away from that drain pipe, Frau Biologist. Thank God more is coming from the cave." He paused, considering her clothes, her midnight appearance. "Or is it? Are you finally ahead of us, Greta? Do you finally know something I don't?"

"That would be difficult, Max, given that you know *everything*." Her expression was one of intense hatred. Also, of triumph.

"Bitch!" His hand cracked across her face and she went flying against the remaining algal containers, knocking several over. The cap snapped off one and its contents began sloshing across the metal deck grating, draining into the bilge. She shook her head dumbly. The blow was so hard she was dazed, her vision blurred.

"Violence seems to be your forte, Max," she said, glancing sideways at the still-full algal containers. Suddenly, she turned and grabbed for the bottles, getting a cap off one before Schmidt was on top of her.

"Get your hands off that!" He seized her by the hair and hauled her backward, trying to strike her with the other fist. His clumsy blows were blocked by the arm she lifted to ward off his attack. He was taller but old and not particularly strong. She twisted and kicked, making him wince. Then they grappled, Greta punching and biting and scratching for her life. He managed to get behind her with an arm around her windpipe and began choking. They stumbled, locked in a pained dance, her voice cut off and Schmidt wheezing as he desperately tried to master a woman thirty years younger than himself. She realized she was beginning to black out and groped wildly with a free hand, looking for a weapon. Her fingers skittered on a glass cylinder, rejected it, then seized it again. Yes! One of his damned hypodermics!

She stabbed. The needle went into Schmidt's shoulder near his neck and the doctor squealed, letting go to claw at the agonizing sting. As he did so she shoved as hard as she could. He lurched sideways and there was a splintering crash. The crude workbench broke from its supports and the beakers, flasks and glass petri dishes with their agar films of plague culture shattered, bits skittering across the laboratory. Like a reproducing fungus, a puff of spores from a broken test tube blossomed into the air.

Schmidt, ensnared in the wreckage, looked goggle-eyed in horror. The hypodermic needle jutted from his shoulder as if sucking at the droplet of bright blood that appeared there. Bits of glass and microbial culture littered his skin. He lifted himself on his elbows. "You've infected me!" he gasped in disbelief. Reaching, he jerked the hypodermic out of his shoulder, groaning. "He was so *weak* to bring you . . ."

She brought the cylinder of algal drug powder down on the doctor's head. There was a solid thud and he fell back, unconscious.

"Shut *up,* you old ghoul." The words were a croak from her sore throat.

She listened, but all she heard was the hum of the ship.

Schmidt would have closed the hatch when he came down. So. *Think. Consider the variables.* She took a shuddering breath. *God what a mess!*

Numbly, almost automatically, she tipped the remaining containers of the cave organism toward the oily bilge. It was the best she could do with her shaking tremble. Schmidt remained still. She had no idea if he was alive or dead and was too frightened to inspect him. Too much in shock to care. *Think!* She hefted the cylinder of the drug. The germs were loose, thrown everywhere by the fight: she probably carried some on her clothes. She needed to treat herself. And Owen. And . . . The hum of the ship. My God. She looked at the ventilator opening, exchanging air, sucking in spores. But if she took the remaining drug with her . . .

If she took it and the submarine turned into a *Bergen,* all these men would die.

The realization made her ashen.

And if she left it? If they lived they could still return to Germany with the disease and enough of the cure organism to begin culture and reproduction. If they lived, they could still hunt Owen and herself down.

Schmidt groaned, stirring. Unless she wanted to kill him right now, she didn't have much time.

What would her nuns say?

What would Owen say?

Schmidt moaned again. Damn him! She brought the cylinder down on his head and he slumped a second time, lying still. She taped his mouth, hands, and ankles. Why hadn't he stayed away? Then, grimly tucking the drug tank under one arm, she climbed out of the U-boat and hurried back to the motor launch, jumping aboard.

"It's done," she whispered.

Owen said she'd done the right thing. The only thing.

"They're murderers, Greta. They tried to kill me." The couple were driving hard for the beach, fearful that Schmidt might somehow stagger out of the laboratory and sound the alarm. Every yard of cold water gave them an added feeling of safety.

"It was the SS that tried to kill you, Owen. Not the sailors." She shivered, her eyes moist.

"Nonsense. Those bastards gave the Nazi salute when Jürgen laid out his plans. They're part of it."

She leaned on him. "I know, I know. But to condemn sixty men, *fellow Germans*, to—"

"They condemned themselves."

"Do you think that will keep them from my dreams?"

"Dreams! What about our waking nightmare! God willing, you've saved millions of people. Millions! The only person you haven't saved yet is yourself."

A white shelf appeared out of the dark: the beach. They crunched against it and Hart cut the motor. "From here we walk." He'd thought about their situation while waiting by the sub for Greta to return. "If we take the launch they'll hunt us by sea but if we leave it they'll comb the island first. That should buy some time."

Her face drained. "If we leave it, Jürgen will reach the submarine."

Owen nodded, looking at her hard. "I *want* him to, Greta."

She said nothing.

"I want him to catch the plague."

She looked out at the night in horror.

"Listen, Greta, I can't make this choice for you. I can't and expect you not to doubt me the rest of our days. So you can take the cylinder back right now, save those men, and sail for Germany. You'll be a savior to those sailors, and far more likely to survive than if you come with me. You can be loyal to the Reich. You can save your husband. Or you can throw it all away—every bit of it—and come with me on this one wild crazy scheme to get away from this island. A chance that will probably kill us both."

She actually smiled at that. "You're so persuasive. So why would I ever come with you?"

"Because I love you."

She nodded. "You make a good argument," she said finally. "It's exactly the one I would make." For an instant she looked up at the stars, seeming to search for something. Then she said: "I go with *you*."

He smiled. "Then let's hurry, before dawn comes. We'll share the antibiotic when we get out of sight of the sub."

Drexler led his men down off the crater rim at dawn, cold and exhausted. The storm was blowing itself out but it had been an abominable night of grim slogging and futile shouts and fired flares. The three SS men had simply disappeared. What a foul island!

Jürgen was frustrated. The mouth of the cave had been blown up as he'd ordered. Had the idiots somehow killed themselves? There was no sign. Or gotten lost in the storm? Again no sign. Something tickled in the back of his mind; some part of their search that remained uncompleted. Yet he couldn't think what it was. Now everyone was half frozen and uneasy. They needed some food and warmth and rest in the submarine.

The launch was where they'd left it, grounded on the beach. But the sentry was missing. Jürgen scowled in disgust.

"Where's Johann?"

The SS sergeant frowned. "He was supposed to stay with the boat. He should be right here."

"*I know* he should be right here! Where is he?"

"Perhaps he went back to the U-boat in the storm?"

"How could he get back to the U-boat without this launch, idiot?"

The sergeant stiffened. "Yes, sir."

Drexler fumed. The elimination of Hart hadn't left him feeling triumphant this time. He dreaded having to face Greta and tell her the American was missing again, lost in the cave or the storm. He doubted she'd believe him. It would be a relief to finally be done with her, he told himself. Yes. A relief.

"This damn island is swallowing my men! I don't like it! I

want to get out of here!" He looked at the others. There was no disagreement. "Well. Into the launch."

They motored to the U-boat. "Have you seen Johann Prien?" Drexler called to the sailors as they climbed wearily aboard.

"Came alongside last night," one replied tiredly. "As you requested."

Drexler frowned. "What?"

"To get the woman. The packs."

"Greta? My wife?"

"Yes. He said you sent a message and then she went with him." He peered curiously at the group, noticing the missing SS men were not there.

"I sent no message." The man looked surprised and a glimmer of dread began to shine on Drexler's brain. "You actually saw Johann?"

"Yes, of course. In the boat."

"I mean, you saw his face? You recognized him?"

The sailor began to comprehend. "No . . . It was dark. No one could recognize anyone last night."

Drexler's men were already dropping down the hatch into the submarine. The colonel's disquiet was growing. "Could this man have been the American?"

"I thought the American was with you."

"Jesus Christ. And Greta went with this man?"

"Yes." The sailor looked at Drexler with a cringe of sympathy.

"Fuck." It was a snarl. "Fuck! Where's Dr. Schmidt?"

"Below, I suppose. I haven't seen him."

Drexler dropped down to the main deck and yanked off his parka, stomping aft in his boots. "Max?" he roared. He found Freiwald. "Where's our damn doctor?"

The captain looked at Drexler with dislike. "I don't keep track of your party, Colonel. How would I know? Try your laboratory."

Drexler peered down. The hatch was closed but that was normal. He climbed down and opened it. "Max?" No answer. There were shards of glass on the deck. The chamber stank. He dropped into it with a premonition of dread. "Great God."

It looked like a bomb had hit. The planks of the workbench had splintered and the deck was littered with shards of petri dishes and their microbial goo. There was a stench reminiscent of the underground lake. All the containers so laboriously carried from the cave were empty. Schmidt lay writhing, trussed in tape. His head was bloody.

The U-boat captain descended the ladder after Drexler and then stopped in fearful shock. "Get out of here," the SS colonel ordered. "Close the hatch."

Jürgen began cutting Schmidt free. As the tape was yanked painfully off his mouth the doctor howled. He gasped for breath.

"Was it Hart, Max? Did that pilot do this?"

Schmidt spat, clutching his head. "Frau Greta Drexler"— Schmidt pronounced the name with acid—"did this. She caught me by surprise and shoved me into the lab bench. She contaminated the ship."

Now Drexler was ashen, remembering the horror of the *Bergen*. "She's a serpent," he muttered. "I married a Medusa."

"Is she insane?"

"She is when the American is around."

"I thought he was supposed to be dead."

Jürgen ignored this. "Do we still have the weapon? Do we still have the cure?"

Schmidt sat up, holding his head, and looked around with a wince. "I secreted the spores away because I remembered her emotional fit the last time. But not the drug. It looks like she dumped what we had and took the concentrate with her. Did you bring more from the cave?"

Drexler felt a tiresome buzzing in his head as he contemplated the wreckage of all his plans, all his hopes. "No. My men never emerged."

"Well, we can get more, yes?"

"No, Max. The cave is demolished. My men may never have gotten out."

"But you just said Hart was out!"

"That's my suspicion." He said it in a small voice. "Greta

would never do this alone." He looked at the splinters of petri dish. "This means we're dead men, Max, unless we catch her. If she has the drug she's our only hope." He swallowed and glanced at the ladder. "I closed the hatch. Maybe it won't spread."

"You must be joking." Schmidt pointed at the vents. "We're talking about escaping germs, not escaping rabbits. It's been sucked all over the ship by now. Everyone is infected. It will be like the *Bergen.* Why on earth did you trust her?"

Drexler looked hollow. "I didn't trust her. I thought I could control her." Then he glared at Schmidt. "Thought *you* could control her! My God, trussed up by a woman?"

"By a sneaking, conniving—"

Drexler held up his hand, suddenly weary. "All right. Enough. Enough recrimination. How much time do we have before the symptoms appear?"

Schmidt shook his head. "Hours. Maybe a day."

"And where did she go? Where on the island did they hide? Another cave?"

"Good point," said Schmidt. "They can't have gone far on an island. Maybe we can find them and get the drug back." He thought a moment. "And they can't operate a submarine, not alone. They can't leave Antarctica without us. If we die, they die, no?"

"I don't think they plan to die. They're too infatuated with each other for self-sacrifice."

"Then they have an alternate plan," Schmidt reasoned. "A radio. A rescue. An airplane . . ."

Mention of the plane jogged Drexler's memory. The lonely Dornier he'd spied on the snowy plateau the last trip, the seaplane that had allowed the American's escape. So there had to be a vehicle this time as well, yes? But where? Ah, of course. Now he remembered! Now he realized what they'd missed on last night's search! The couple's furtive discussion at the cave mouth! The tiny bay they'd surveyed together. That was their escape hatch! There was something there. Something to get them out. That was where they'd run.

He hauled up Schmidt. "I know where they're going, I think. A bay on the other side of the volcano below the new cave. We can intercept them there. Not over the rim: that takes too long. Around by sea. If we do that, we live."

Schmidt looked at the SS colonel with hope. They banged open the hatch and climbed out. "Freiwald!"

The captain was in the control room looking worried. "Aren't you letting out the—"

"It's already out," Drexler said brusquely. "It's all over the ship. You're breathing it now." The submariner looked aghast. "Never mind that. How soon can we get underway?"

"Our plan was not to go for a day or two."

"Our plans have obviously changed."

The captain frowned. "I had the engineers strip the diesels. We're doing some routine maintenance. It will take several hours to put them back together."

"What?"

"We can't sail before noon."

Schmidt looked dumbly at his watch. "Good God."

"We can't wait that long," Jürgen said. "I'll take the motor launch and my men to catch them. You follow in the submarine. Captain, if you don't get this boat moving soon, all of you are going to die. Do you understand? Owen Hart and my wife have escaped with the antibiotic and they're our only hope."

Freiwald nodded fearfully and opened his mouth to say something.

Instead, he sneezed.

"God bless you," said Schmidt.

CHAPTER THIRTY-SEVEN

The slender reed that supported the couple's hope of escape looked to Greta's weary mind like a cradle in the snow, a refuge into which she wanted to curl and sleep until they were far, far away. It wouldn't be that easy, of course. The lifeboat's very presence was a grim reminder of how difficult it might prove to get away from the Antarctic island. The two surviving Norwegians from the *Bergen* had tried and failed.

When Hart first crawled out of the cave six years ago it was utter exhaustion that had allowed him to spot the craft. He'd collapsed on the lava ledge too tired to even lift his head and as his eyes adjusted to the stark polar light he found them idly tracing the fractal geometry of the shoreline far below. It was the leaf-shaped regularity of the abandoned boat's gunwale that caught his eye. He'd risked the time for inspection and found that the artifact was the Norwegian lifeboat, perfectly preserved by the Antarctic dry freeze. The memory had stuck in his mind ever since.

The overturned craft now remained impervious to time. Its wood was bleached gray but it seemed as sound as when it had first left the *Bergen*. The craft's fittings were only lightly rusted. A few cans of food, a blanket, and a seaman's wool watch cap were frozen onto its bottom floorboards in defiance of gravity. Even the lines were still there, stiff with cold but little decayed. The mast had been unstepped and hastily lashed to the thwarts and its fringe of tattered canvas told what must have happened. The Norwegians' sail had blown out in a storm and they'd been driven back to the island. Either a wave had tossed the boat high on shore or the whalers themselves had dragged the boat away from the reach of the sea. Then the men had disappeared. The pilot supposed they were somewhere nearby, entombed in snow.

"It's not the best of boats to change our luck in," he admitted to Greta.

"I think it's beautiful because it's ours," she replied. "The first part of our new life."

They used ice axes to chop the boat free from its frozen fusion and then rolled it onto its keel. Hart stepped the mast, fastened the boom, and tied on the sail he'd liberated from the motor launch, using as rigging both the lines in the boat and additional ones Greta had stuffed in their packs. The fit was inexact but would serve. Then they put their shoulders to the stern and pushed.

"Heave!" Hart shouted. "Heave with all your might!"

She leaned and let out a Valkyrie cry. The lifeboat broke free and tobogganed into the water, Owen snaring the stern line to keep it from drifting away.

She glanced back up the volcanic slope above the cove. No sign of Jürgen. "They haven't found us yet. We might just make it."

"If we hurry. We're a long ways from the open sea and we'll have to row quite a distance to weave out of this pack ice."

"Do you still have strength for rowing?"

"I'll row to New York to get away from here."

The floating pack ice was a problem for the German launch as well. After motoring out of the caldera entrance Drexler and his SS detachment of five surviving men had to swing wide around

the flank of the island to avoid its encircling rind. Being outside
the protective crater and on the open sea made Drexler nervous.
He really didn't like Antarctica's expansive emptiness, he admitted to himself. The excitement he'd felt about the continent when
the *Schwabenland* had first cast off from Germany had long since
disappeared. What made it such a dreadful place, he thought, was
that it was beyond human control. Not a house nor a light nor a
refuge nor a path. To his mind, there was nothing liberating
about such wilderness: he felt like he had to squeeze himself to
prevent being pulled apart by Antarctica's vacuum, pieces of him
sailing off in all directions like an explosion in space.
Accordingly, he'd been looking forward to the cubbyhole embrace of the steel submarine on the long voyage home, his victory
ensured in ranks of neatly labeled bottles of a revolutionary biology. Now he was driving through water so cold it was like dark
syrup, a sea so chill that the snow which fell on it didn't melt but
instead undulated on its top like gray skin. A monstrous place!

He was struggling to fight off gloom. The antibiotic was gone,
the cave destroyed, and the U-boat contaminated. The other volcano was smoking more than ever and a full-scale eruption might
make a return impossible. Which meant his dreams had been utterly imperiled by the woman he'd loved. Almost *destroyed!* Lord,
how he hated her.

There was a rattle and he looked down to see bits of ice rasp
along the side of the launch. He shivered. He still couldn't swim
and he wondered how deep the ocean was here. It seemed bottomless.

"Seals." One of the storm troopers pointed.

There was a group of them on an ice floe, as indolent as ever.
Drexler remembered that Greta had claimed some of them were
fierce predators, huge and swift. The thought was absurd! The
sluggish beasts barely moved except to yawn and defecate. They
stank and whelped and did nothing more. Worst of all, they were
indifferent to the Germans, caring nothing for what they were up
against. It was a kind of arrogance that annoyed him. It was like
the indifference of God.

"Give me your gun."

"My gun?"

"Give it to me!"

The lazy animals had no fear of man. That must change. He pulled back the lever on the submachine gun to arm it and fired a burst, the rattle surprisingly clamorous in the hushed whiteness. One of the seals recoiled, barking in surprise and pain, and suddenly the snow was bright with blood. In a flash the animals slithered off the ice and into the water.

"Damned slugs." Drexler threw the gun back at the soldier.

The storm troopers looked at one another uneasily. Bad luck.

"What was that?" Greta's head had come up.

Hart looked around uneasily. "Maybe just a glacier calving. Or a breakup of ice." He frowned. It had sounded like a burst of gunshots.

They'd been rowing slowly and carefully, picking their way through the ice toward the open sea. Now the pilot clambered forward to where the mast was stepped, pulling himself up its short length and clinging with his legs.

"Careful!" Greta warned. The boat rocked dangerously.

Hart squinted across the ice. He didn't see the German boat so much as spy movement: motion in a place that otherwise was calm and still. He slid down, heartsick.

"It's *them.* In the motor launch. Somehow they saw us, or realized what we're doing. They're trying to cut us off by sea. How did they figure it out?"

She looked pained, then determined. "Jürgen always figures it out. But I'm not going back with them."

"We're not to that point yet. I'm going to raise the sail. Maybe we can outrun them in this ice."

There was just breeze enough to fill the canvas. He hoisted the sail and it caught, the lifeboat heeling slightly. They'd lashed the rudder amidships and now he untied it and began to steer, meanwhile grasping the boom line. "Stay on the upward side of the boat to help balance."

She nodded. "I've sailed. I can help tack when you give the word."

They began coasting, dark water gurgling up from the stern. How many thousands of miles to go? Hart looked in the direction of the Germans.

"And Greta? You'd better unlash the submachine gun."

She nodded. "They may be surprised that we have it."

"Colonel! A sail!"

The SS men were pointing and Drexler lifted his binoculars. It was them, trying to ghost away as if they were making a pleasure sail on the Havel outside Berlin. He could imagine them laughing together, thinking they'd infected all the tiresome Germans and joking about the fool they'd made of the cuckold Jürgen Drexler. Except that Jürgen Drexler wasn't ill, not yet. And even if he already was—even if he felt perhaps the murmur of fever in his brain—it was still just a whisper. He had plenty of time to catch them and punish them and swallow the cure.

"Full power! Full speed!" The engine roared as the helmsman gunned it. "Watch for ice! But go, go, go!"

The added breeze from their acceleration was colder. While the helmsman steered, the other SS men checked their weapons and then crouched low behind the gunwales for shelter, a peeking pride of lions.

"Speed, dammit!" A small floe banged against the hull and Drexler was forcibly reminded of the *Schwabenland*'s mishap. "But be careful!"

He spotted a wide patch of open water to port and pointed. "Go there!" They were faster than the sailboat and could afford to loop around the unpowered craft, blocking the fugitives from the ocean. With that pathetic mast sticking upward like a pointing flag the adulterous lovers couldn't hope to hide. He had them! Oh, he had them.

The Germans charged across the open water, spray arcing off their prow, a tendril of greasy engine smoke drifting behind. Each swell that lifted gave a better view of the fleeing sail, tacking first this way and then that. Predator and prey, strong and weak. The way of the world! Now the storm troopers were between the lifeboat and the open sea. Owen and Greta were caught against the island.

"Now, that way! Into that lead there! We'll pin them!"

The motor launch wake churned the flat water of the ice lead, its wake heaving the floes up and down. The sail was getting tantalizingly close, flapping aimlessly now as the couple hunted for fickle wind. He could imagine their panic. He could feel their dread. It was sweet revenge, imagining what they must feel like as the soldiers inexorably gained on them. Would she weep at the end? If she did, it would no longer move him. He was sure of it.

They churned through a tiny connecting channel and then they were in the same polynya of open water as the sailboat. Where had they gotten the craft? Drexler suddenly looked around as if the American might have allies ready to attempt a rescue. But no, the horizons were empty. Still, it was as if Hart was some kind of magician, able to conjure improbable escapes and sudden resources at the last moment. It baffled him: the pilot had been a plague since that first night at Karinhall. Well, the showdown had finally come. No more tricks.

The sail abruptly dropped and the pair unshipped their oars; they were going to try to reach the edge of the ice and escape on foot. Drexler calculated. The Nazis would catch them a few feet short of their goal. "Faster!"

Suddenly there was a burp of gunfire in Drexler's ear. Spouts of seawater flew up near the fleeing lifeboat. One of the SS men had opened fire.

Drexler cuffed him. "Not yet, you fool! Not until we've recovered the drug!" Morons. Was he the only person on this voyage capable of thought?

Then Hart bent, sat up, and there was a flicker of muzzle flash in return. "He's got a gun!" the helmsman cried as water and wood splinters filled the air and one of the SS men cried out. The motor launch veered abruptly away, lurching toward the ice on the opposite side of the watery channel. They hit with a glancing blow and Drexler and the other men landed in a tangle on the bottom.

"Get off me, dammit!" He struggled upward. The pair were rowing again, taking advantage of the Nazi confusion. The couple hit the other side of the ice and scrambled out, dragging their packs behind them.

"Damn! Make for them!" But Hart had already staked their boat to a line and the two were jogging away like a pair of taunting foxes.

"Fuck! Now we'll have to catch them on foot." There was a groan, and Drexler looked down in irritation. It was Walther, one of his SS men. He was hit in the stomach and spewing blood all over the damn boat. Well, he'd be envied if they didn't recover the drug. And if they did it would be too late to save him anyway. The groaning would stop soon enough.

"We're leaking!" one of the men cried, watching water stream into the motor launch from a bullet hole.

"No matter," Drexler said. "We'll have their boat."

Chapter Thirty-Eight

It occurred to Greta that perhaps she was trapped in a dream. The chase had the hallucinatory, slow-motion quality of an unending nightmare. The world was a monochrome of black and white. The ice under her feet cracked and sighed as they painfully trotted across its powdery coverlet of snow. Her head was dizzy from the constant gasping of brittle air. For mere minutes, it seemed, they'd been free. Then Jürgen had materialized again as if he read every thought in her head, knew every plan she laid. She longed to wake up—to have it be over with.

The Germans were following them like a pack of wolves, five in all. Owen said he thought he'd counted six at first, so perhaps he'd hit one. Not that it mattered. How could they fight so many?

"Owen, I can't go on much longer."

She was panting, her pack as heavy as the Cross. They'd be run down in minutes.

He nodded. "Me neither. We have to leave the packs and lose the soldiers, then circle back. Maybe I can slow them down first."

They stopped at a fissure where the pressure of the shifting ice had heaved several blocks into the air. The barrier briefly shielded them from view.

"We'll put the packs here," Hart said. "Take the cylinder with the antidote and go ahead, aiming for that trapped iceberg. I'm going to give them something to think about." He threw down his pack and untangled the machine gun. "Are you all right?"

She nodded, tense. "Try not to be late."

There was an eruption of shots behind Greta and she could hear shouts and screams from the pursuing Germans. The soldiers let loose with a fusillade of their own, the bullets kicking up a small blizzard at the top of the ice blocks. Then Owen was away and running low after her, faster now without his pack and gun.

"I got one of the bastards and the others went flat," he reported. "The gun is empty and so is my stock of ideas."

"We still have a chance," she said hopefully. "They should have the disease. If we can just keep away long enough it should begin to slow them down."

"I hope that bacteria hurries. They look pretty damn healthy to me."

The iceberg was a gnarled hill of ice that had drifted in the sea until ensnared in the flat pack ice. The vise that held it was made of two large islands of ice separated by a dark lead of water that stretched hundreds of yards in either direction. The iceberg was the only bridge across this channel. Hart hesitated, glancing back. The Germans had paused to fall on the couple's packs like ravenous dogs, looking for the drug. Not finding it, they were loping after them again more warily, their guns ready. They didn't know Hart had hidden his empty submachine gun in the snow.

"Owen, come on! Why are we stopping?"

He glanced ahead. "Icebergs can sometimes be unstable. They slowly melt and as they change shape their center of gravity shifts and they roll. Sometimes the weight of a person or a seal or even a penguin can make the final difference. If we climb onto it and go into the water we're dead."

She looked impatient. "If we wait here we're dead."

"I know, I know. You go first then, to minimize the weight. I think if I stand here they'll hesitate in case I have a gun. Then I'll follow."

Now it was she who hesitated.

"Go. Quickly!"

Greta leaped a thin crevice of seawater and began scrambling across the iceberg, trying to ignore its ominous rock. As Owen had expected, the pursuing Germans slowed cautiously when they saw him standing there. One fired a tentative burst but the distance was still too great: the bullets went wide. Hart looked the other way. Greta had disappeared over the crest of the berg.

He leaped and the iceberg heaved unsteadily beneath him. Hart followed in Greta's tracks, praying their bridge would stay stable. More bullets whipped around him as he scrambled over the crest. Then he was sliding down the other side toward a gap of dark water and jumped again. The flatter ice cracked as he landed on it but didn't give way.

Greta seized his hand. "Hurry!"

On they went, the world a white miasma. They had no sense of direction except to get away.

"Hart! Oweeennnn Hart!"

They looked back. It was Drexler, standing on the crest of the iceberg and hoisting a machine gun. "Your lives in return for the drug, Hart! It isn't too late to make a bargain!"

They stopped to confer. "If we agree," said Greta, "they might survive to take the microbe back to Germany."

"And kill us anyway." Hart raised his arm.

Drexler lifted his binoculars, focusing. A middle finger came into view. Bastard!

The Nazi charged down the iceberg after them then, his men swarming over the crest just behind. The Germans came down in a tight group, neared the edge . . .

The iceberg rolled.

The movement was as spectacular as it was sudden. The hill of ice upended like a sinking ship, the end nearest Owen and Greta dipping into the water. The storm troopers screamed as they tumbled, desperately trying to claw away from the gulping water.

Drexler leaped, his legs churning, his arms outspread. He landed flat on the stable pack ice, the air going out of him with a whoosh. The iceberg continued to roll behind him and the three remaining storm troopers slid into the sea, thousands of tons of ice flipping to drive them deep. Their scream was chopped off as abruptly as the fall of an ax.

"Jesus," Hart whispered. "I'd heard of it, but never seen it."

The overturned iceberg was pitching uneasily now, seeking a new equilibrium. Seawater poured off its flanks in a hundred small waterfalls.

Drexler slowly got to his hands and knees.

Then one of his soldiers surfaced like a cork, thrashing. "Save me!" The sound exploded from his lungs but was thin and frail across the broad expanse of sea ice. Jürgen looked dully back over his shoulder. The man's hand was clutching at the air.

"He has no chance," Hart said. "The water's too cold."

The soldier had flailed his way to the edge of the pack ice and frantically hauled himself up on it, flopping like a fish. He was pleading, saying something to Drexler that they couldn't hear. The Nazi didn't respond at first. But as the soldier began to crawl pitifully toward Jürgen the SS colonel finally got to his feet. The soldier was slowing. A rime of ice was forming on his clothes.

Drexler regarded the man solemnly and then walked over to point his submachine gun. The storm trooper lifted his head. There was a short burst and the soaked soldier jerked and lay still.

Then the SS colonel looked at the two fugitives a hundred yards away across the ice. Grimly, he began trotting after them again.

The U-boat sounded like a tuberculosis ward. Men were hacking and sneezing, sweat beginning to dot their flushed faces. Schmidt felt ill as well but for his own protection from angry sailors he stayed near Freiwald in the control room, clutching the periscope. At least the submarine was beginning to move again. They'd find Drexler's motor launch, learn where Hart had gone, hunt down the antibiotic . . . He looked around the enclosing chamber bleakly. Time. Time.

He noticed a calendar near the helm. Almost Christmas. Rocket assembly should have begun by now. Laboratory space was being readied in the mines of the Ruhr. Warheads were being test-fired with anthrax. They were so close. So close! How he longed to squeeze the life out of that traitorous bitch.

"How late in the disease can we take the antidote and live, Doctor?" Freiwald asked.

He shrugged. "Who knows?"

"You'd better damn well know!"

Schmidt sighed. "The rabbits lived. A seaman on the first voyage drank some after infection and lived. Hart, damn his soul, lived. So. We have to hope."

The captain looked bleak. "Myself I don't care about. But my men . . . If they start to die, Doctor, they'll blame you. For bringing the spores aboard. You know that."

Schmidt nodded. "No matter. I'm older, less resistant. And I was infected first." He smiled broadly, lips drawn back from yellow teeth. "I'll beat them all to hell."

"Oh my God, Owen. Only open water."

They stopped, panting. They'd run and run and run, always the remorseless dark figure of Jürgen Drexler tagging behind as tireless as a shadow. They'd run until their clothes were soaked with sweat in the bitter cold, run until their lungs were on fire and their sides ached. Now they could run no more. The ice pack had ended in a wide lead of water as dark and shiny as tar. There was no way around. They were pinned between Jürgen Drexler and the sea.

The couple looked back. Their pursuer had slowed to a weary walk himself now, his submachine gun leveled lest they try to dash along the edge of the ice. He had to be as exhausted as they were. He had to be feeling the plague. But they'd run out of time to wait for his collapse.

Hart glanced around. The world was a gauzy gray, chill and

bleak. The ice was an inhospitable plain, its only mark the trail of their footprints. The volcano behind was smoking more furiously and for the first time they could hear its low rumble. Had they succeeded they would have gotten away from the damnable island just in time, he thought. Hell was breathing. Fire and ice.

"I'm sorry, Greta. I don't have a weapon. I don't even have any strength." He looked at her fondly, sadly. At least I knew her, he thought. And because of that I've had a good life.

"It's all right, Owen," she replied, as if reading his thoughts. She held his hand.

Jürgen stopped twenty feet short, pinning them on a small peninsula of ice. His breath steamed, his parka covered with frost. He looked ill.

"So. We come together for the final time."

"Give it up, Jürgen," Hart tiredly tried. "Your men are dead. The submarine is contaminated. It's over."

"No, Hart." He coughed. "What you don't understand—what you've never understood—is that it isn't over until *I* say so. Do you really think I'm going to let you destroy my work and sail off with my wife? I don't know which to be more impressed by: your irredeemable stupidity or your irrepressible persistence. A lesser man would have surrendered by now, you know. Perhaps you're not such a coward after all."

"Excuse me if I don't give a damn."

Drexler nodded. "No, at times like this other things seem more important, yes? I'm sick, you're helpless. We all think of what might have been."

"Jürgen, please," Greta pleaded. "We can still choose life . . ."

"Life?" He looked at her in amazement. "Life? My command butchered? My crew poisoned? Life, in this *wasteland?* Look around you, Greta. Do you see anything alive, anywhere, in this kingdom of the dead?" He coughed again, then swung the machine gun at Owen's chest. "So, I'll give you a final choice, Hart. You can be shot down. Or drown."

"Go to hell."

Greta glanced away as Drexler spoke, studying the opening of dark water. Something had moved to catch her eye, producing a dark eddy. Then it sank soundlessly. She slid her hand inside her parka and pulled out the steel tank. "Jürgen, wait. If you kill Owen I'll throw the drug into the sea. You'll die of plague, a horrible death."

He was still breathing hard. "Then give it here."

"You can have it for the gun. Then we'll all live."

He licked his lips. "No. Give it here or I'll simply shoot you and take it."

"Do you promise not to kill us?"

"I promise to kill you if you *don't* hand that over."

She glanced at Owen. He shook his head. She cocked her arm.

"No!" said Drexler. "Don't throw it!"

She threw.

"God damn you!"

The cylinder landed in the snow at the edge of the water, almost going in. Neither man was certain if she'd been aiming for the water or Drexler. "I'm sorry. I was never good at throwing."

"Pathetic bitch." Keeping the machine gun aimed, he sidled to pick it up. "My life was ruined from the moment I met you, do you realize that? You never understood anything: not me, not Germany, not science—" He bent.

The water exploded.

Hart jumped back as if he'd been shot. There was an astonishing blur and the momentary flicker of a yawning pink mouth with white teeth. Then with a scream and a titanic splash, Jürgen Drexler was gone.

"Christ!" the pilot cried.

"Leopard seal," said Greta grimly. "It thought he was a penguin."

The cold was like fire, the shock so powerful that Drexler didn't even notice the animal's teeth had punctured his thigh. The gun and the tank of drug slipped away. Then, dismayed by the strange mouthful of cloth and flesh it had seized, the seal let go. The Nazi couldn't swim but the shock drove instinct. He thrashed toward the surface in a cloud of blood, erupting with a shriek.

"Save me!"

Hart considered only for a moment. Then he sprang forward and grabbed.

"Owen, no!"

The pilot ignored her. He heaved and Drexler slithered up on the ice, gasping.

"Why did you *do* that?"

"Because he has something that belongs to us."

Ice was forming on Drexler's clothes. His body was shaking uncontrollably, his strength and coordination ebbing, his brain shutting down. "Please . . ."

"I'll never understand you, Jürgen," Hart said, squatting. "You had heaven. You had Greta. And you chose hell." He yanked open the German's parka and began feeling his pockets. "Where is it, dammit?"

"Please . . ."

"Owen, the cylinder went in the water with him. It's gone." She looked at the smoking volcano. "God's will, perhaps."

"That's not what I'm looking for." He hoisted Drexler up off the snow and ripped open the flap of his chest pocket. "Here!" Then he dropped the German and backed away.

Drexler's lips were blue, his mouth still open. His eyes had lost focus. The pulse of blood from his bite wound had become sluggish. His movements were ending.

Greta stared without expression. "I don't feel anything except release, Owen," she confessed. "My compassion has died."

"He killed it. And in the end he's luckier than he deserves. The plague would have killed him more slowly." He turned to her and opened his hand. It was the penguin locket. "This is why I pulled him out. He showed me he'd kept the thing, to gloat." Yanking his gloves off with his teeth he opened it, inspecting. "Lost the pebble, I see." He unfastened the chain. "Put your hood down."

She did so and bent her head. Tenderly, he reached around and hooked the locket. She let it dangle a minute on the outside of her parka so he could see it.

"I gave the pebble to my father," she said. "So he could keep it safely for us."

"You trusted him not to sell it?" It was a grin.

"He wouldn't sell it. Not anymore."

Hart pulled her hood back up. "We need to conserve every bit of heat and energy we can now." They glanced down at Drexler's body. "You're a widow again."

She nodded—not with sadness but release. "Yes. But a widow with *prospects*." Her look was shy.

His look was a combination of pleasure and apprehension. "I should say so. *If* we can survive the sea."

CHAPTER THIRTY-NINE

Owen and Greta were quiet on the long walk back to the boat. Exhaustion was taking its toll and the trek was grim. They skirted the frozen soldier by the iceberg, rounded the open water, and worked back to their packs where they gathered their supplies. They passed the body of the other man that Hart had shot and found a third lying in the half-sunken motor launch. The pilot had hoped to transfer to that larger craft and use its engine to get clear of the ice but his gunfire had holed it. The dead storm trooper lay in pink water that had risen halfway up to the gunwales, its surface freezing into slush. So the couple restowed their gear in the whaler's lifeboat and pushed off from the pack ice, rowing numbly.

After several hundred yards they stopped and Hart tethered the boat to another ice island. They crawled into the bottom of the boat and covered themselves with a blanket and tarp. A light snow was falling and it dusted the covering. They kissed wearily in their cocoon and cupped like spoons, Greta nested into Owen. Then they slept. For the first time in weeks, dark dreams did not plague them.

The pair woke stiff but somewhat recovered, crawling out from under the tarp like burrowing animals. Hart looked around. The panorama was gray, water the color of lead. The ice was dull under a ceiling of cloud. He'd no idea what time it was, or even what day it was. Time had stopped, or become irrelevant. Atropos Island continued to thunder, the volcanic plume bulging under the overcast like a sagging belly. Mist fogged the distant glaciers and flakes of snow spat at them in lazy fashion. Everywhere Hart looked there was utter emptiness, a land and seascape absolutely vacuumed of life, of warmth, of history. They were in a frozen limbo and the only sound in all that chilly vastness was the drum of their own pumping blood, the only sparks of heat the ones each carried in their core. All that mattered in the end, he realized, was each other.

"I feel like we're the last living things on earth," he told her.

She was biting off a piece of bread, her eyes shining. To have awakened this morning was like awakening from her terrible dream. She'd never felt such relief.

"No, Owen. The sea is still alive. Look." She pointed.

There was a hiss. A cloud of rank vapor, evidence of another huge beating heart, puffed above the water. The surface roiled as the small hillock of a whale's back appeared. Then it submerged again and the tail broke the surface, waving. Beckoning them to the sea.

"It's a good sign," she promised. "That despite all the kilometers ahead we're going to make it."

Hart unhooked the boat from the ice and they began to row, following the whale. Slowly they worked out of the pack ice that clung to the island.

As they neared the open ocean the wind began to pick up. They hoisted the sail and huddled for warmth in the stern, the lifeboat taking on an easy motion as it slid up and down the swells. An iceberg passed by on the starboard side and they saw penguins standing on it. Yes, there was life after all.

"How far to land?" she asked.

"About four thousand kilometers to Africa."

"My God." The impossibility was obvious.

"We have to try."

They sailed on. Strangely, their mood was not despair but contentment. They were alone and with each other. It was enough. The sea was gray, the swells cresting with foam but not yet threatening to overpower their little boat. Seabirds appeared and began trailing them, riding the wind in long, looping circles. The overcast broke and a tantalizing rift of blue showed through. Behind, the island began to look simply like a gigantic dark cloud.

Hours passed. Greta dozed in Owen's arms, lulled by the roll of the sea. Then she lazily came awake again, watching the water. It was hypnotic, swells marking a timeless rhythm. She squinted, her gaze caught on something that broke the pattern. Something above the surface. Something hard. "My God. Is that a ship?" She pointed.

He followed her arm eagerly, then looked uneasy. "I think it's the submarine. I think it's the *U-4501*."

"No." She put her arms around him. "This is too much."

He studied the craft. "It would be. Except it isn't trying to intercept us, I think."

"Hasn't it spotted us? Should we drop the sail to hide?"

"No," he said, now more puzzled than alarmed. "That's not it. The sub isn't trying to do anything. I think it's dead."

"Dead?"

"Plague." He aimed for the vessel.

The U-boat was wallowing sluggishly, drifting as if it had lost all power. The main deck was awash, only the conning tower clear of the sea. It rocked back and forth like a lonely buoy.

"I don't see anybody," Greta said quietly.

Owen hove to and then watched the submarine for a while in grim wonder. "No," he replied. "I suspect there's no one to see. It's a ghost ship now, like the *Bergen*."

"So I really killed them. I'm looking at their tomb."

"No, they killed themselves."

She crossed herself. He turned the rudder and began sailing away.

"The conning tower looks like it's slowly sinking," she judged, staring after the disappearing U-boat.

"Maybe Freiwald's taking her to the bottom. Maybe there's a leak."

"So it's really over, isn't it?"

"That part is."

They sailed on, the day getting late. They took turns eating and steering, catching snatches of sleep. Both felt immensely tired. The euphoria of escape was wearing off and life's insistence at worrying about the next danger was pecking persistently at their mood. Night fell, a cloudy one as dark as the cave, and then the gray dawn revealed mostly empty ocean. A few icebergs drifted miles from their position but the island was lost below the southern horizon.

"I want to talk about our future," Greta said. "A future that will keep my spirits up."

"All right." Hart thought a moment. "What kind of house shall we have?"

"A sunny one," she said promptly. "With a tree, and a table under the tree. Not big, like I had in Berlin. But bright."

He laughed. "It sounds affordable. And what kind of car?"

"Do ordinary people really have cars in America?"

"Yes, some of them. You need one. The country's big."

"Well then, I want one of those too. But not black. A happy color."

"Like in a children's book?"

"Exactly."

The clouds parted briefly and for a while the horizon sparkled. Then the weather closed again and the wind began to rise ominously. The tiny boat was like a leaf on a prairie, the sea slowly building and breaking white. The sky was darkening. Hart shortened sail.

"They call this latitude the Furious Fifties," he said. "Now we'll see why."

The boat was beginning to toboggan down one side of the swells and climb laboriously up the next, the wind singing in the rigging. Spray breaking across the prow began to wet them. It would be a long second night.

Greta looked across the cold seascape, her hair blowing past her cheeks with a sad, faraway look that reminded the pilot of their days on the *Schwabenland*. He wondered what her picture of America was, and what she would think of it if they ever got there. The boat rolled steeply and she shifted her body automatically to help balance. A streak of foam hissed away from their stern. She began to bail, barely keeping pace with the rain of spray.

"We're not going to make it, are we, Owen?" she asked finally when she rested. "We could never make it. Like you said."

He was looking out across the water, his eyes narrow, his mouth in its half smile of concentration. "I was wrong. We'll make it."

"Ah, the optimistic American." She couldn't help smiling. "You don't give up easily, do you?"

"Not anymore."

"And how do you *know* that we'll make it, Mr. Hart?"

"Well, for one thing, we've only got three thousand and nine hundred kilometers to go. Much less if you count in nautical miles."

She laughed. "I hadn't realized we were so close!"

"And for another thing, you have an angel on your shoulder."

"Oh really?" She turned to look. "Very small, I think. But that's what your Eskimo friend promised, yes?"

Hart nodded. "And Elmer was right."

She slumped in the bottom of the boat, huddling against the cold. "I wish he was but I don't see this angel, Owen. The angels have deserted me, I suspect."

"No they haven't." He pointed. "*I* can see it."

She didn't bother to look this time. Her eyes closed.

"Greta?" he said impatiently.

"Hmmmm?"

"Please get out the flare gun you packed."

"What?" Her eyes opened wide.

"For your angel." He pointed again. And this time she swung to look.

There was a gray shape on the horizon. Another ship.

"My God. It's true!"

Owen was beaming now, his face stung with spray, his hair whipping in the wind. "Of course it's true. Because of the person I'm with, I suspect." He leaned and seized and kissed her, passionately happy. "Get out the flare, dammit!"

She did so and a red star shot skyward in the gloom. They waited a few minutes. Then another.

The ship began pointing toward them.

Owen whooped, waving his hand wildly as if they could see it at such a distance. Then he beamed at his companion. "Did I ever tell you that women are good luck?"

The American destroyer *Reuben Gray* picked them up at dusk. Greta went up the rope ladder first, sailors eagerly lifting her the last few feet and marveling at the novelty of a woman.

Then a sailor pointed to the ladder urgently and gestured at Hart.

"Speak English, kid!" the pilot asked.

His mouth dropped open. "You sound American!"

"Montanan. Never thought I'd see so much fucking water in my life." The Norwegian lifeboat was heavy with it, he realized, accumulated spray sloshing under the floorboards. They wouldn't have lasted the night. He grabbed the ladder and hoisted himself aboard.

"Where'd you come from?" The sailor's wide eyes looked out at an empty sea.

"Heaven. And hell."

Hart looked down at the lifeboat a last time with appreciation. On its second chance it had done its job.

"Big wave!" someone called from the deck, pointing. The two

men looked. A dark hill was mounding, aiming for the destroyer's stern quarter.

"Hang on!" the sailor shouted, shoving Hart. The pilot needed no encouragement. He wrapped an arm around a metal rack. The stern of the ship dipped, a mountain of gray water looming over it. Then the wave broke, spray crashing against the stern like breakers on a rocky coast.

There was a splintering crack. The stern rose, twisted, dropped again. The destroyer tilted as it sought equilibrium.

Hart let go and looked back over the side. The Norwegian lifeboat had been hurled against the steel ship's side and shattered. It was gone, except for a scrap of wood attached to one line. The destroyer began to accelerate and steered a more favorable course into the waves, steadying. And at last the island seemed reassuringly remote. They were safe. But what was an American destroyer doing way down here?

Owen walked across the fantail to a hatchway where yellow light beckoned. Greta was there, her hood down and a halo of illumination around her hair. And there was someone else too.

"Fortune is curious, isn't it, Mr. Hart?"

"I don't believe it."

Otto Kohl smiled like the proprietor of a private yacht. "You're lucky we found you in time. And I'm lucky you found us. I think the captain was ready to pitch me overboard if I didn't find a submarine to sink or an island to invade. And I feared I was going to help him kill the two of you. Instead I saved you. Now perhaps you can convince him of the truth of what I've been saying."

Hart stepped inside, feeling himself sagging in the relative warmth. "I'll try. But what are you *doing* here?"

"I went to the Americans. I confessed all. They didn't believe me until they intercepted a radio signal from your U-boat. Then they made me a captive guide, exhibiting a sorry mistrust I've only slowly been overcoming."

"Well, it's too late to guide them, Otto. They're all dead, even Jürgen. The submarine is gone, the island volcano erupting, the disease and cure lost. Forever, I hope. It would be insane to go back there."

"The submarine . . . gone?"

"It was full of plague and slowly sinking the last time we saw it. This destroyer can look in hopes of practicing its naval gunnery, but I don't think they'll find it."

"And was anything salvaged from this vessel?"

"Of course not. You want a souvenir?"

Kohl sighed. "No. Just that Jürgen was holding some . . . papers of mine."

"Ah. I saw those come aboard. Important?"

The German thought about that. Then he shook his head. "No. Not important. Not anymore. Because life goes on, I think. Because it's time to start over and make up for the past, no?"

Hart nodded. "Admiral Byrd once remarked that Antarctica can provide a man with a chance to remake himself. Maybe he was right. But I'm sorry about your papers, Otto. I don't know what other evidence we have to back up your story."

He shrugged. "Yourselves, certainly. How else did you come to be down here in an open boat?"

The pilot nodded. "There's that."

"And one other thing." Greta fished into her clothes and pulled out her bottle. "An algae or a sponge, a strange organism. Perhaps some scientist will confirm its novelty."

"Greta! You saved some?" The pilot was surprised.

"Just this raw sample, when I destroyed the rest. I'm curious. As a scientist, you know."

Otto peered. "This is what all the fuss has been about?"

"This and how humans could misuse it."

Kohl nodded. "That I understand." He paused then, considering the way the couple looked at each other. "Well. Would an engagement present be appropriate?"

"It would be *very* appropriate," Hart said. Greta smiled.

"Good. Because I've been carrying this halfway around the world and don't have a clue as to why." He reached into a pocket and took out a scrap of soiled ribbon, handing it to Greta. "But I kept it as you asked."

She looked happy as she unwrapped the pebble.

"What the devil *is* that rock?"

She lifted the locket out of her clothes and unsnapped it. "It's memory, Papa." She slipped the pebble in and closed the tiny container. "It goes here, near the heart."

Her father nodded. "And now you two go on to . . . ?"

"California, I hope." Greta looked shyly at Owen. "It's warmer than Montana, I hear. And I want to be near the sea to study whales. Not to hunt them, but to learn from them."

"And you, Owen?"

"I think commercial aviation is going to increase after the war. I want to fly and I suspect California will be as good a place to start as any. I once spent some time there."

"Good. And I think I want to help rebuild some of what we destroyed after the Reich finally dies. They will need Otto Kohl, I think."

An ensign stepped into the room. "The captain wants to talk to you three. You have a lot of explaining to do."

"Of course, of course!" Kohl nodded. "What a story we have to tell! Lead the way, young man!" He put a cautious hand on Hart's shoulder. "Captain Reynolds and I are slowly becoming the best of friends," he whispered. "It's taking time but he's warming to me, I think. So you, of course, must let me do most of the talking."

As the trio climbed toward the vessel's bridge, Owen Hart slipped his arm around the woman he loved.

AUTHOR'S NOTE

This book was inspired by a true incident. In 1938–39, Germany's Hermann Göring did send an expedition to Antarctica on the seaplane tender *Schwabenland.* Its pilots were the first to fly over the coastal ranges of Queen Maud Land and they assigned some names to the region that persist today. The Germans did drop swastika-engraved darts from their flying boats to establish a claim to the continent, and did greet curious penguins with a "Heil Hitler!" They named the area New Schwabenland.

Except for Hermann Göring, however, all the characters in this novel are imagined. None are meant to represent the actual members of the *Schwabenland* expedition. The history recounted here is solely the author's invention. To the degree possible, however, this novel's descriptions are based on historic accounts of the places, times, people, and mores of the Nazi era.

Those readers familiar with Antarctic history and geography will recognize some sources of the novel's ideas. Atropos Island is inspired by real-life Deception Island, for example. Dry valleys such as the one described do exist. So do leopard seals. The disease depicted is fiction but scientists have recently discovered underground ecosystems of bacteria fed by chemicals and the earth's heat energy. The drug was suggested by the story of penicillin, discovered accidentally in 1928 when mold spores blew through a scientist's window and fell on plates of bacteria. The strain that was developed as an antibiotic in World War II, *Penicillin chrysogenum,* came from a single moldy cantaloupe found by a researcher in a supermarket garbage bin in Peoria, Illinois. Proving again that truth is at least as strange as fiction.

This book would not have been possible without the opportunity to make two visits to Antarctica as a science journalist writing for the *Seattle Times*, under a fellowship program of the National Science Foundation. I am grateful to the *Times,* the NSF, and all the people I met there. They and the southern continent affected me deeply.

Antarctica is an extraordinary place, which tends to have an enormous impact on those who visit it. No continent on earth has quite its combination of hostility and beauty. In the twenty-first century Antarctica is likely to come under heavy pressure from nations eager to exploit its resources. It is imperative this unique place be preserved as the wilderness and research park it is today.

I am in debt to the encouragement of my agent, Kris Dahl, and the patient guidance and support of my editor, Rick Horgan. And I am at a loss to adequately thank my wife, Holly, for her help with this book. She became my collaborator on this novel under difficult circumstances. Across a vast distance we became closer, and I will always be grateful for that.

ATROPOS ISLAND

E

N ← → S

W

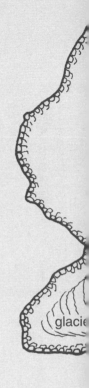

glacie

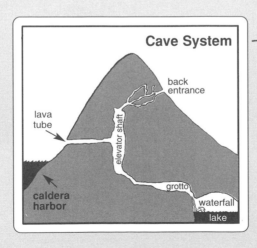

Cave System

back
entrance

lava
tube

elevator shaft

caldera
harbor

grotto

waterfall

lake